NINJAK

OPERATION DEADSIDE

MATT KINDT | DOUG BRAITHWAITE | JUAN JOSÉ RYP | BRIAN REBER

CONTENTS

Collection Cover Art: Doug Braithwaite

Consulting Editor: Tom Brennan
(Associate Editor, #10)
Editor: Warren Simons

VALIANT.

Peter Cuneo
Chairman

Dinesh Shamdasani
CEO & Chief Creative Officer

Gavin Cuneo
Chief Operating Officer & CFO

Fred Pierce
Publisher

Warren Simons
VP Editor-in-Chief

Walter Black
VP Operations

Hunter Gorinson
Director of Marketing,
Communications & Digital Media

Atom! Freeman
Director of Sales

Matthew Klein
Andy Liegl
John Petrie
Sales Managers

Josh Johns
Associate Director of Digital Media and Development

Travis Escarfullery
Jeff Walker
Production & Design Managers

Tom Brennan
Editor

Kyle Andrukiewicz
Editor and Creative Executive

Peter Stern
Publishing & Operations Manager

Andrew Steinbeiser
Marketing & Communications Manager

Danny Khazem
Editorial Operations Manager

Ivan Cohen
Collection Editor

Steve Blackwell
Collection Designer

Lauren Hitzhusen
Editorial Assistant

Rian Hughes/Device
Trade Dress & Book Design

Russell Brown
President, Consumer Products,
Promotions and Ad Sales

Geeta Singh
Licensing Manager

VALIANT

#10

NINJAK

PART 1

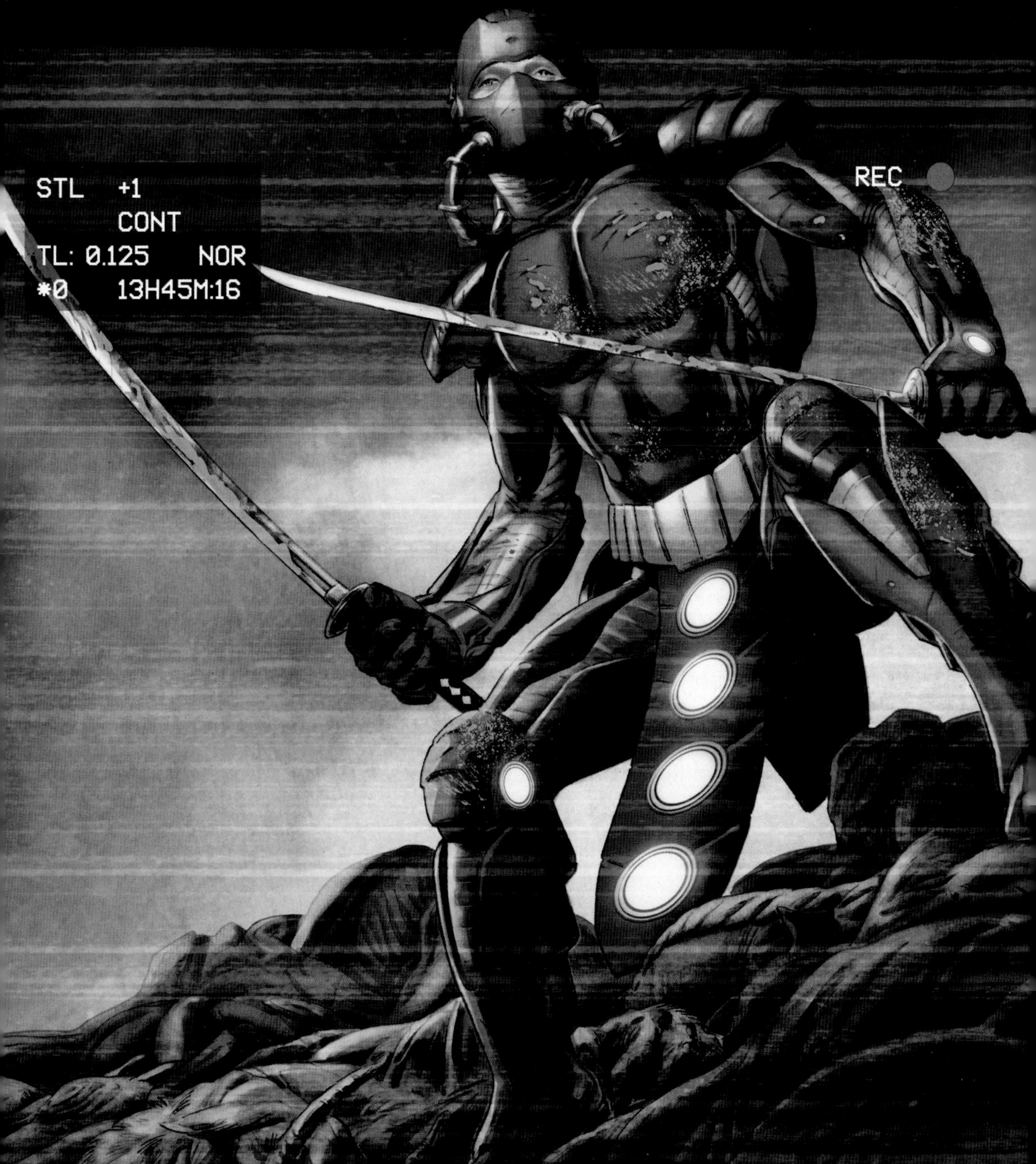

STL +1
CONT
TL: 0.125 NOR
*0 13H45M:16
REC

OPERATION DEADSIDE:

RECORDING: 01/04

MATT KINDT · DOUG BRAITHWAITE · JUAN JOSÉ RYP · BRIAN REBER

His name is Ninjak, spy and mercenary for hire. He is also Colin King, wealthy son of privilege. He works for the highest bidder, though his conscience often aligns him with the good guys. He is an expert in combat and espionage. He is as ruthless as he is charming. He is...

NINJAK®

OPERATION DEADSIDE:

PART 1

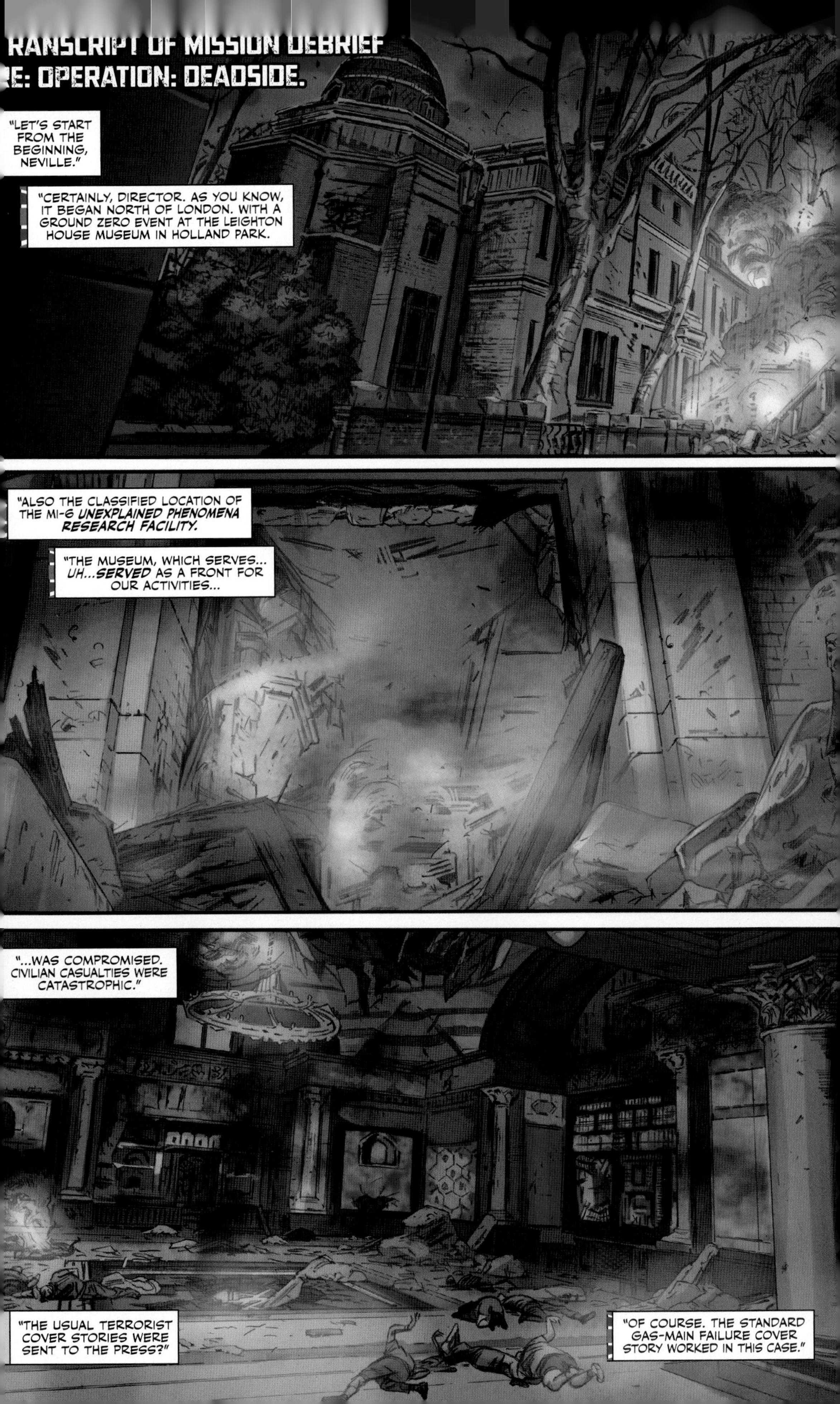
RANSCRIPT OF MISSION DEBRIEF
E: OPERATION: DEADSIDE.
"LET'S START FROM THE BEGINNING, NEVILLE."
"CERTAINLY, DIRECTOR. AS YOU KNOW, IT BEGAN NORTH OF LONDON. WITH A GROUND ZERO EVENT AT THE LEIGHTON HOUSE MUSEUM IN HOLLAND PARK.
"ALSO THE CLASSIFIED LOCATION OF THE MI-6 UNEXPLAINED PHENOMENA RESEARCH FACILITY.
"THE MUSEUM, WHICH SERVES... UH...SERVED AS A FRONT FOR OUR ACTIVITIES...
"...WAS COMPROMISED. CIVILIAN CASUALTIES WERE CATASTROPHIC."
"THE USUAL TERRORIST COVER STORIES WERE SENT TO THE PRESS?"
"OF COURSE. THE STANDARD GAS-MAIN FAILURE COVER STORY WORKED IN THIS CASE."

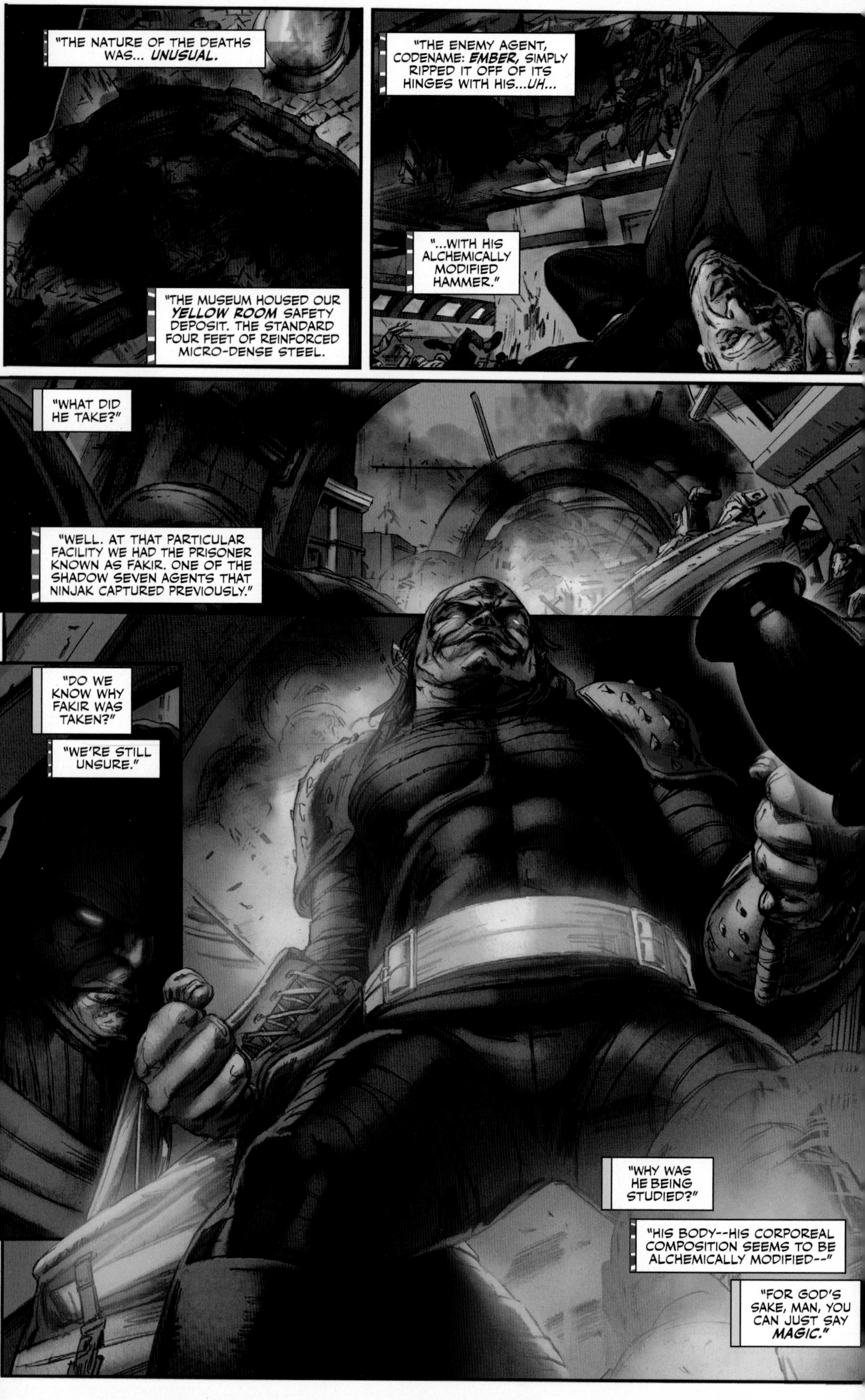
"THE NATURE OF THE DEATHS WAS... *UNUSUAL.*
"THE MUSEUM HOUSED OUR *YELLOW ROOM* SAFETY DEPOSIT. THE STANDARD FOUR FEET OF REINFORCED MICRO-DENSE STEEL.
"THE ENEMY AGENT, CODENAME: *EMBER,* SIMPLY RIPPED IT OFF OF ITS HINGES WITH HIS...*UH...*
"...WITH HIS ALCHEMICALLY MODIFIED HAMMER."
"WHAT DID HE TAKE?"
"WELL. AT THAT PARTICULAR FACILITY WE HAD THE PRISONER KNOWN AS FAKIR. ONE OF THE SHADOW SEVEN AGENTS THAT NINJAK CAPTURED PREVIOUSLY."
"DO WE KNOW WHY FAKIR WAS TAKEN?"
"WE'RE STILL UNSURE."
"WHY WAS HE BEING STUDIED?"
"HIS BODY--HIS CORPOREAL COMPOSITION SEEMS TO BE ALCHEMICALLY MODIFIED--"
"FOR GOD'S SAKE, MAN, YOU CAN JUST SAY *MAGIC.*"

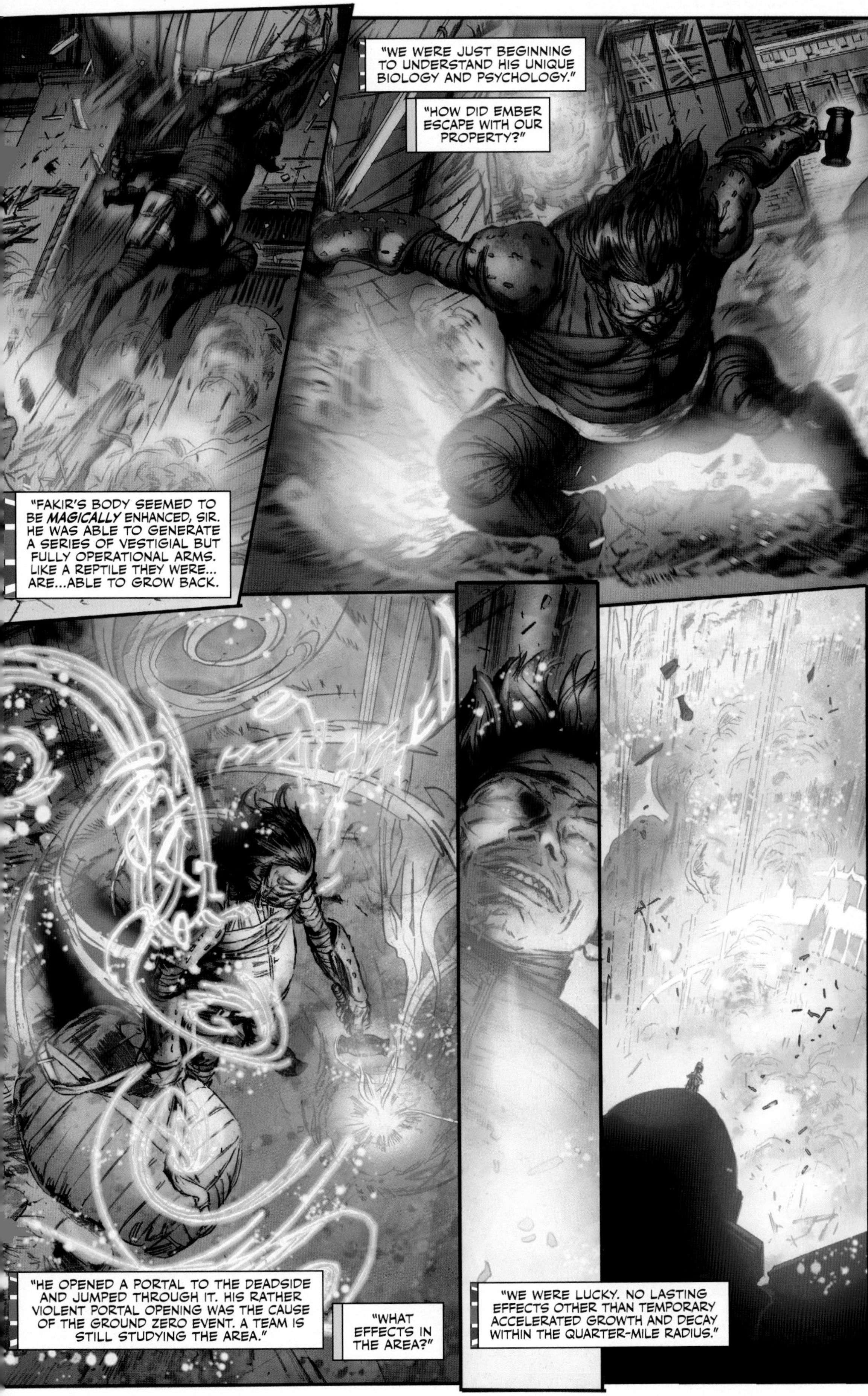
"WE WERE JUST BEGINNING TO UNDERSTAND HIS UNIQUE BIOLOGY AND PSYCHOLOGY."
"HOW DID EMBER ESCAPE WITH OUR PROPERTY?"
"FAKIR'S BODY SEEMED TO BE *MAGICALLY* ENHANCED, SIR. HE WAS ABLE TO GENERATE A SERIES OF VESTIGIAL BUT FULLY OPERATIONAL ARMS. LIKE A REPTILE THEY WERE... ARE...ABLE TO GROW BACK.
"HE OPENED A PORTAL TO THE DEADSIDE AND JUMPED THROUGH IT. HIS RATHER VIOLENT PORTAL OPENING WAS THE CAUSE OF THE GROUND ZERO EVENT. A TEAM IS STILL STUDYING THE AREA."
"WHAT EFFECTS IN THE AREA?"
"WE WERE LUCKY. NO LASTING EFFECTS OTHER THAN TEMPORARY ACCELERATED GROWTH AND DECAY WITHIN THE QUARTER-MILE RADIUS."

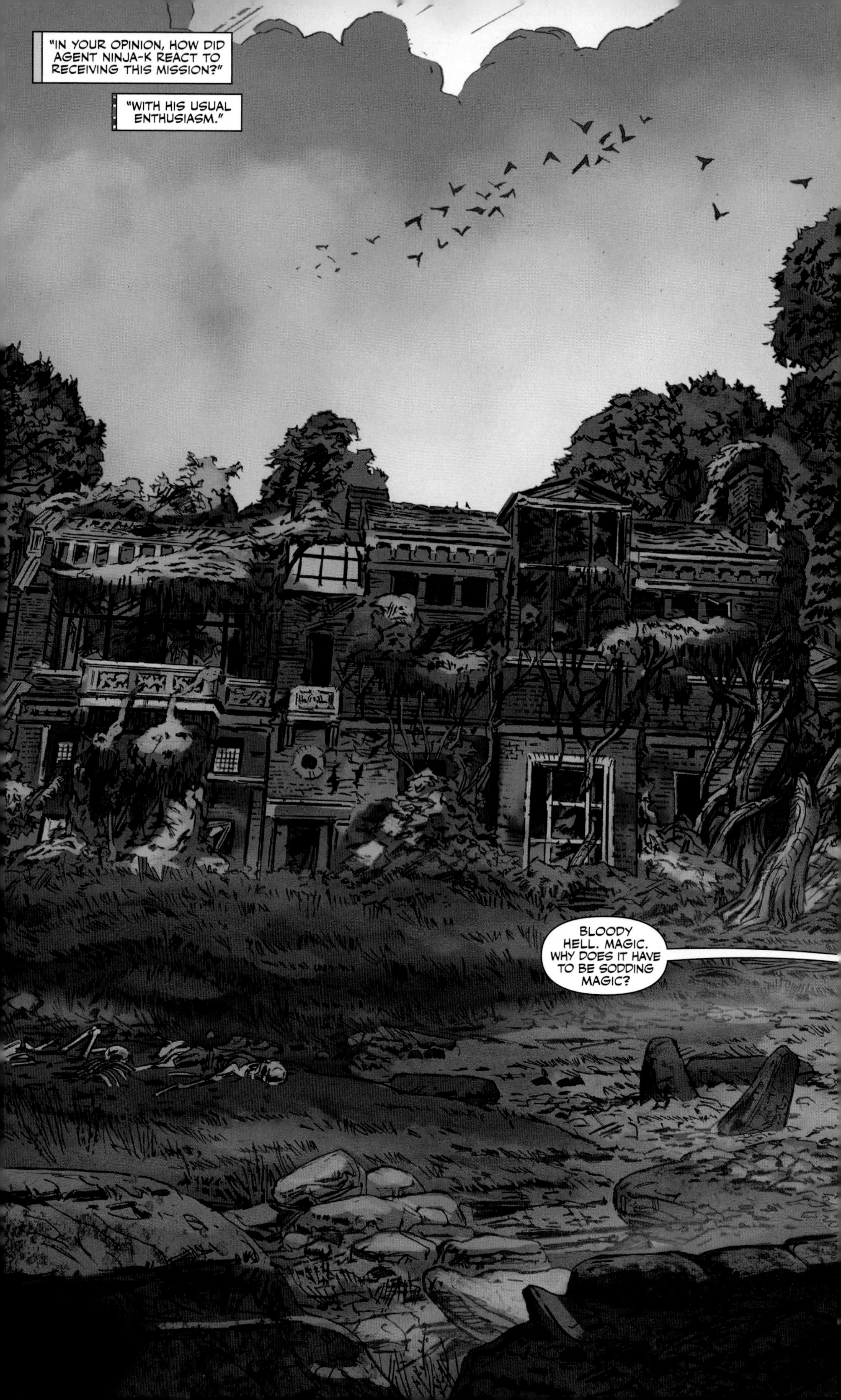
"IN YOUR OPINION, HOW DID AGENT NINJA-K REACT TO RECEIVING THIS MISSION?"
"WITH HIS USUAL ENTHUSIASM."
BLOODY HELL. MAGIC. WHY DOES IT HAVE TO BE SODDING MAGIC?

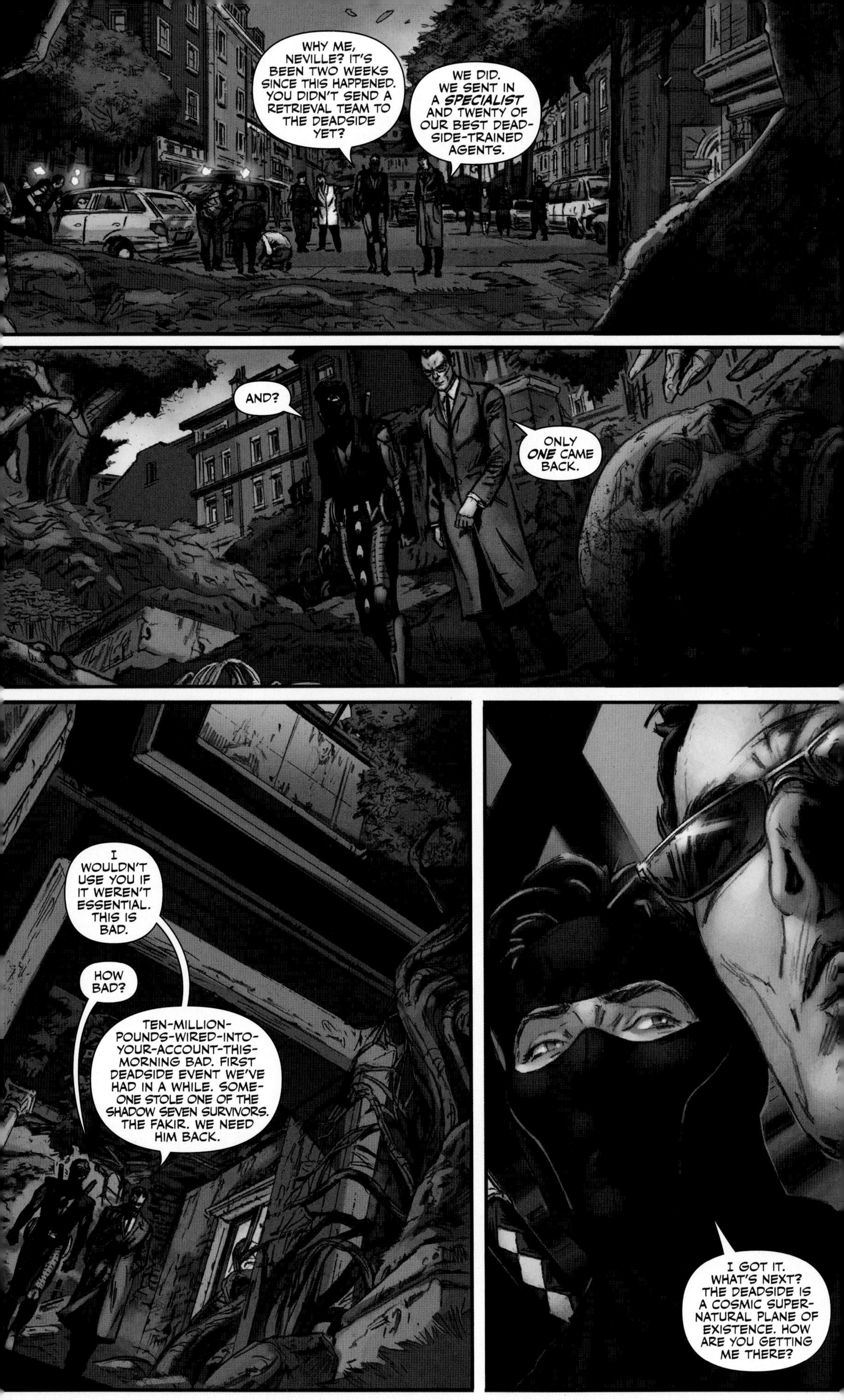
WHY ME, NEVILLE? IT'S BEEN TWO WEEKS SINCE THIS HAPPENED. YOU DIDN'T SEND A RETRIEVAL TEAM TO THE DEADSIDE YET?
WE DID. WE SENT IN A *SPECIALIST* AND TWENTY OF OUR BEST DEAD-SIDE-TRAINED AGENTS.
AND?
ONLY *ONE* CAME BACK.
I WOULDN'T USE YOU IF IT WEREN'T ESSENTIAL. THIS IS BAD.
HOW BAD?
TEN-MILLION-POUNDS-WIRED-INTO-YOUR-ACCOUNT-THIS-MORNING BAD. FIRST DEADSIDE EVENT WE'VE HAD IN A WHILE. SOME-ONE STOLE ONE OF THE SHADOW SEVEN SURVIVORS. THE FAKIR. WE NEED HIM BACK.
I GOT IT. WHAT'S NEXT? THE DEADSIDE IS A COSMIC SUPER-NATURAL PLANE OF EXISTENCE. HOW ARE YOU GETTING ME THERE?

"NINJAK WAS PUT INTO CONTACT WITH OUR DEADSIDE SPECIALIST IN LONDON.

"THE IDEA WAS TO KEEP THE TEAM SMALL THIS TIME. QUIET."

"HAD THE TWO AGENTS EVER WORKED TOGETHER BEFORE?"

"IN A...LIMITED CAPACITY."

NOK NOK

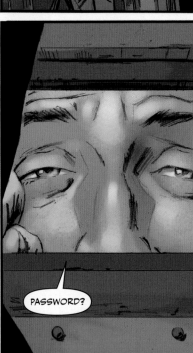

PASSWORD?

...FURRY CHAPS.

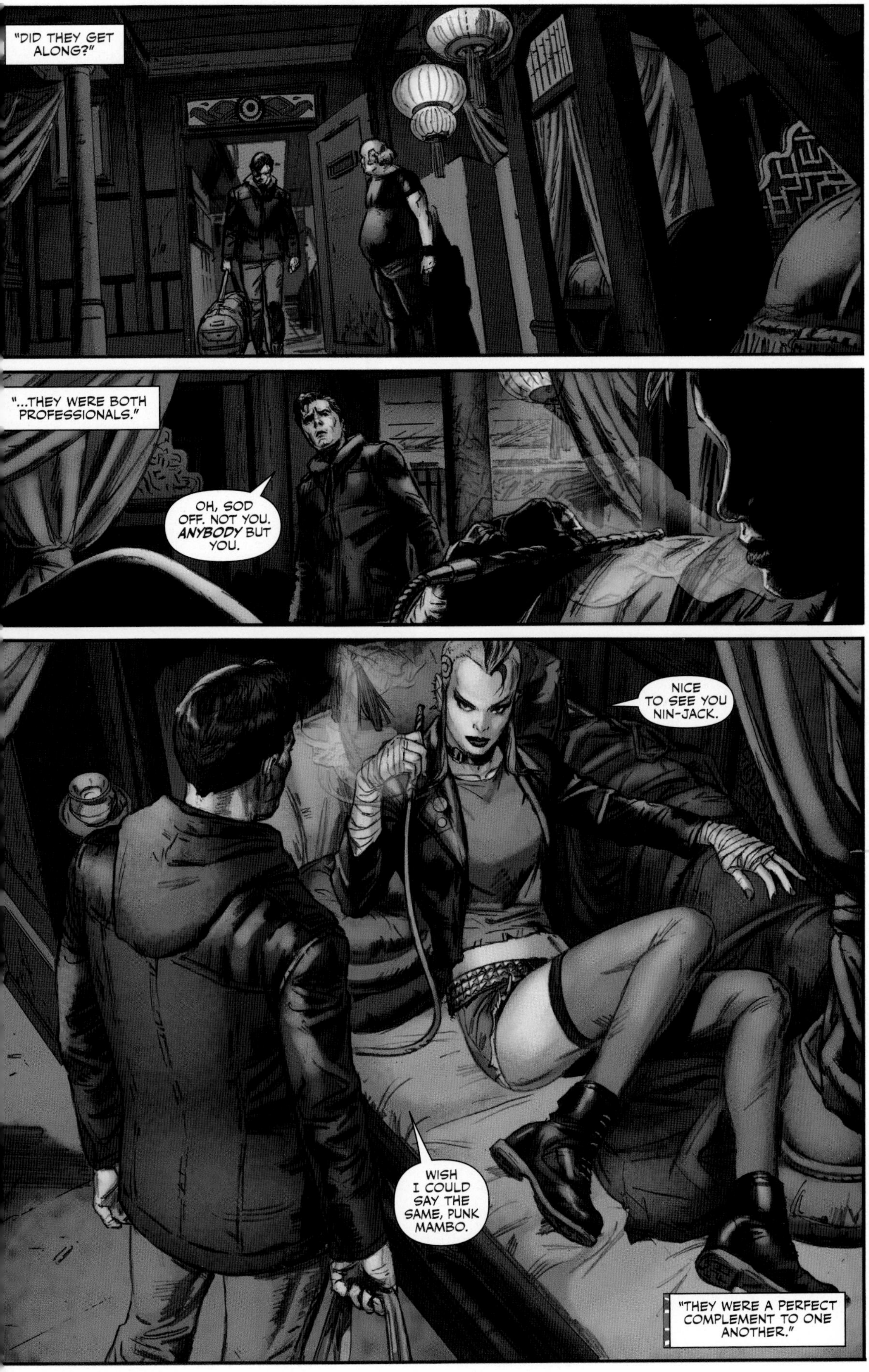
"DID THEY GET ALONG?"
"...THEY WERE BOTH PROFESSIONALS."
OH, SOD OFF. NOT YOU. *ANYBODY* BUT YOU.
NICE TO SEE YOU NIN-JACK.
WISH I COULD SAY THE SAME, PUNK MAMBO.
"THEY WERE A PERFECT COMPLEMENT TO ONE ANOTHER."

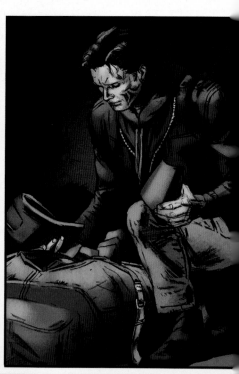

SO YOU'RE MY CONTACT? OKAY. OPEN THE PORTAL AND LET'S GET THIS OVER WITH.

FSH

PROBLEM?

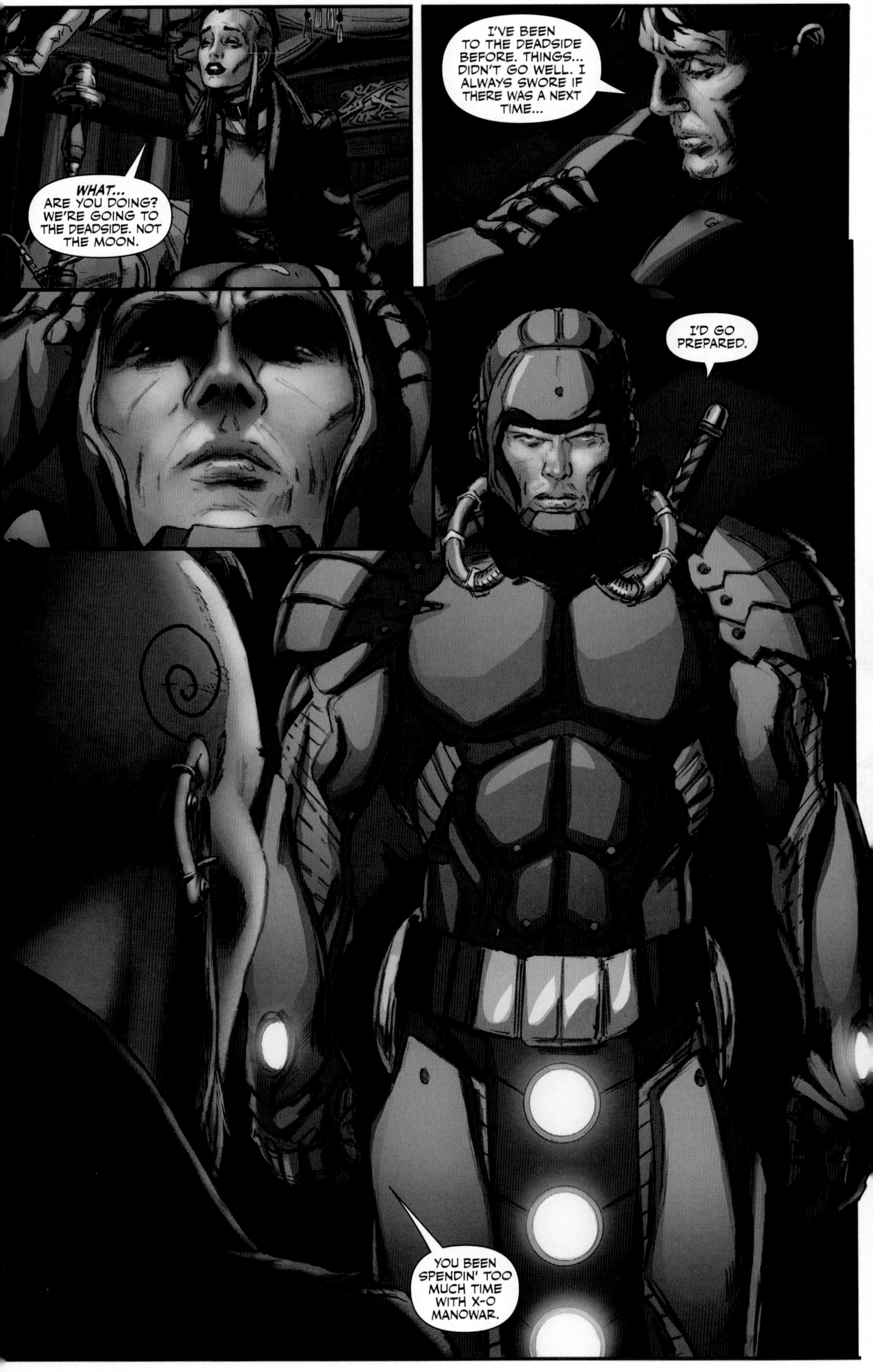
WHAT... ARE YOU DOING? WE'RE GOING TO THE DEADSIDE. NOT THE MOON.
I'VE BEEN TO THE DEADSIDE BEFORE. THINGS... DIDN'T GO WELL. I ALWAYS SWORE IF THERE WAS A NEXT TIME...
I'D GO PREPARED.
YOU BEEN SPENDIN' TOO MUCH TIME WITH X-O MANOWAR.

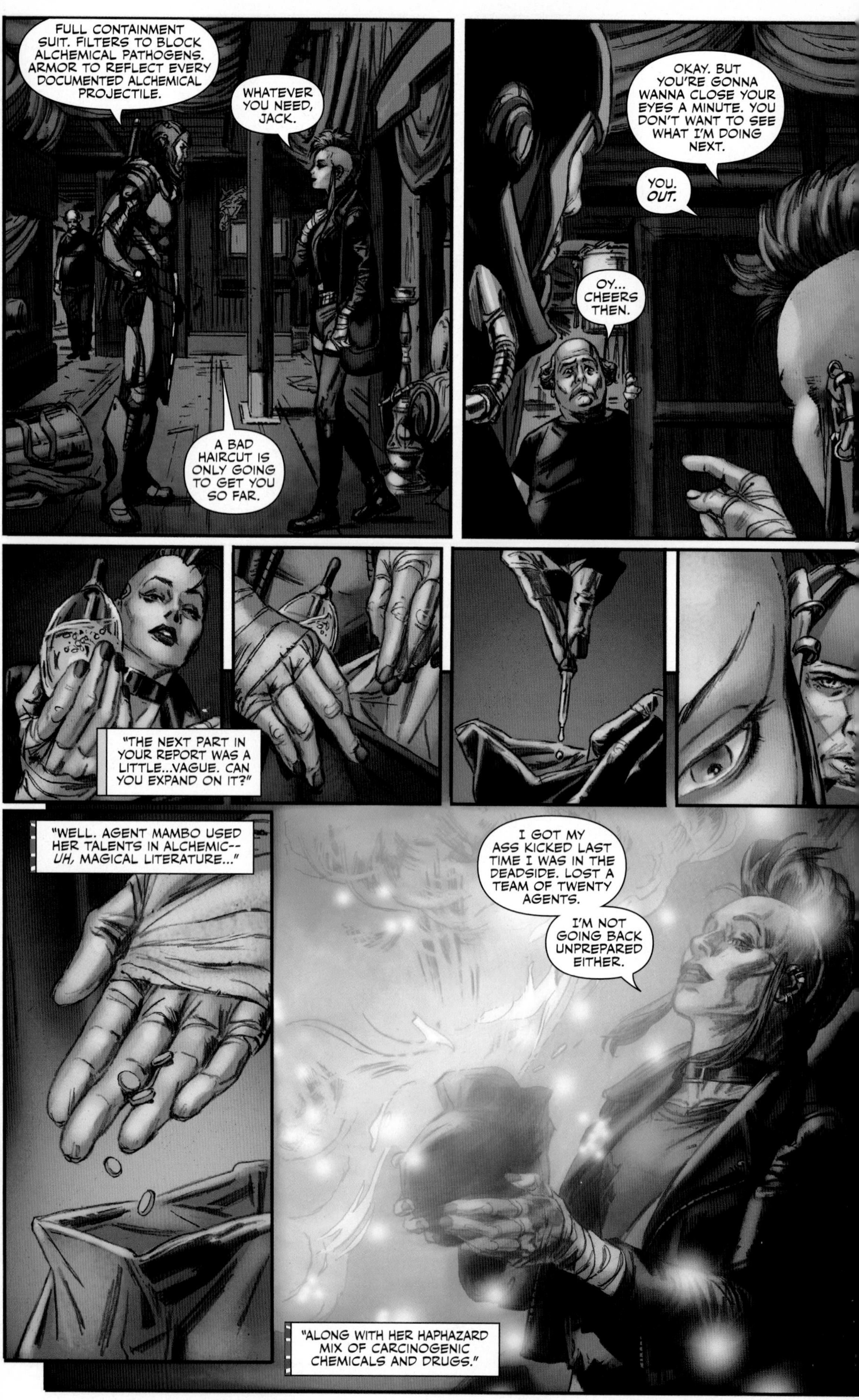

FULL CONTAINMENT SUIT. FILTERS TO BLOCK ALCHEMICAL PATHOGENS. ARMOR TO REFLECT EVERY DOCUMENTED ALCHEMICAL PROJECTILE.
WHATEVER YOU NEED, JACK.
A BAD HAIRCUT IS ONLY GOING TO GET YOU SO FAR.
OKAY. BUT YOU'RE GONNA WANNA CLOSE YOUR EYES A MINUTE. YOU DON'T WANT TO SEE WHAT I'M DOING NEXT.
YOU. *OUT.*
OY... CHEERS THEN.
"THE NEXT PART IN YOUR REPORT WAS A LITTLE...VAGUE. CAN YOU EXPAND ON IT?"
"WELL. AGENT MAMBO USED HER TALENTS IN ALCHEMIC-- *UH,* MAGICAL LITERATURE..."
I GOT MY ASS KICKED LAST TIME I WAS IN THE DEADSIDE. LOST A TEAM OF TWENTY AGENTS.
I'M NOT GOING BACK UNPREPARED EITHER.
"ALONG WITH HER HAPHAZARD MIX OF CARCINOGENIC CHEMICALS AND DRUGS."

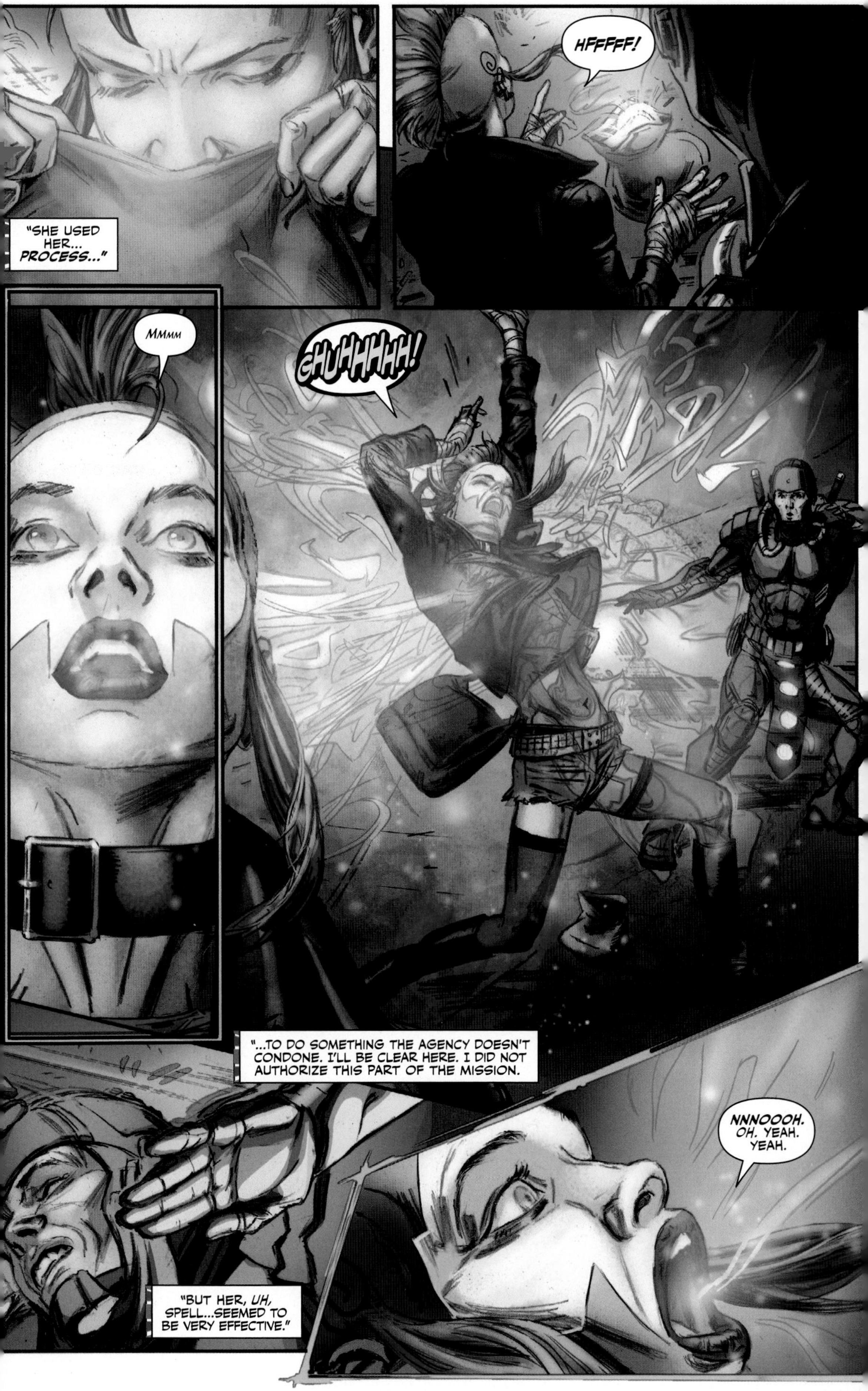

"SHE USED HER... PROCESS..."
HFFFFF!
MMMM
CHUHHHHH!
"...TO DO SOMETHING THE AGENCY DOESN'T CONDONE. I'LL BE CLEAR HERE. I DID NOT AUTHORIZE THIS PART OF THE MISSION.
NNNOOOH. OH. YEAH. YEAH.
"BUT HER, UH, SPELL...SEEMED TO BE VERY EFFECTIVE."

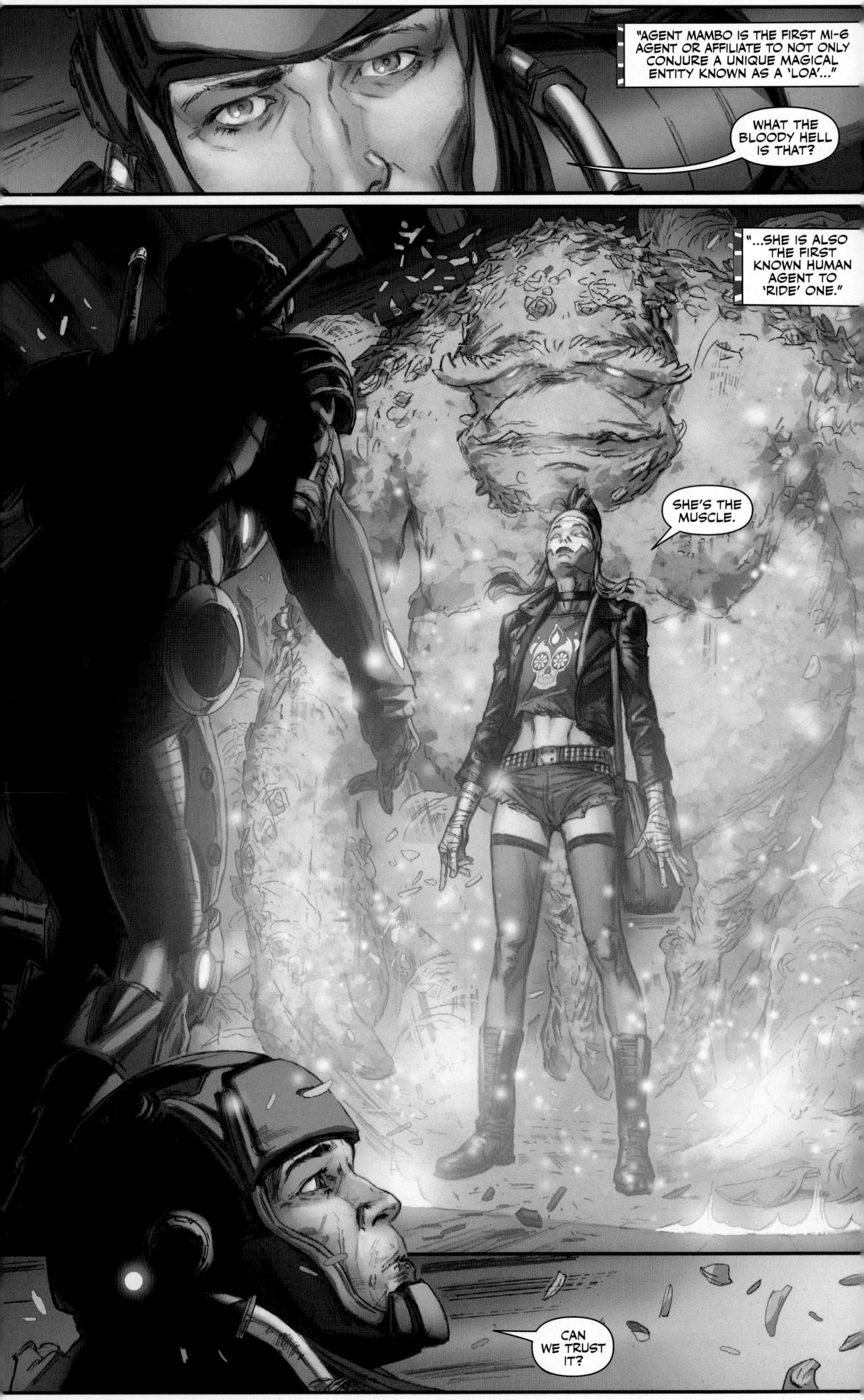
"AGENT MAMBO IS THE FIRST MI-6 AGENT OR AFFILIATE TO NOT ONLY CONJURE A UNIQUE MAGICAL ENTITY KNOWN AS A 'LOA'..."
WHAT THE BLOODY HELL IS THAT?
"...SHE IS ALSO THE FIRST KNOWN HUMAN AGENT TO 'RIDE' ONE."
SHE'S THE MUSCLE.
CAN WE TRUST IT?

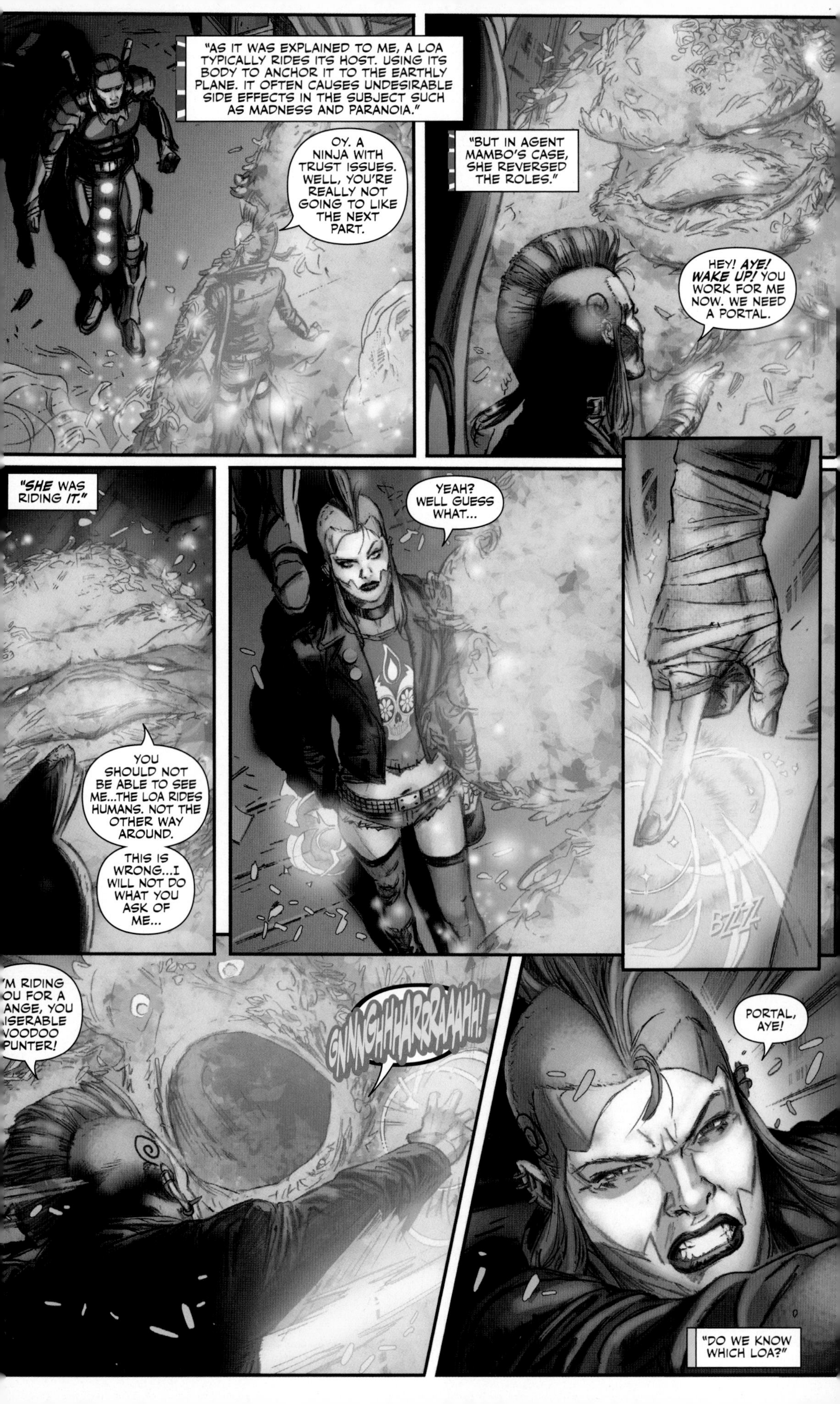
"AS IT WAS EXPLAINED TO ME, A LOA TYPICALLY RIDES ITS HOST. USING ITS BODY TO ANCHOR IT TO THE EARTHLY PLANE. IT OFTEN CAUSES UNDESIRABLE SIDE EFFECTS IN THE SUBJECT SUCH AS MADNESS AND PARANOIA."
OY. A NINJA WITH TRUST ISSUES. WELL, YOU'RE REALLY NOT GOING TO LIKE THE NEXT PART.
"BUT IN AGENT MAMBO'S CASE, SHE REVERSED THE ROLES."
HEY! ***AYE! WAKE UP!*** YOU WORK FOR ME NOW. WE NEED A PORTAL.
"***SHE*** WAS RIDING ***IT.***"
YOU SHOULD NOT BE ABLE TO SEE ME...THE LOA RIDES HUMANS. NOT THE OTHER WAY AROUND.
THIS IS WRONG...I WILL NOT DO WHAT YOU ASK OF ME...
YEAH? WELL GUESS WHAT...
BZZZZ
'M RIDING OU FOR A ANGE, YOU ISERABLE VOODOO PUNTER!
GNNNGHHHARRRAAAHH!
PORTAL, AYE!
"DO WE KNOW WHICH LOA?"

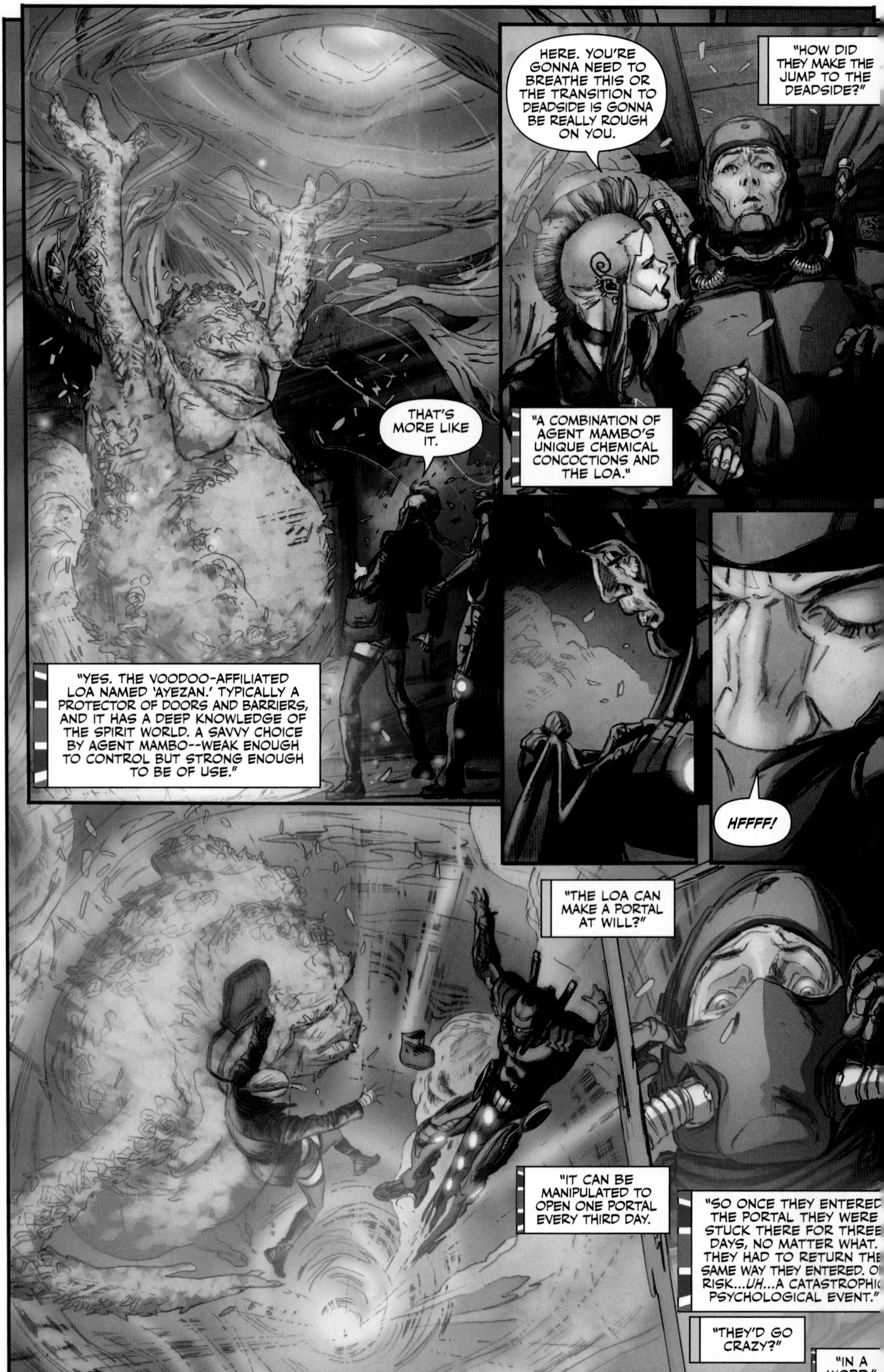

HERE. YOU'RE GONNA NEED TO BREATHE THIS OR THE TRANSITION TO DEADSIDE IS GONNA BE REALLY ROUGH ON YOU.
"HOW DID THEY MAKE THE JUMP TO THE DEADSIDE?"
THAT'S MORE LIKE IT.
"A COMBINATION OF AGENT MAMBO'S UNIQUE CHEMICAL CONCOCTIONS AND THE LOA."
"YES. THE VOODOO-AFFILIATED LOA NAMED 'AYEZAN.' TYPICALLY A PROTECTOR OF DOORS AND BARRIERS, AND IT HAS A DEEP KNOWLEDGE OF THE SPIRIT WORLD. A SAVVY CHOICE BY AGENT MAMBO--WEAK ENOUGH TO CONTROL BUT STRONG ENOUGH TO BE OF USE."
HFFFF!
"THE LOA CAN MAKE A PORTAL AT WILL?"
"IT CAN BE MANIPULATED TO OPEN ONE PORTAL EVERY THIRD DAY.
"SO ONCE THEY ENTERED THE PORTAL THEY WERE STUCK THERE FOR THREE DAYS, NO MATTER WHAT. THEY HAD TO RETURN THE SAME WAY THEY ENTERED. OR RISK...*UH*...A CATASTROPHIC PSYCHOLOGICAL EVENT."
"THEY'D GO CRAZY?"
"IN A WORD."

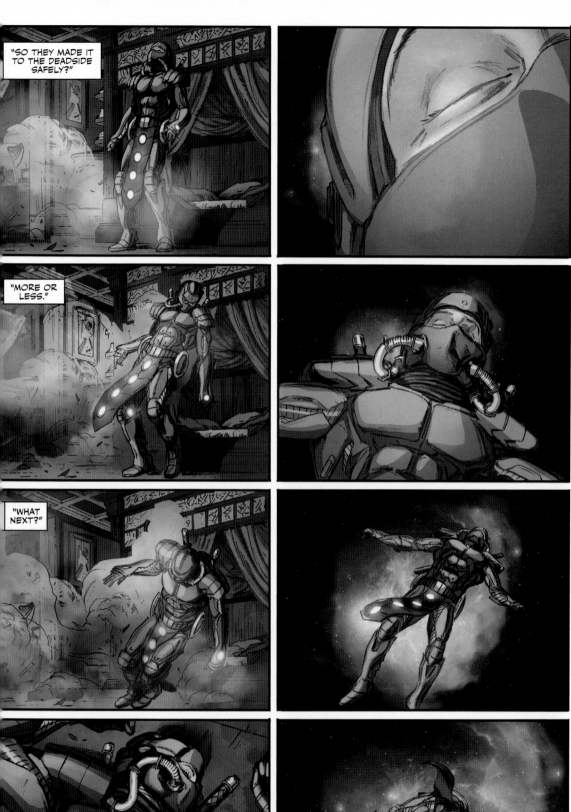

"SO THEY MADE IT TO THE DEADSIDE SAFELY?"

"MORE OR LESS."

"WHAT NEXT?"

"WITHOUT EVER HAVING BEEN TO THE DEADSIDE...IT MIGHT BE A LITTLE HARD TO EXPLAIN IT..."

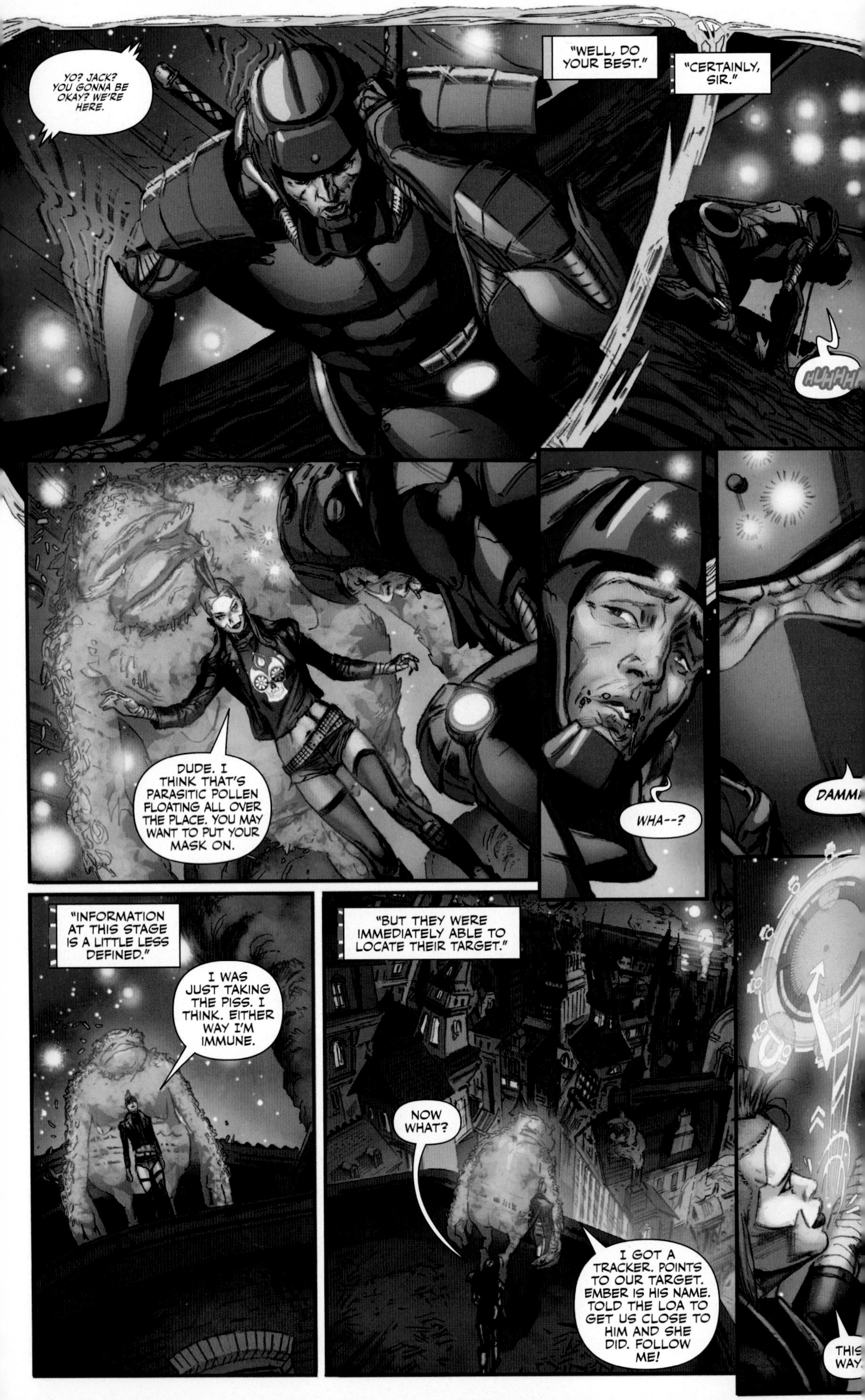
YO? JACK? YOU GONNA BE OKAY? WE'RE HERE.
"WELL, DO YOUR BEST."
"CERTAINLY, SIR."
HUHHH
DUDE. I THINK THAT'S PARASITIC POLLEN FLOATING ALL OVER THE PLACE. YOU MAY WANT TO PUT YOUR MASK ON.
WHA--?
DAMM
"INFORMATION AT THIS STAGE IS A LITTLE LESS DEFINED."
I WAS JUST TAKING THE PISS. I THINK. EITHER WAY I'M IMMUNE.
"BUT THEY WERE IMMEDIATELY ABLE TO LOCATE THEIR TARGET."
NOW WHAT?
I GOT A TRACKER. POINTS TO OUR TARGET. EMBER IS HIS NAME. TOLD THE LOA TO GET US CLOSE TO HIM AND SHE DID. FOLLOW ME!
THIS WAY.

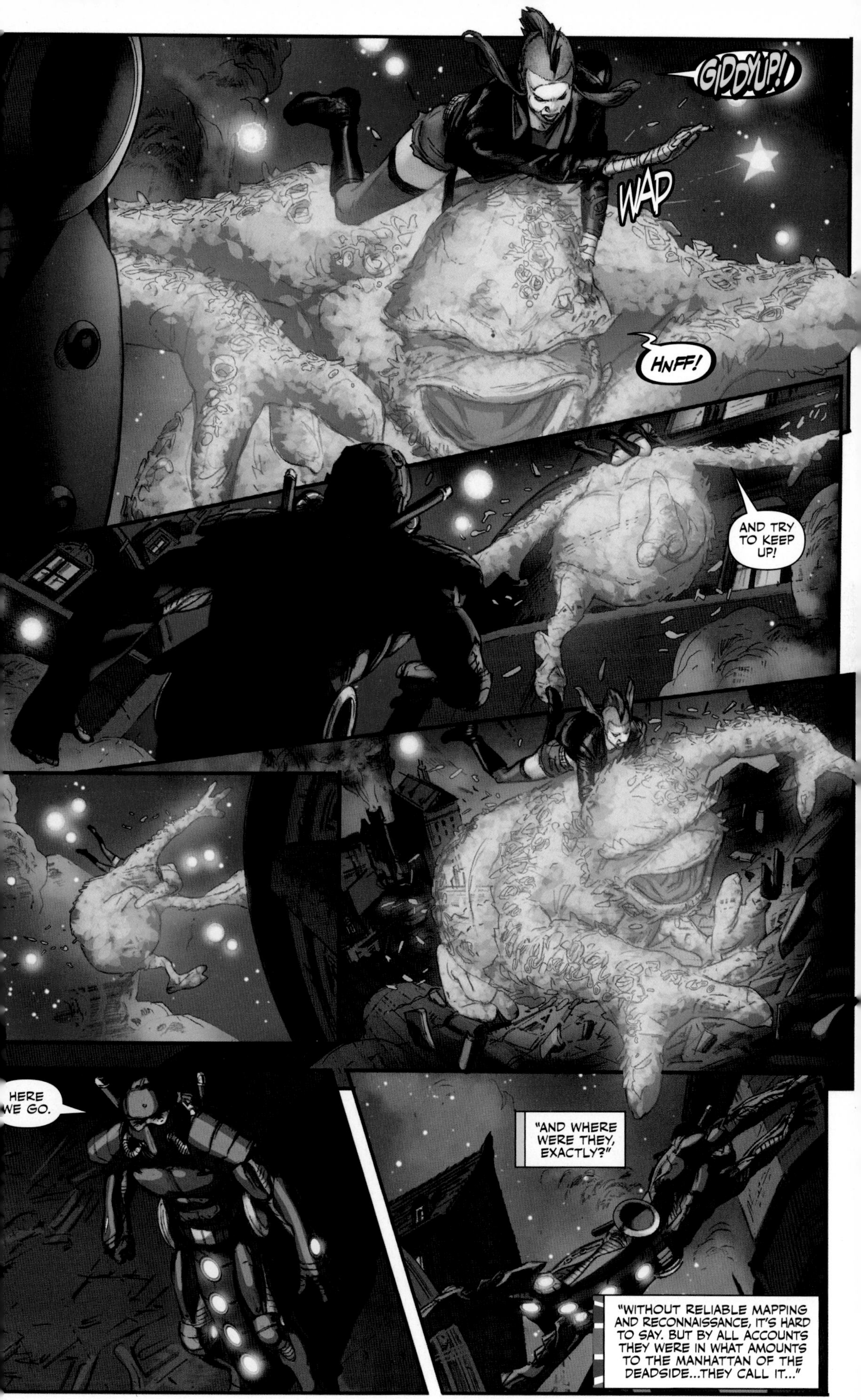
GIDDYUP!
WAP
HNFF!
AND TRY TO KEEP UP!
HERE WE GO.
"AND WHERE WERE THEY, EXACTLY?"
"WITHOUT RELIABLE MAPPING AND RECONNAISSANCE, IT'S HARD TO SAY. BUT BY ALL ACCOUNTS THEY WERE IN WHAT AMOUNTS TO THE MANHATTAN OF THE DEADSIDE...THEY CALL IT..."

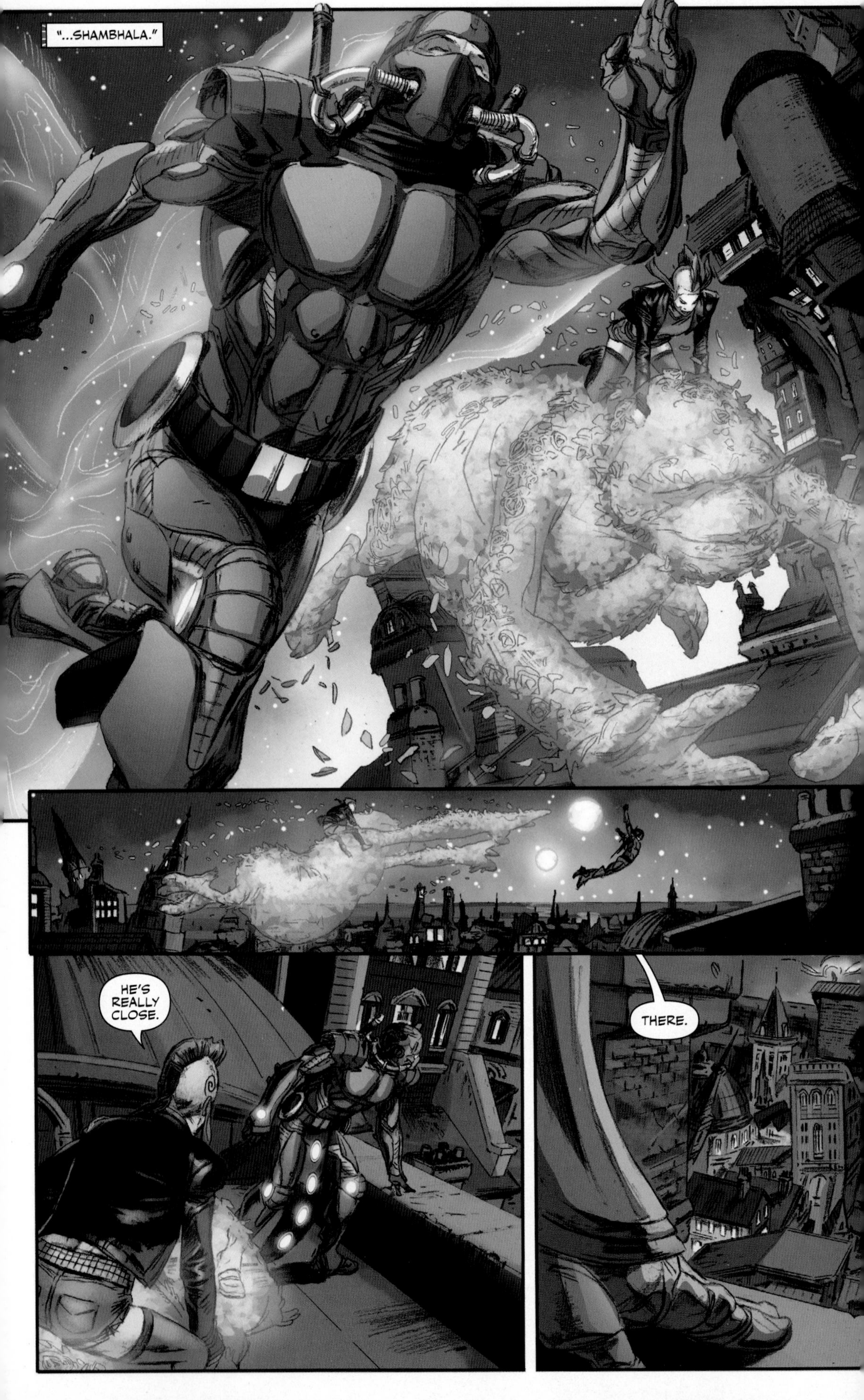
"...SHAMBHALA."
HE'S REALLY CLOSE.
THERE.

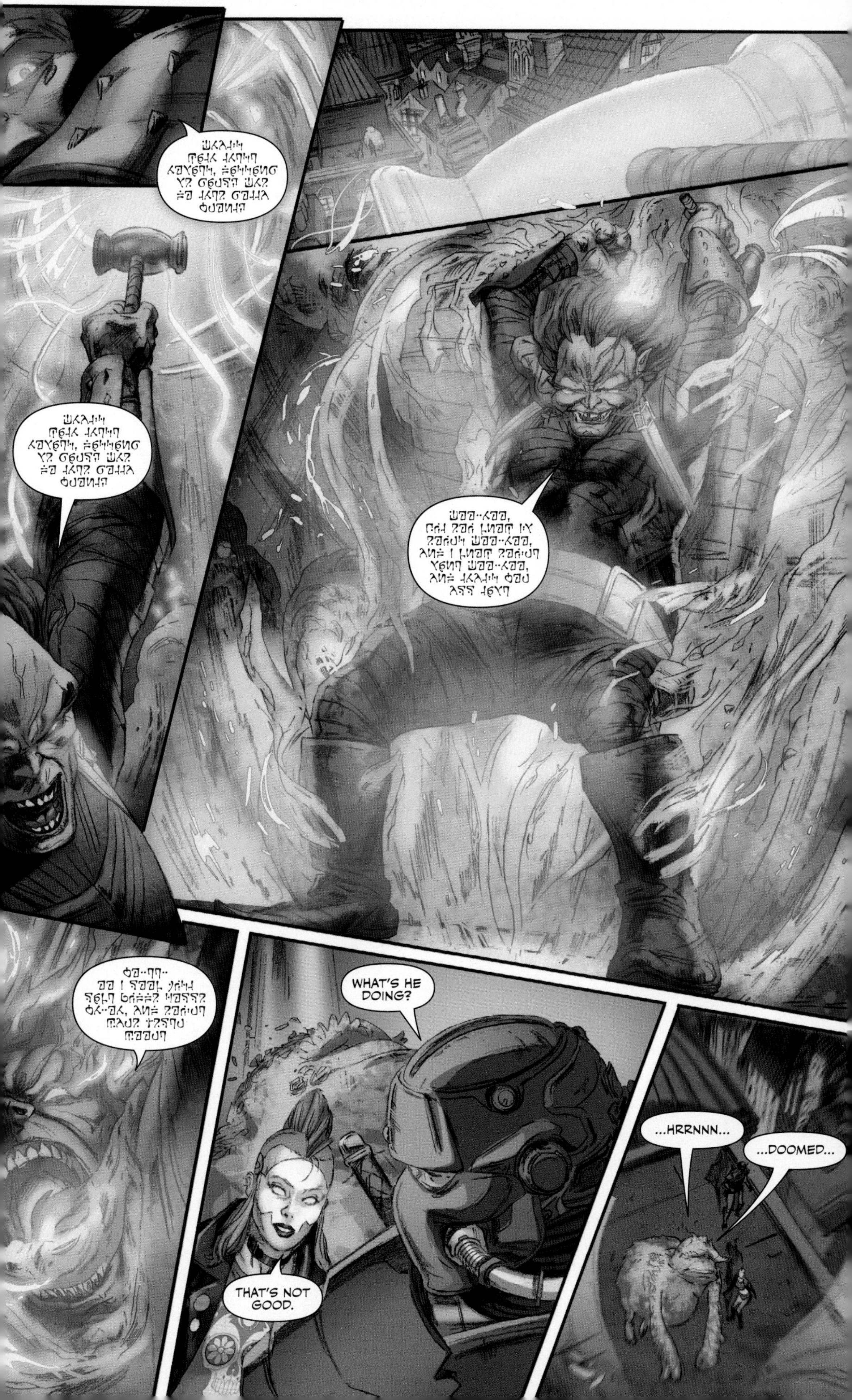
WHAT'S HE DOING?
THAT'S NOT GOOD.
...HRRNNN...
...DOOMED...

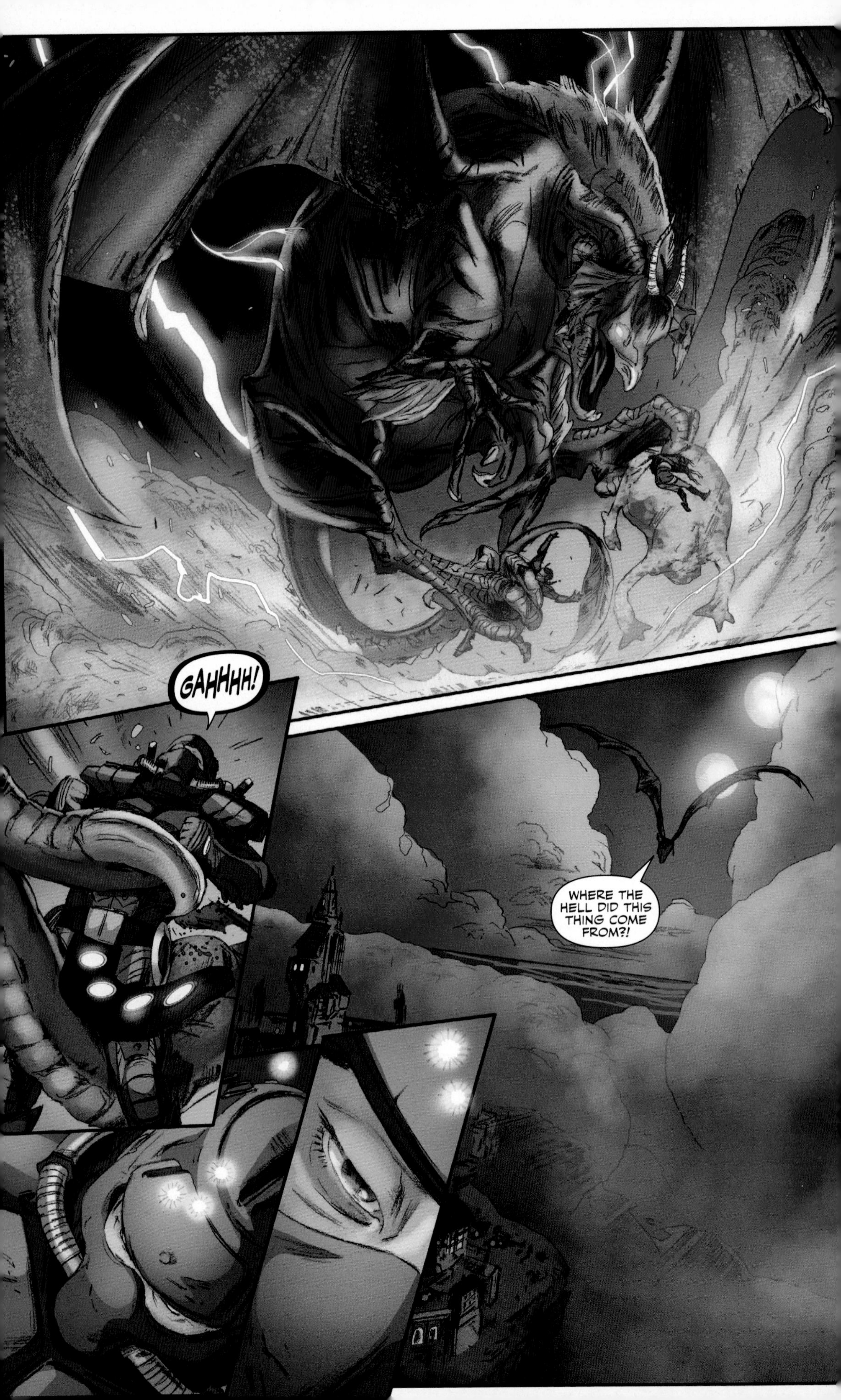
GAHHHH!
WHERE THE HELL DID THIS THING COME FROM?!

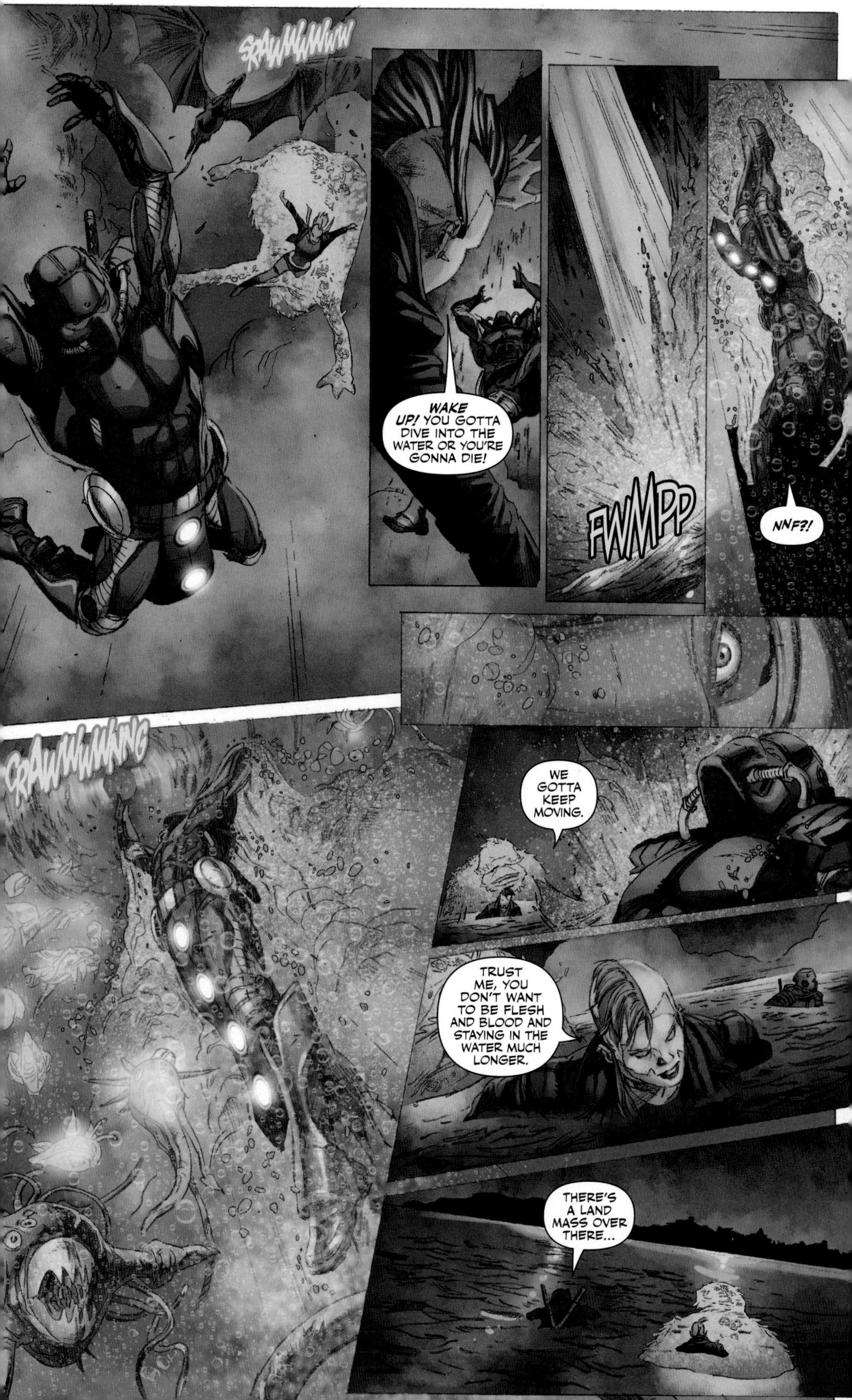
SRAWWWWWW
WAKE UP! YOU GOTTA DIVE INTO THE WATER OR YOU'RE GONNA DIE!
FWMPP
NNF?!
CRAWWWWWWNG
WE GOTTA KEEP MOVING.
TRUST ME, YOU DON'T WANT TO BE FLESH AND BLOOD AND STAYING IN THE WATER MUCH LONGER.
THERE'S A LAND MASS OVER THERE...

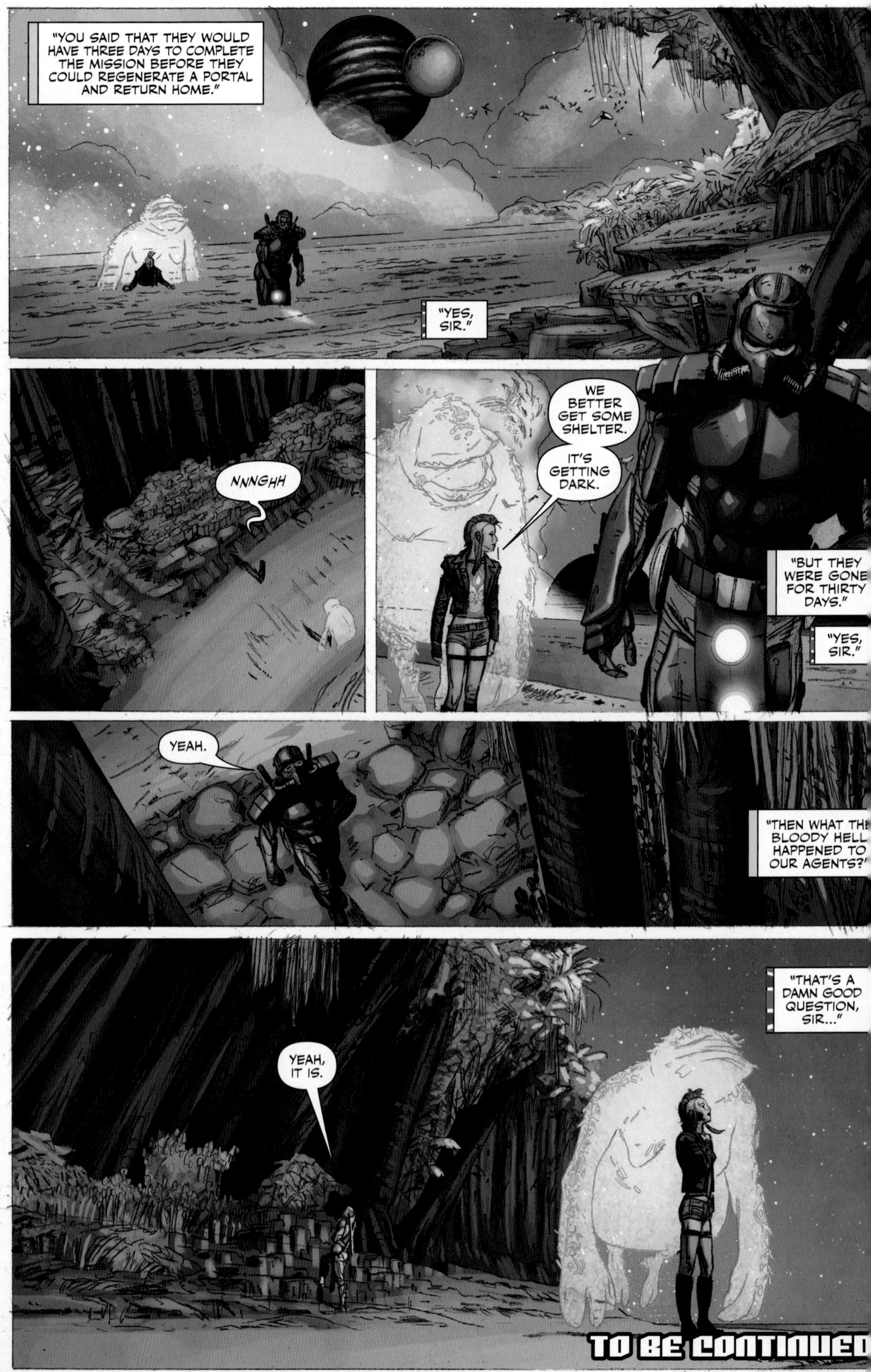
"YOU SAID THAT THEY WOULD HAVE THREE DAYS TO COMPLETE THE MISSION BEFORE THEY COULD REGENERATE A PORTAL AND RETURN HOME."
"YES, SIR."
NNNGHH
WE BETTER GET SOME SHELTER.
IT'S GETTING DARK.
"BUT THEY WERE GONE FOR THIRTY DAYS."
"YES, SIR."
YEAH.
"THEN WHAT THE BLOODY HELL HAPPENED TO OUR AGENTS?"
"THAT'S A DAMN GOOD QUESTION, SIR..."
YEAH, IT IS.
TO BE CONTINUED

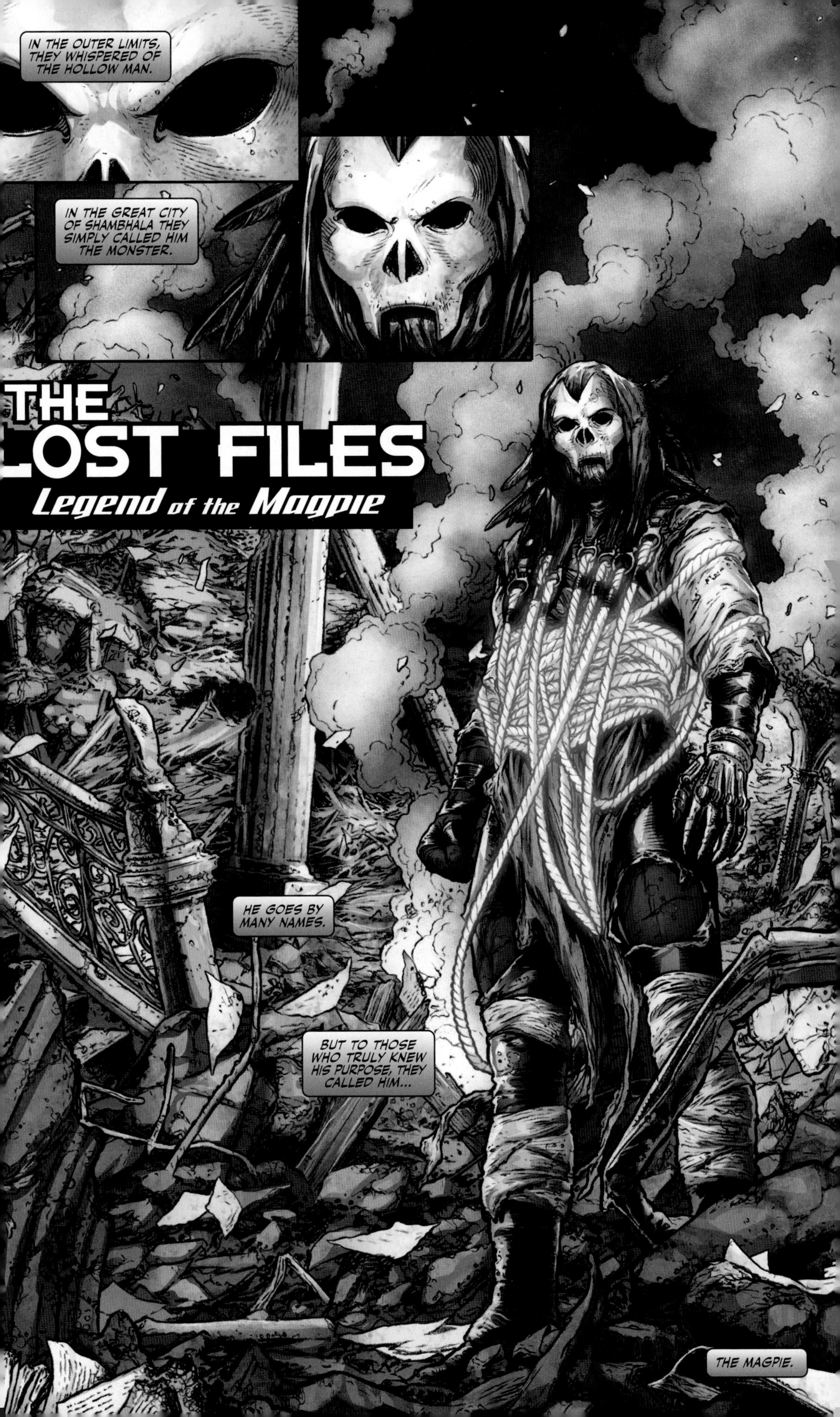
IN THE OUTER LIMITS, THEY WHISPERED OF THE HOLLOW MAN.
IN THE GREAT CITY OF SHAMBHALA THEY SIMPLY CALLED HIM THE MONSTER.
THE LOST FILES
Legend of the Magpie
HE GOES BY MANY NAMES.
BUT TO THOSE WHO TRULY KNEW HIS PURPOSE, THEY CALLED HIM...
THE MAGPIE.

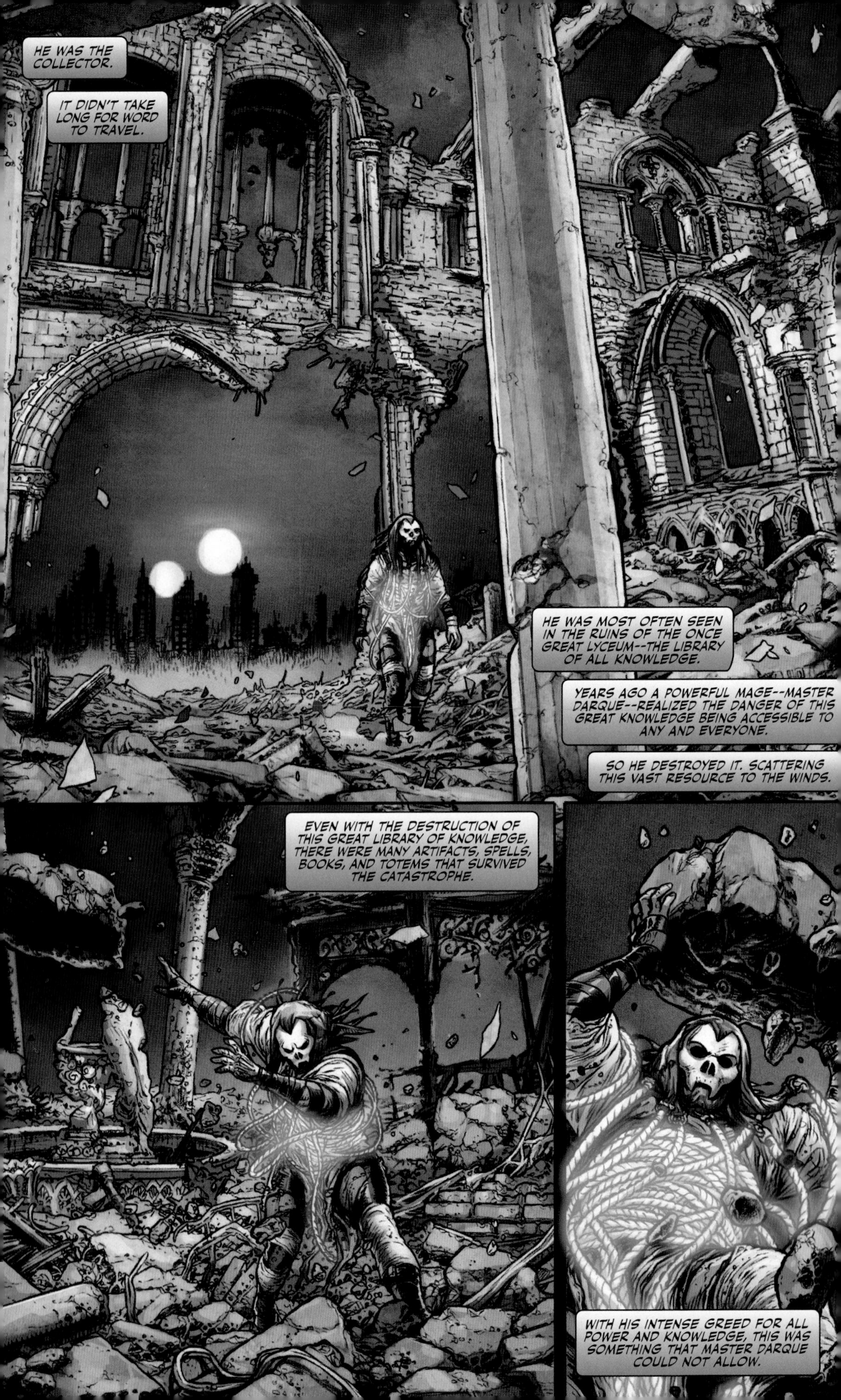
HE WAS THE COLLECTOR.
IT DIDN'T TAKE LONG FOR WORD TO TRAVEL.
HE WAS MOST OFTEN SEEN IN THE RUINS OF THE ONCE GREAT LYCEUM--THE LIBRARY OF ALL KNOWLEDGE.
YEARS AGO A POWERFUL MAGE--MASTER DARQUE--REALIZED THE DANGER OF THIS GREAT KNOWLEDGE BEING ACCESSIBLE TO ANY AND EVERYONE.
SO HE DESTROYED IT. SCATTERING THIS VAST RESOURCE TO THE WINDS.
EVEN WITH THE DESTRUCTION OF THIS GREAT LIBRARY OF KNOWLEDGE, THERE WERE MANY ARTIFACTS, SPELLS, BOOKS, AND TOTEMS THAT SURVIVED THE CATASTROPHE.
WITH HIS INTENSE GREED FOR ALL POWER AND KNOWLEDGE, THIS WAS SOMETHING THAT MASTER DARQUE COULD NOT ALLOW.

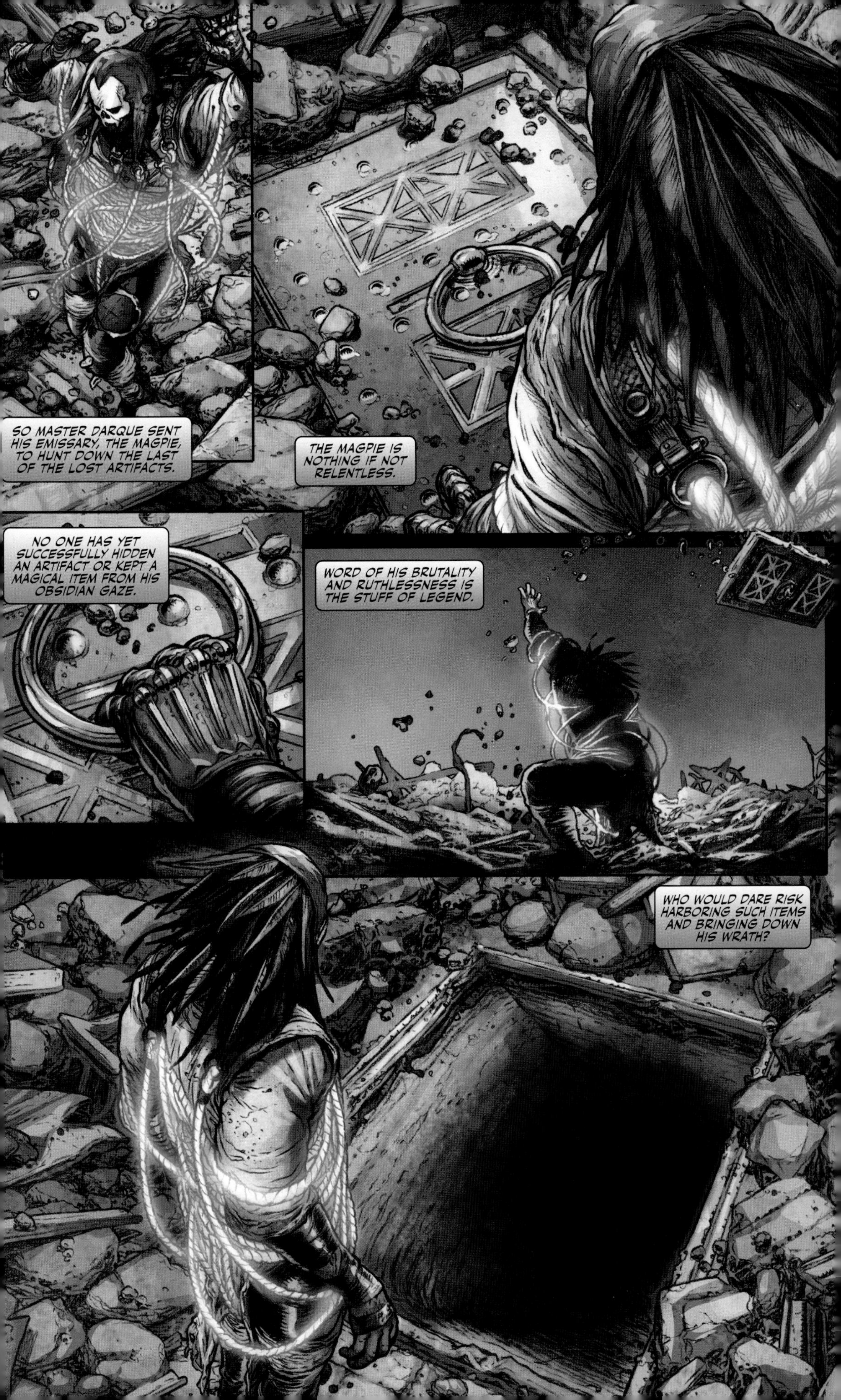
SO MASTER DARQUE SENT HIS EMISSARY, THE MAGPIE, TO HUNT DOWN THE LAST OF THE LOST ARTIFACTS.
THE MAGPIE IS NOTHING IF NOT RELENTLESS.
NO ONE HAS YET SUCCESSFULLY HIDDEN AN ARTIFACT OR KEPT A MAGICAL ITEM FROM HIS OBSIDIAN GAZE.
WORD OF HIS BRUTALITY AND RUTHLESSNESS IS THE STUFF OF LEGEND.
WHO WOULD DARE RISK HARBORING SUCH ITEMS AND BRINGING DOWN HIS WRATH?

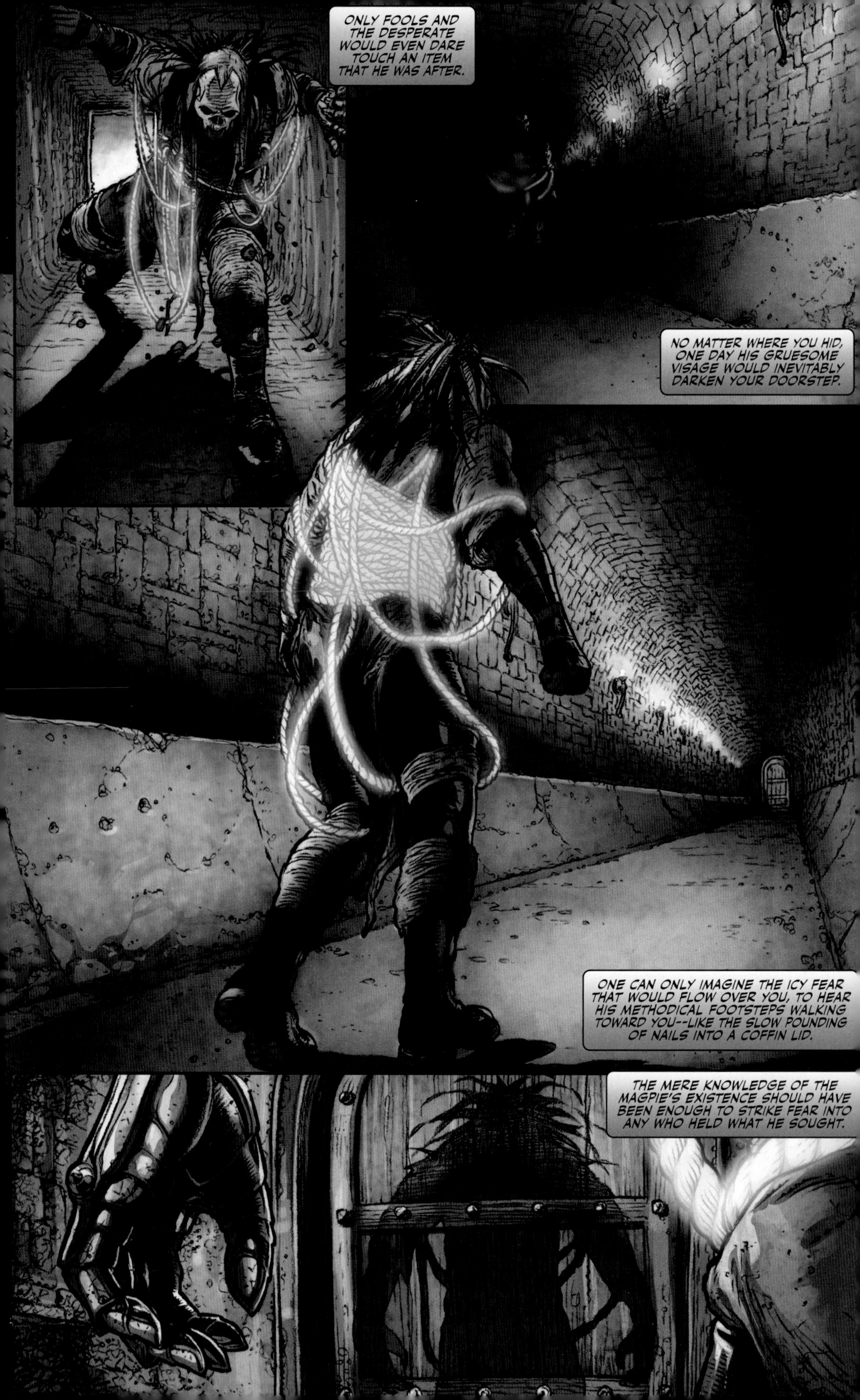
ONLY FOOLS AND THE DESPERATE WOULD EVEN DARE TOUCH AN ITEM THAT HE WAS AFTER.
NO MATTER WHERE YOU HID, ONE DAY HIS GRUESOME VISAGE WOULD INEVITABLY DARKEN YOUR DOORSTEP.
ONE CAN ONLY IMAGINE THE ICY FEAR THAT WOULD FLOW OVER YOU, TO HEAR HIS METHODICAL FOOTSTEPS WALKING TOWARD YOU--LIKE THE SLOW POUNDING OF NAILS INTO A COFFIN LID.
THE MERE KNOWLEDGE OF THE MAGPIE'S EXISTENCE SHOULD HAVE BEEN ENOUGH TO STRIKE FEAR INTO ANY WHO HELD WHAT HE SOUGHT.

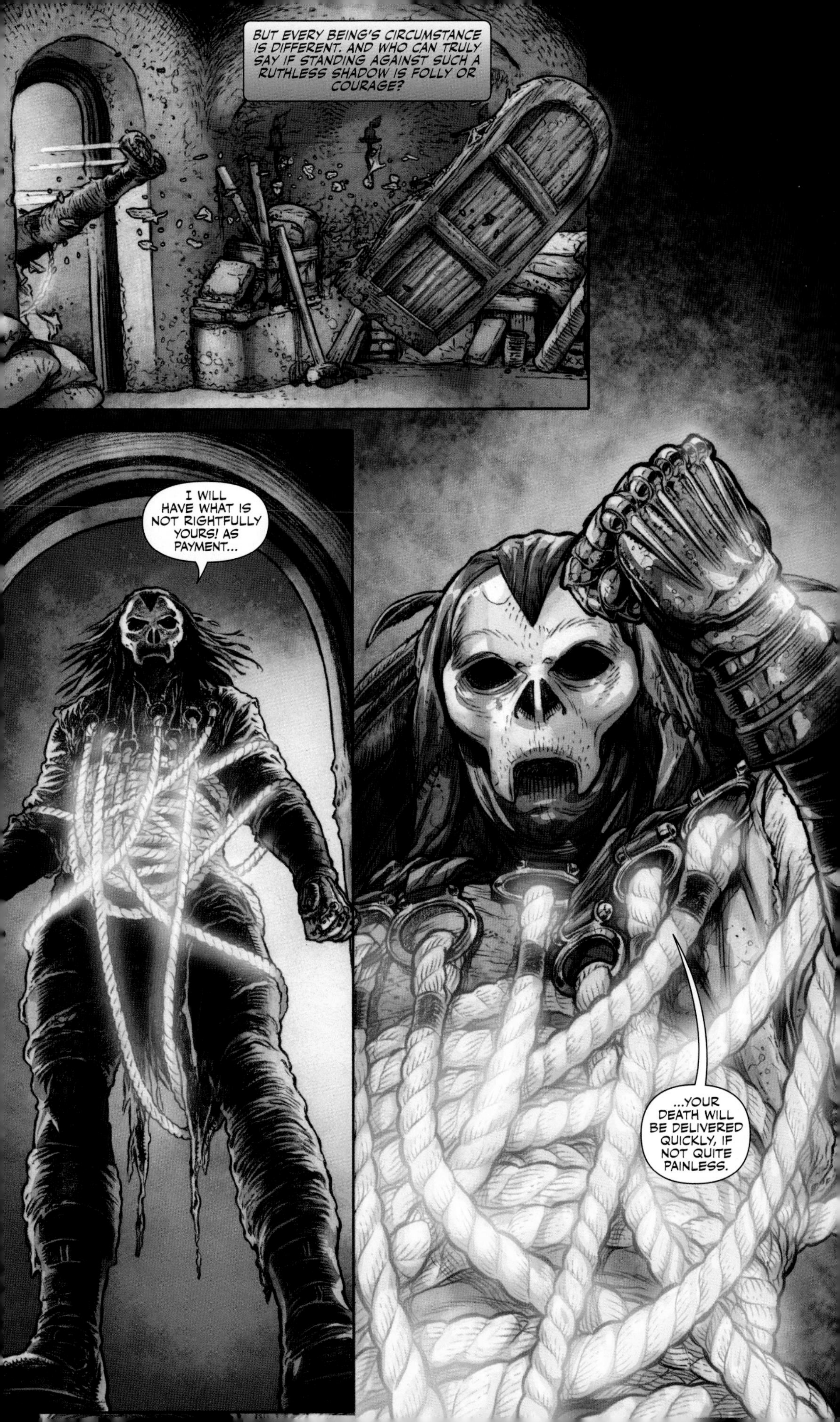
BUT EVERY BEING'S CIRCUMSTANCE IS DIFFERENT. AND WHO CAN TRULY SAY IF STANDING AGAINST SUCH A RUTHLESS SHADOW IS FOLLY OR COURAGE?
I WILL HAVE WHAT IS NOT RIGHTFULLY YOURS! AS PAYMENT...
...YOUR DEATH WILL BE DELIVERED QUICKLY, IF NOT QUITE PAINLESS.

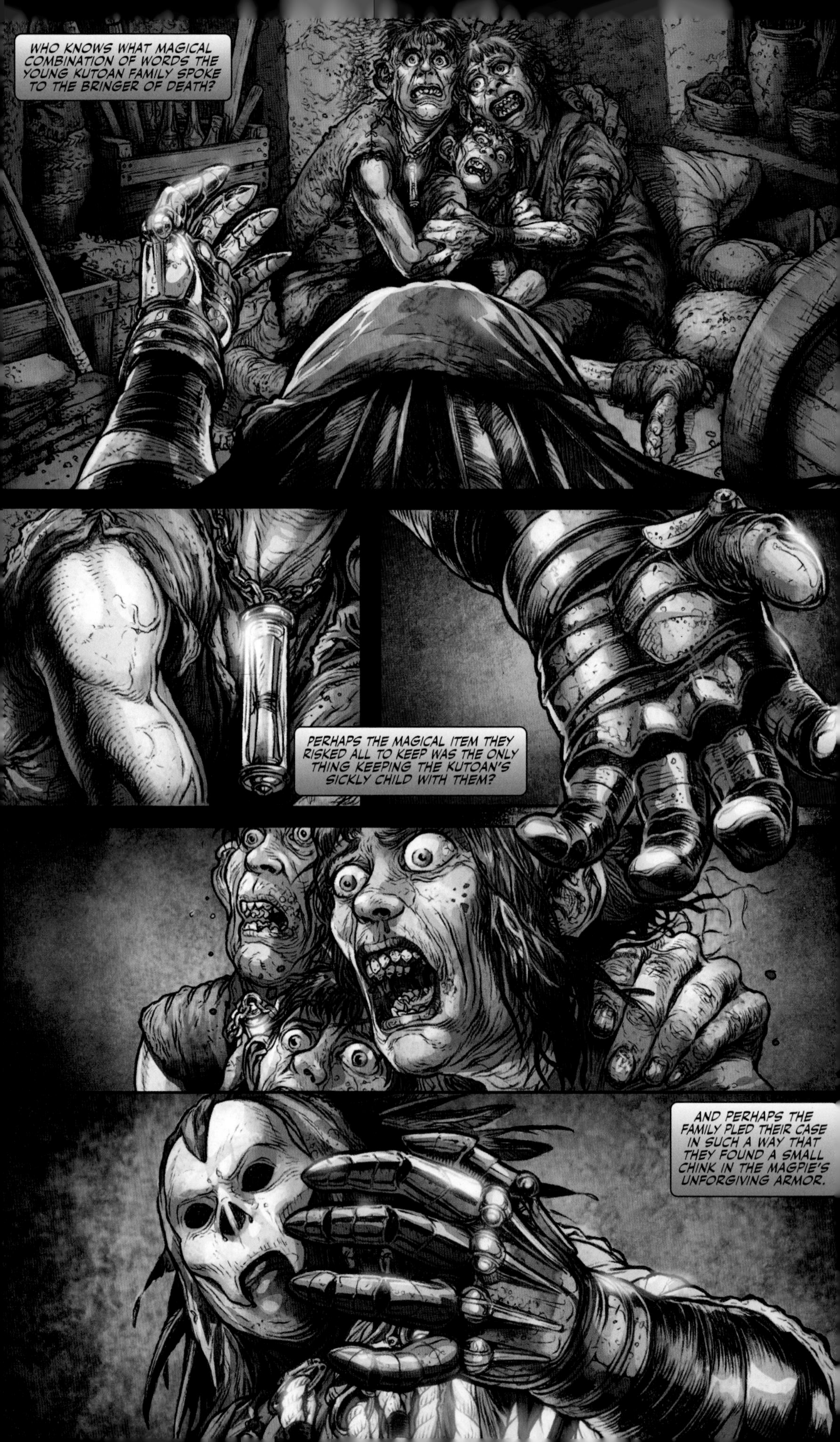
WHO KNOWS WHAT MAGICAL COMBINATION OF WORDS THE YOUNG KUTOAN FAMILY SPOKE TO THE BRINGER OF DEATH?
PERHAPS THE MAGICAL ITEM THEY RISKED ALL TO KEEP WAS THE ONLY THING KEEPING THE KUTOAN'S SICKLY CHILD WITH THEM?
AND PERHAPS THE FAMILY PLED THEIR CASE IN SUCH A WAY THAT THEY FOUND A SMALL CHINK IN THE MAGPIE'S UNFORGIVING ARMOR.

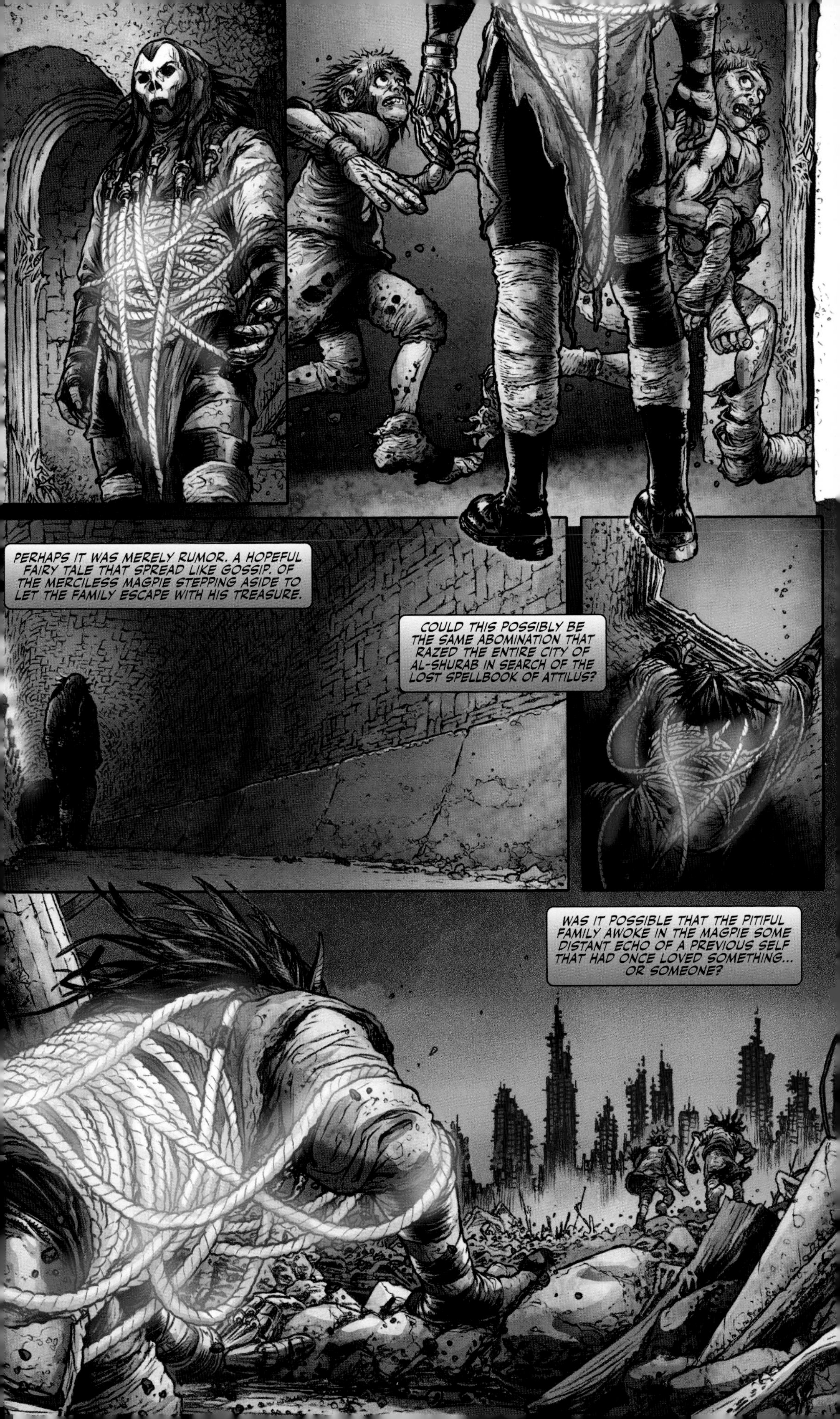
PERHAPS IT WAS MERELY RUMOR. A HOPEFUL FAIRY TALE THAT SPREAD LIKE GOSSIP. OF THE MERCILESS MAGPIE STEPPING ASIDE TO LET THE FAMILY ESCAPE WITH HIS TREASURE.
COULD THIS POSSIBLY BE THE SAME ABOMINATION THAT RAZED THE ENTIRE CITY OF AL-SHURAB IN SEARCH OF THE LOST SPELLBOOK OF ATTILUS?
WAS IT POSSIBLE THAT THE PITIFUL FAMILY AWOKE IN THE MAGPIE SOME DISTANT ECHO OF A PREVIOUS SELF THAT HAD ONCE LOVED SOMETHING... OR SOMEONE?

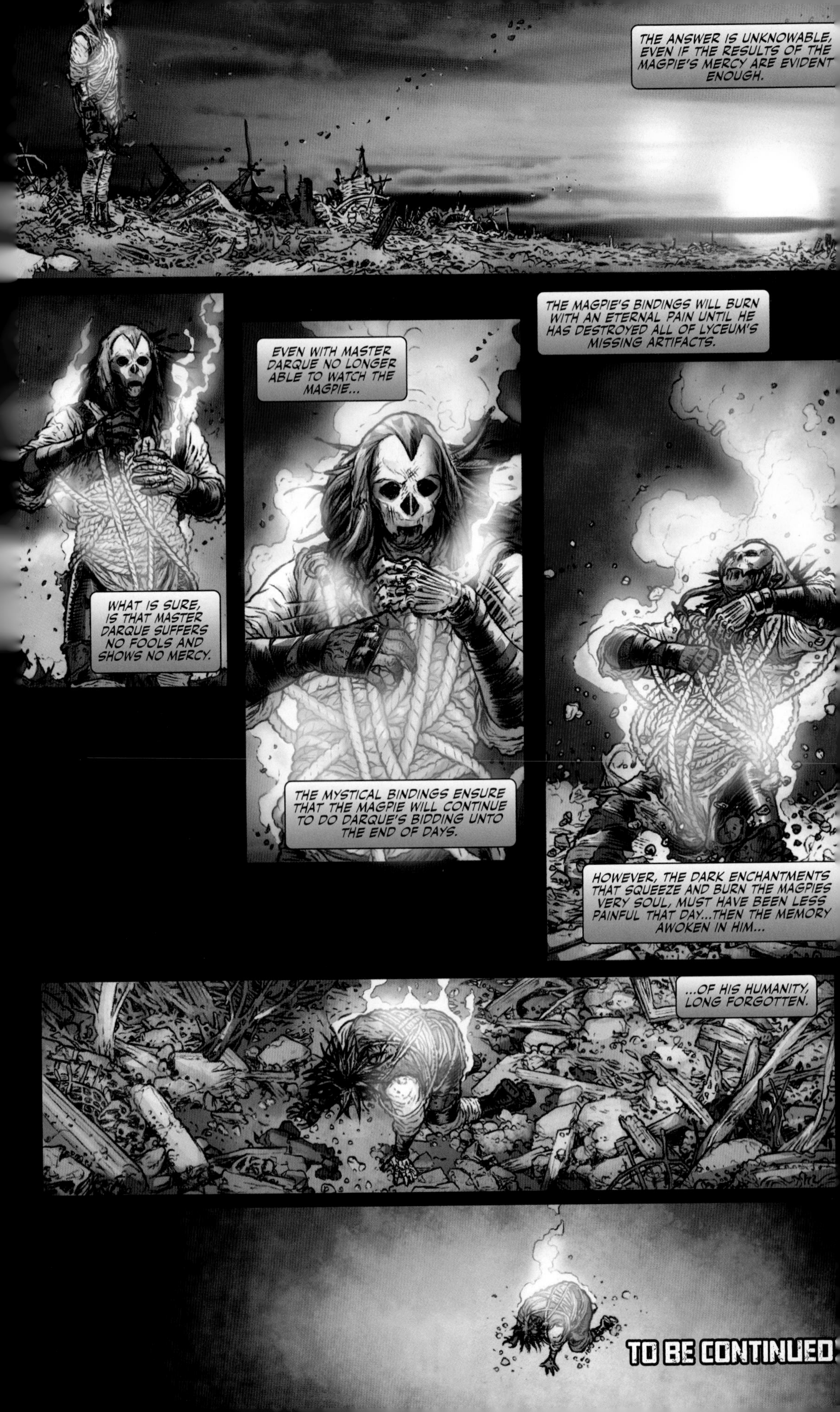

THE ANSWER IS UNKNOWABLE, EVEN IF THE RESULTS OF THE MAGPIE'S MERCY ARE EVIDENT ENOUGH.
WHAT IS SURE, IS THAT MASTER DARQUE SUFFERS NO FOOLS AND SHOWS NO MERCY.
EVEN WITH MASTER DARQUE NO LONGER ABLE TO WATCH THE MAGPIE...
THE MYSTICAL BINDINGS ENSURE THAT THE MAGPIE WILL CONTINUE TO DO DARQUE'S BIDDING UNTO THE END OF DAYS.
THE MAGPIE'S BINDINGS WILL BURN WITH AN ETERNAL PAIN UNTIL HE HAS DESTROYED ALL OF LYCEUM'S MISSING ARTIFACTS.
HOWEVER, THE DARK ENCHANTMENTS THAT SQUEEZE AND BURN THE MAGPIES VERY SOUL, MUST HAVE BEEN LESS PAINFUL THAT DAY...THEN THE MEMORY AWOKEN IN HIM...
...OF HIS HUMANITY, LONG FORGOTTEN.
TO BE CONTINUED

VALIANT

#11

NINJAK

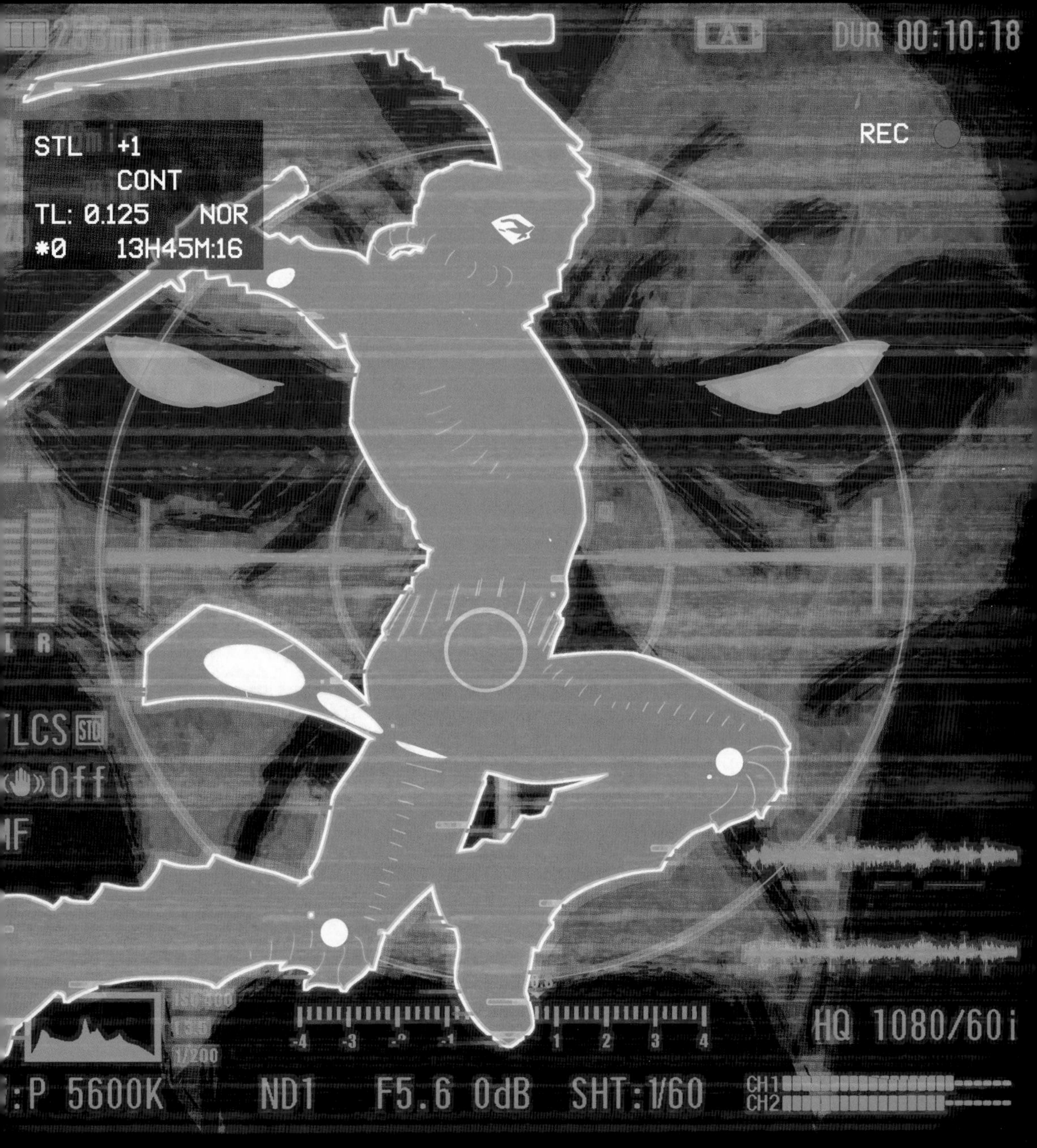
DUR 00:10:18
REC
STL +1
CONT
TL: 0.125 NOR
*0 13H45M:16
TLCS
Off
HQ 1080/60i
:P 5600K
ND1
F5.6 0dB
SHT:1/60
CH1
CH2

OPERATION DEADSIDE:

RECORDING: 02/04

MATT KINDT · DOUG BRAITHWAITE · JUAN JOSÉ RYP · BRIAN REBER

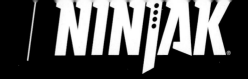

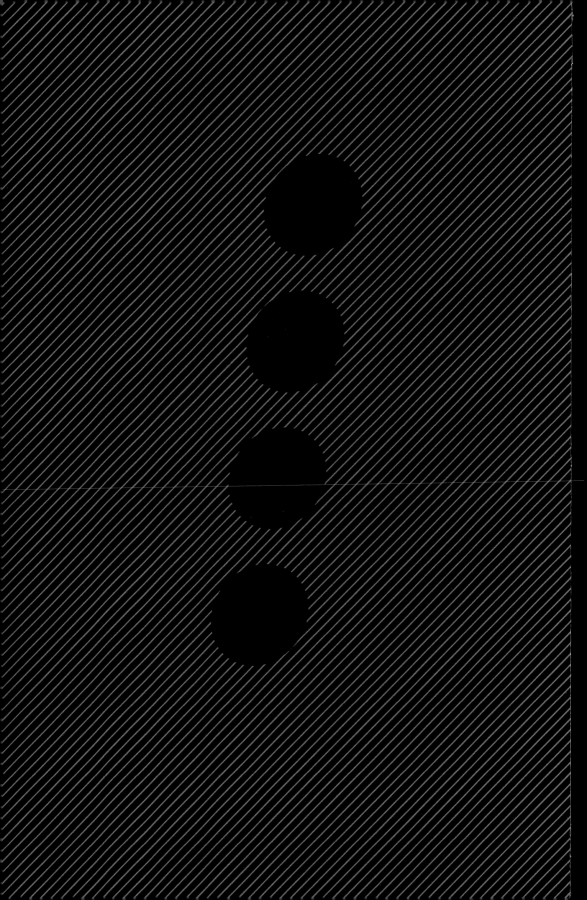

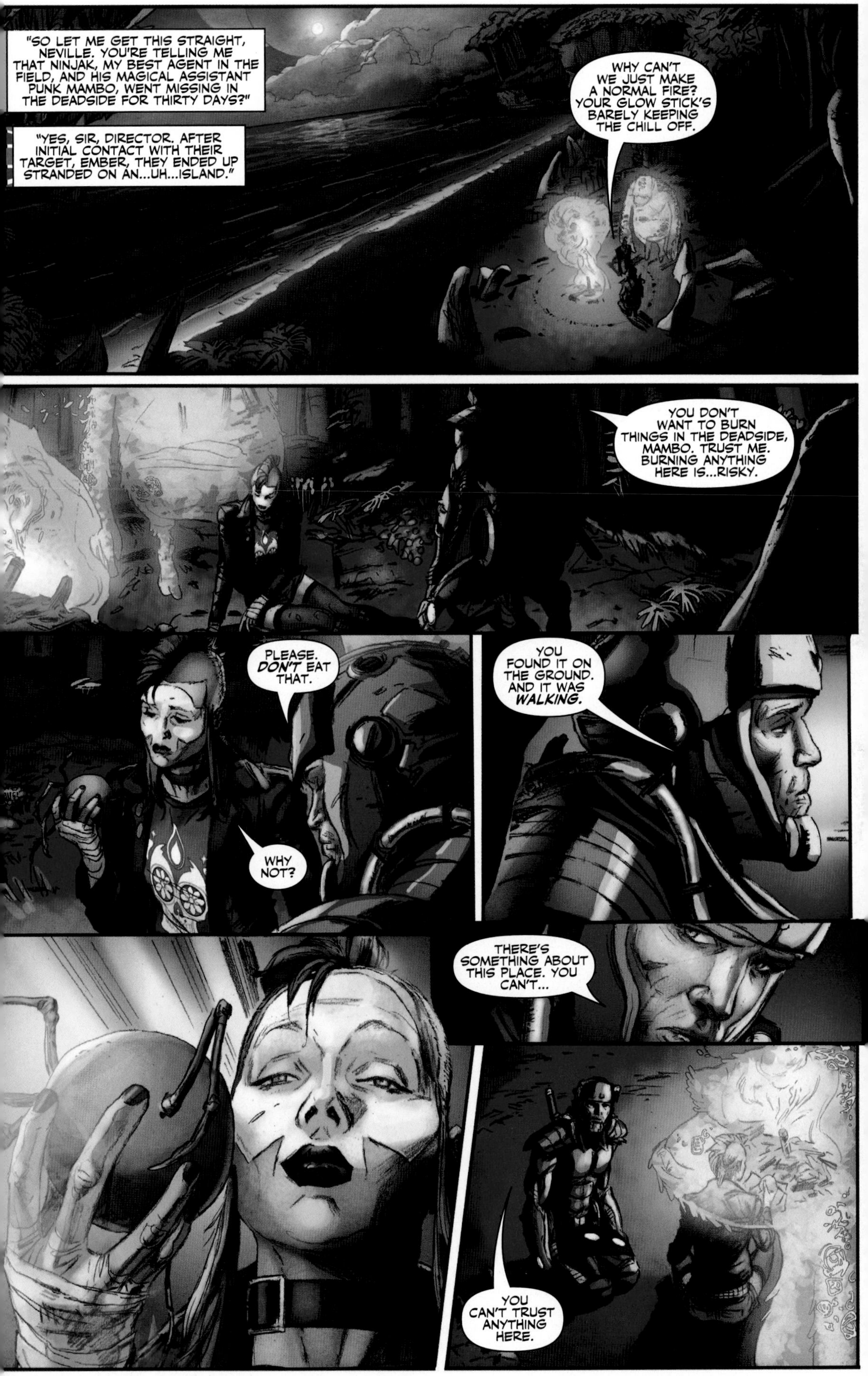
"SO LET ME GET THIS STRAIGHT, NEVILLE. YOU'RE TELLING ME THAT NINJAK, MY BEST AGENT IN THE FIELD, AND HIS MAGICAL ASSISTANT PUNK MAMBO, WENT MISSING IN THE DEADSIDE FOR THIRTY DAYS?"
"YES, SIR, DIRECTOR. AFTER INITIAL CONTACT WITH THEIR TARGET, EMBER, THEY ENDED UP STRANDED ON AN...UH...ISLAND."
WHY CAN'T WE JUST MAKE A NORMAL FIRE? YOUR GLOW STICK'S BARELY KEEPING THE CHILL OFF.
YOU DON'T WANT TO BURN THINGS IN THE DEADSIDE, MAMBO. TRUST ME. BURNING ANYTHING HERE IS...RISKY.
PLEASE. *DON'T* EAT THAT.
WHY NOT?
YOU FOUND IT ON THE GROUND. AND IT WAS *WALKING.*
THERE'S SOMETHING ABOUT THIS PLACE. YOU CAN'T...
YOU CAN'T TRUST ANYTHING HERE.

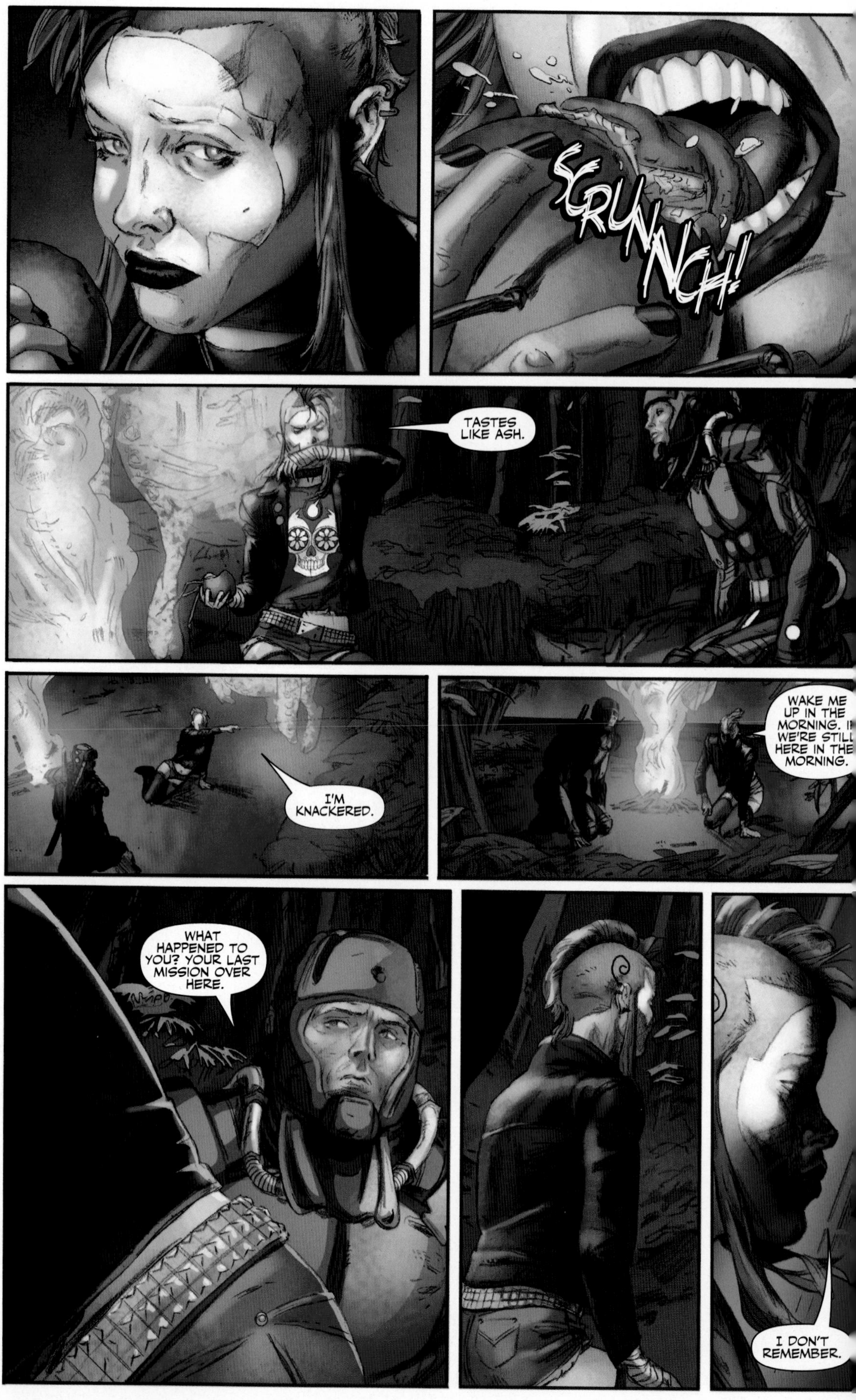
SCRUNNNCH!
TASTES LIKE ASH.
I'M KNACKERED.
WAKE ME UP IN THE MORNING. IF WE'RE STILL HERE IN THE MORNING.
WHAT HAPPENED TO YOU? YOUR LAST MISSION OVER HERE.
I DON'T REMEMBER.

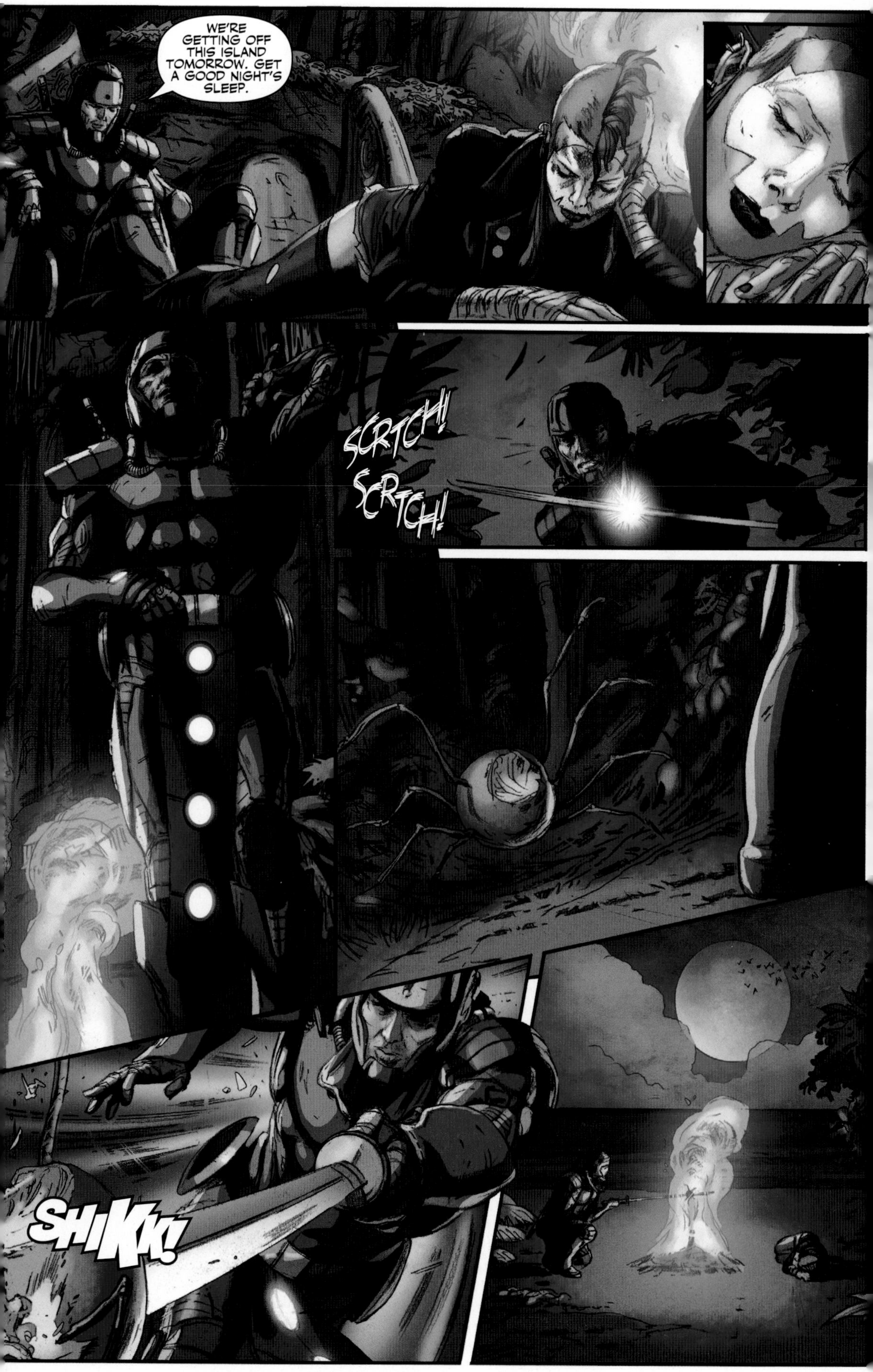
WE'RE GETTING OFF THIS ISLAND TOMORROW. GET A GOOD NIGHT'S SLEEP.
SCRTCH! SCRTCH!
SHIKK!

"WE DIDN'T EXPECT A PROLONGED ENGAGEMENT. THE TWO RAN OUT OF SUPPLIES QUICKLY....AND WHILE NINJA-K WAS EQUIPPED WITH A HOST OF EXPERIMENTAL TECH OF HIS OWN DESIGN, NONE OF IT WAS DESIGNED FOR AIR OR SEA TRAVEL."

WHILE YOU SLEPT, I PUT A MINI-SATELLITE CAMERA TOGETHER WITH MY EXISTING TECH.

WE NEED TO GET TO A CLEARING SO I CAN LAUNCH IT. THEN WE GET TO HIGH GROUND.

"NAVIGATION IN THE DEADSIDE IS PROBLEMATIC. THE CONSTELLATIONS ARE UNCHARTED. TRADITIONAL NAVIGATION TECHNIQUES ARE USELESS."

THE CAMERA WILL BOUNCE IMAGES BACK DOWN TO ME. THEN WE'LL KNOW WHICH WAY BACK TO SHAMBHALA.

"SO EVEN IF THEY HAD A WAY OFF THE ISLAND, NAVIGATING THEIR WAY BACK TO THE TARGET'S LOCATION IN SHAMBHALA WOULD BE STRICTLY GUESSWORK."

WE GET A CLEAR PICTURE OF THIS BLOOD PLACE. THEN W' GET OUT OF HERE.

YOU THINK YOU HAVE AN ANSWER FOR EVERYTHING, DON'T YOU? NOT EVERYTHING HAS AN ANSWER, TRUST ME. THIS PLACE...DOES *NOT* HAVE AN ANSWER.

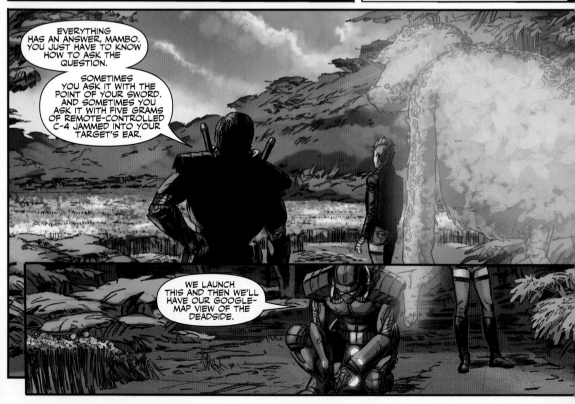

EVERYTHING HAS AN ANSWER, MAMBO. YOU JUST HAVE TO KNOW HOW TO ASK THE QUESTION.

SOMETIMES YOU ASK IT WITH THE POINT OF YOUR SWORD. AND SOMETIMES YOU ASK IT WITH FIVE GRAMS OF REMOTE-CONTROLLED C-4 JAMMED INTO YOUR TARGET'S EAR.

WE LAUNCH THIS AND THEN WE'LL HAVE OUR GOOGLE-MAP VIEW OF THE DEADSIDE.

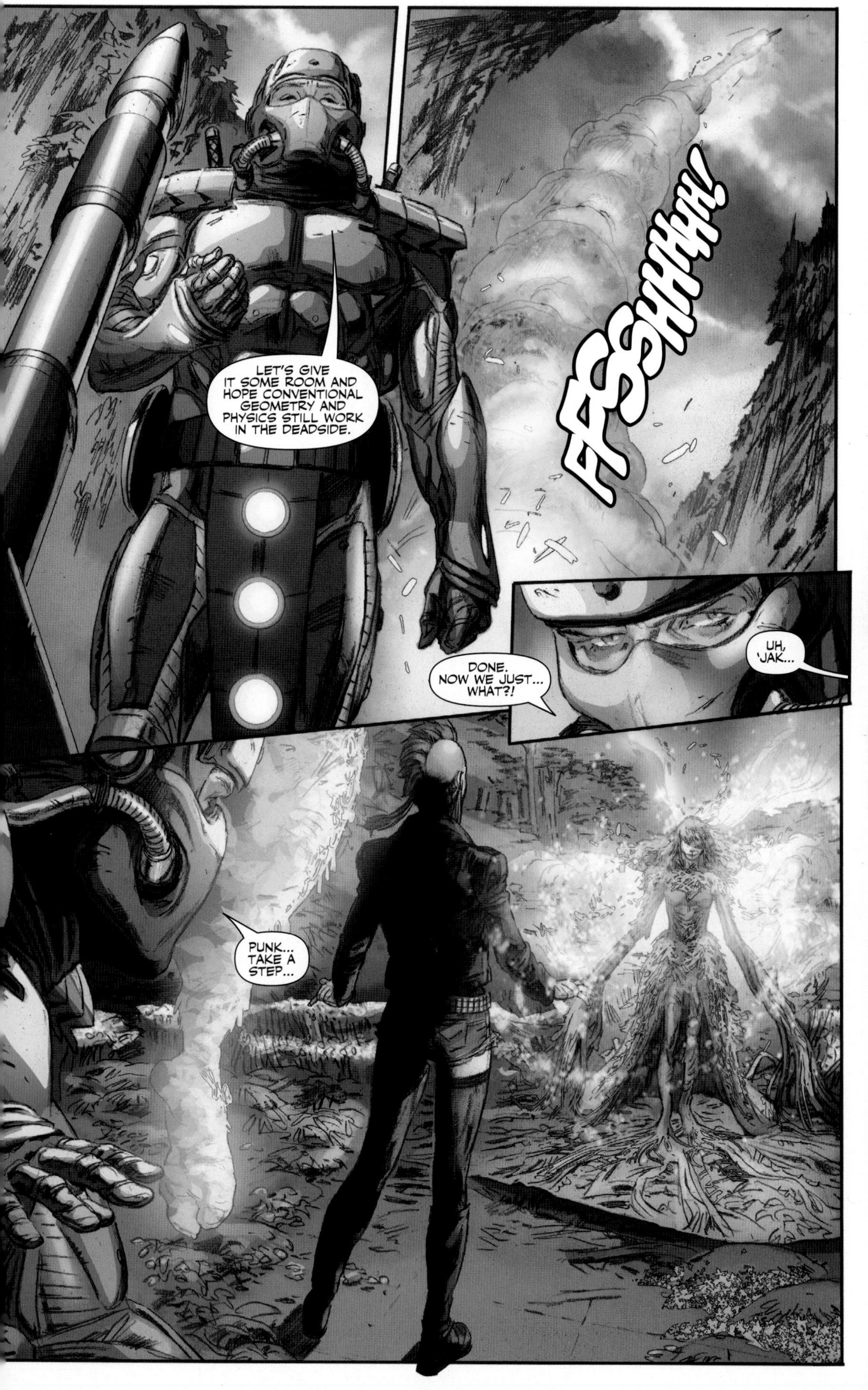
LET'S GIVE IT SOME ROOM AND HOPE CONVENTIONAL GEOMETRY AND PHYSICS STILL WORK IN THE DEADSIDE.
FFSSHHHHH!
DONE. NOW WE JUST... WHAT?!
UH, 'JAK...
PUNK... TAKE A STEP...

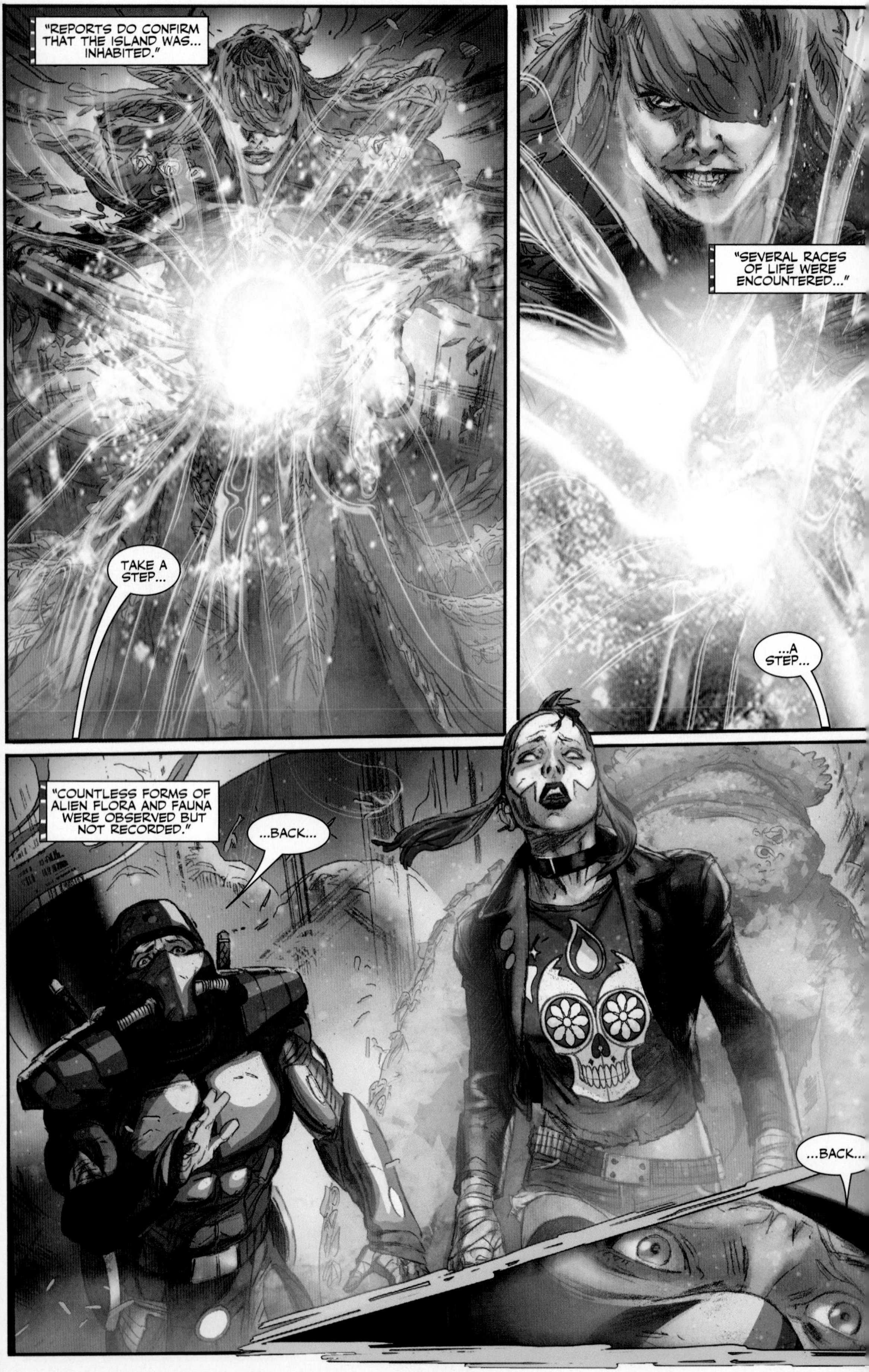
"REPORTS DO CONFIRM THAT THE ISLAND WAS... INHABITED."
TAKE A STEP...
"SEVERAL RACES OF LIFE WERE ENCOUNTERED..."
...A STEP...
"COUNTLESS FORMS OF ALIEN FLORA AND FAUNA WERE OBSERVED BUT NOT RECORDED."
...BACK...
...BACK...

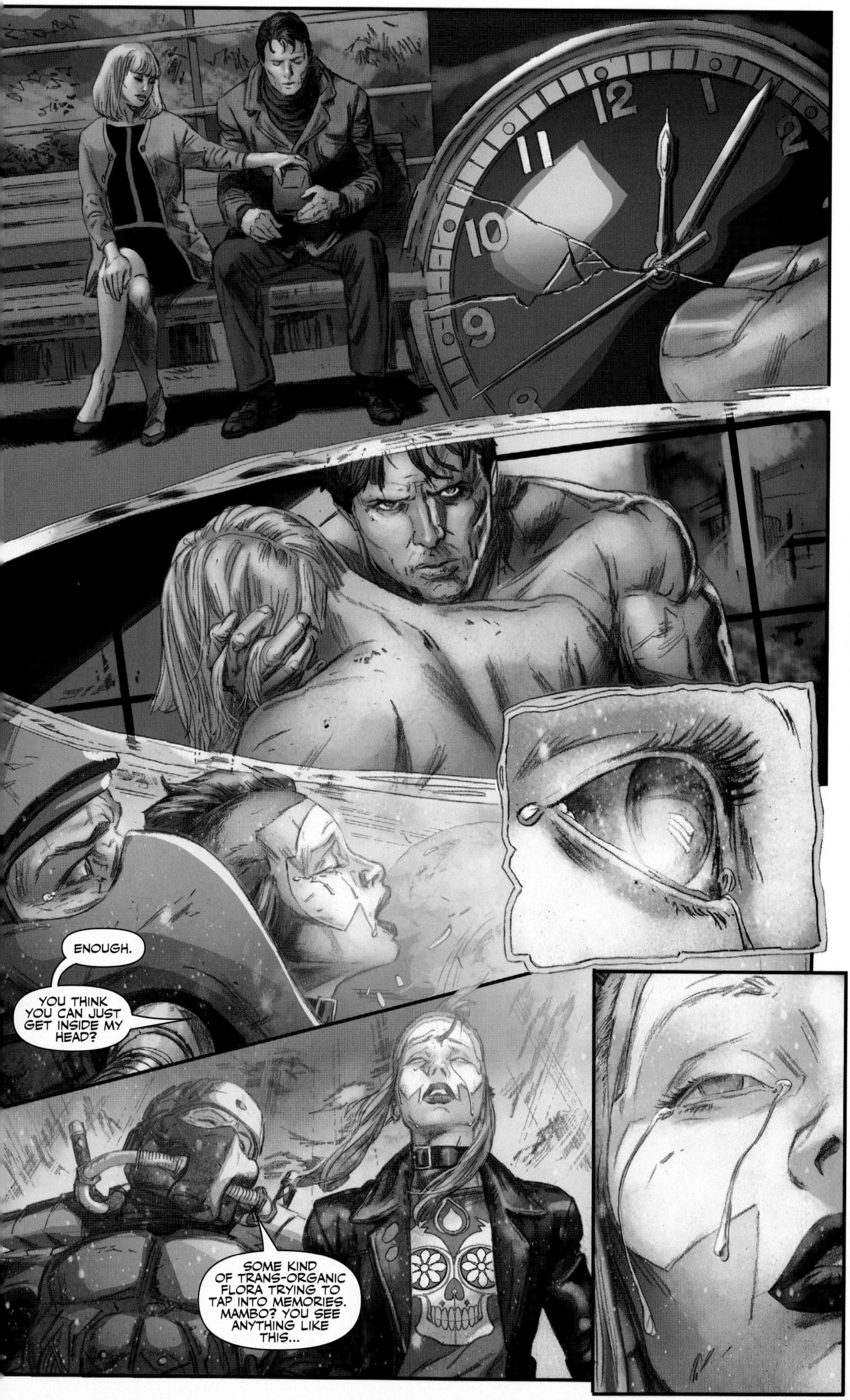
ENOUGH.
YOU THINK YOU CAN JUST GET INSIDE MY HEAD?
SOME KIND OF TRANS-ORGANIC FLORA TRYING TO TAP INTO MEMORIES. MAMBO? YOU SEE ANYTHING LIKE THIS...

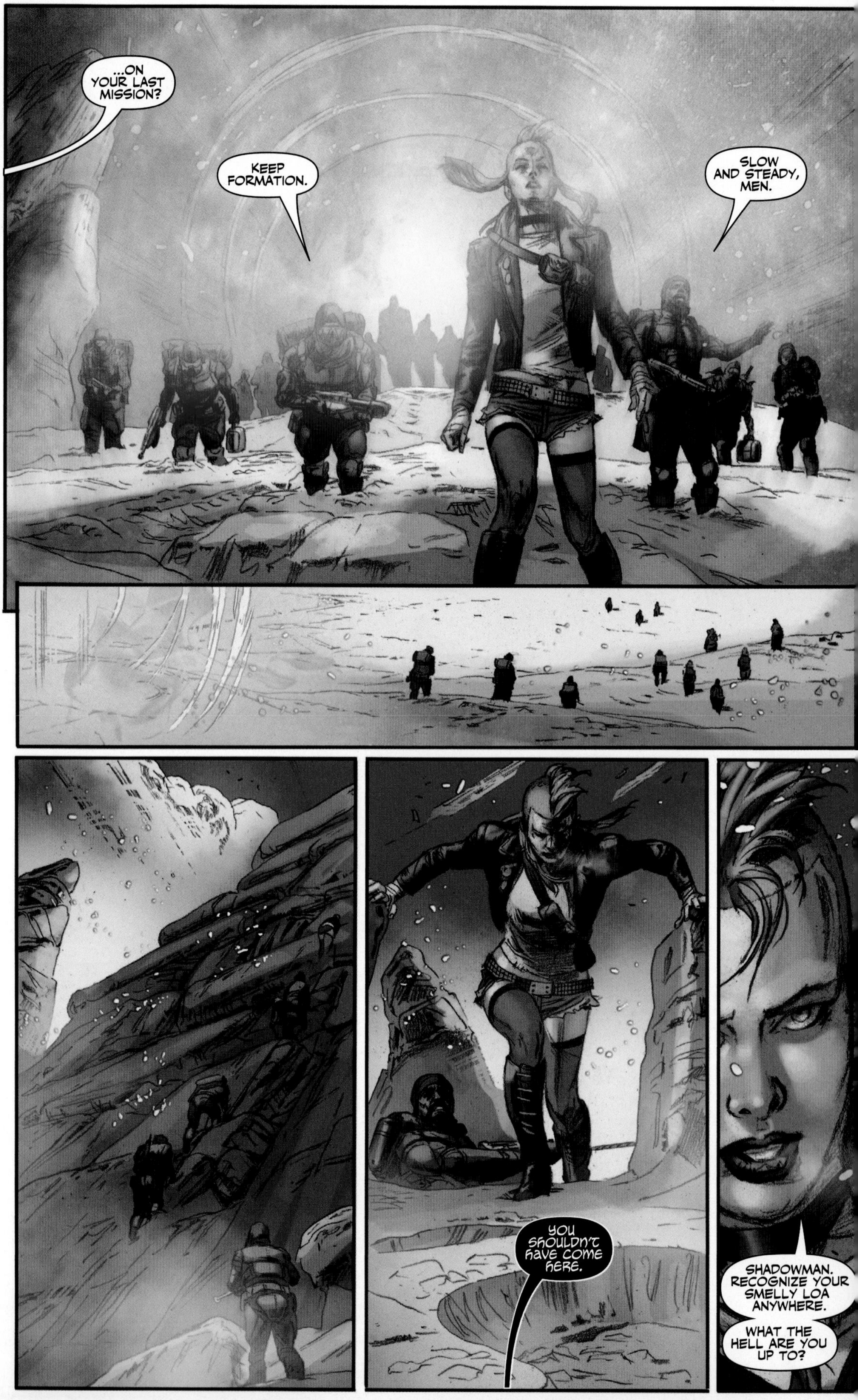
...ON YOUR LAST MISSION?
KEEP FORMATION.
SLOW AND STEADY, MEN.
YOU SHOULDN'T HAVE COME HERE.
SHADOWMAN. RECOGNIZE YOUR SMELLY LOA ANYWHERE.
WHAT THE HELL ARE YOU UP TO?

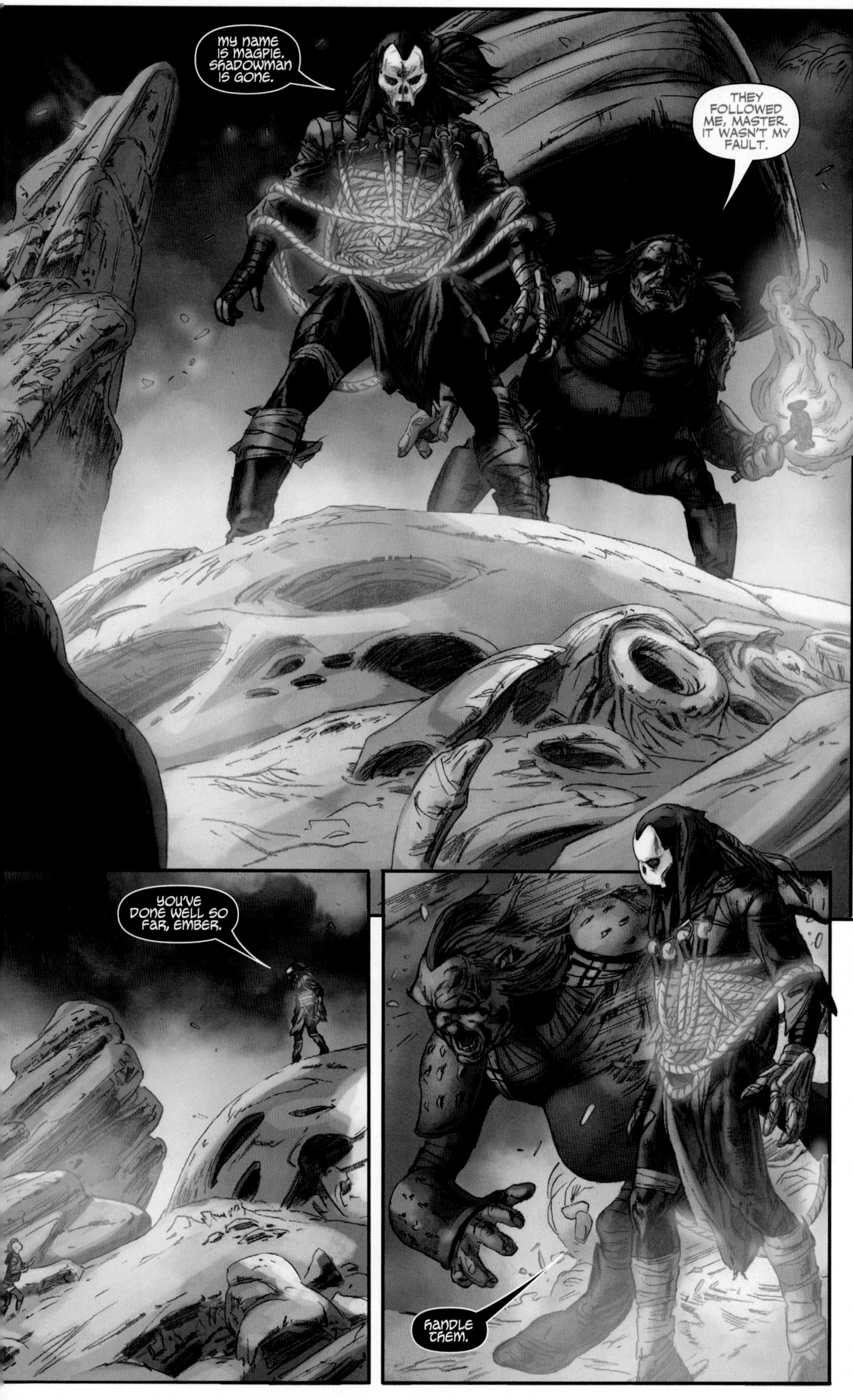
MY NAME IS MAGPIE. SHADOWMAN IS GONE.
THEY FOLLOWED ME, MASTER. IT WASN'T MY FAULT.
YOU'VE DONE WELL SO FAR, EMBER.
HANDLE THEM.

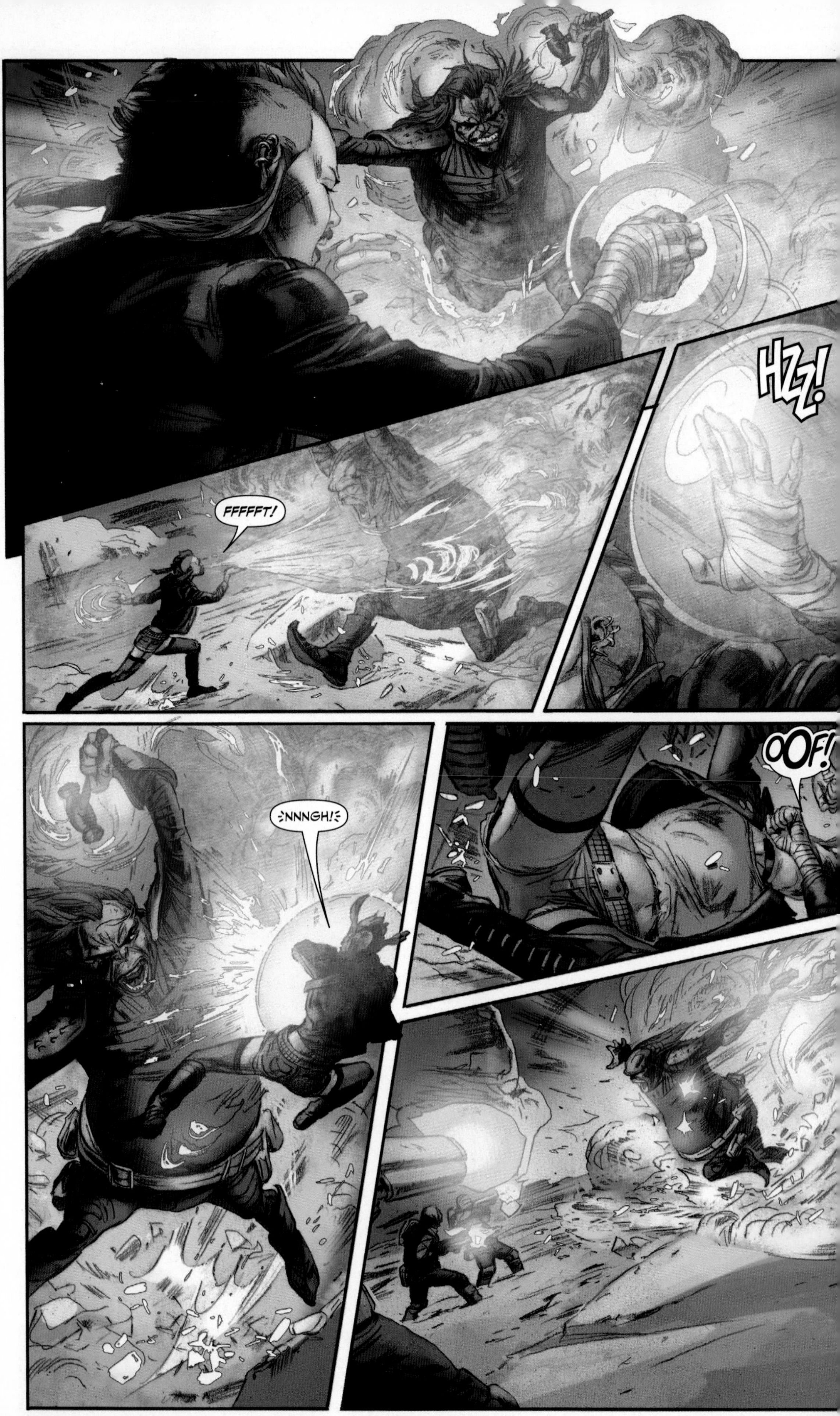
HZZ!
FFFFFT!
NNNGH!
OOF!

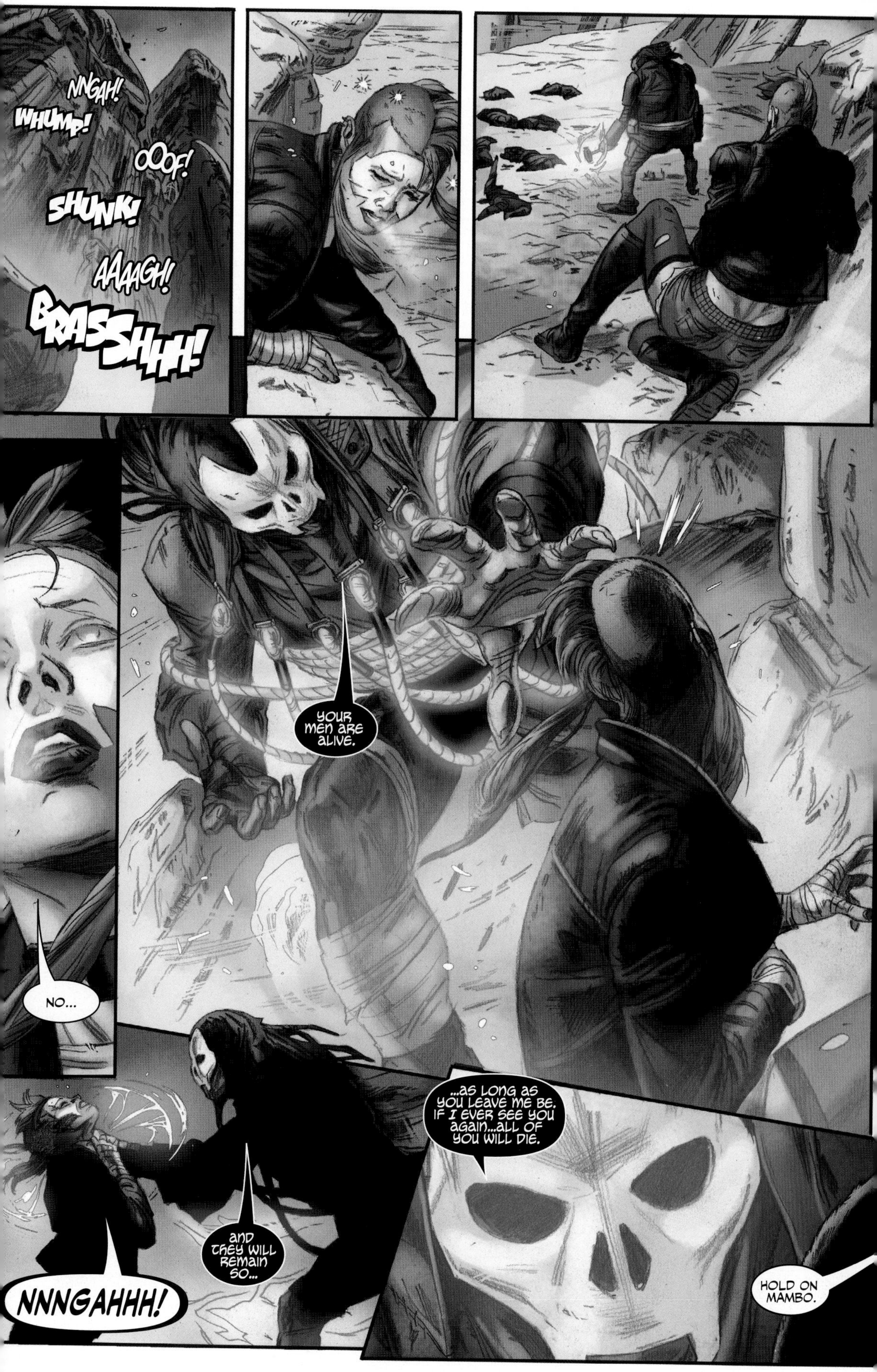

NNGAH!
WHUMP!
OOOF!
SHUNK!
AAAAGH!
BRASSHHH!
YOUR MEN ARE ALIVE.
NO...
AND THEY WILL REMAIN SO...
NNNGAHHH!
...AS LONG AS YOU LEAVE ME BE. IF I EVER SEE YOU AGAIN...ALL OF YOU WILL DIE.
HOLD ON MAMBO.

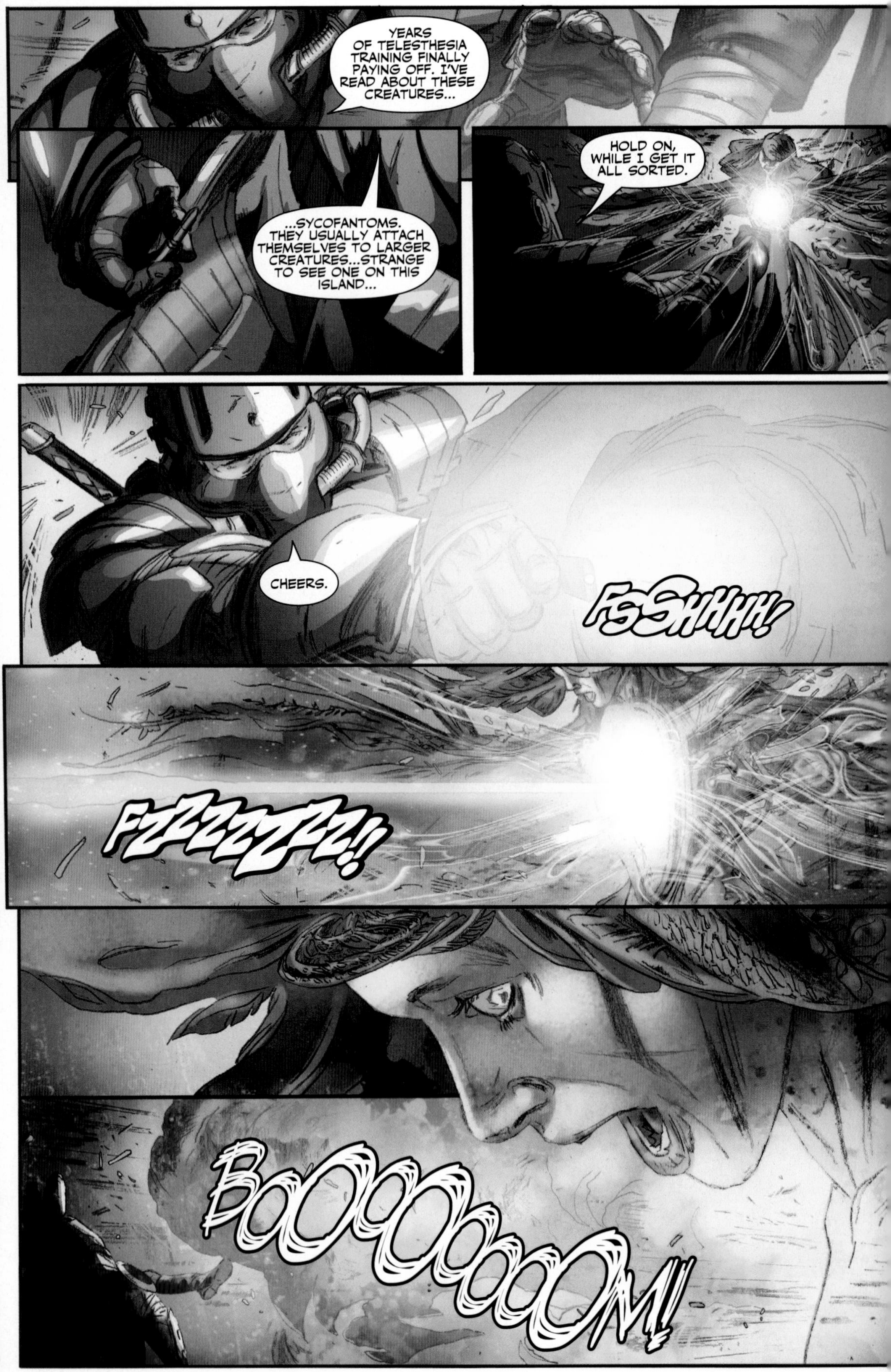
YEARS OF TELESTHESIA TRAINING FINALLY PAYING OFF. I'VE READ ABOUT THESE CREATURES...
...SYCOFANTOMS. THEY USUALLY ATTACH THEMSELVES TO LARGER CREATURES...STRANGE TO SEE ONE ON THIS ISLAND...
HOLD ON, WHILE I GET IT ALL SORTED.
CHEERS.
FSSHHHH!
FZZZZZZZ!!
BOOOOOOOOOM!!

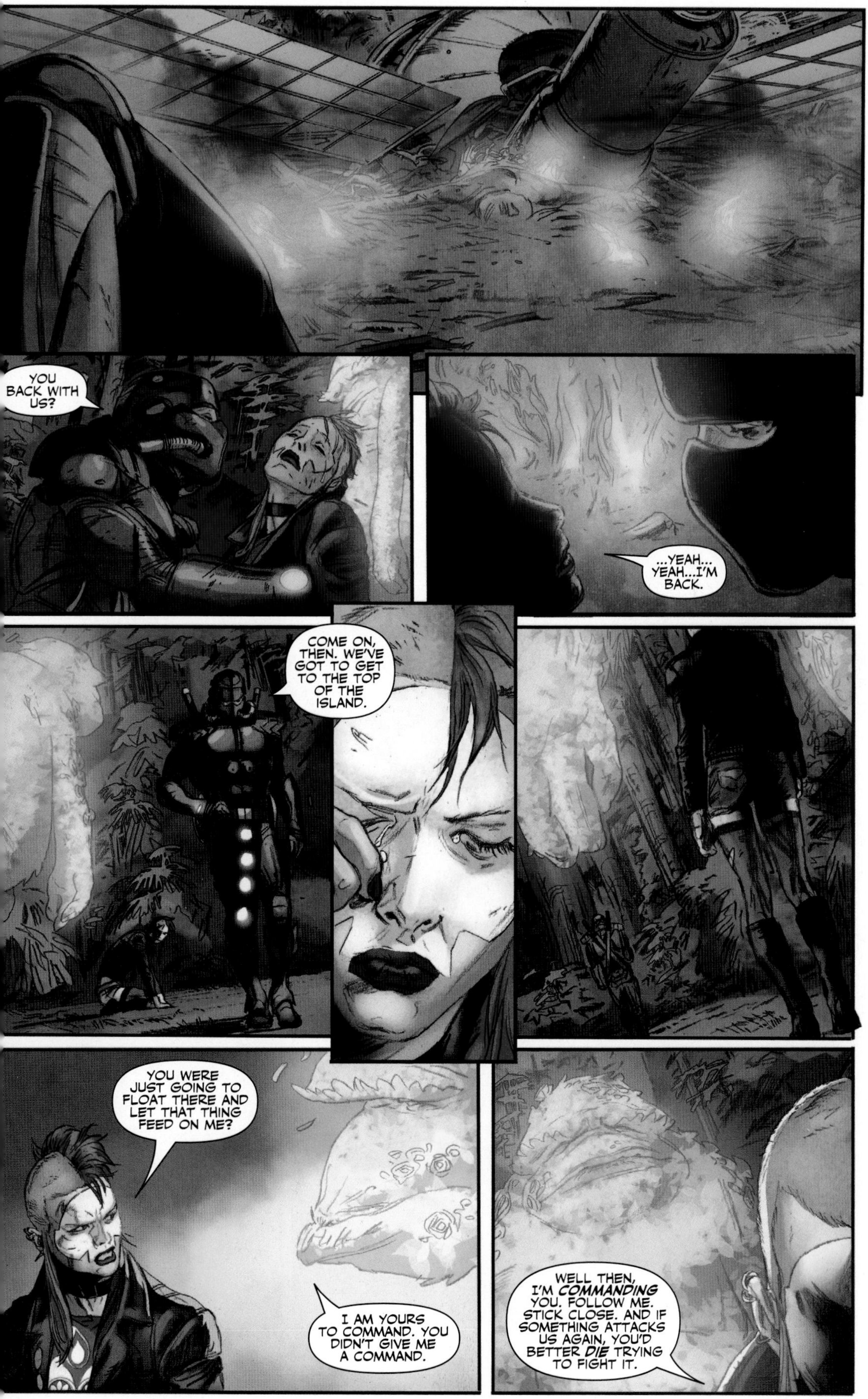
YOU BACK WITH US?
...YEAH... YEAH...I'M BACK.
COME ON, THEN. WE'VE GOT TO GET TO THE TOP OF THE ISLAND.
YOU WERE JUST GOING TO FLOAT THERE AND LET THAT THING FEED ON ME?
I AM YOURS TO COMMAND. YOU DIDN'T GIVE ME A COMMAND.
WELL THEN, I'M COMMANDING YOU. FOLLOW ME. STICK CLOSE. AND IF SOMETHING ATTACKS US AGAIN, YOU'D BETTER DIE TRYING TO FIGHT IT.

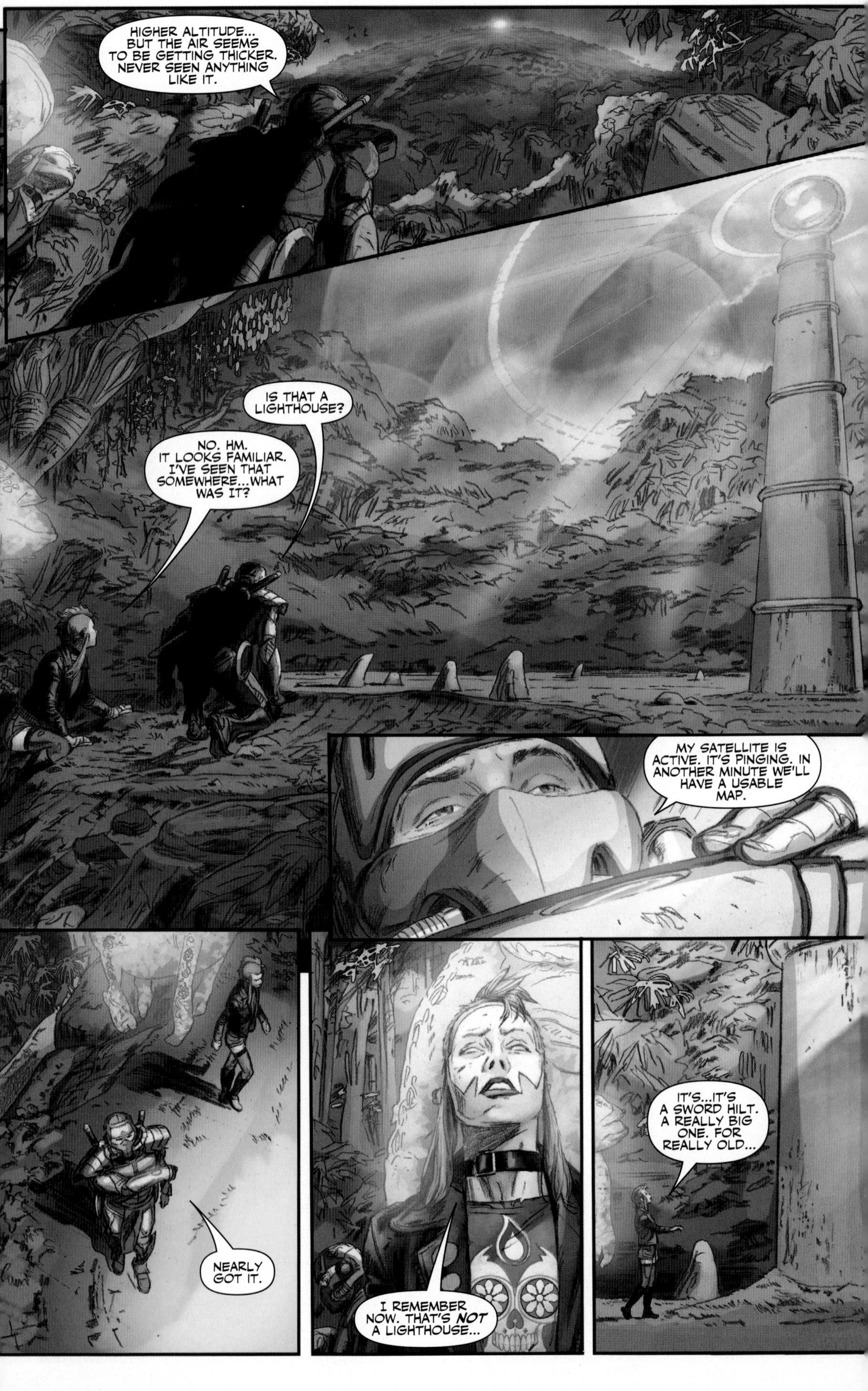
HIGHER ALTITUDE... BUT THE AIR SEEMS TO BE GETTING THICKER. NEVER SEEN ANYTHING LIKE IT.
IS THAT A LIGHTHOUSE?
NO. HM. IT LOOKS FAMILIAR. I'VE SEEN THAT SOMEWHERE...WHAT WAS IT?
MY SATELLITE IS ACTIVE. IT'S PINGING. IN ANOTHER MINUTE WE'LL HAVE A USABLE MAP.
NEARLY GOT IT.
I REMEMBER NOW. THAT'S NOT A LIGHTHOUSE...
IT'S...IT'S A SWORD HILT. A REALLY BIG ONE. FOR REALLY OLD...

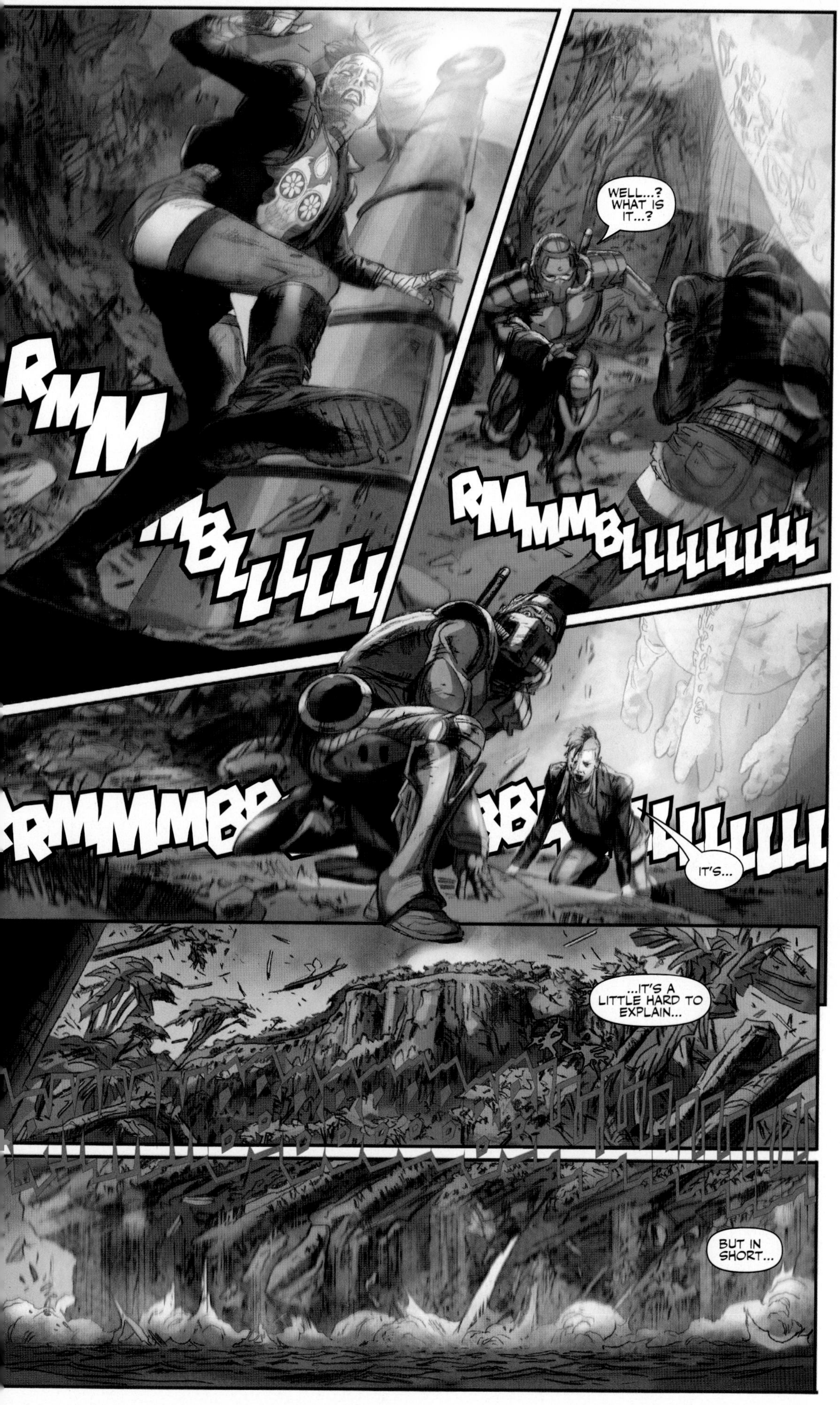
RMM
MBLLLLL
WELL...? WHAT IS IT...?
RMMMMBLLLLLLLLL
RMMMMBR
BRLLLLLLL
IT'S...
...IT'S A LITTLE HARD TO EXPLAIN...
BUT IN SHORT...

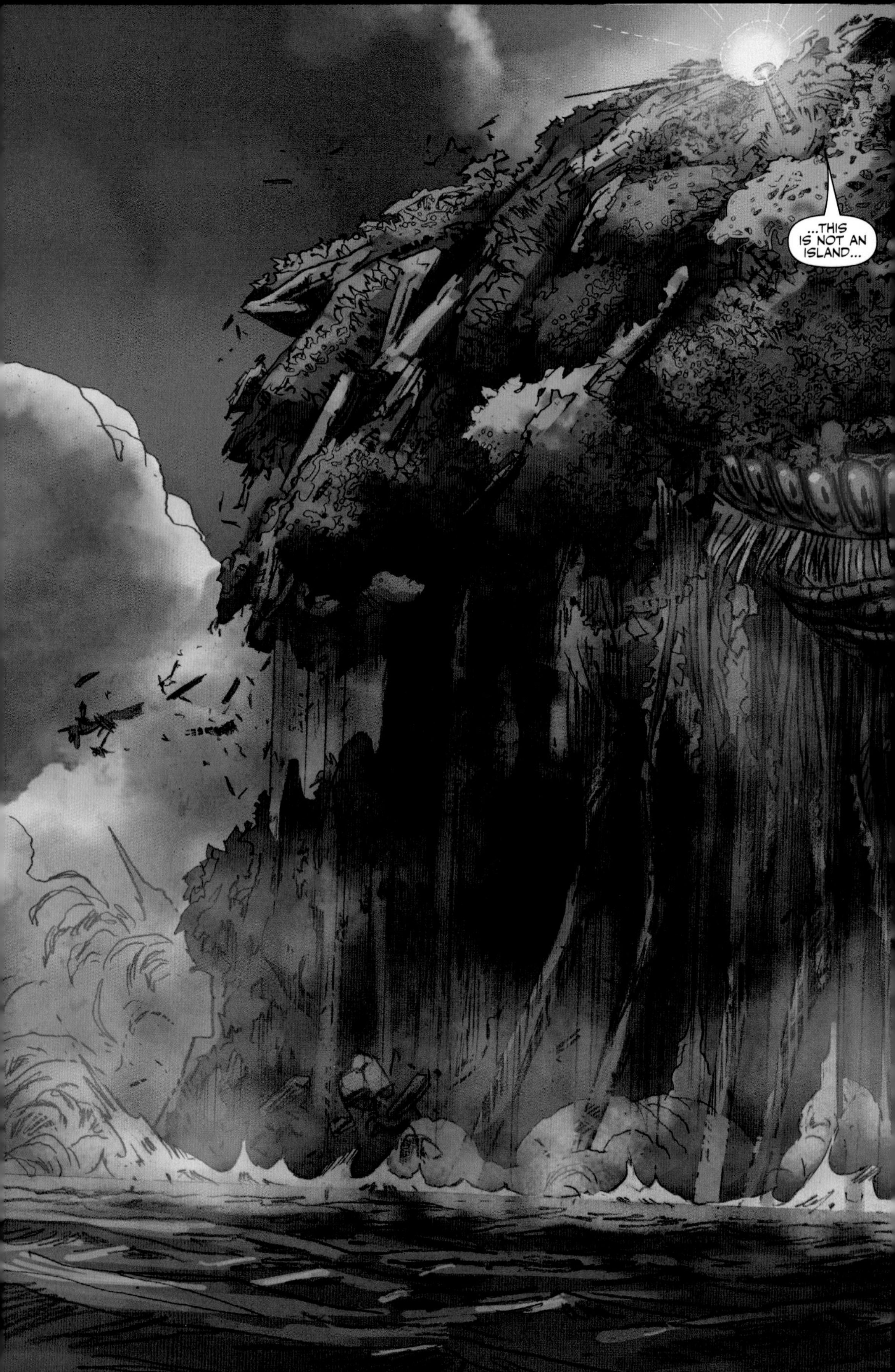
...THIS IS NOT AN ISLAND...

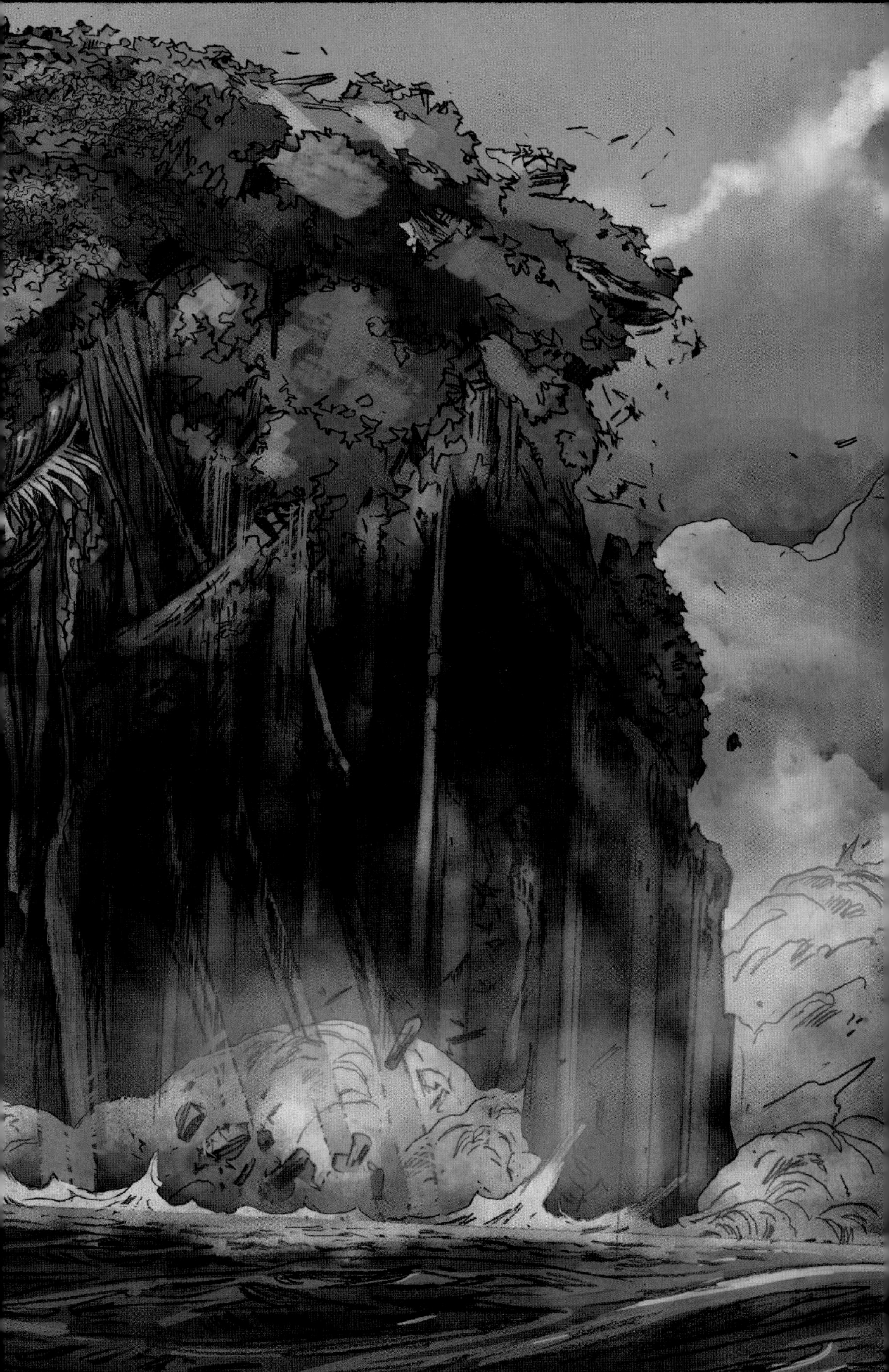

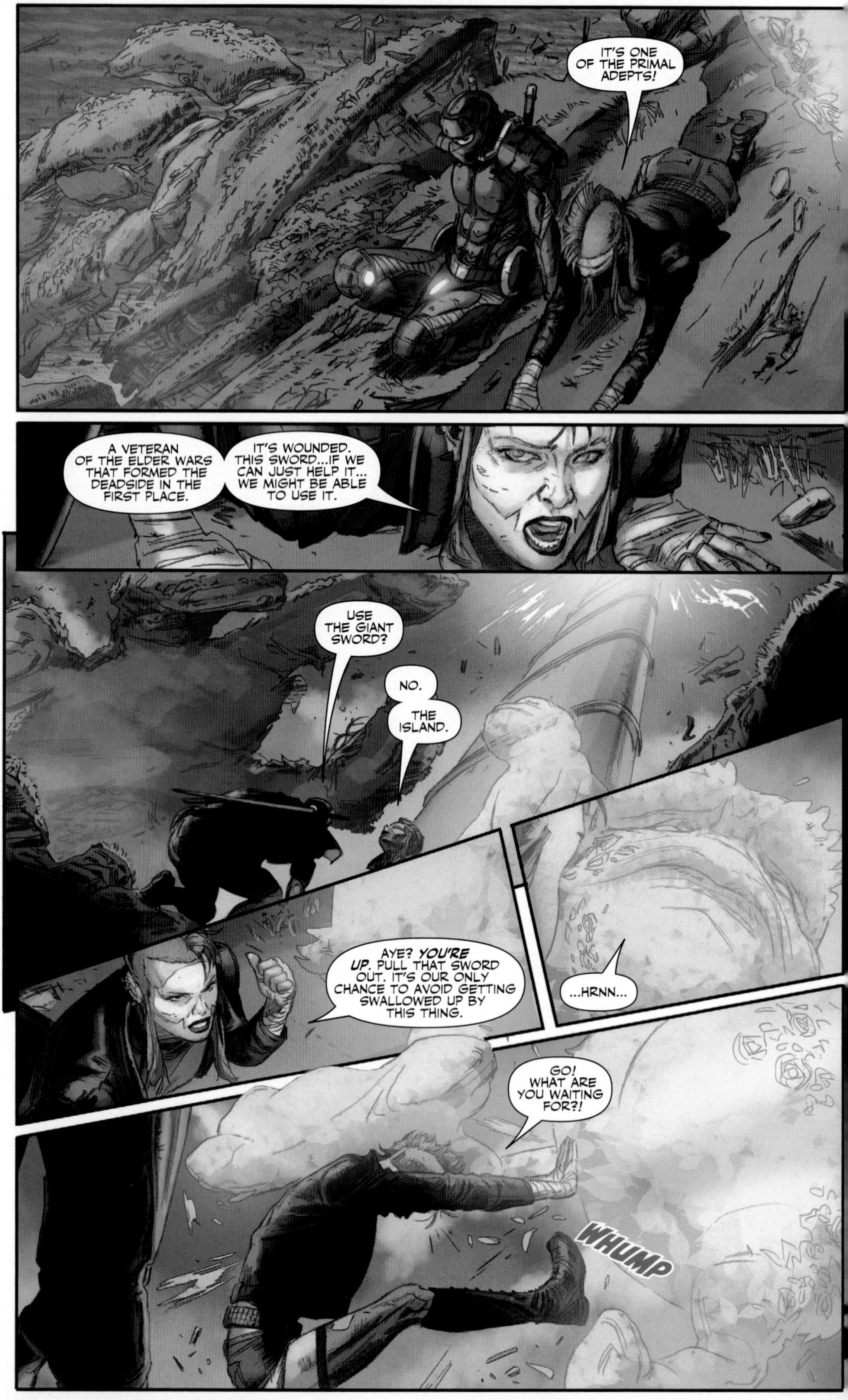
IT'S ONE OF THE PRIMAL ADEPTS!
A VETERAN OF THE ELDER WARS THAT FORMED THE DEADSIDE IN THE FIRST PLACE.
IT'S WOUNDED. THIS SWORD...IF WE CAN JUST HELP IT... WE MIGHT BE ABLE TO USE IT.
USE THE GIANT SWORD?
NO.
THE ISLAND.
AYE? YOU'RE UP. PULL THAT SWORD OUT. IT'S OUR ONLY CHANCE TO AVOID GETTING SWALLOWED UP BY THIS THING.
...HRNN...
GO! WHAT ARE YOU WAITING FOR?!
WHUMP

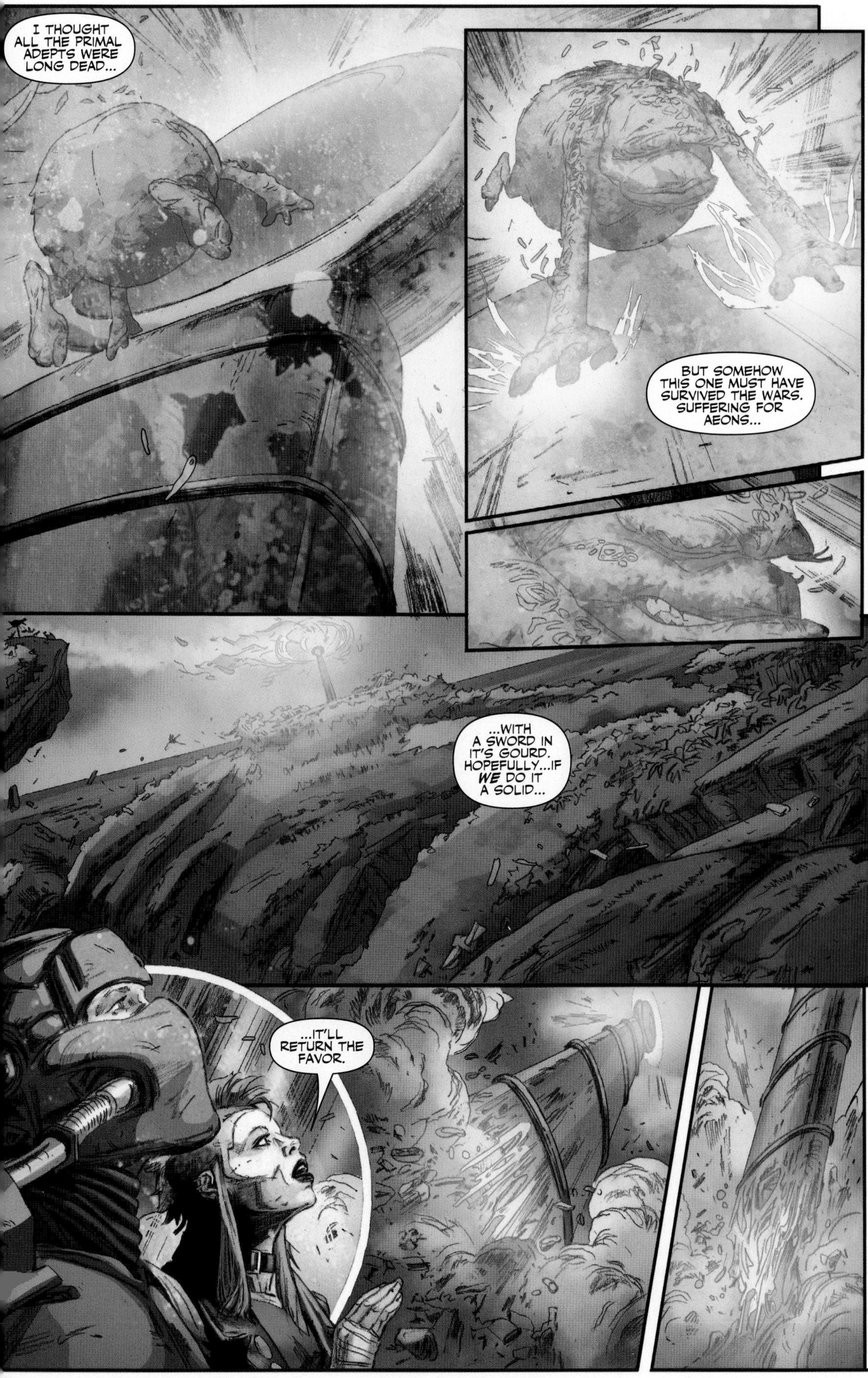
I THOUGHT ALL THE PRIMAL ADEPTS WERE LONG DEAD...
BUT SOMEHOW THIS ONE MUST HAVE SURVIVED THE WARS. SUFFERING FOR AEONS...
...WITH A SWORD IN IT'S GOURD. HOPEFULLY...IF WE DO IT A SOLID...
...IT'LL RETURN THE FAVOR.

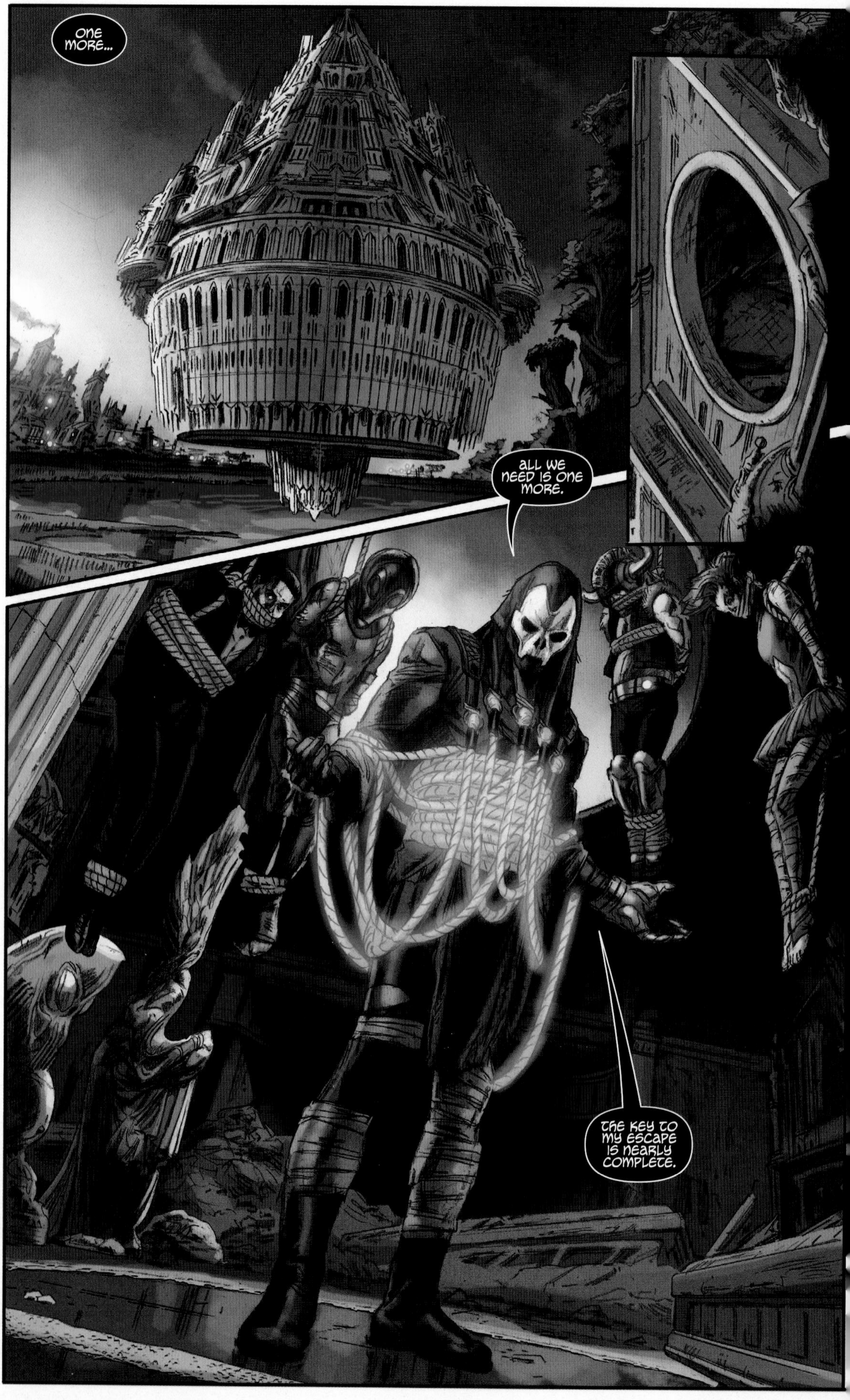
ONE MORE...
ALL WE NEED IS ONE MORE.
THE KEY TO MY ESCAPE IS NEARLY COMPLETE.

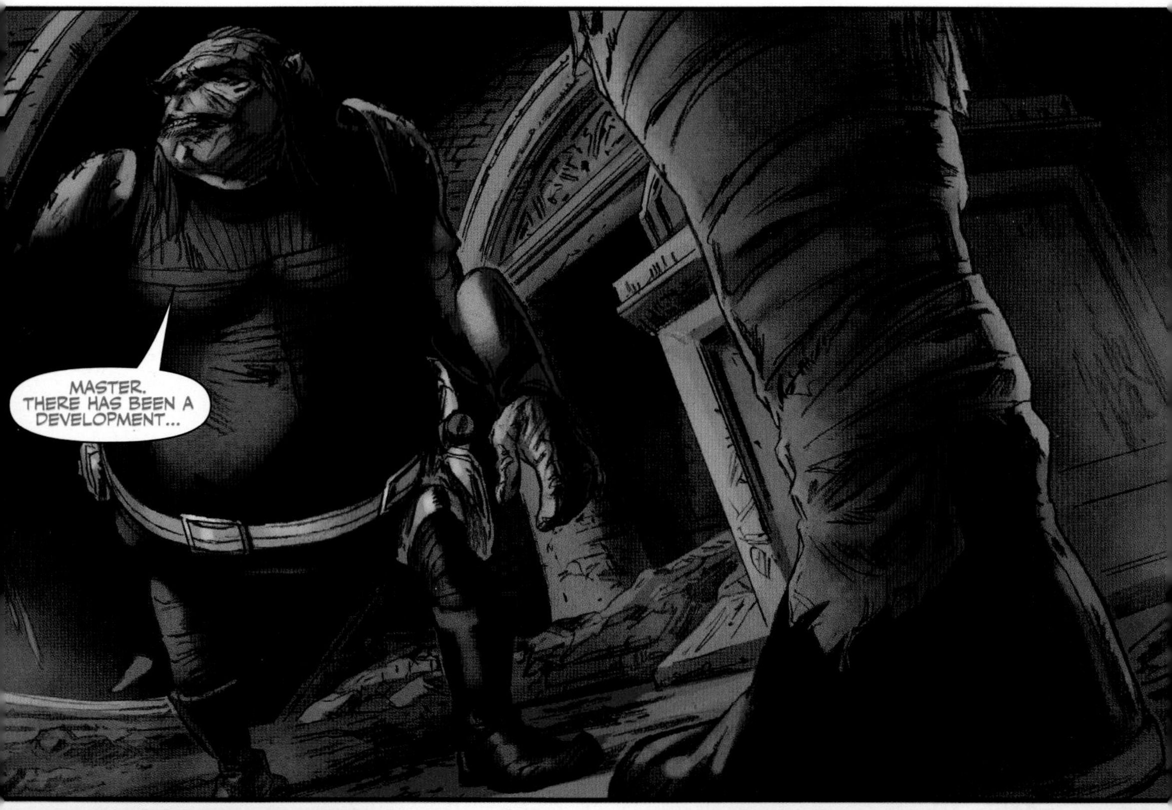
MASTER. THERE HAS BEEN A DEVELOPMENT...

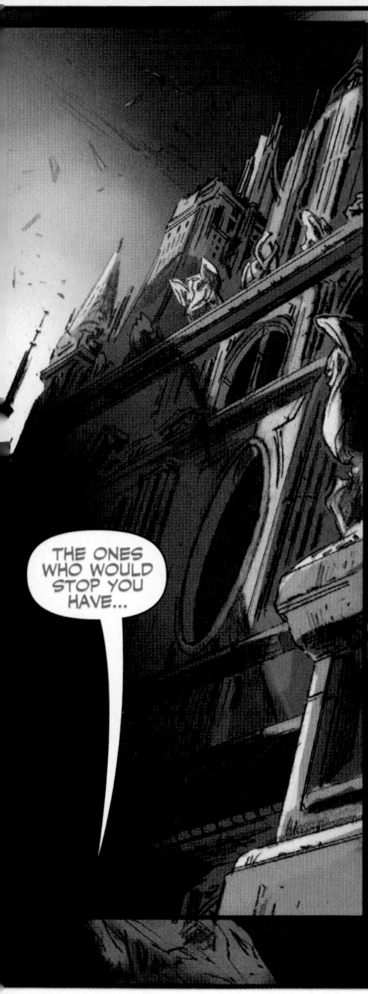
THE ONES WHO WOULD STOP YOU HAVE...

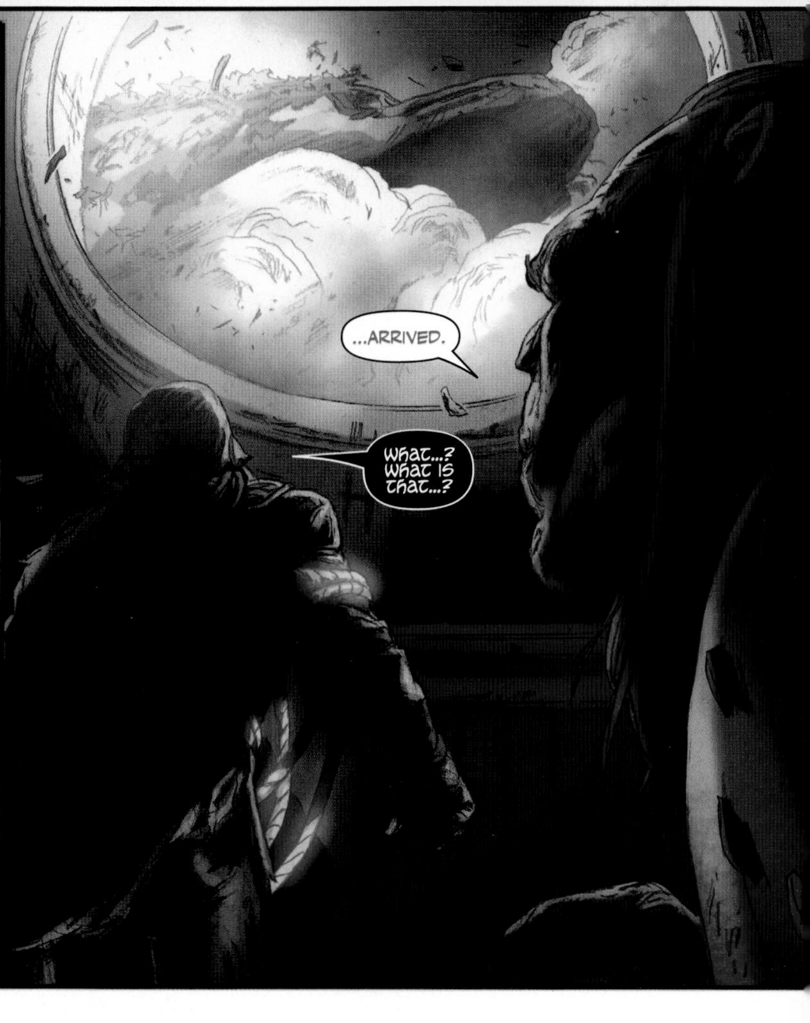
...ARRIVED.
What...? What is that...?

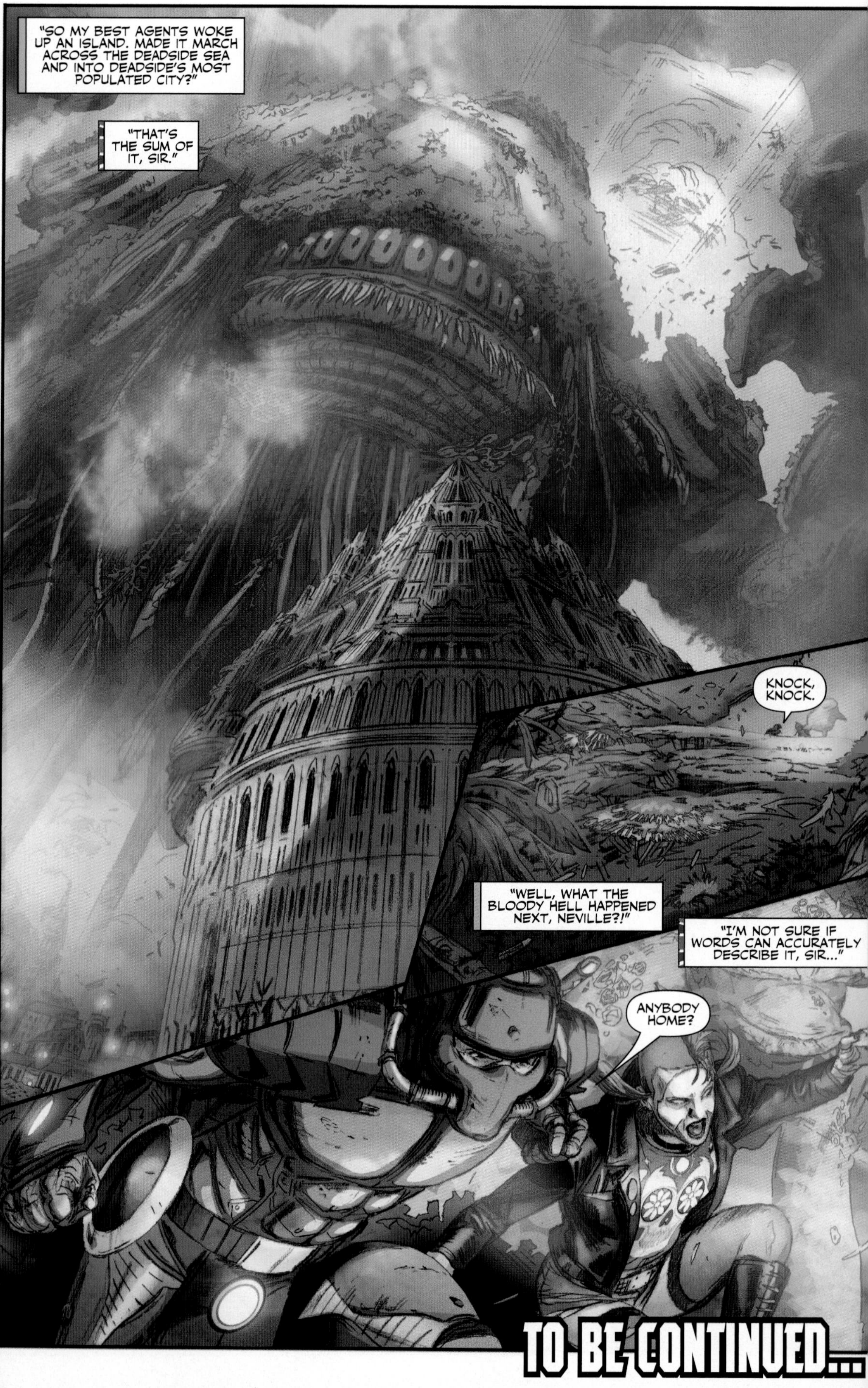
"SO MY BEST AGENTS WOKE UP AN ISLAND. MADE IT MARCH ACROSS THE DEADSIDE SEA AND INTO DEADSIDE'S MOST POPULATED CITY?"
"THAT'S THE SUM OF IT, SIR."
KNOCK, KNOCK.
"WELL, WHAT THE BLOODY HELL HAPPENED NEXT, NEVILLE?!"
"I'M NOT SURE IF WORDS CAN ACCURATELY DESCRIBE IT, SIR..."
ANYBODY HOME?
TO BE CONTINUED...

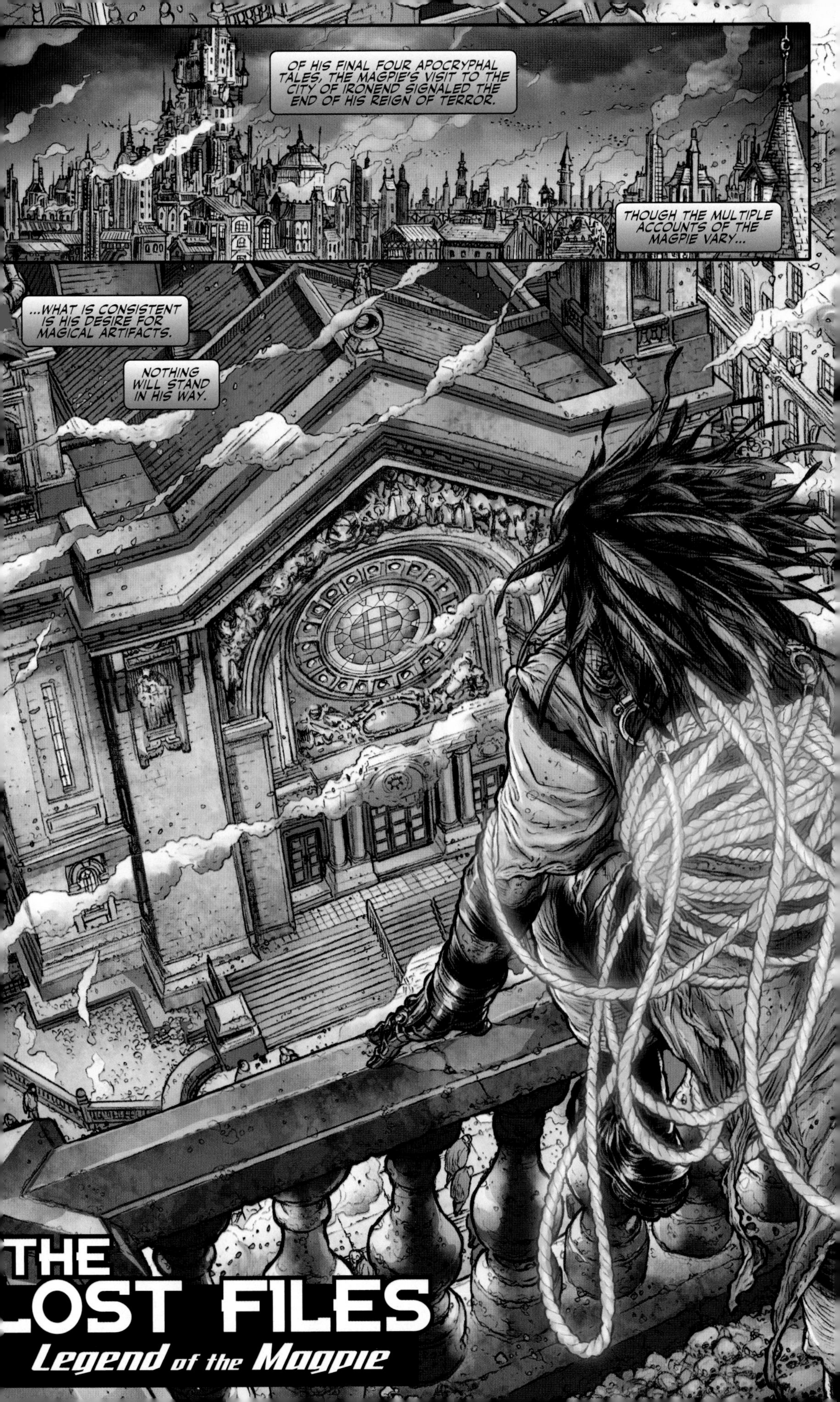

OF HIS FINAL FOUR APOCRYPHAL TALES, THE MAGPIE'S VISIT TO THE CITY OF IRONEND SIGNALED THE END OF HIS REIGN OF TERROR.
THOUGH THE MULTIPLE ACCOUNTS OF THE MAGPIE VARY...
...WHAT IS CONSISTENT IS HIS DESIRE FOR MAGICAL ARTIFACTS.
NOTHING WILL STAND IN HIS WAY.
THE LOST FILES
Legend of the Magpie

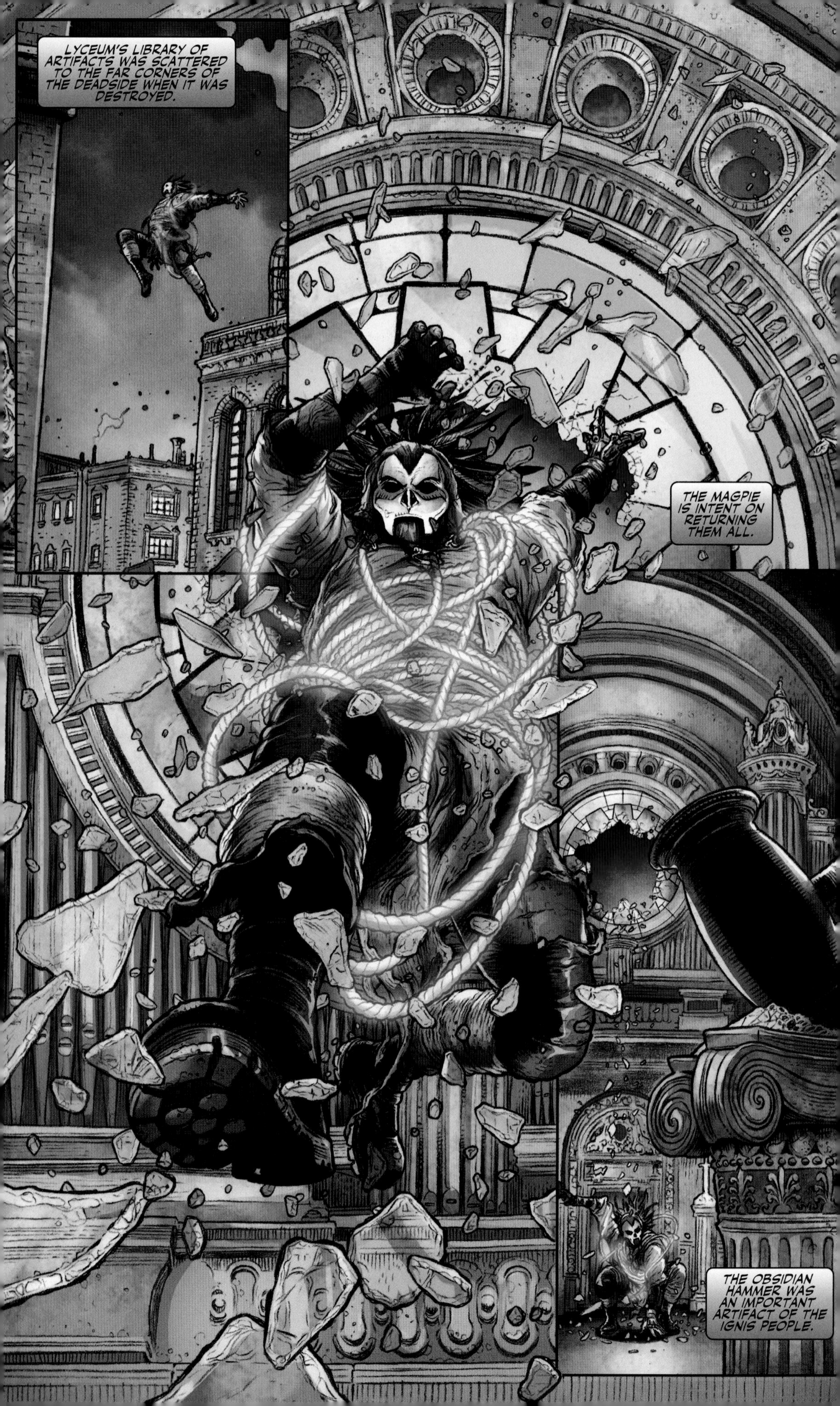
LYCEUM'S LIBRARY OF ARTIFACTS WAS SCATTERED TO THE FAR CORNERS OF THE DEADSIDE WHEN IT WAS DESTROYED.
THE MAGPIE IS INTENT ON RETURNING THEM ALL.
THE OBSIDIAN HAMMER WAS AN IMPORTANT ARTIFACT OF THE IGNIS PEOPLE.

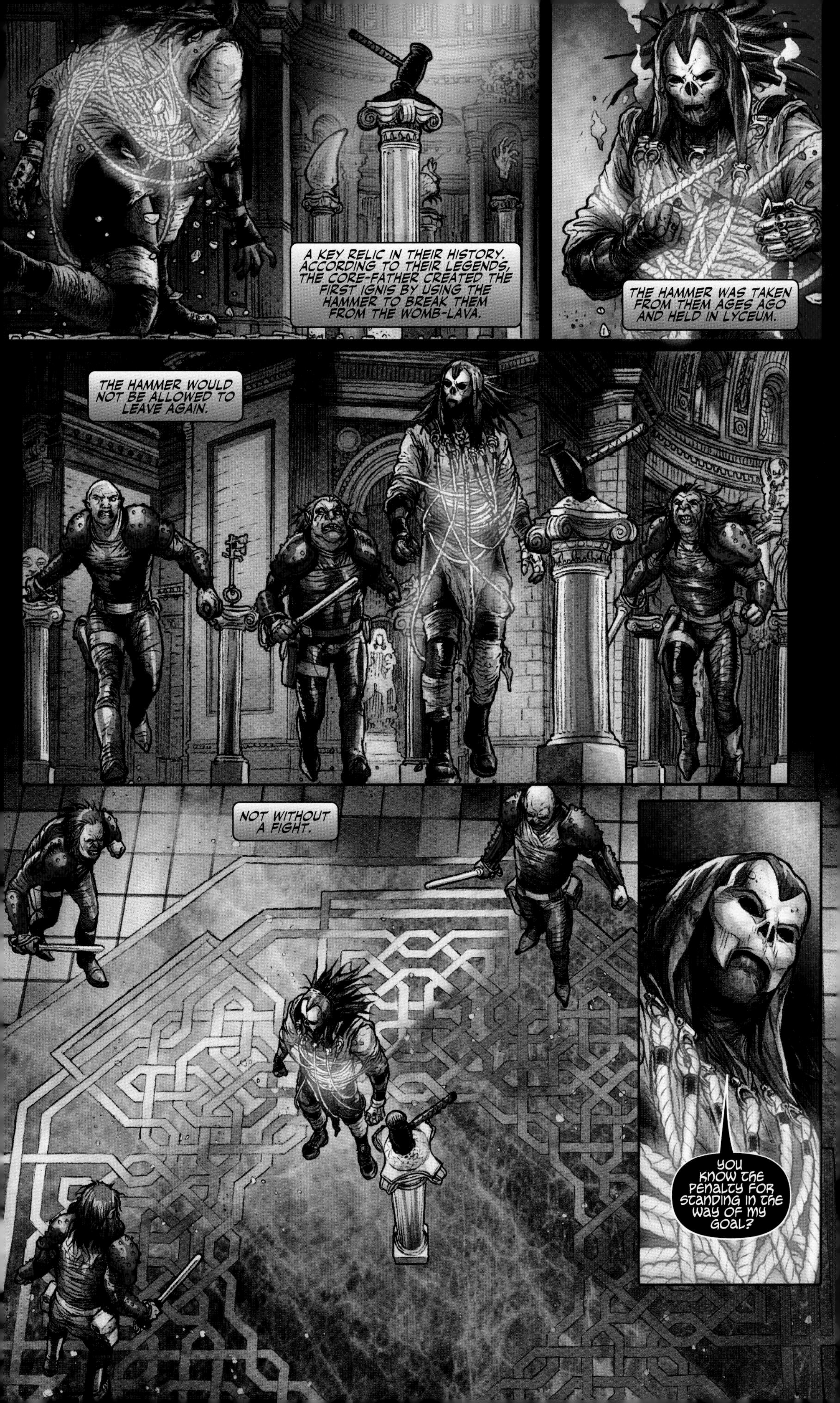
A KEY RELIC IN THEIR HISTORY. ACCORDING TO THEIR LEGENDS, THE CORE-FATHER CREATED THE FIRST IGNIS BY USING THE HAMMER TO BREAK THEM FROM THE WOMB-LAVA.
THE HAMMER WAS TAKEN FROM THEM AGES AGO AND HELD IN LYCEUM.
THE HAMMER WOULD NOT BE ALLOWED TO LEAVE AGAIN.
NOT WITHOUT A FIGHT.
YOU KNOW THE PENALTY FOR STANDING IN THE WAY OF MY GOAL?

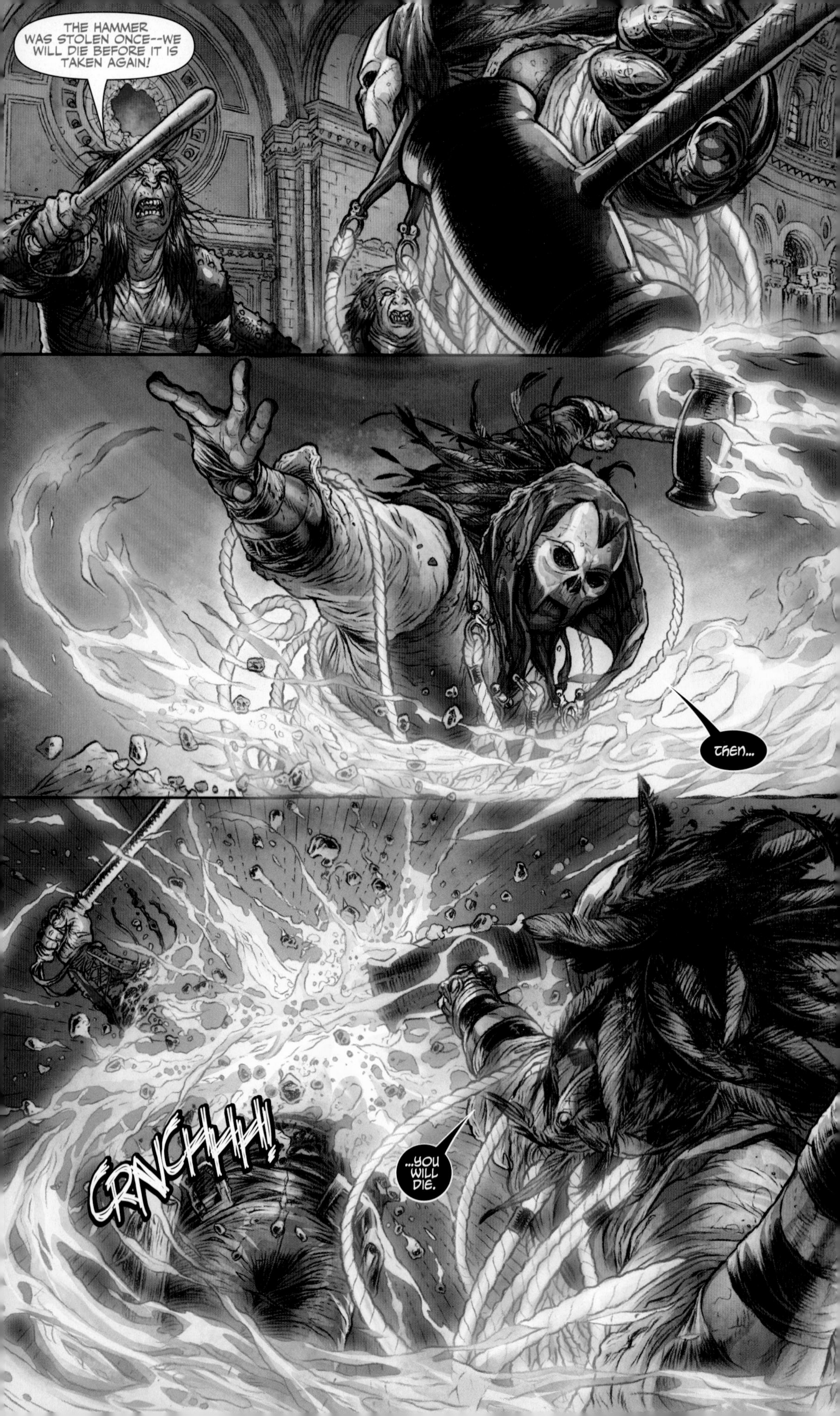
THE HAMMER WAS STOLEN ONCE--WE WILL DIE BEFORE IT IS TAKEN AGAIN!
THEN...
CRNCHHH!
...YOU WILL DIE.

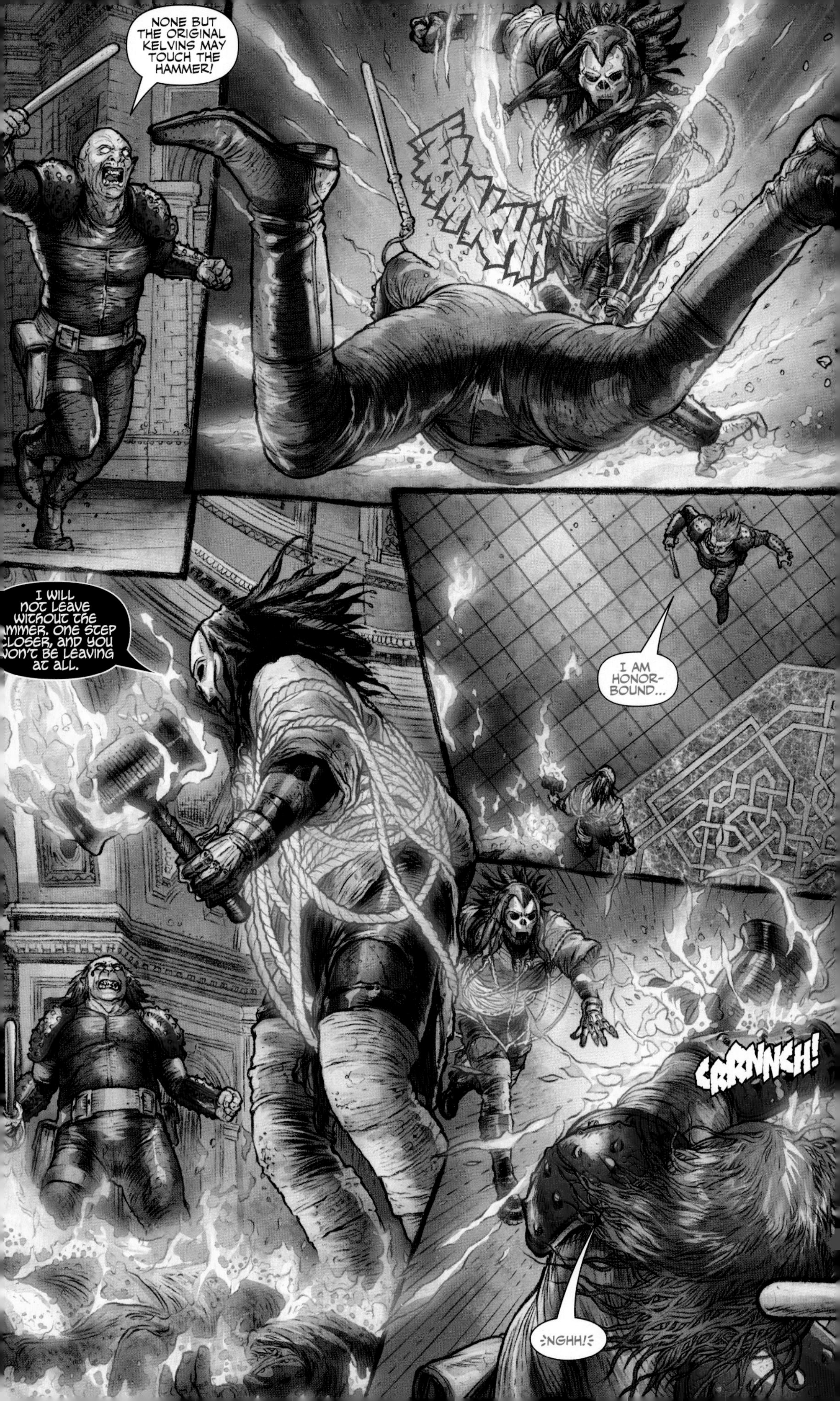

NONE BUT THE ORIGINAL KELVINS MAY TOUCH THE HAMMER!
I WILL NOT LEAVE WITHOUT THE HAMMER. ONE STEP CLOSER, AND YOU WON'T BE LEAVING AT ALL.
I AM HONOR-BOUND...
CRRNNCH!
NGHH!

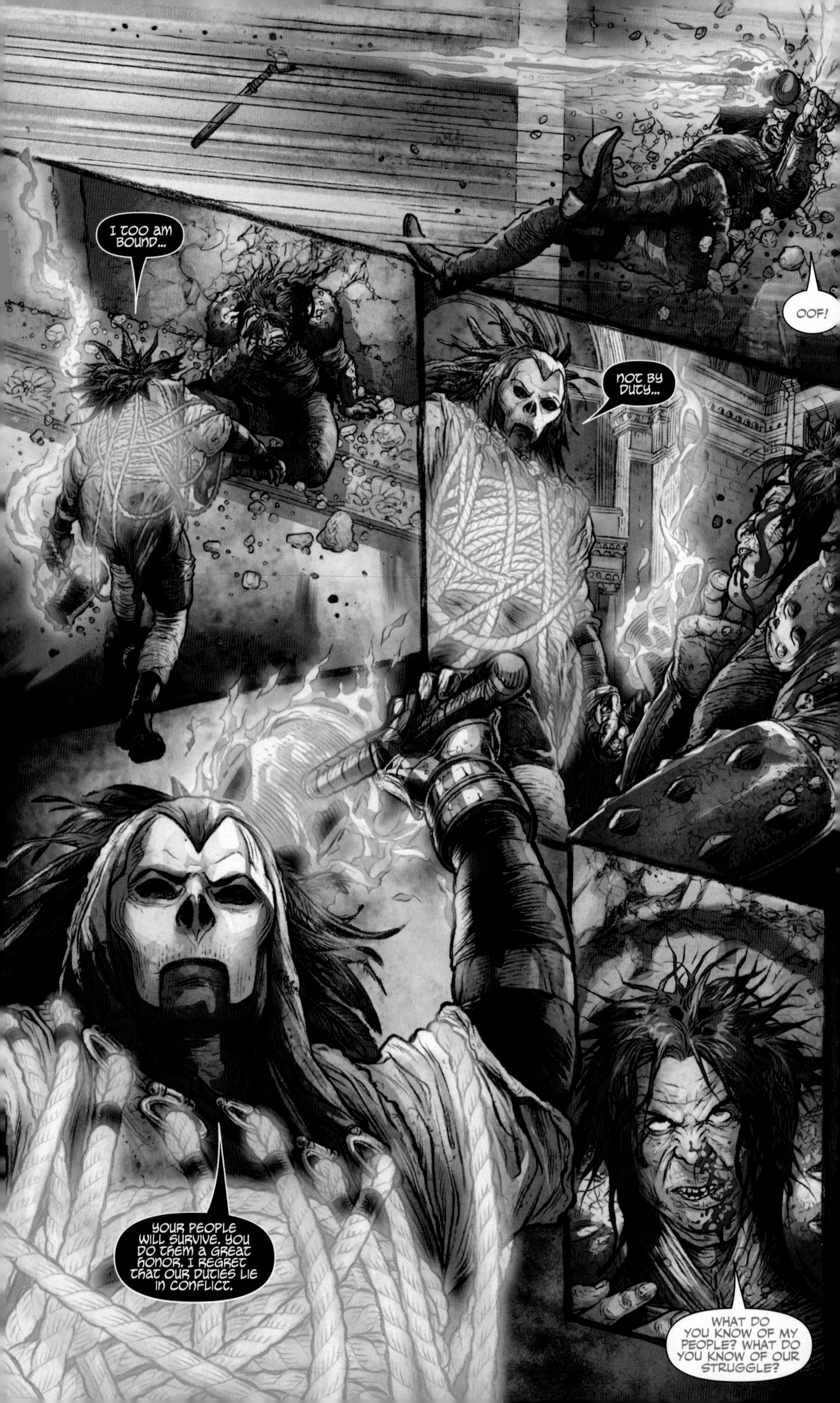
OOF!
I TOO AM BOUND...
NOT BY DUTY...
YOUR PEOPLE WILL SURVIVE. YOU DO THEM A GREAT HONOR. I REGRET THAT OUR DUTIES LIE IN CONFLICT.
WHAT DO YOU KNOW OF MY PEOPLE? WHAT DO YOU KNOW OF OUR STRUGGLE?

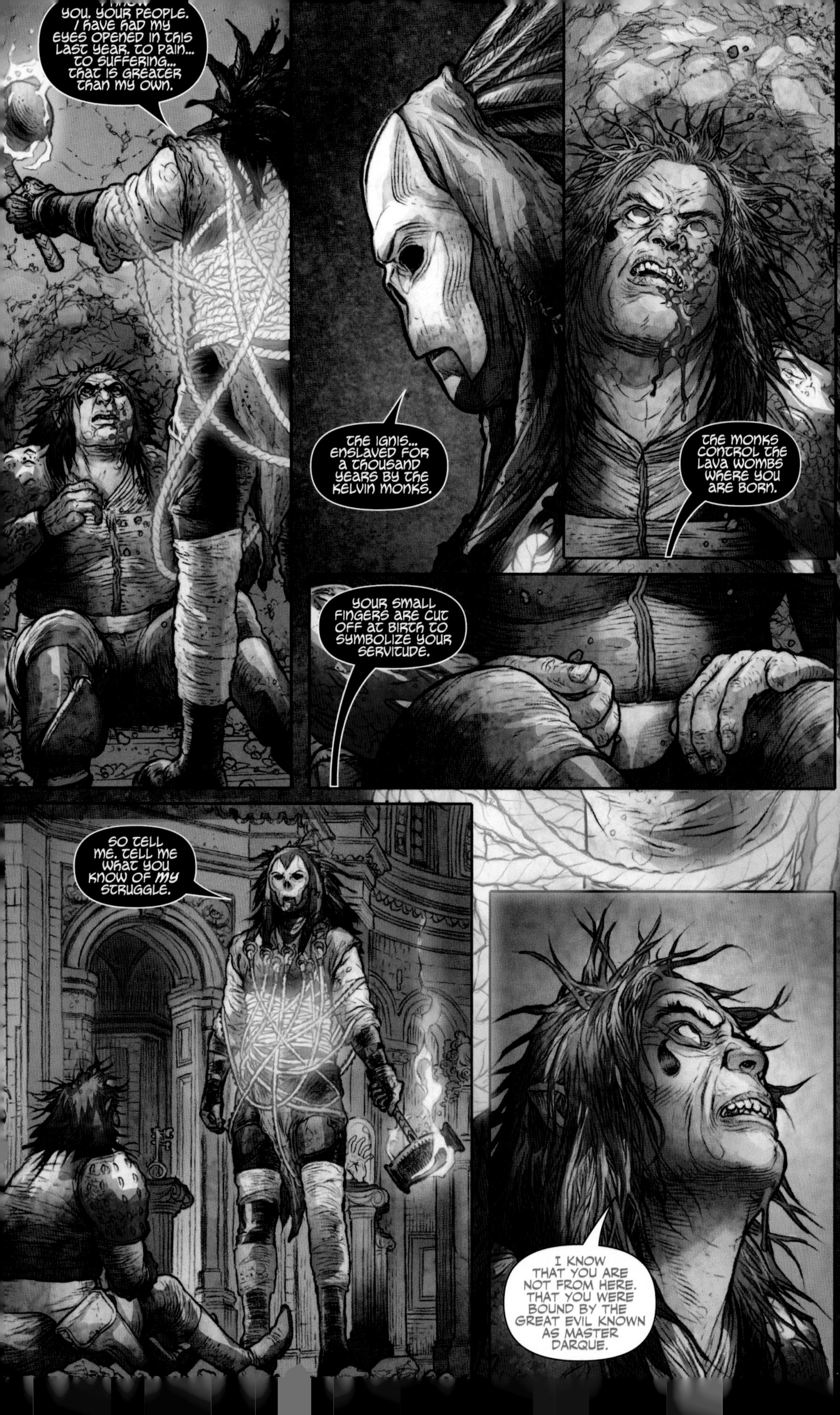
YOU. YOUR PEOPLE. I HAVE HAD MY EYES OPENED IN THIS LAST YEAR. TO PAIN... TO SUFFERING... THAT IS GREATER THAN MY OWN.
THE IGNIS... ENSLAVED FOR A THOUSAND YEARS BY THE KELVIN MONKS.
THE MONKS CONTROL THE LAVA WOMBS WHERE YOU ARE BORN.
YOUR SMALL FINGERS ARE CUT OFF AT BIRTH TO SYMBOLIZE YOUR SERVITUDE.
SO TELL ME. TELL ME WHAT YOU KNOW OF *MY* STRUGGLE.
I KNOW THAT YOU ARE NOT FROM HERE. THAT YOU WERE BOUND BY THE GREAT EVIL KNOWN AS MASTER DARQUE.

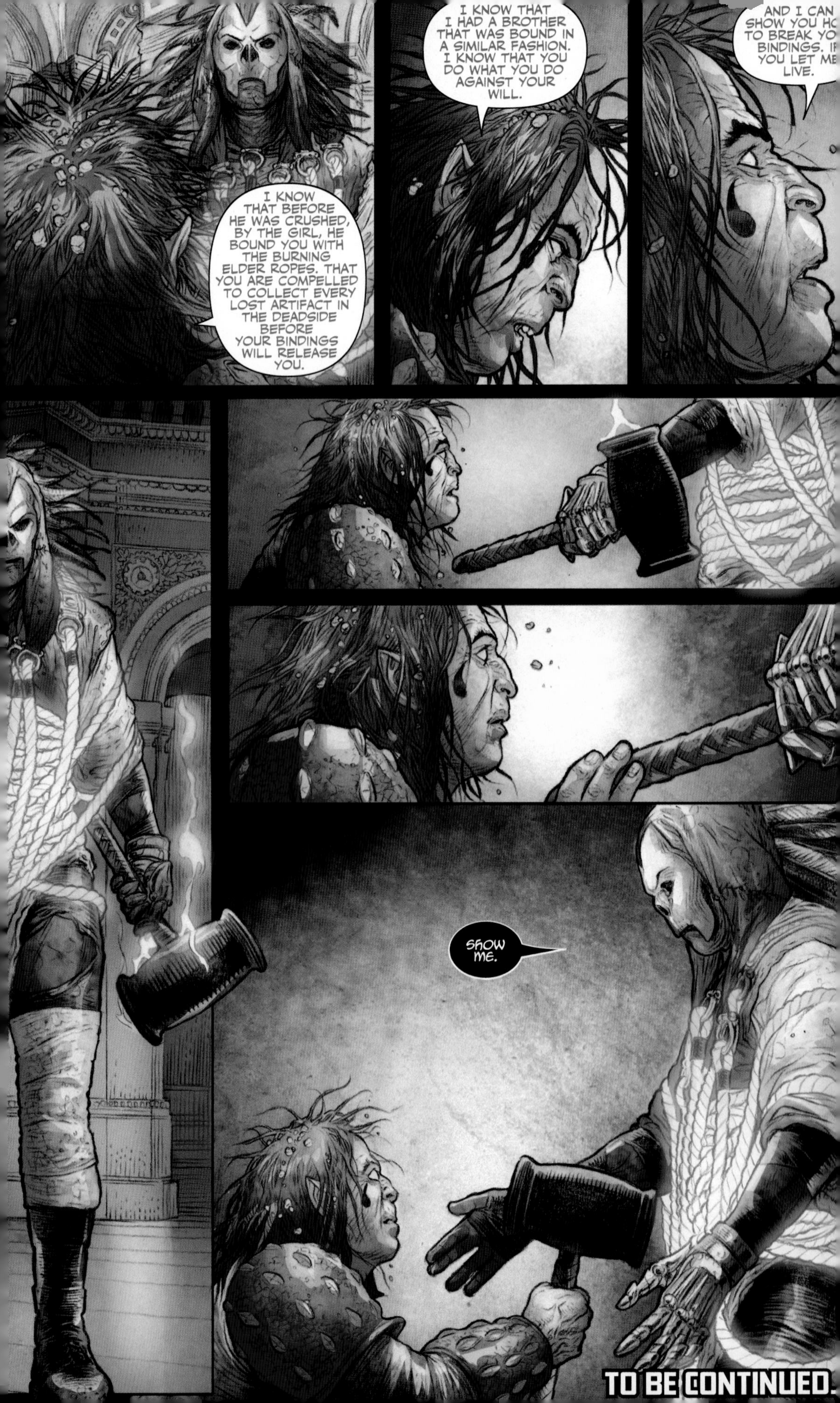
I KNOW THAT BEFORE HE WAS CRUSHED, BY THE GIRL, HE BOUND YOU WITH THE BURNING ELDER ROPES. THAT YOU ARE COMPELLED TO COLLECT EVERY LOST ARTIFACT IN THE DEADSIDE BEFORE YOUR BINDINGS WILL RELEASE YOU.
I KNOW THAT I HAD A BROTHER THAT WAS BOUND IN A SIMILAR FASHION. I KNOW THAT YOU DO WHAT YOU DO AGAINST YOUR WILL.
AND I CAN SHOW YOU HO TO BREAK YO BINDINGS. IF YOU LET ME LIVE.
SHOW ME.
TO BE CONTINUED...

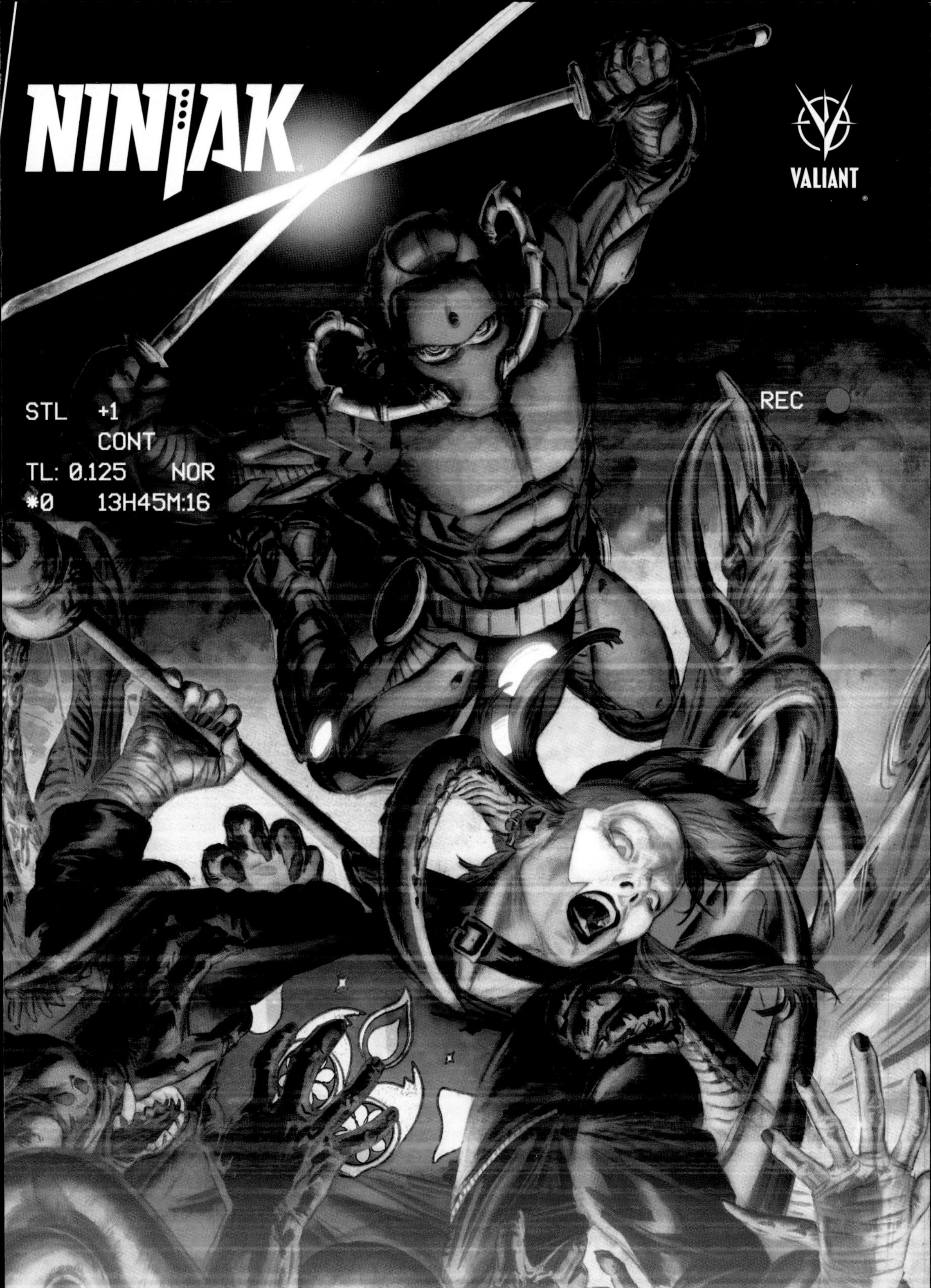
NINJAK
VALIANT
STL +1
CONT
TL: 0.125 NOR
*0 13H45M:16
REC

OPERATION

DEADSIDE:

#12

RECORDING: 03/04

MATT KINDT : DOUG BRAITHWAITE : JUAN JOSÉ RYP : BRIAN REBER

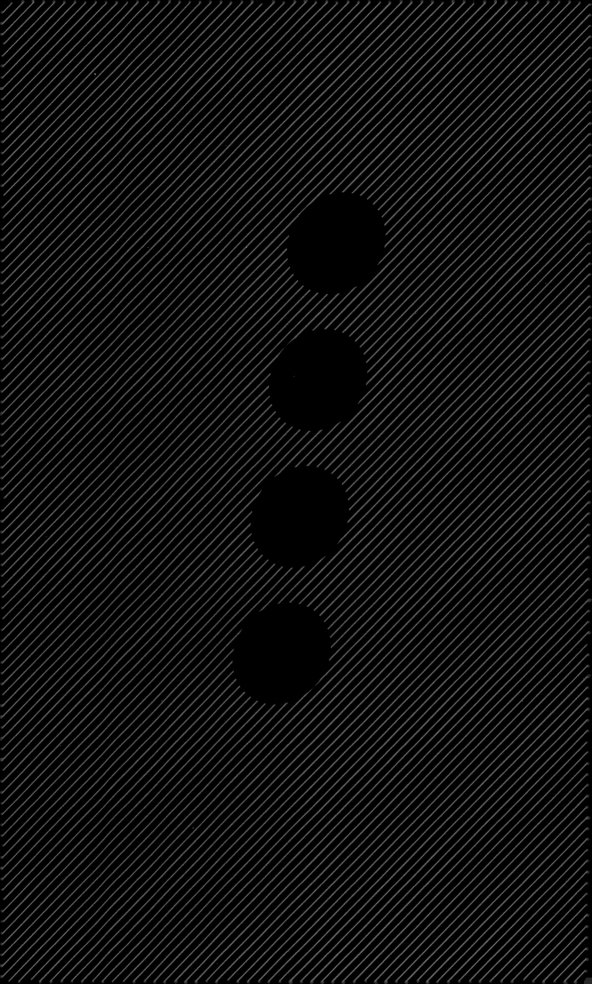

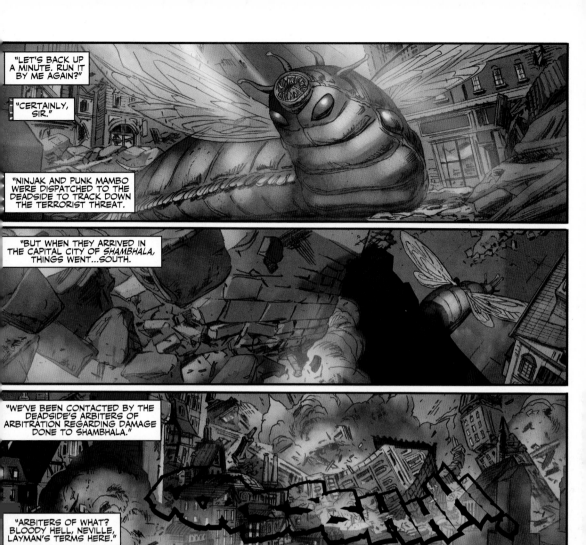

"LET'S BACK UP A MINUTE. RUN IT BY ME AGAIN?"

"CERTAINLY, SIR."

"NINJAK AND PUNK MAMBO WERE DISPATCHED TO THE DEADSIDE TO TRACK DOWN THE TERRORIST THREAT.

"BUT WHEN THEY ARRIVED IN THE CAPITAL CITY OF *SHAMBHALA*, THINGS WENT...SOUTH.

"WE'VE BEEN CONTACTED BY THE DEADSIDE'S ARBITERS OF ARBITRATION REGARDING DAMAGE DONE TO SHAMBHALA."

"ARBITERS OF WHAT? BLOODY HELL, NEVILLE, LAYMAN'S TERMS HERE."

"ARBITERS OF ARBITRATION... BASICALLY THEY'RE BARRISTERS. *DEMON* BARRISTERS."

"YOU'RE KIDDING."

"AFRAID NOT, SIR. WE HAVE *DR. MIRAGE* REPRESENTING US. SHE'S CONFIDENT THAT MOST OF THEIR CLAIMS ARE *SPURIOUS*."

CRSSHHH!

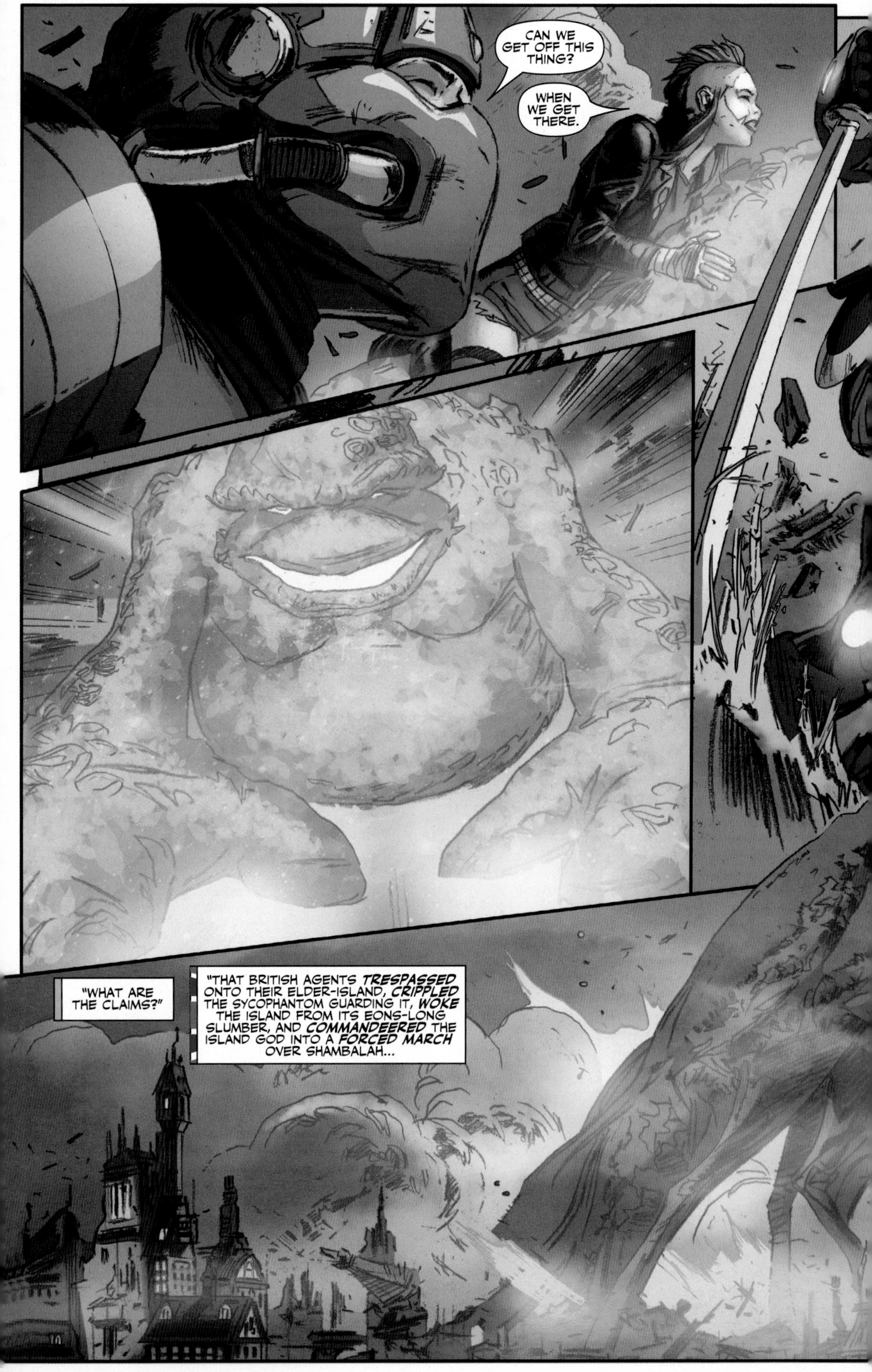
CAN WE GET OFF THIS THING?
WHEN WE GET THERE.
"WHAT ARE THE CLAIMS?"
"THAT BRITISH AGENTS TRESPASSED ONTO THEIR ELDER-ISLAND, CRIPPLED THE SYCOPHANTOM GUARDING IT, WOKE THE ISLAND FROM ITS EONS-LONG SLUMBER, AND COMMANDEERED THE ISLAND GOD INTO A FORCED MARCH OVER SHAMBALAH...

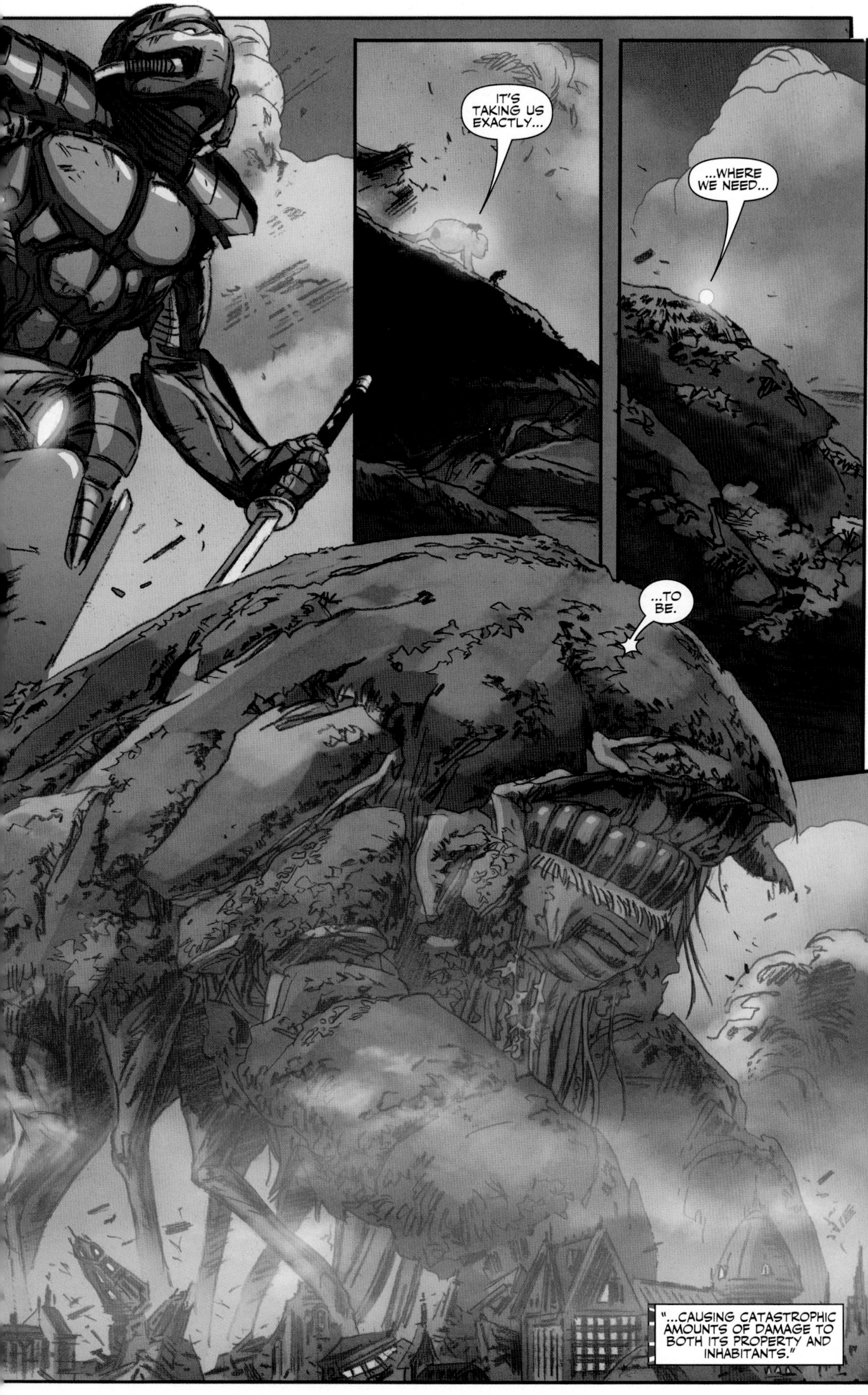
IT'S TAKING US EXACTLY...
...WHERE WE NEED...
...TO BE.
"...CAUSING CATASTROPHIC AMOUNTS OF DAMAGE TO BOTH ITS PROPERTY AND INHABITANTS."

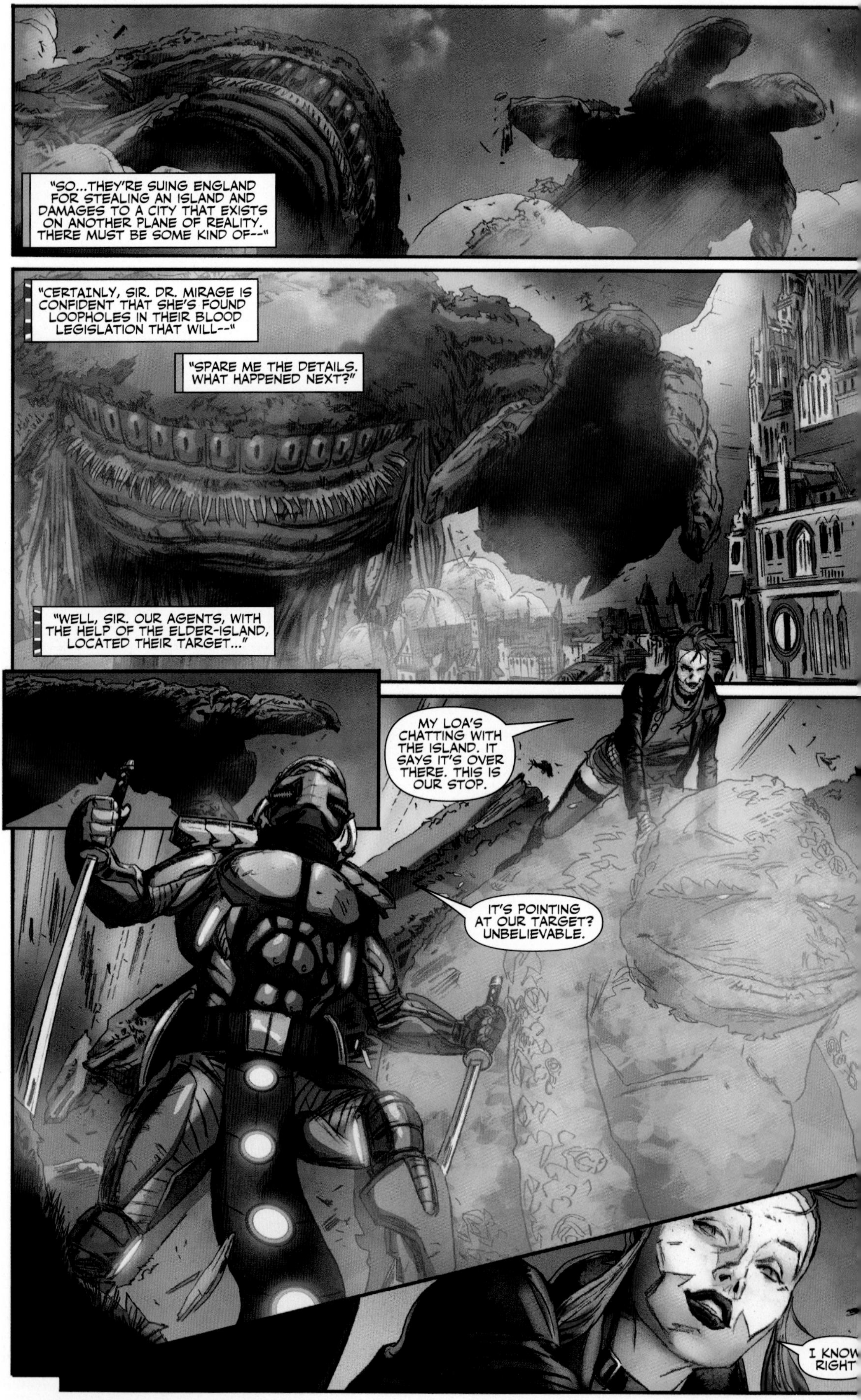
"SO...THEY'RE SUING ENGLAND FOR STEALING AN ISLAND AND DAMAGES TO A CITY THAT EXISTS ON ANOTHER PLANE OF REALITY. THERE MUST BE SOME KIND OF--"
"CERTAINLY, SIR. DR. MIRAGE IS CONFIDENT THAT SHE'S FOUND LOOPHOLES IN THEIR BLOOD LEGISLATION THAT WILL--"
"SPARE ME THE DETAILS. WHAT HAPPENED NEXT?"
"WELL, SIR. OUR AGENTS, WITH THE HELP OF THE ELDER-ISLAND, LOCATED THEIR TARGET..."
MY LOA'S CHATTING WITH THE ISLAND. IT SAYS IT'S OVER THERE. THIS IS OUR STOP.
IT'S POINTING AT OUR TARGET? UNBELIEVABLE.
I KNOW RIGHT

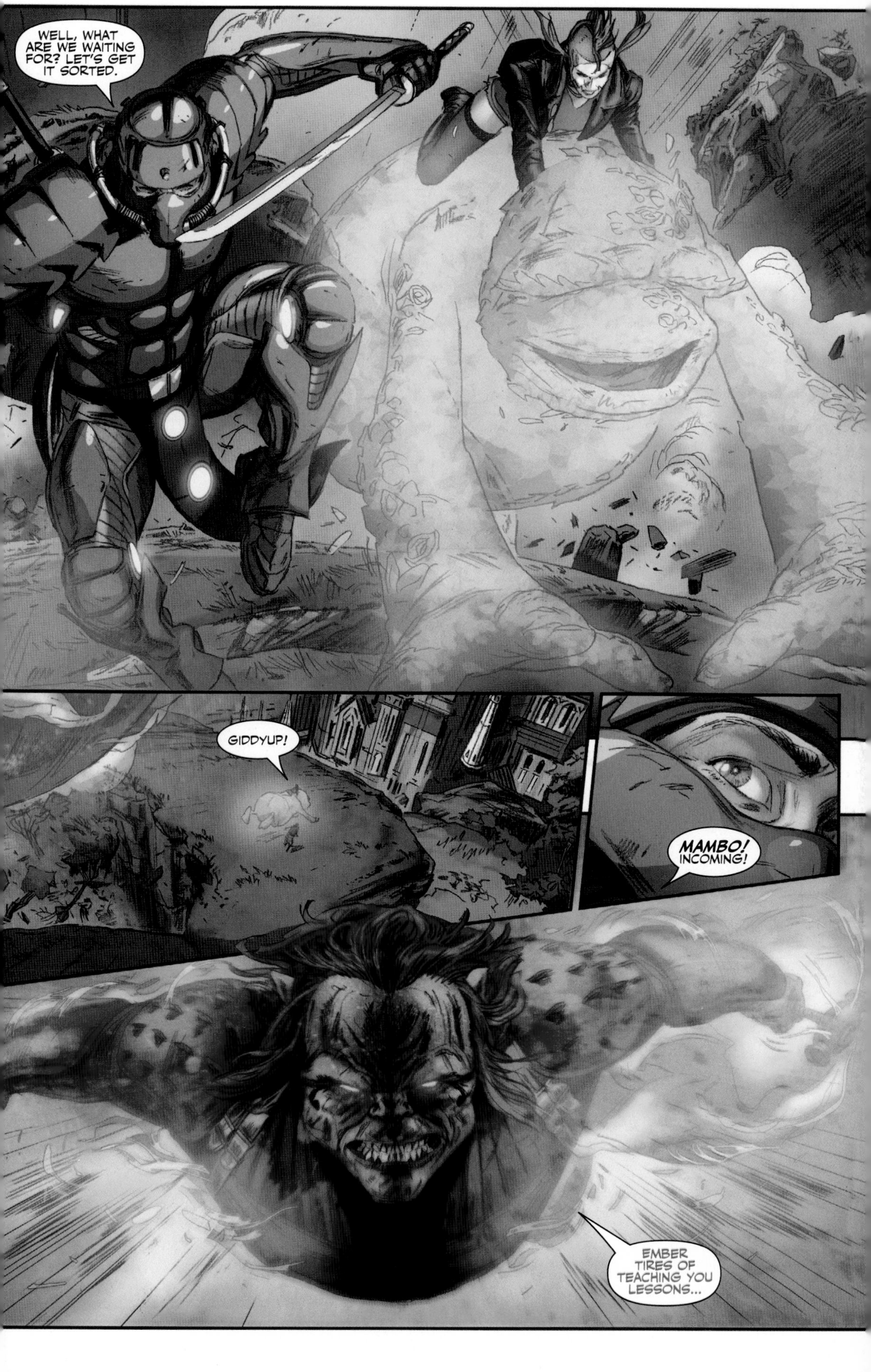

WELL, WHAT ARE WE WAITING FOR? LET'S GET IT SORTED.
GIDDYUP!
MAMBO! INCOMING!
EMBER TIRES OF TEACHING YOU LESSONS...

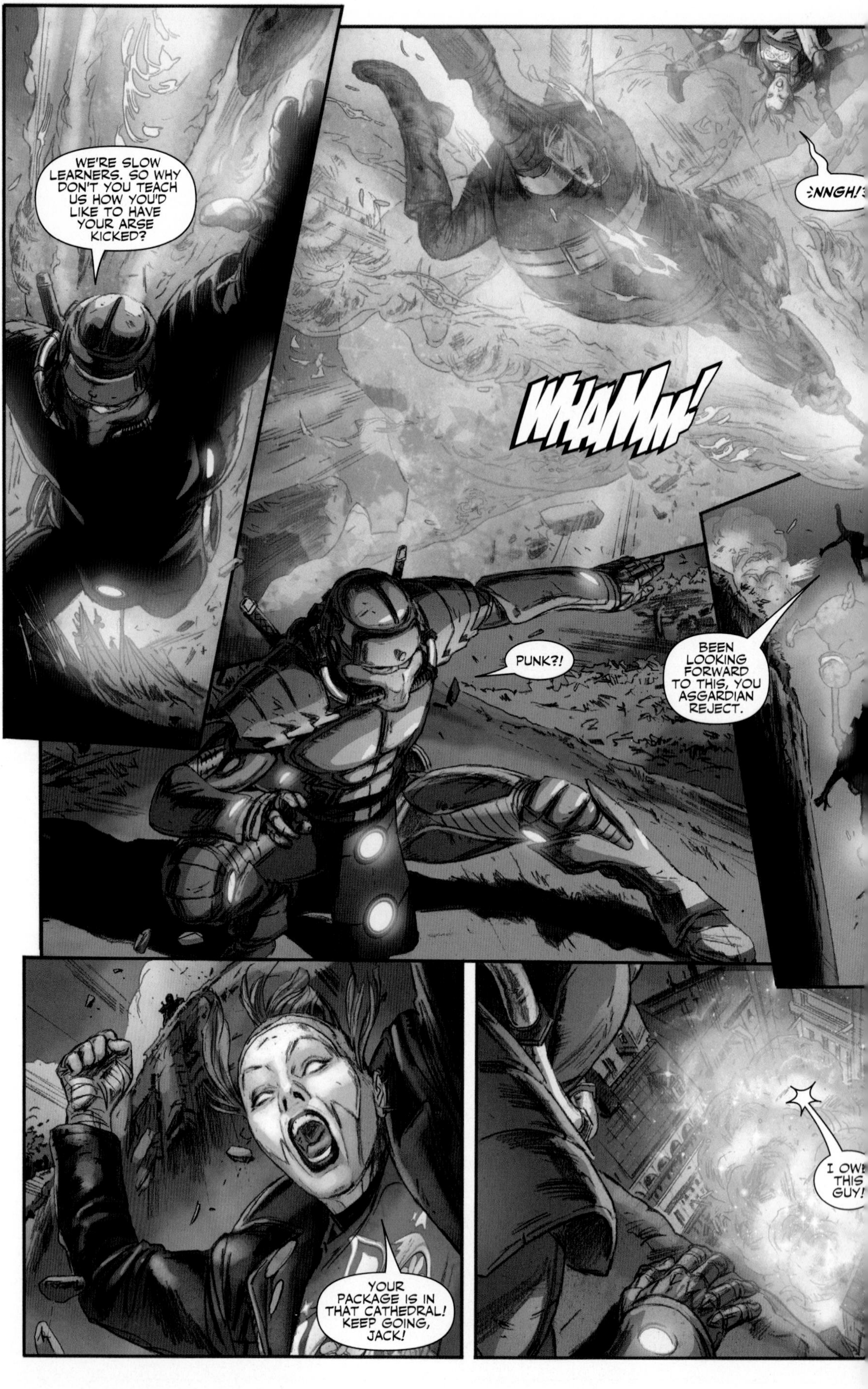

WE'RE SLOW LEARNERS. SO WHY DON'T YOU TEACH US HOW YOU'D LIKE TO HAVE YOUR ARSE KICKED?
NNGH!
WHAMM!
PUNK?!
BEEN LOOKING FORWARD TO THIS, YOU ASGARDIAN REJECT.
YOUR PACKAGE IS IN THAT CATHEDRAL! KEEP GOING, JACK!
I OWE THIS GUY!

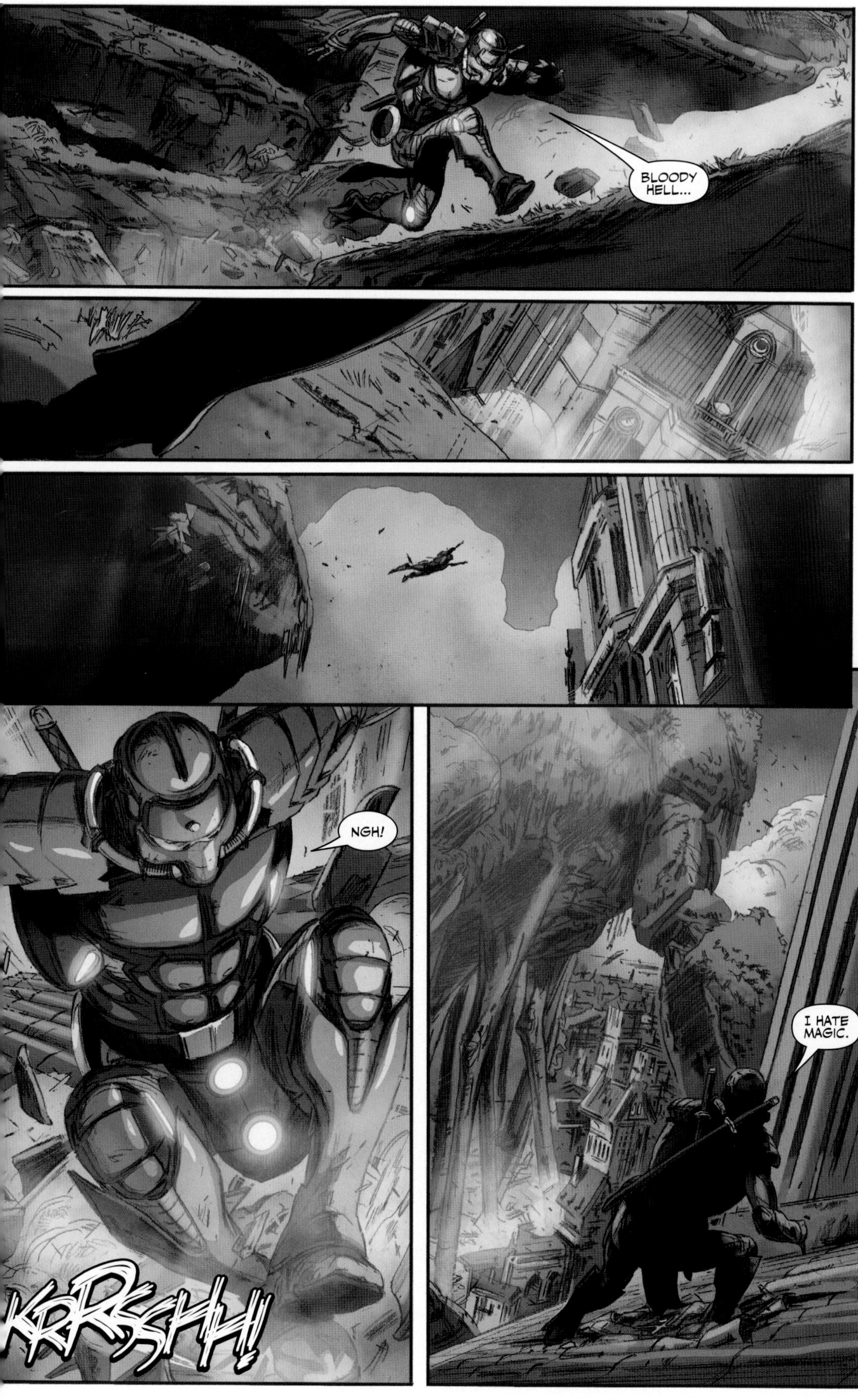
BLOODY HELL...
NGH!
KRRSSHH!
I HATE MAGIC.

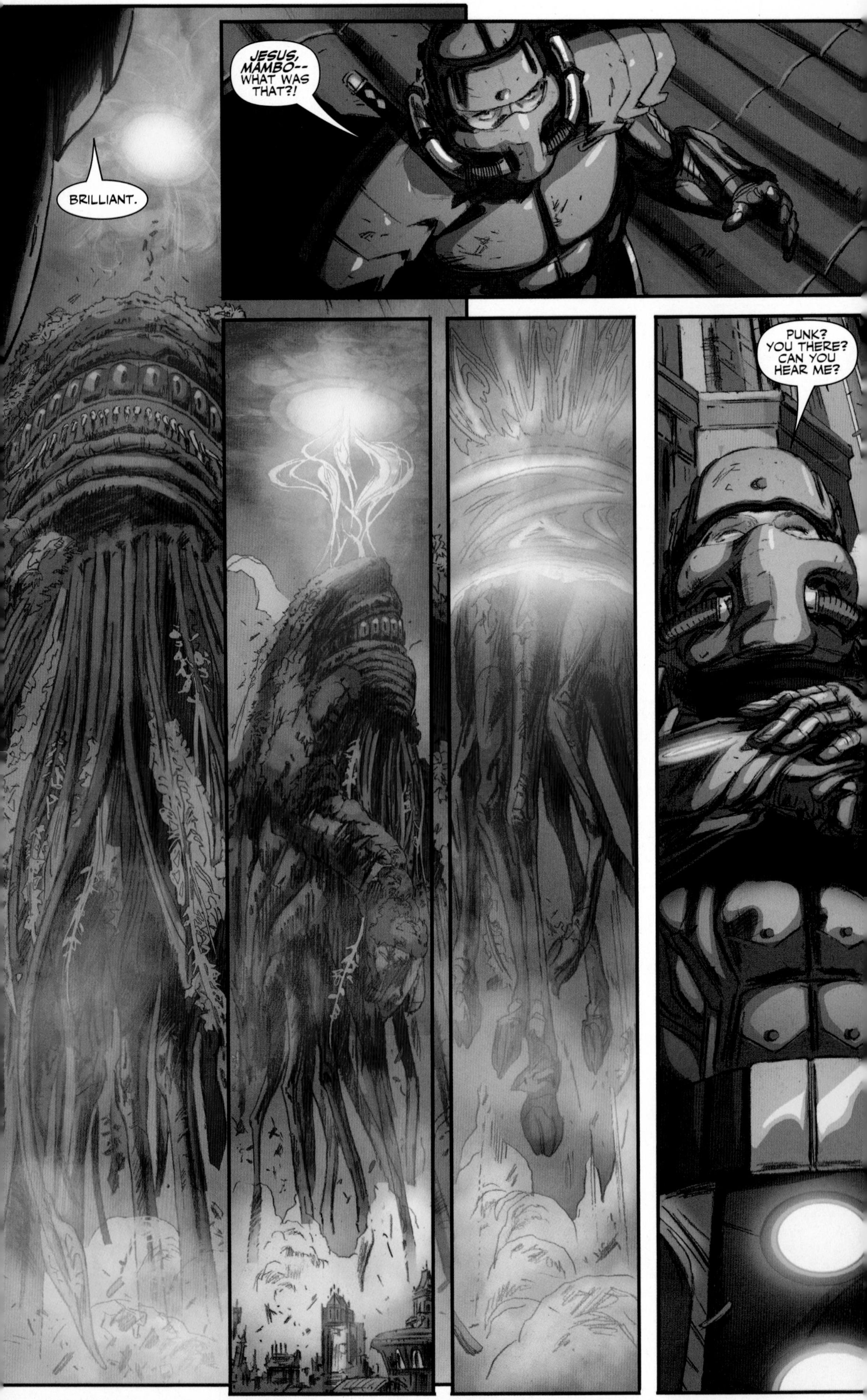
JESUS, MAMBO-- WHAT WAS THAT?!
BRILLIANT.
PUNK? YOU THERE? CAN YOU HEAR ME?

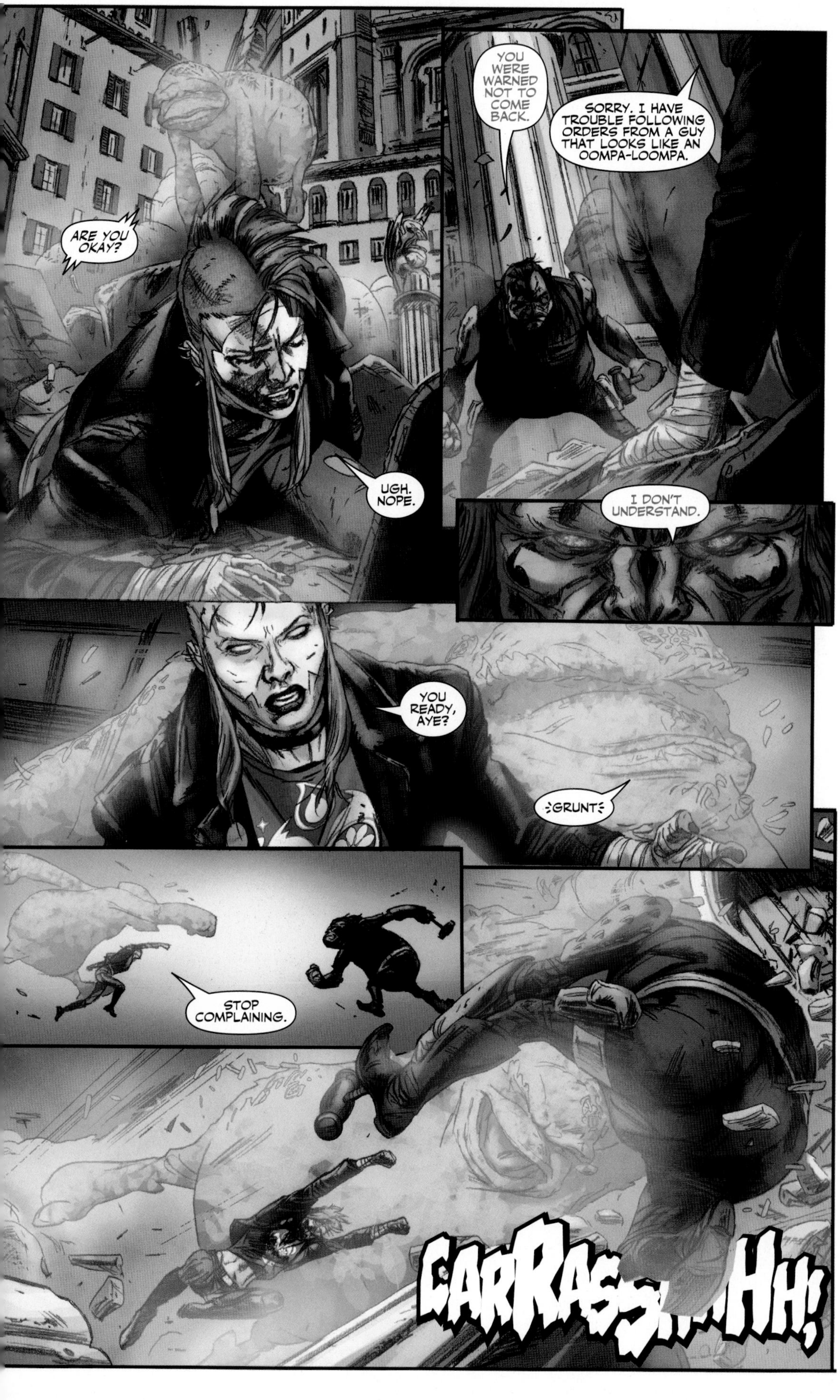
ARE YOU OKAY?
UGH. NOPE.
YOU WERE WARNED NOT TO COME BACK.
SORRY. I HAVE TROUBLE FOLLOWING ORDERS FROM A GUY THAT LOOKS LIKE AN OOMPA-LOOMPA.
I DON'T UNDERSTAND.
YOU READY, AYE?
GRUNT
STOP COMPLAINING.
CARRASSHHH!

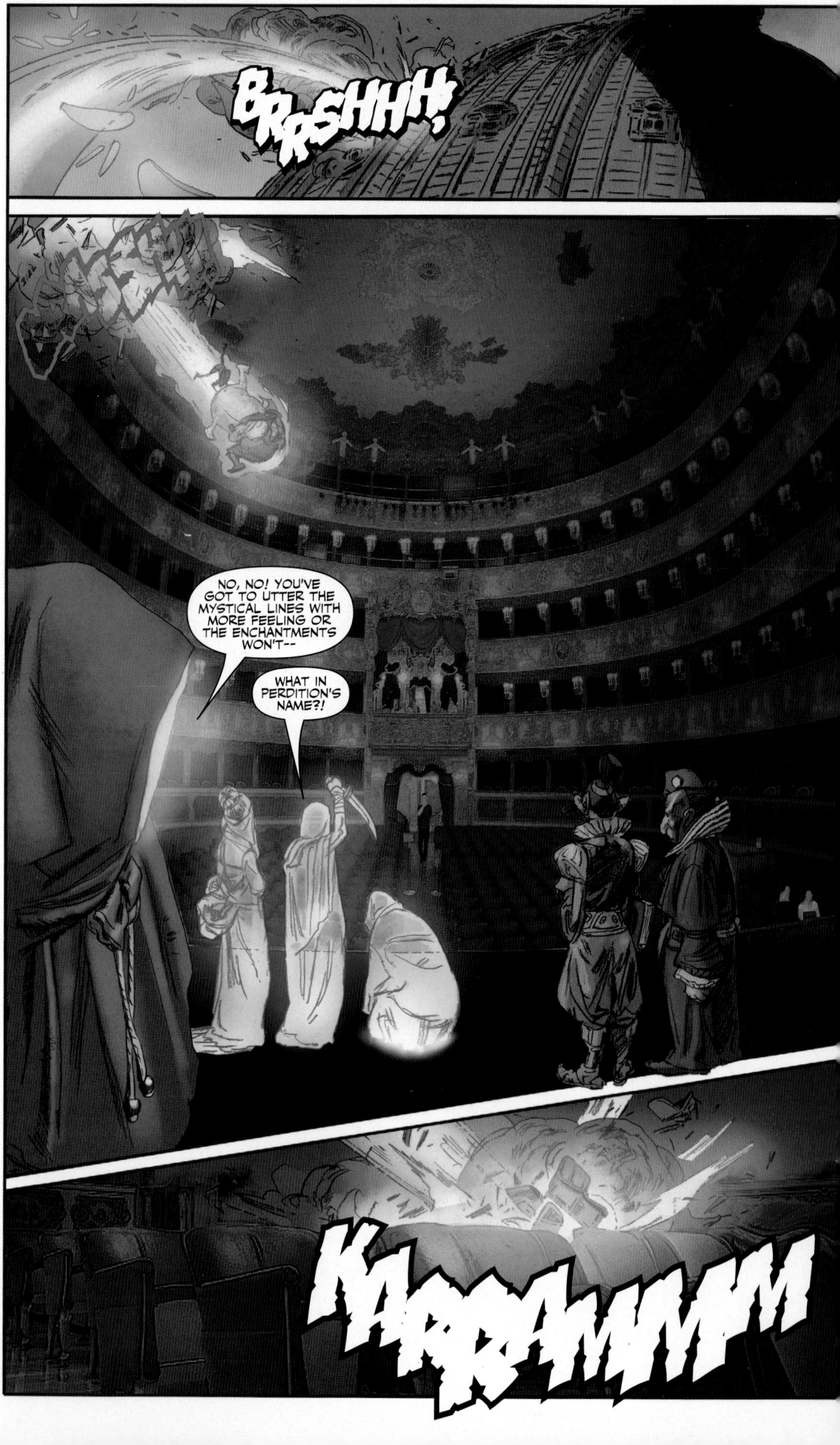
BRRSHHH!
NO, NO! YOU'VE GOT TO UTTER THE MYSTICAL LINES WITH MORE FEELING OR THE ENCHANTMENTS WON'T--
WHAT IN PERDITION'S NAME?!
KARRAMMM

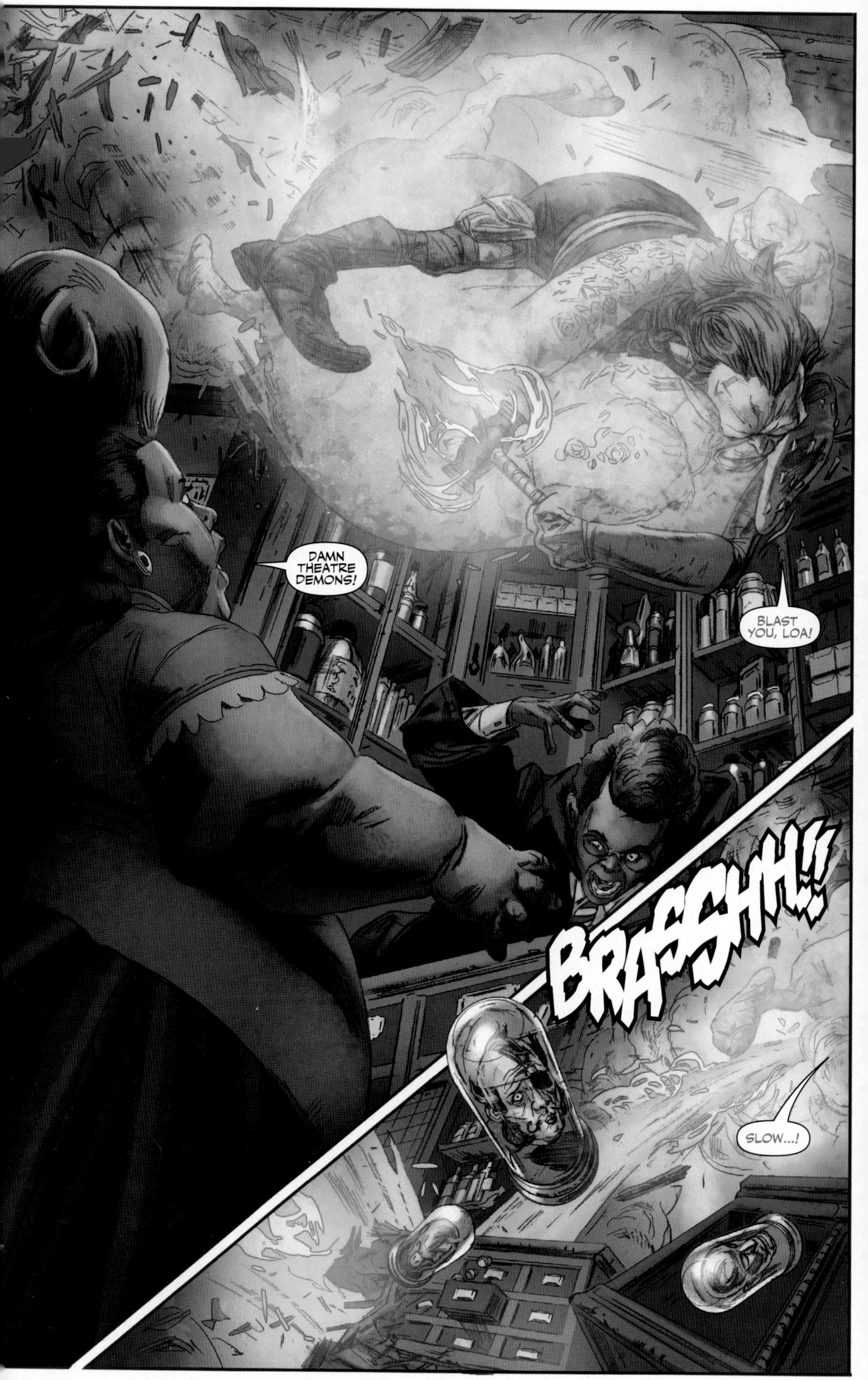
DAMN THEATRE DEMONS!
BLAST YOU, LOA!
BRASSHH!!
SLOW...!

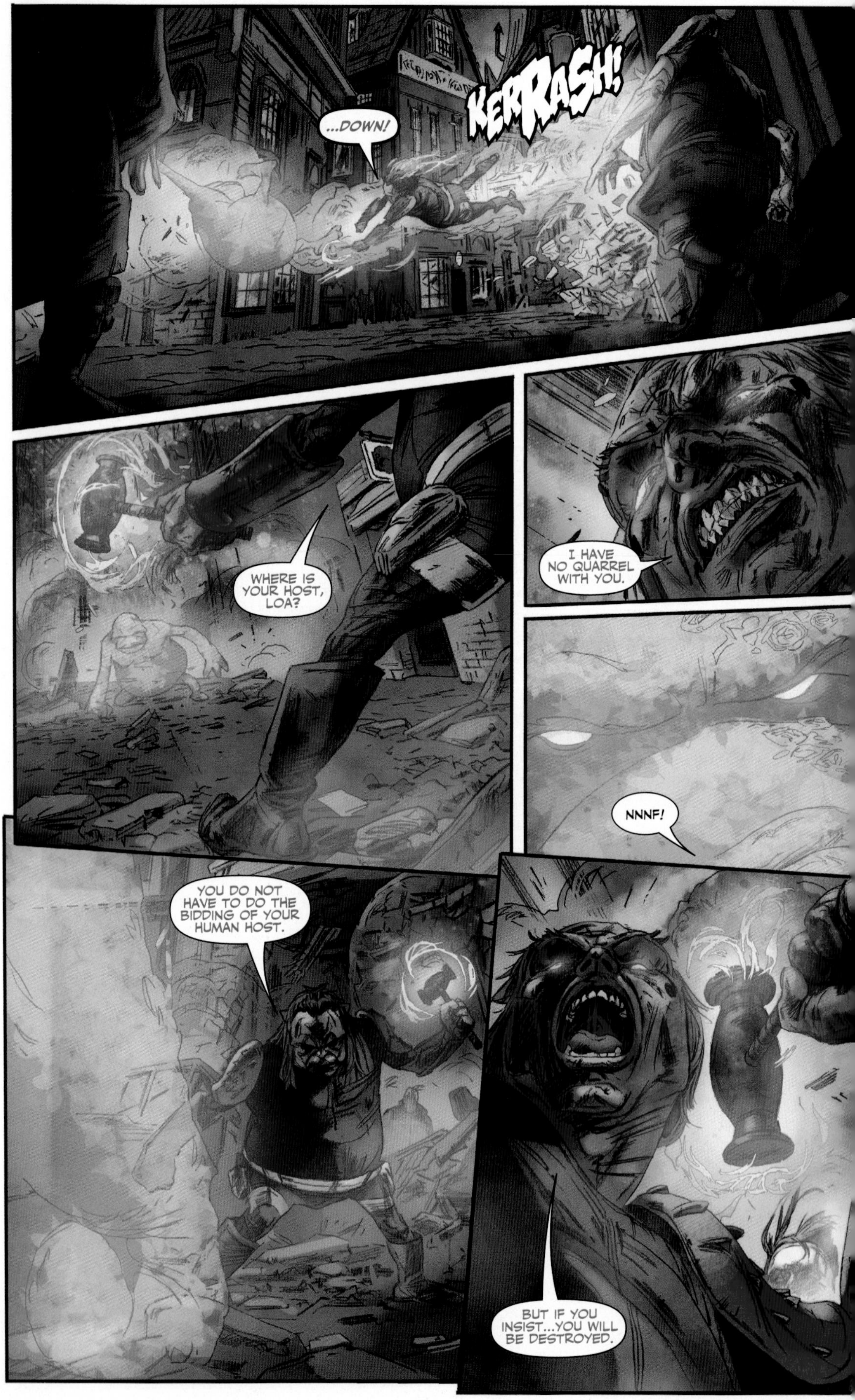
KERRASH!
...DOWN!
WHERE IS YOUR HOST, LOA?
I HAVE NO QUARREL WITH YOU.
NNNF!
YOU DO NOT HAVE TO DO THE BIDDING OF YOUR HUMAN HOST.
BUT IF YOU INSIST...YOU WILL BE DESTROYED.

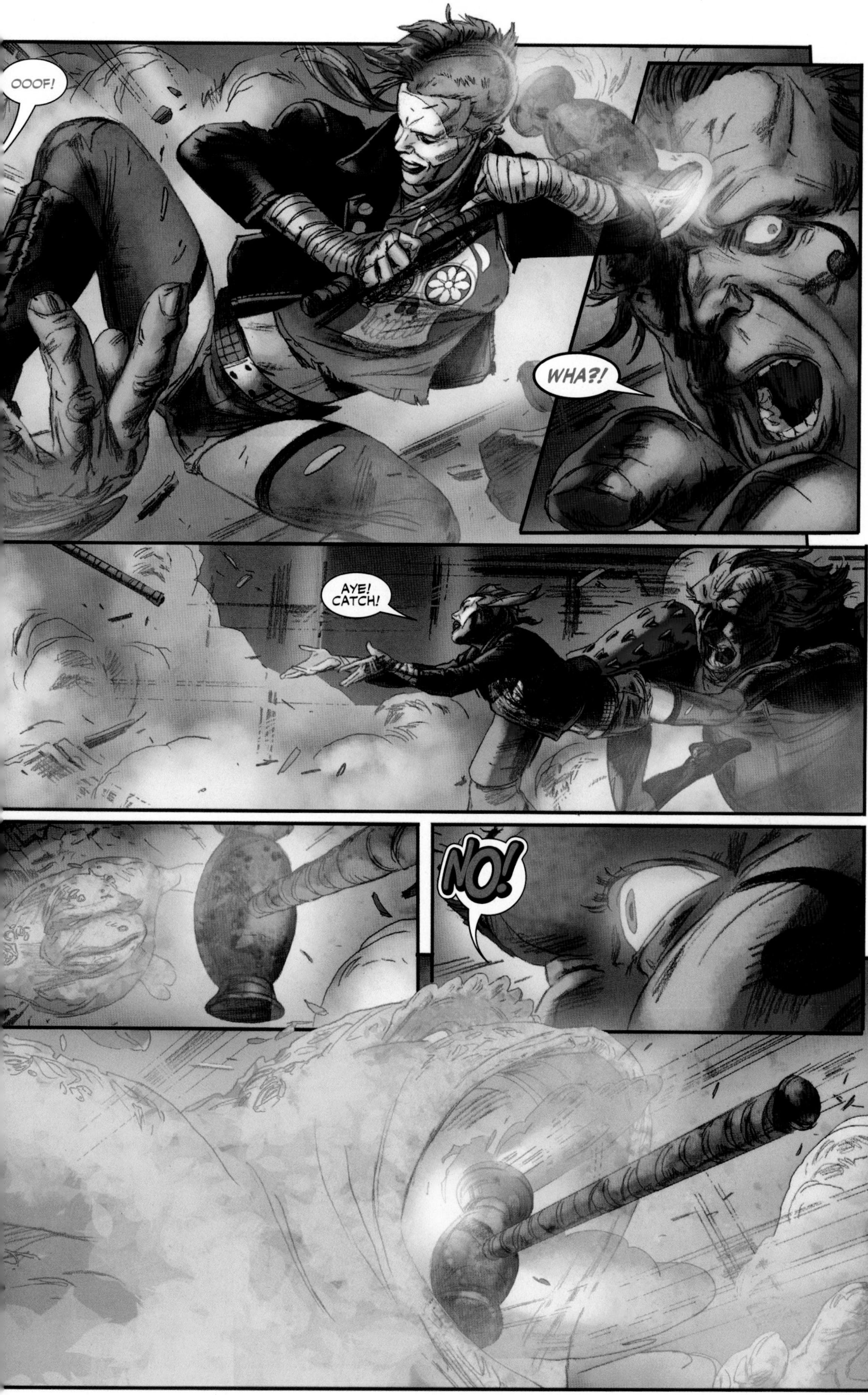

OOOF!
WHA?!
AYE! CATCH!
NO!

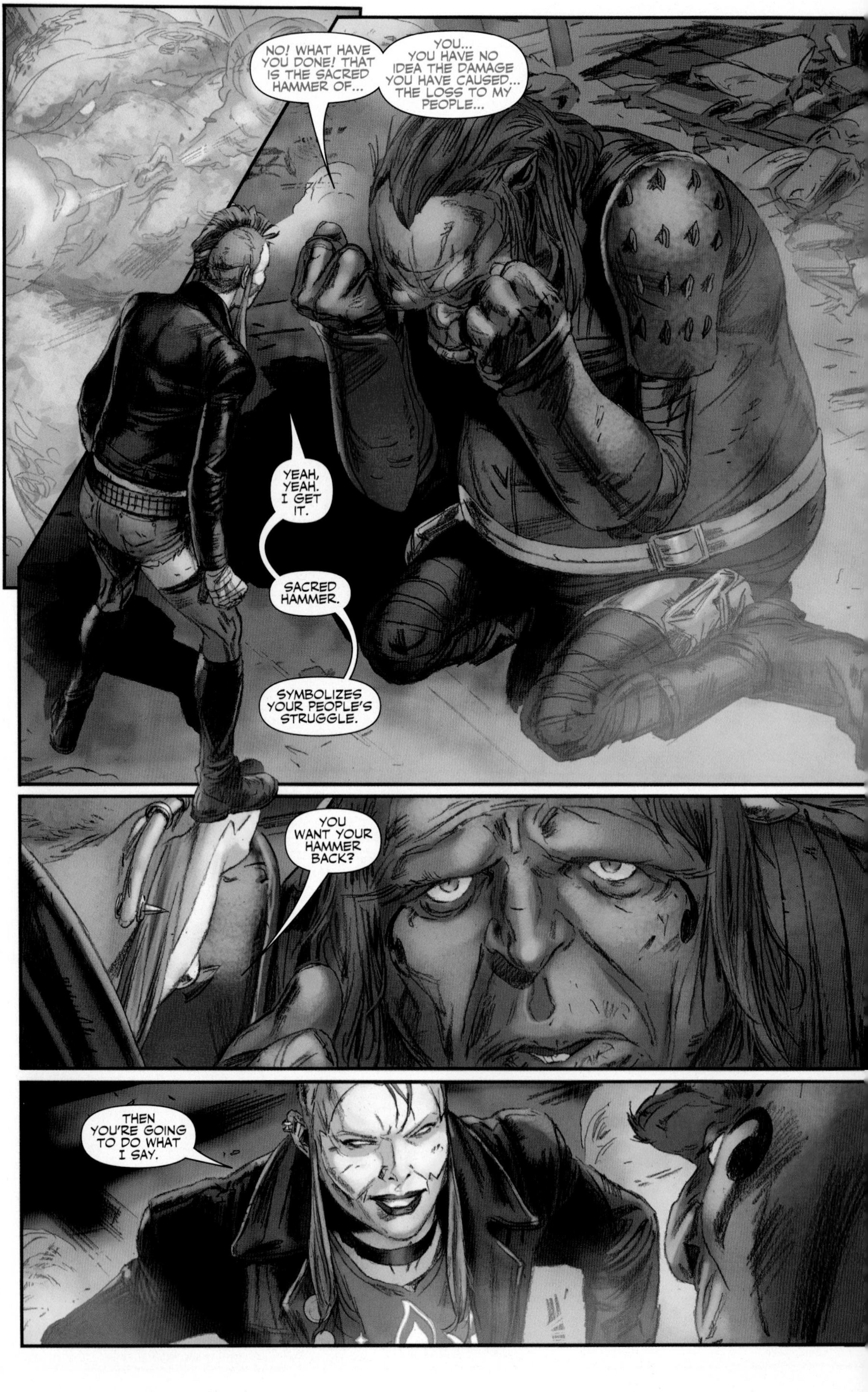
NO! WHAT HAVE YOU DONE! THAT IS THE SACRED HAMMER OF...
YOU... YOU HAVE NO IDEA THE DAMAGE YOU HAVE CAUSED... THE LOSS TO MY PEOPLE...
YEAH, YEAH. I GET IT.
SACRED HAMMER.
SYMBOLIZES YOUR PEOPLE'S STRUGGLE.
YOU WANT YOUR HAMMER BACK?
THEN YOU'RE GOING TO DO WHAT I SAY.

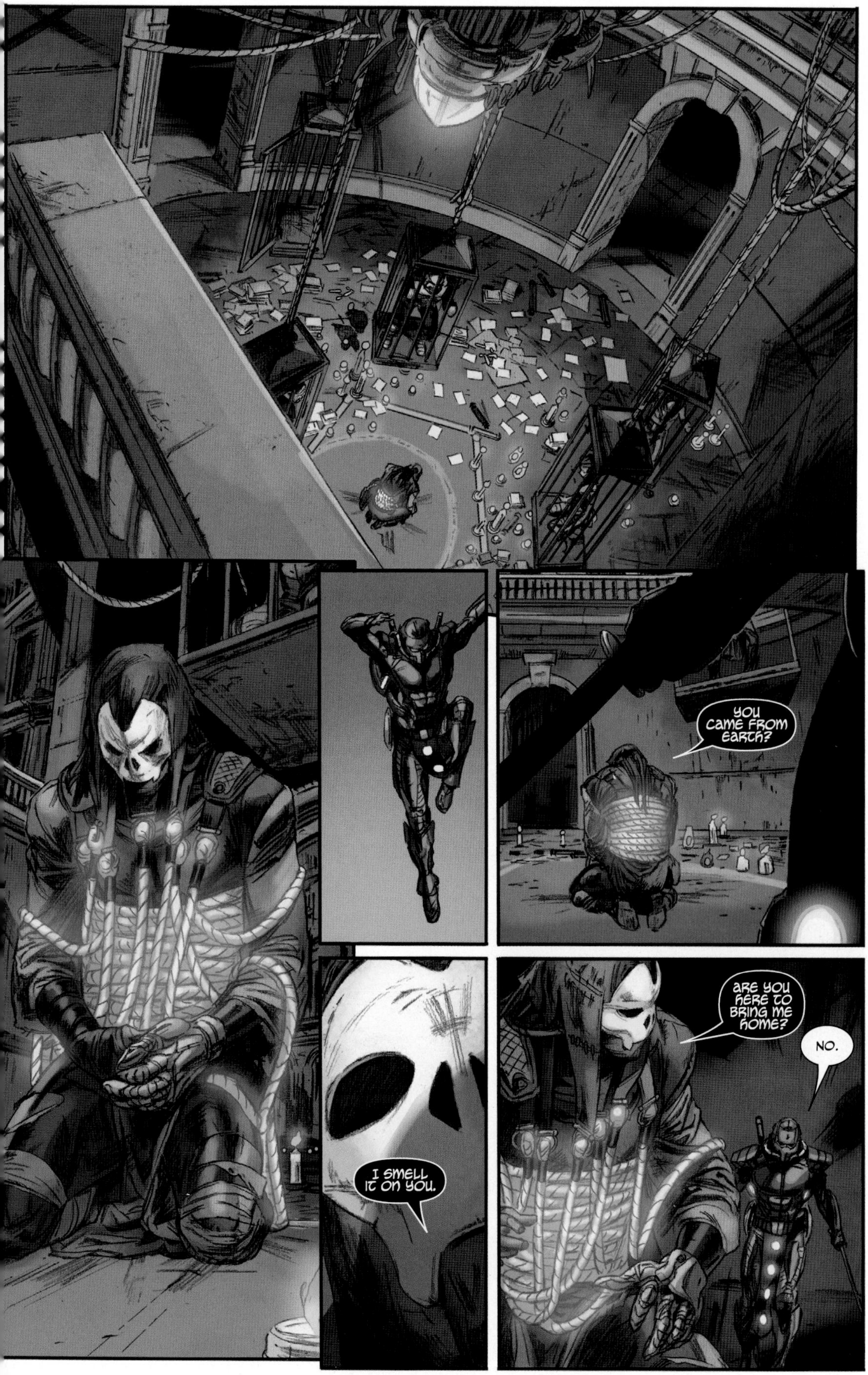
YOU CAME FROM EARTH?
I SMELL IT ON YOU.
ARE YOU HERE TO BRING ME HOME?
NO.

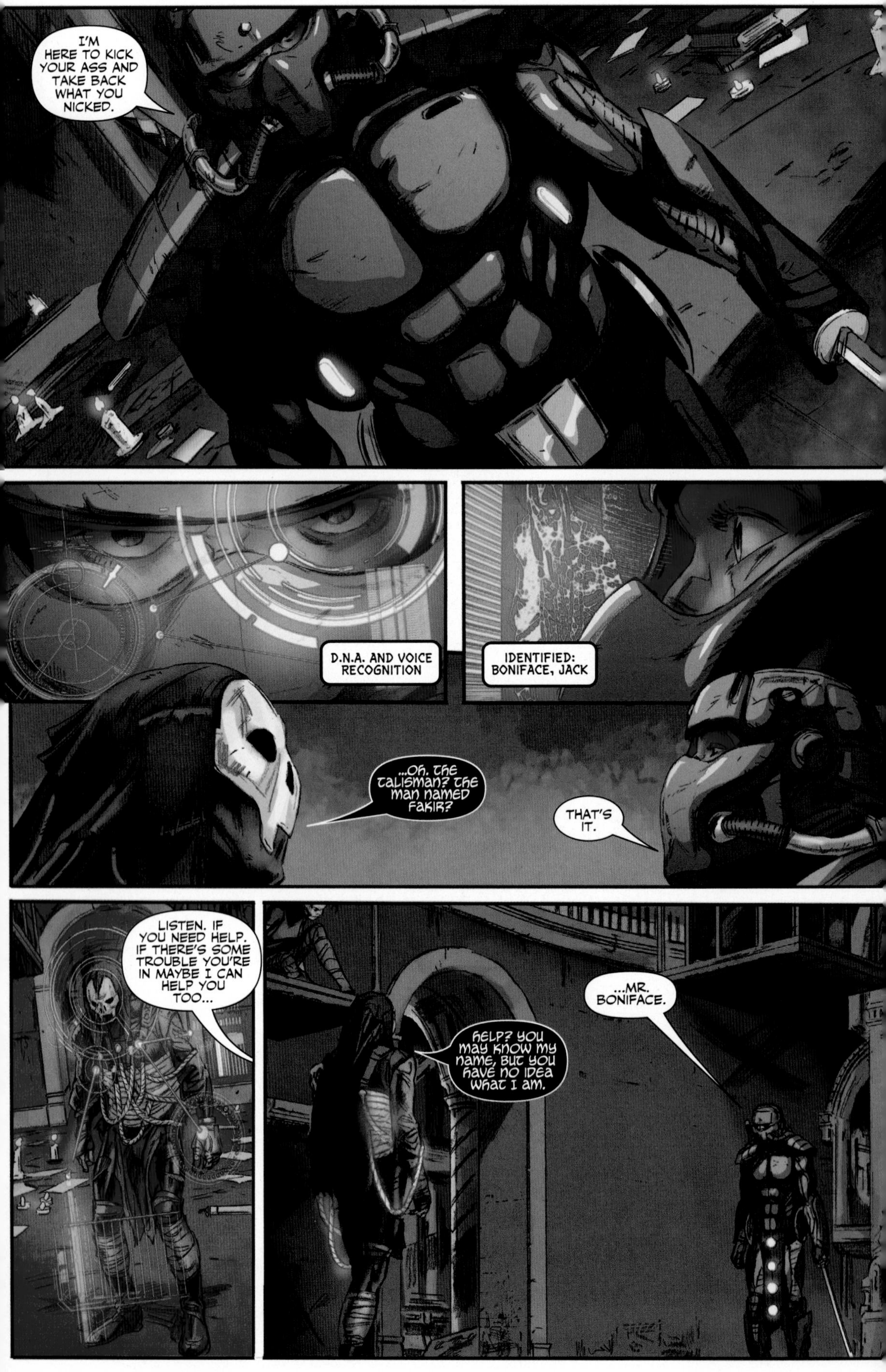
I'M HERE TO KICK YOUR ASS AND TAKE BACK WHAT YOU NICKED.
D.N.A. AND VOICE RECOGNITION
IDENTIFIED: BONIFACE, JACK
...OH. THE TALISMAN? THE MAN NAMED FAKIR?
THAT'S IT.
LISTEN. IF YOU NEED HELP. IF THERE'S SOME TROUBLE YOU'RE IN MAYBE I CAN HELP YOU TOO...
...MR. BONIFACE.
HELP? YOU MAY KNOW MY NAME, BUT YOU HAVE NO IDEA WHAT I AM.

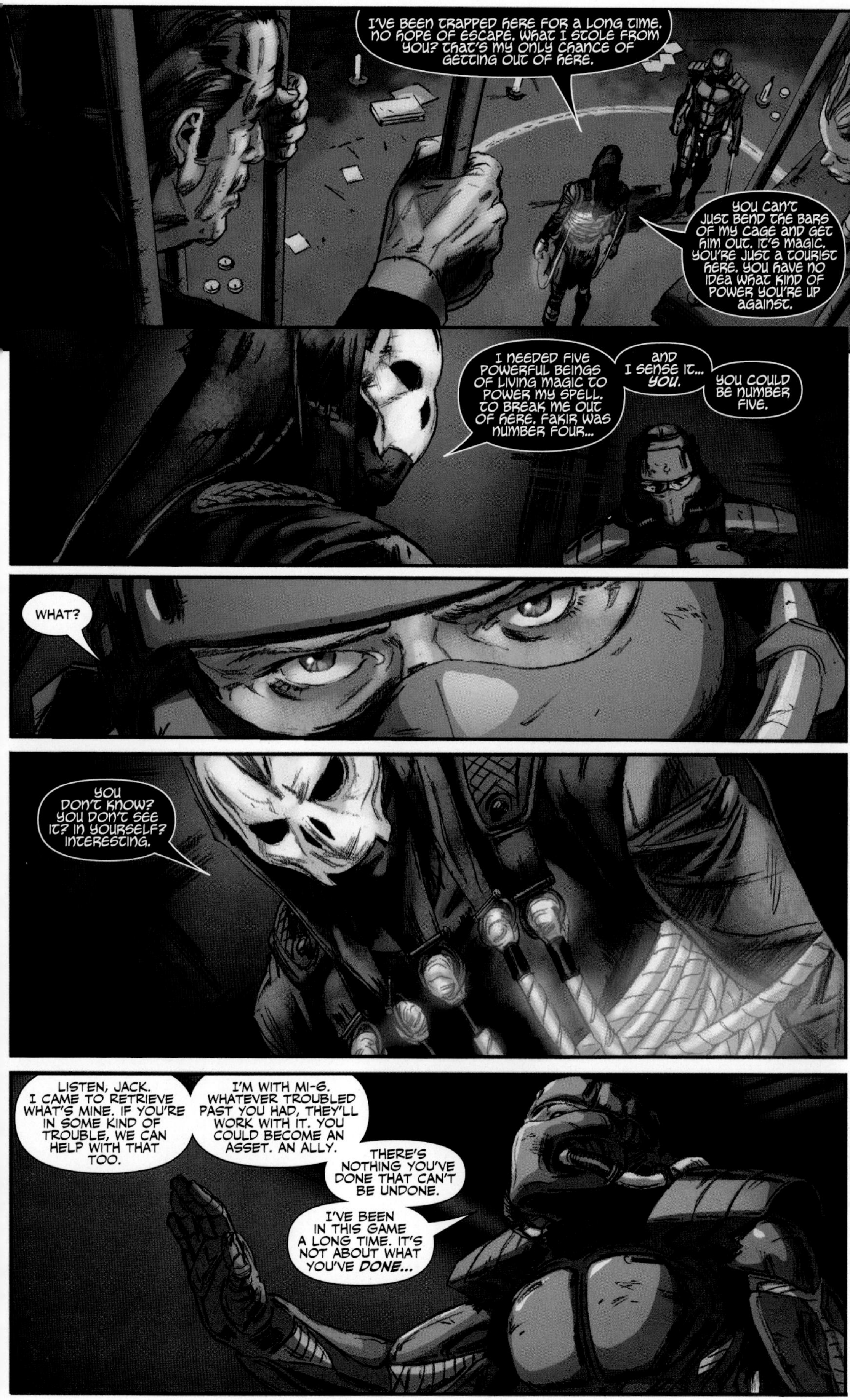
I'VE BEEN TRAPPED HERE FOR A LONG TIME. NO HOPE OF ESCAPE. WHAT I STOLE FROM YOU? THAT'S MY ONLY CHANCE OF GETTING OUT OF HERE.
YOU CAN'T JUST BEND THE BARS OF MY CAGE AND GET HIM OUT. IT'S MAGIC. YOU'RE JUST A TOURIST HERE. YOU HAVE NO IDEA WHAT KIND OF POWER YOU'RE UP AGAINST.
I NEEDED FIVE POWERFUL BEINGS OF LIVING MAGIC TO POWER MY SPELL. TO BREAK ME OUT OF HERE. FAKIR WAS NUMBER FOUR...
AND I SENSE IT... *YOU.*
YOU COULD BE NUMBER FIVE.
WHAT?
YOU DON'T KNOW? YOU DON'T SEE IT? IN YOURSELF? INTERESTING.
LISTEN, JACK. I CAME TO RETRIEVE WHAT'S MINE. IF YOU'RE IN SOME KIND OF TROUBLE, WE CAN HELP WITH THAT TOO.
I'M WITH MI-6. WHATEVER TROUBLED PAST YOU HAD, THEY'LL WORK WITH IT. YOU COULD BECOME AN ASSET. AN ALLY.
THERE'S NOTHING YOU'VE DONE THAT CAN'T BE UNDONE.
I'VE BEEN IN THIS GAME A LONG TIME. IT'S NOT ABOUT WHAT YOU'VE *DONE...*

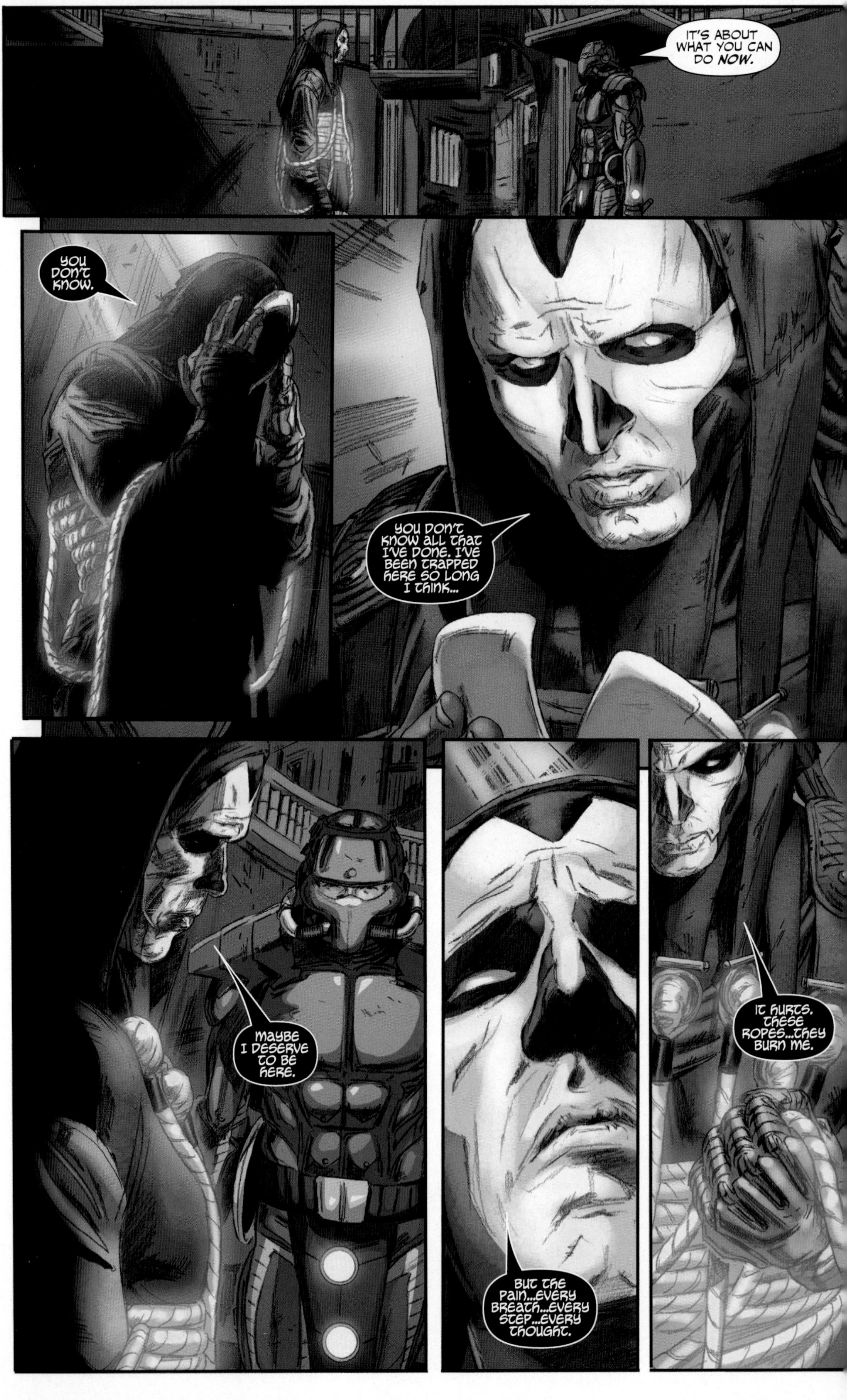
IT'S ABOUT WHAT YOU CAN DO NOW.
YOU DON'T KNOW.
YOU DON'T KNOW ALL THAT I'VE DONE. I'VE BEEN TRAPPED HERE SO LONG I THINK...
MAYBE I DESERVE TO BE HERE.
BUT THE PAIN...EVERY BREATH...EVERY STEP...EVERY THOUGHT.
IT HURTS. THESE ROPES...THEY BURN ME.

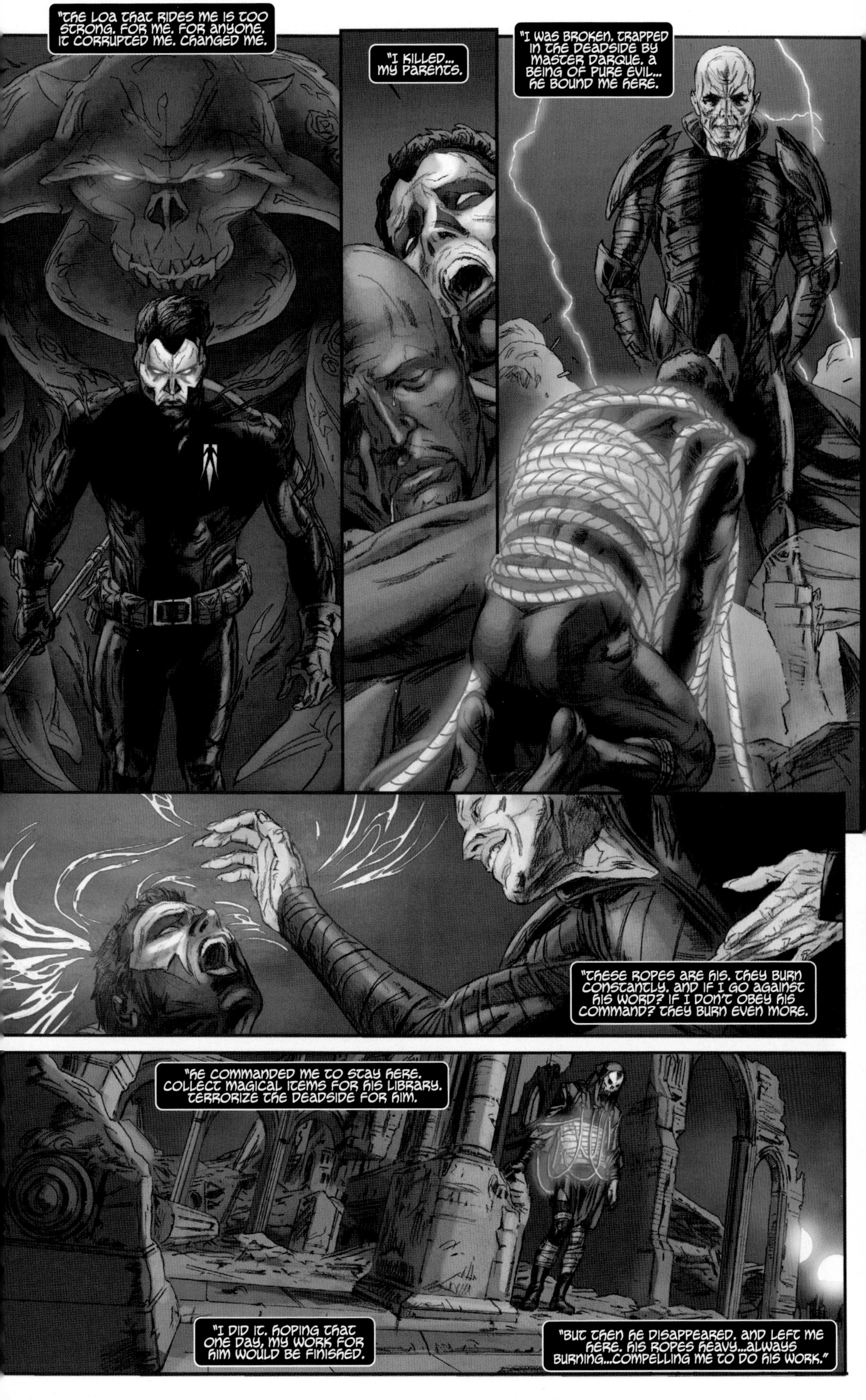

"THE LOA THAT RIDES ME IS TOO STRONG. FOR ME. FOR ANYONE. IT CORRUPTED ME. CHANGED ME.
"I KILLED... MY PARENTS.
"I WAS BROKEN. TRAPPED IN THE DEADSIDE BY MASTER DARQUE. A BEING OF PURE EVIL... HE BOUND ME HERE.
"THESE ROPES ARE HIS. THEY BURN CONSTANTLY. AND IF I GO AGAINST HIS WORD? IF I DON'T OBEY HIS COMMAND? THEY BURN EVEN MORE.
"HE COMMANDED ME TO STAY HERE. COLLECT MAGICAL ITEMS FOR HIS LIBRARY. TERRORIZE THE DEADSIDE FOR HIM.
"I DID IT. HOPING THAT ONE DAY, MY WORK FOR HIM WOULD BE FINISHED.
"BUT THEN HE DISAPPEARED. AND LEFT ME HERE. HIS ROPES HEAVY...ALWAYS BURNING...COMPELLING ME TO DO HIS WORK."

YOU REALIZE? THEY BURN EVEN NOW. THE PAIN IS CONSTANT... ONLY RELENTING WHEN I AM DOING HIS BIDDING. TALKING TO YOU NOW... THE PAIN IS...NEARLY UNBEARABLE...

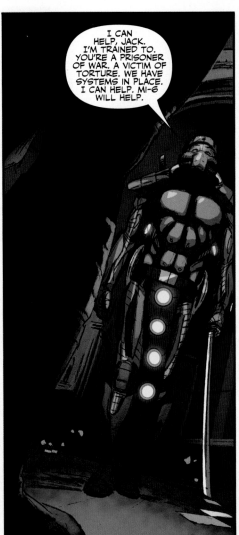

I CAN HELP, JACK. I'M TRAINED TO. YOU'RE A PRISONER OF WAR. A VICTIM OF TORTURE. WE HAVE SYSTEMS IN PLACE. I CAN HELP. MI-6 WILL HELP.

TRUST ME...

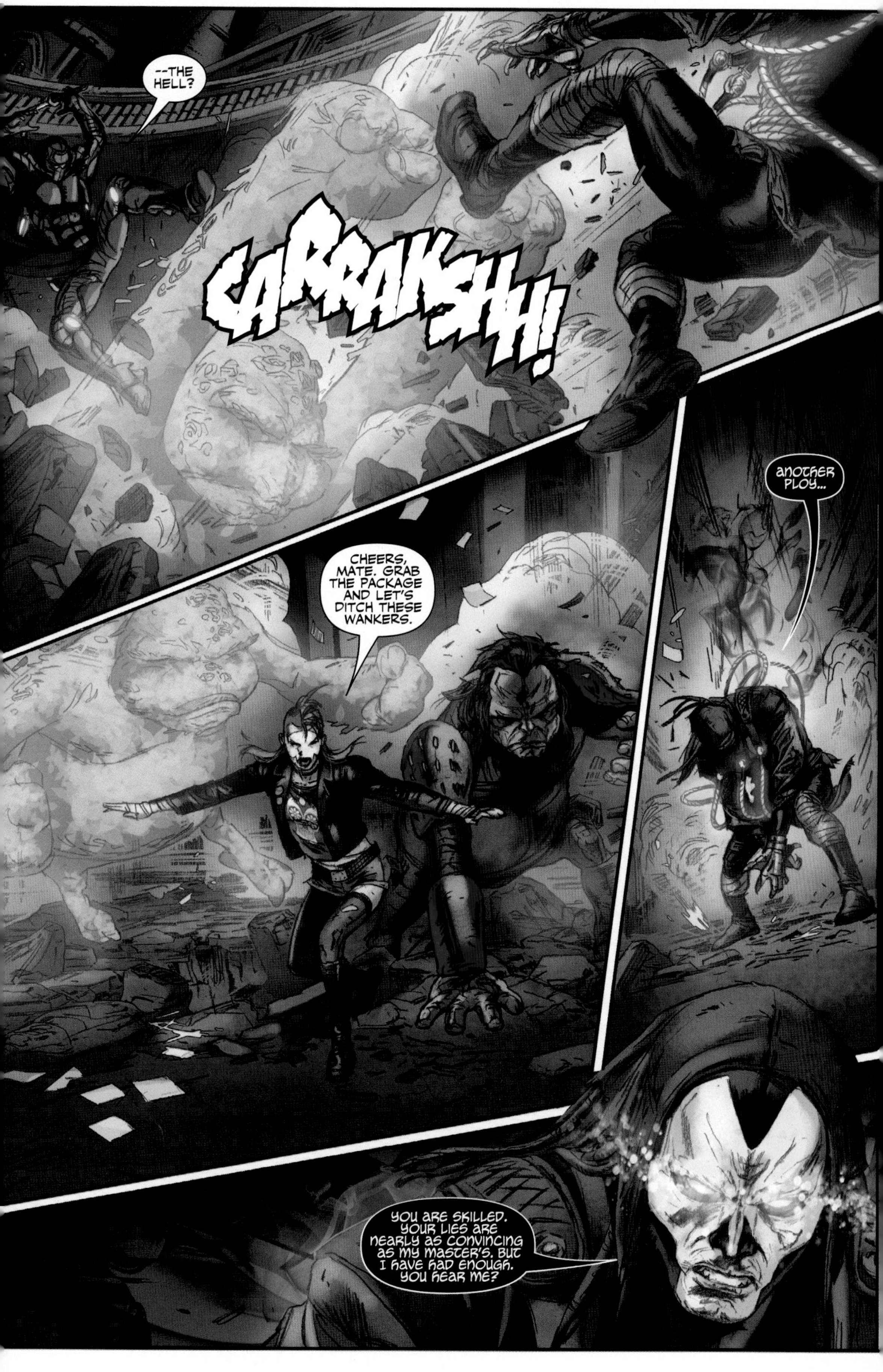
--THE HELL?
CARRAKSHH!
CHEERS, MATE. GRAB THE PACKAGE AND LET'S DITCH THESE WANKERS.
ANOTHER PLOY...
YOU ARE SKILLED. YOUR LIES ARE NEARLY AS CONVINCING AS MY MASTER'S. BUT I HAVE HAD ENOUGH. YOU HEAR ME?

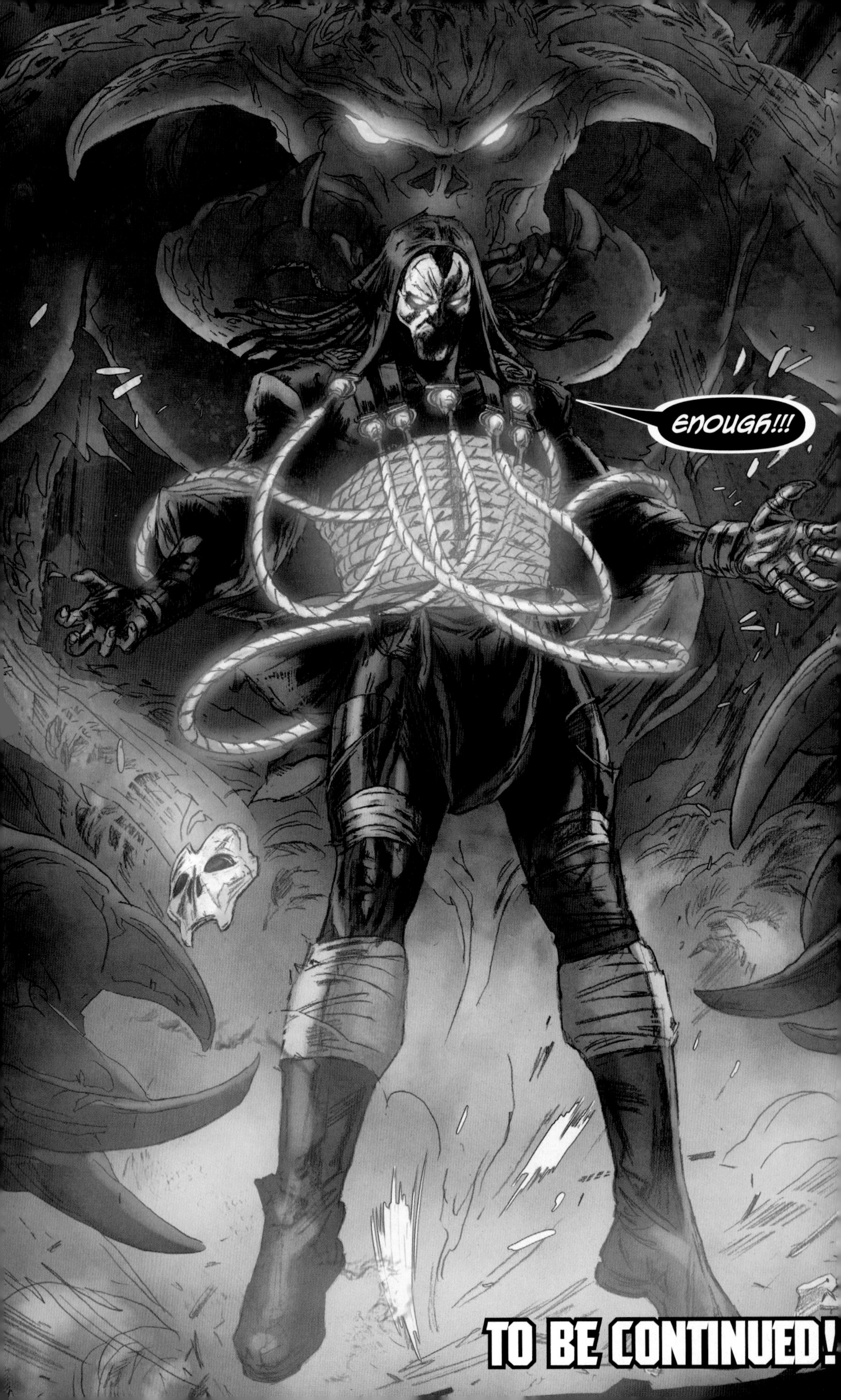
ENOUGH!!!
TO BE CONTINUED!

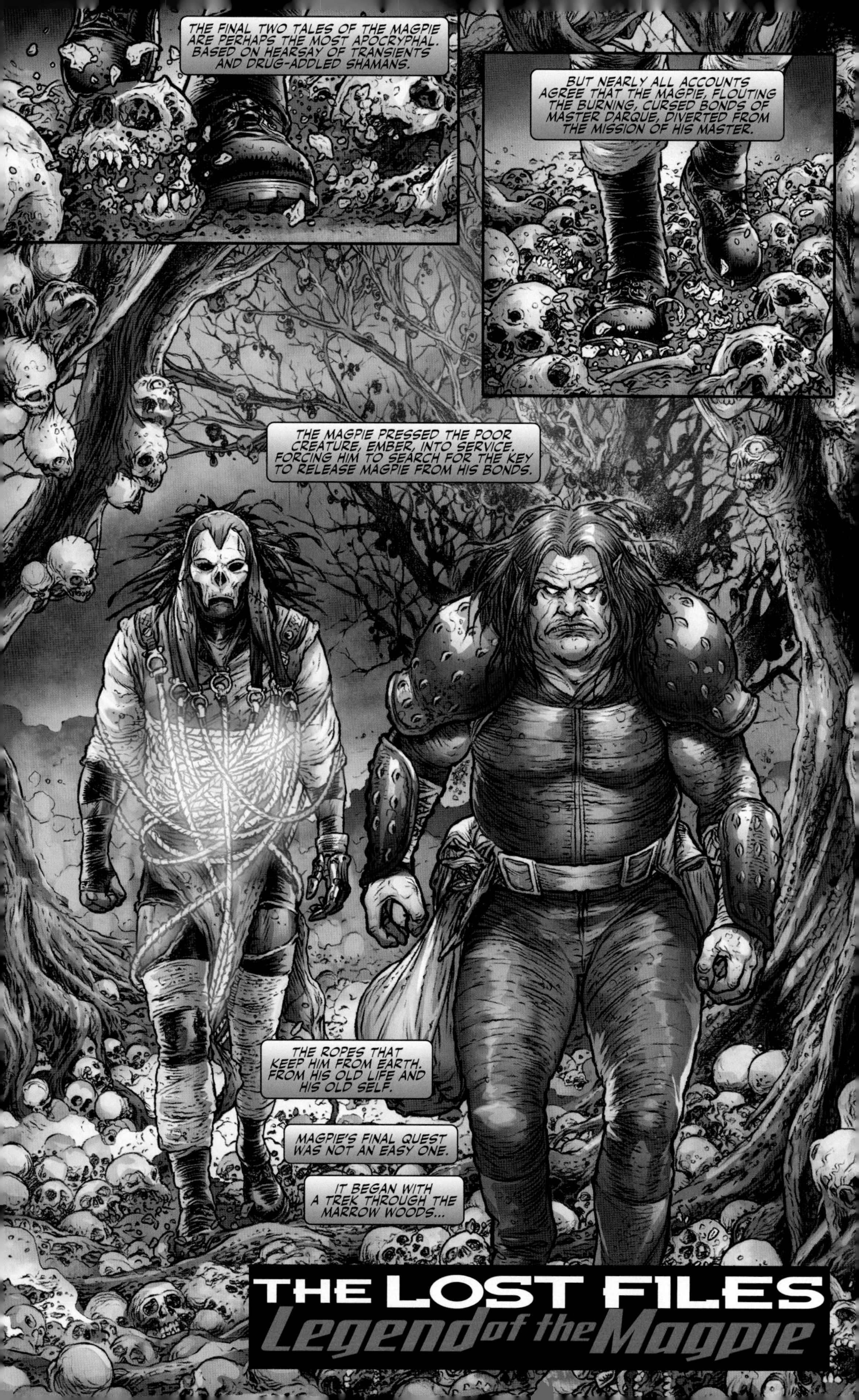
THE FINAL TWO TALES OF THE MAGPIE ARE PERHAPS THE MOST APOCRYPHAL. BASED ON HEARSAY OF TRANSIENTS AND DRUG-ADDLED SHAMANS.
BUT NEARLY ALL ACCOUNTS AGREE THAT THE MAGPIE, FLOUTING THE BURNING, CURSED BONDS OF MASTER DARQUE, DIVERTED FROM THE MISSION OF HIS MASTER.
THE MAGPIE PRESSED THE POOR CREATURE, EMBER, INTO SERVICE. FORCING HIM TO SEARCH FOR THE KEY TO RELEASE MAGPIE FROM HIS BONDS.
THE ROPES THAT KEEP HIM FROM EARTH. FROM HIS OLD LIFE AND HIS OLD SELF.
MAGPIE'S FINAL QUEST WAS NOT AN EASY ONE.
IT BEGAN WITH A TREK THROUGH THE MARROW WOODS...
THE LOST FILES
Legend of the Magpie

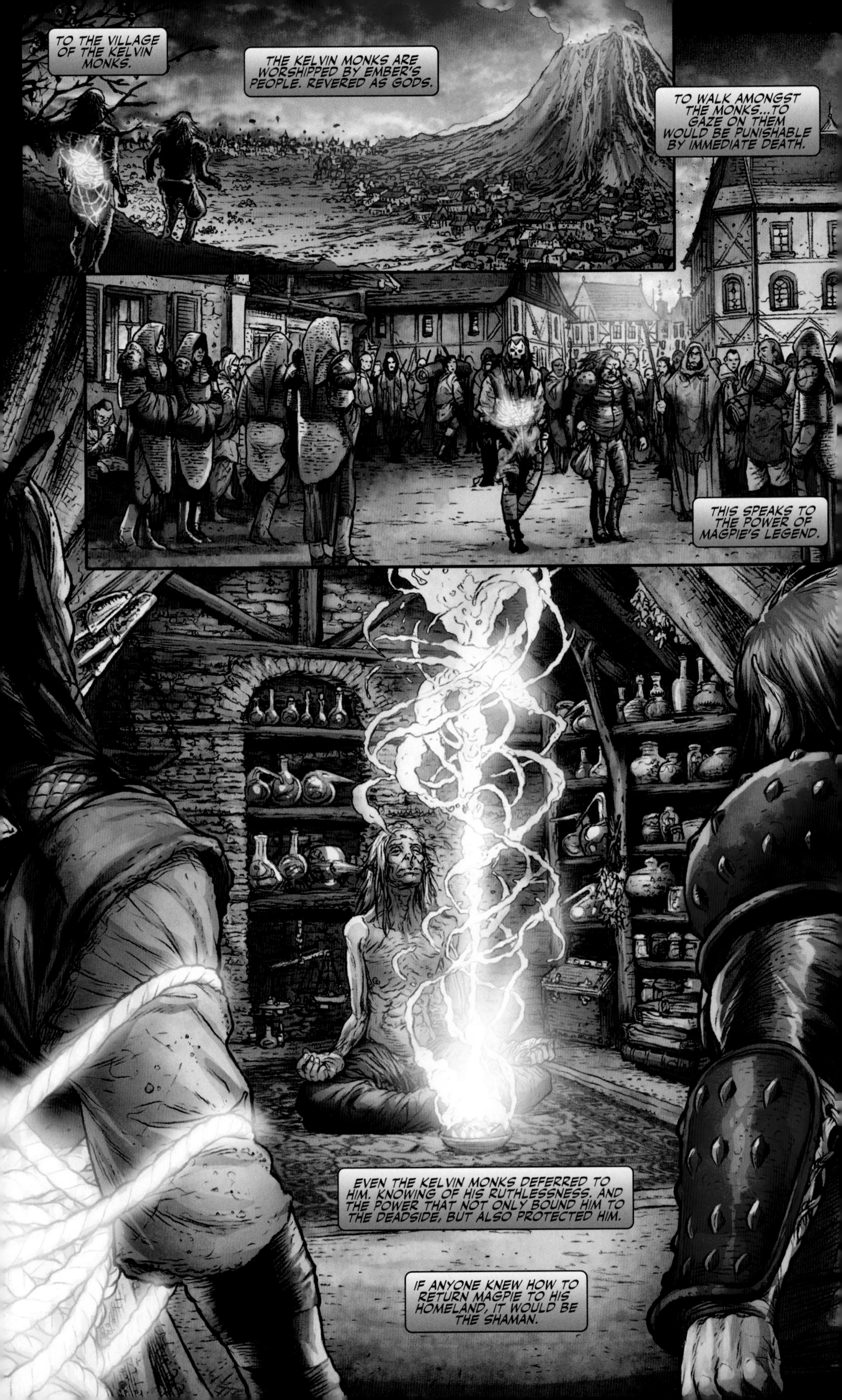
TO THE VILLAGE OF THE KELVIN MONKS.
THE KELVIN MONKS ARE WORSHIPPED BY EMBER'S PEOPLE. REVERED AS GODS.
TO WALK AMONGST THE MONKS...TO GAZE ON THEM WOULD BE PUNISHABLE BY IMMEDIATE DEATH.
THIS SPEAKS TO THE POWER OF MAGPIE'S LEGEND.
EVEN THE KELVIN MONKS DEFERRED TO HIM. KNOWING OF HIS RUTHLESSNESS. AND THE POWER THAT NOT ONLY BOUND HIM TO THE DEADSIDE, BUT ALSO PROTECTED HIM.
IF ANYONE KNEW HOW TO RETURN MAGPIE TO HIS HOMELAND, IT WOULD BE THE SHAMAN.

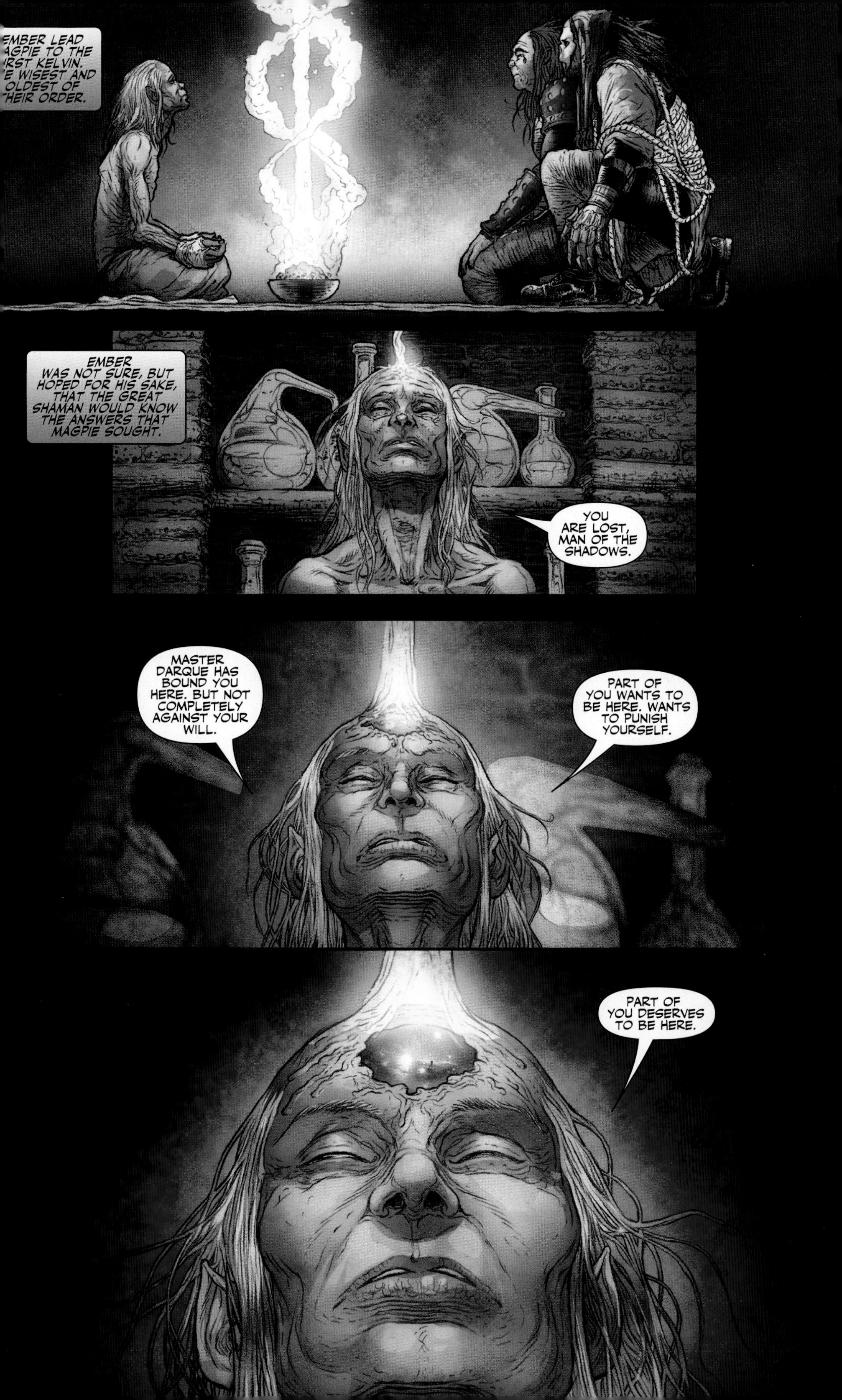
EMBER LEAD
AGPIE TO THE
IRST KELVIN.
E WISEST AND
OLDEST OF
THEIR ORDER.
EMBER WAS NOT SURE, BUT HOPED FOR HIS SAKE, THAT THE GREAT SHAMAN WOULD KNOW THE ANSWERS THAT MAGPIE SOUGHT.
YOU ARE LOST, MAN OF THE SHADOWS.
MASTER DARQUE HAS BOUND YOU HERE. BUT NOT COMPLETELY AGAINST YOUR WILL.
PART OF YOU WANTS TO BE HERE. WANTS TO PUNISH YOURSELF.
PART OF YOU DESERVES TO BE HERE.

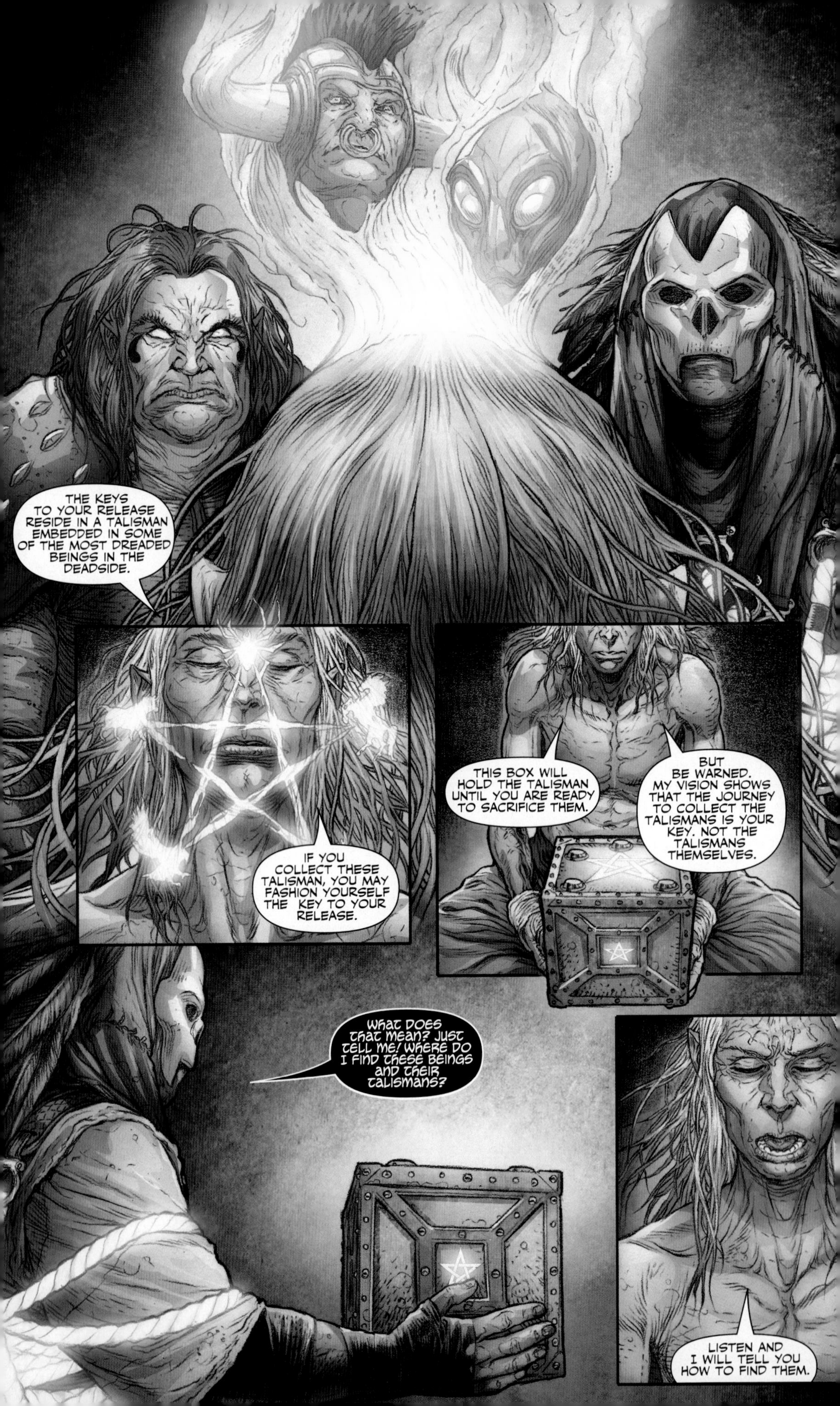
THE KEYS TO YOUR RELEASE RESIDE IN A TALISMAN EMBEDDED IN SOME OF THE MOST DREADED BEINGS IN THE DEADSIDE.
IF YOU COLLECT THESE TALISMAN, YOU MAY FASHION YOURSELF THE KEY TO YOUR RELEASE.
THIS BOX WILL HOLD THE TALISMAN UNTIL YOU ARE READY TO SACRIFICE THEM.
BUT BE WARNED. MY VISION SHOWS THAT THE JOURNEY TO COLLECT THE TALISMANS IS YOUR KEY. NOT THE TALISMANS THEMSELVES.
WHAT DOES THAT MEAN? JUST TELL ME! WHERE DO I FIND THESE BEINGS AND THEIR TALISMANS?
LISTEN AND I WILL TELL YOU HOW TO FIND THEM.

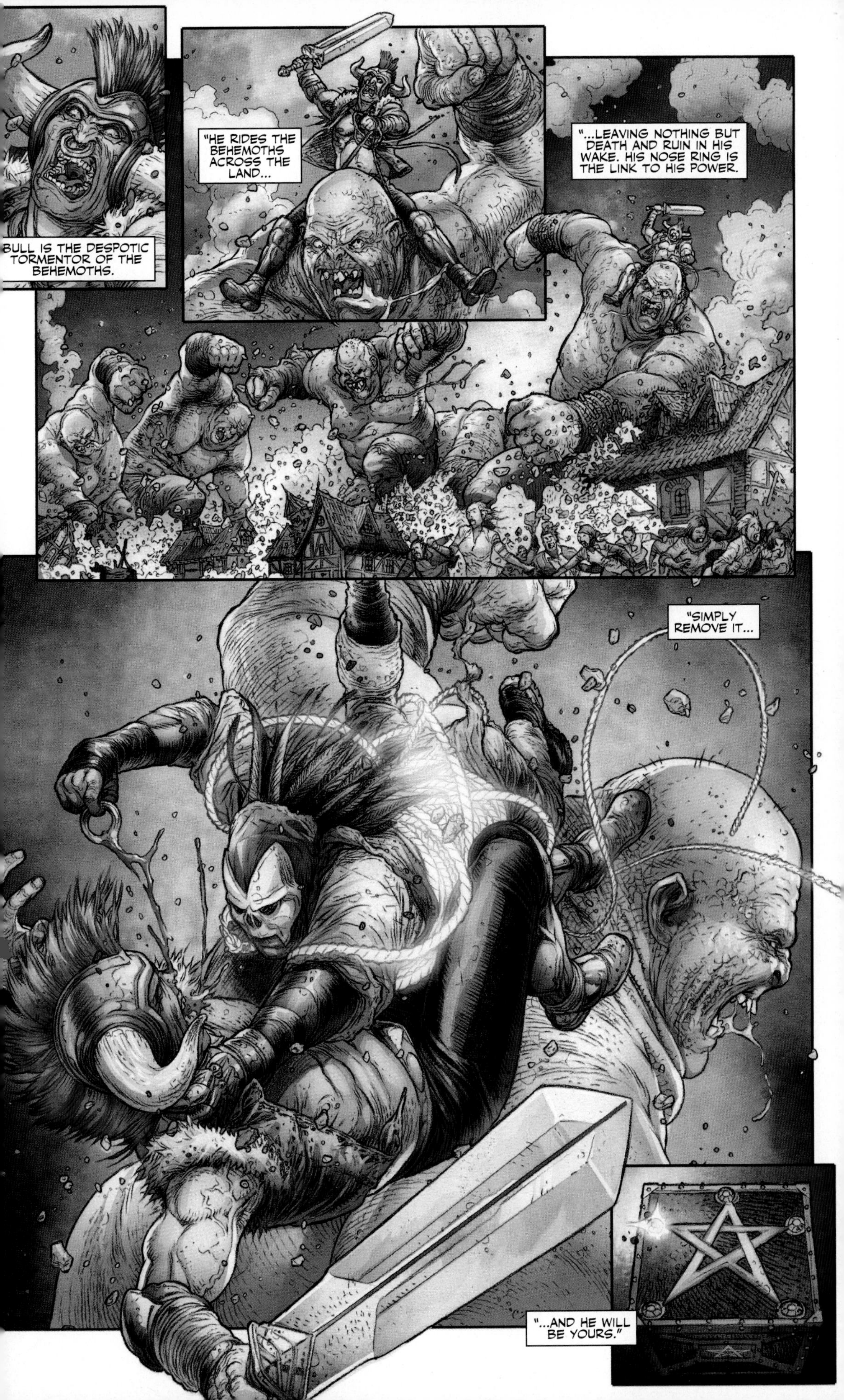
BULL IS THE DESPOTIC TORMENTOR OF THE BEHEMOTHS.
"HE RIDES THE BEHEMOTHS ACROSS THE LAND...
"...LEAVING NOTHING BUT DEATH AND RUIN IN HIS WAKE. HIS NOSE RING IS THE LINK TO HIS POWER.
"SIMPLY REMOVE IT...
"...AND HE WILL BE YOURS."

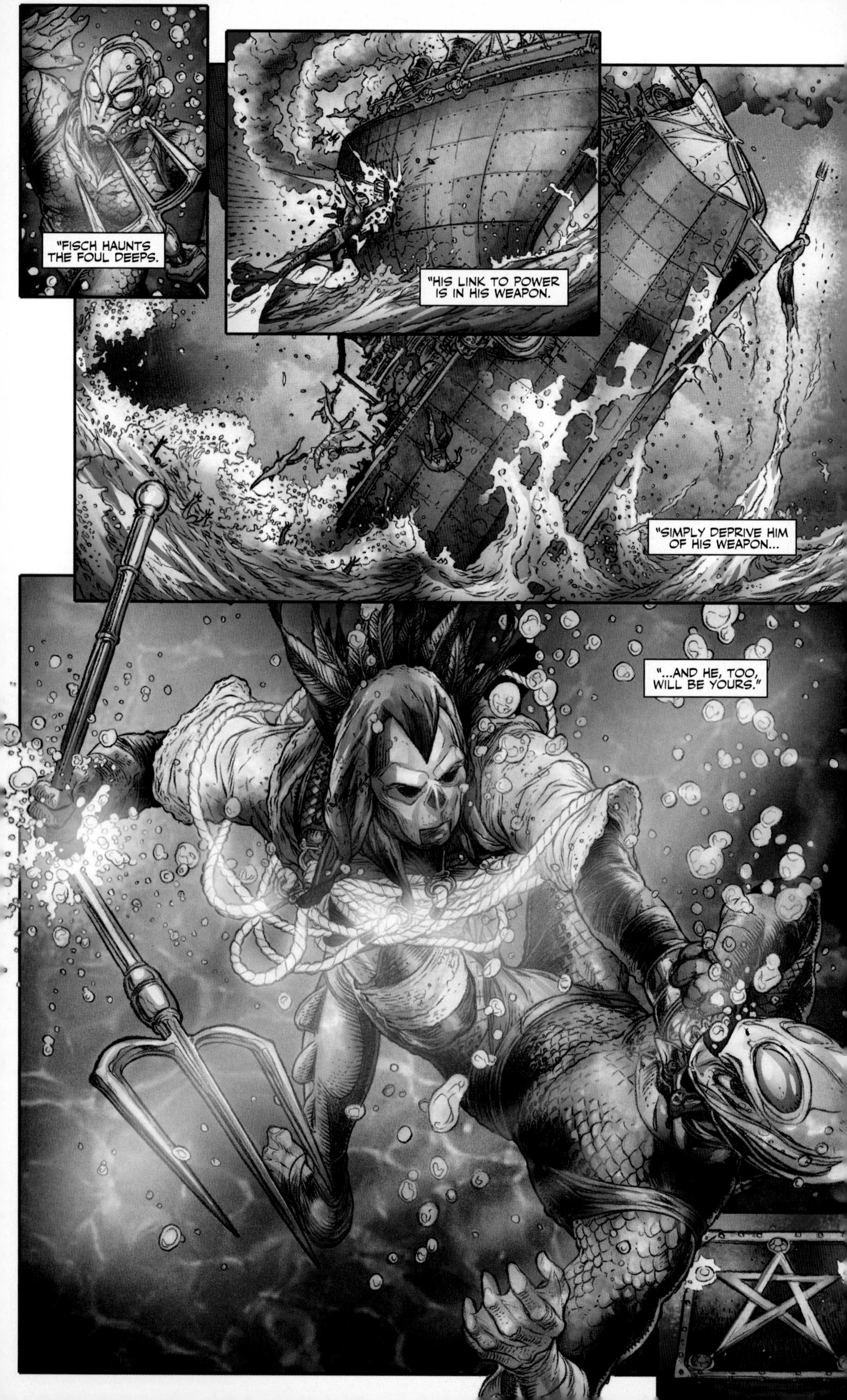
"FISCH HAUNTS THE FOUL DEEPS.
"HIS LINK TO POWER IS IN HIS WEAPON.
"SIMPLY DEPRIVE HIM OF HIS WEAPON...
"...AND HE, TOO, WILL BE YOURS."

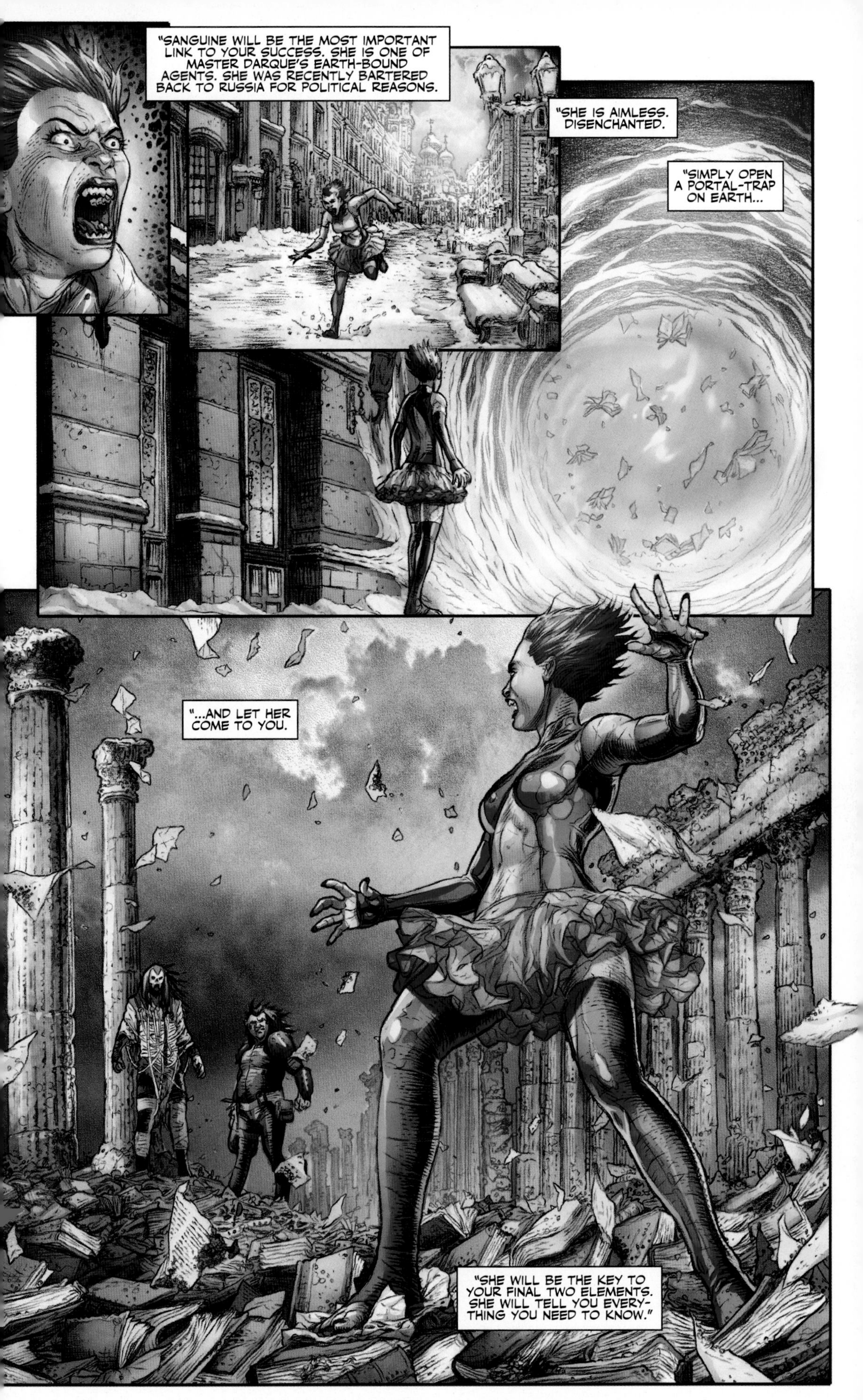
"SANGUINE WILL BE THE MOST IMPORTANT LINK TO YOUR SUCCESS. SHE IS ONE OF MASTER DARQUE'S EARTH-BOUND AGENTS. SHE WAS RECENTLY BARTERED BACK TO RUSSIA FOR POLITICAL REASONS.
"SHE IS AIMLESS. DISENCHANTED.
"SIMPLY OPEN A PORTAL-TRAP ON EARTH...
"...AND LET HER COME TO YOU.
"SHE WILL BE THE KEY TO YOUR FINAL TWO ELEMENTS. SHE WILL TELL YOU EVERY-THING YOU NEED TO KNOW."

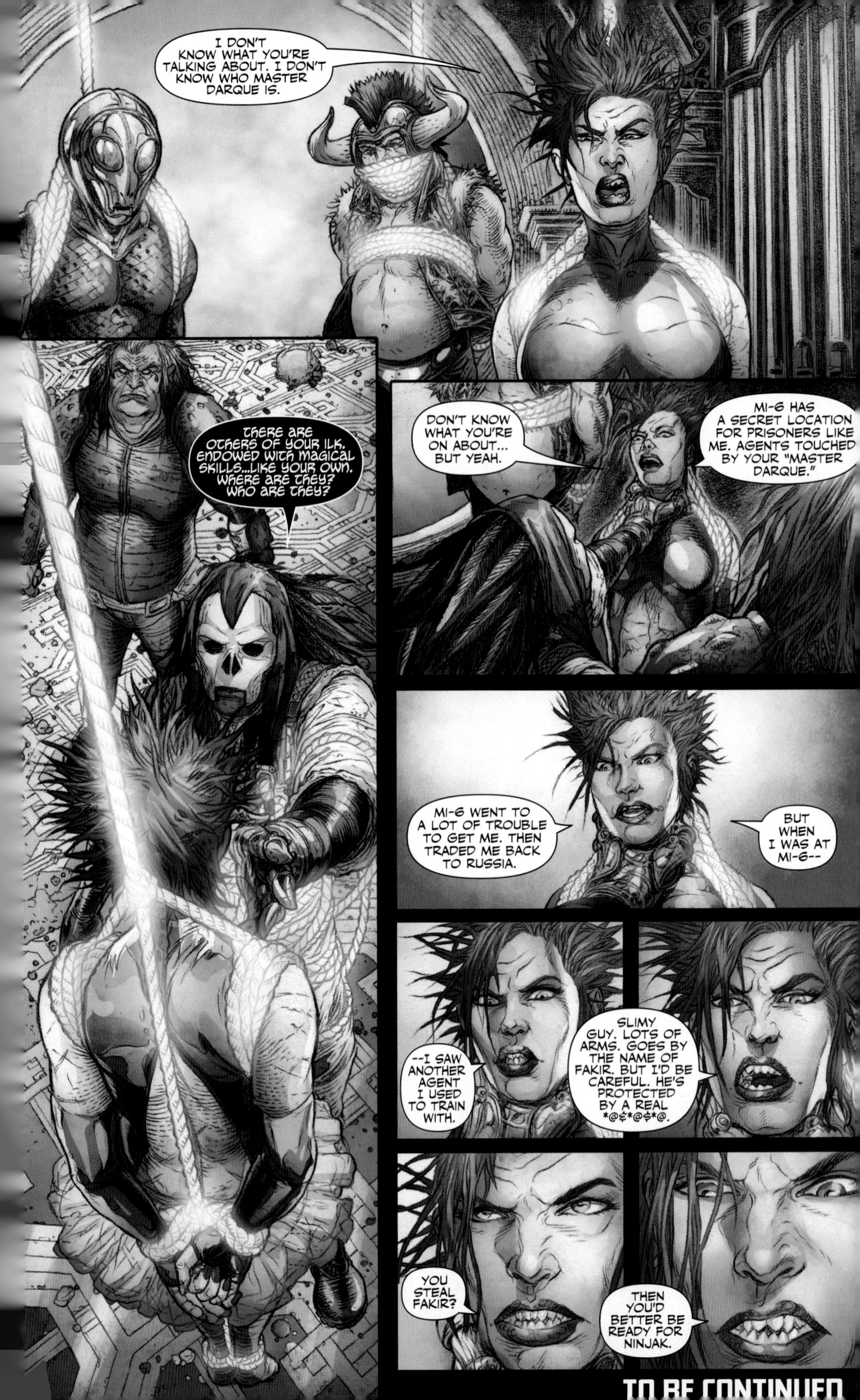
I DON'T KNOW WHAT YOU'RE TALKING ABOUT. I DON'T KNOW WHO MASTER DARQUE IS.
THERE ARE OTHERS OF YOUR ILK, ENDOWED WITH MAGICAL SKILLS...LIKE YOUR OWN. WHERE ARE THEY? WHO ARE THEY?
DON'T KNOW WHAT YOU'RE ON ABOUT... BUT YEAH.
MI-6 HAS A SECRET LOCATION FOR PRISONERS LIKE ME. AGENTS TOUCHED BY YOUR "MASTER DARQUE."
MI-6 WENT TO A LOT OF TROUBLE TO GET ME. THEN TRADED ME BACK TO RUSSIA.
BUT WHEN I WAS AT MI-6--
--I SAW ANOTHER AGENT I USED TO TRAIN WITH.
SLIMY GUY. LOTS OF ARMS. GOES BY THE NAME OF FAKIR. BUT I'D BE CAREFUL. HE'S PROTECTED BY A REAL *@$*@$*@.
YOU STEAL FAKIR?
THEN YOU'D BETTER BE READY FOR NINJAK.
TO BE CONTINUED

VALIANT

#13

NINJAK

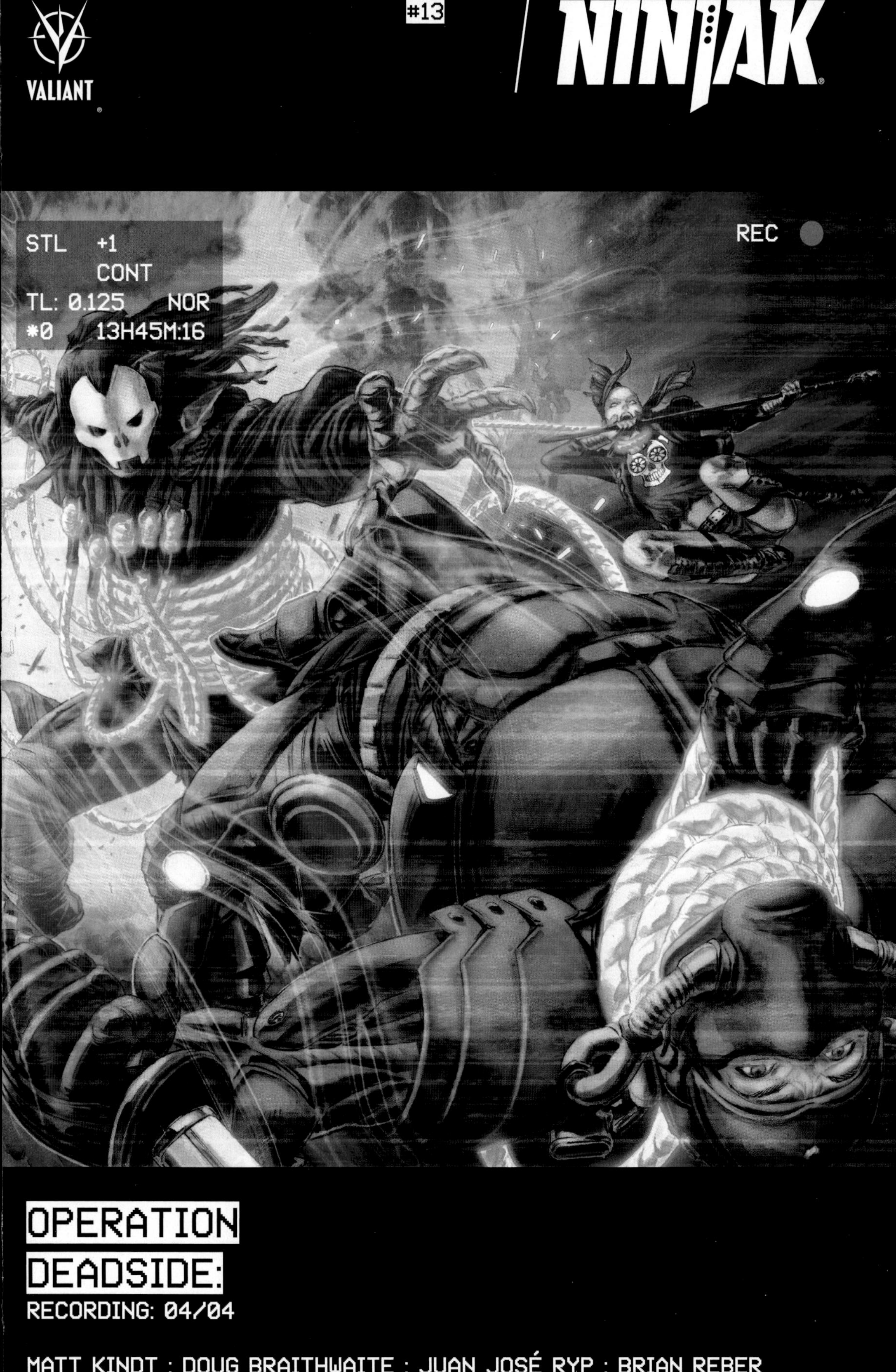
STL +1
CONT
TL: 0.125 NOR
*0 13H45M:16
REC

OPERATION DEADSIDE:

RECORDING: 04/04

MATT KINDT : DOUG BRAITHWAITE : JUAN JOSÉ RYP : BRIAN REBER

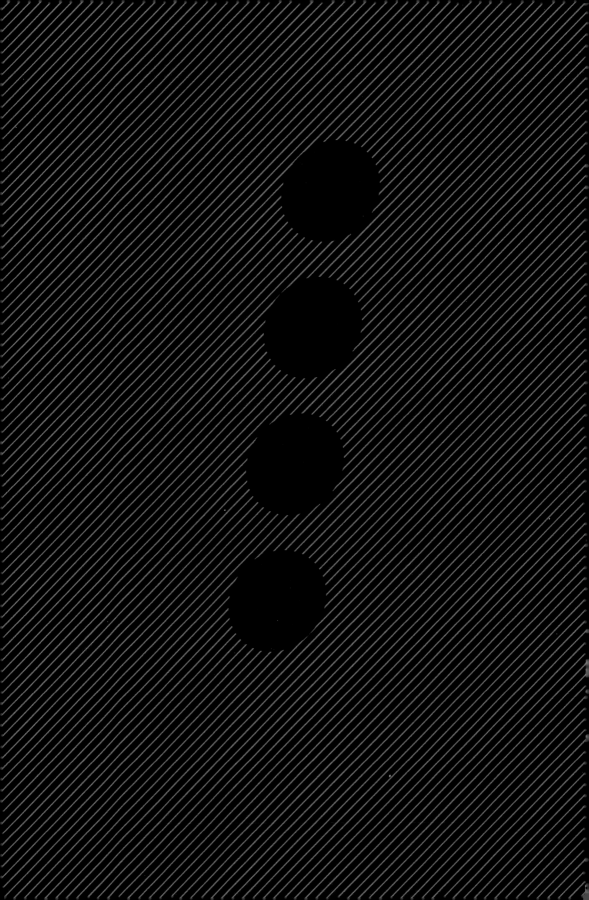

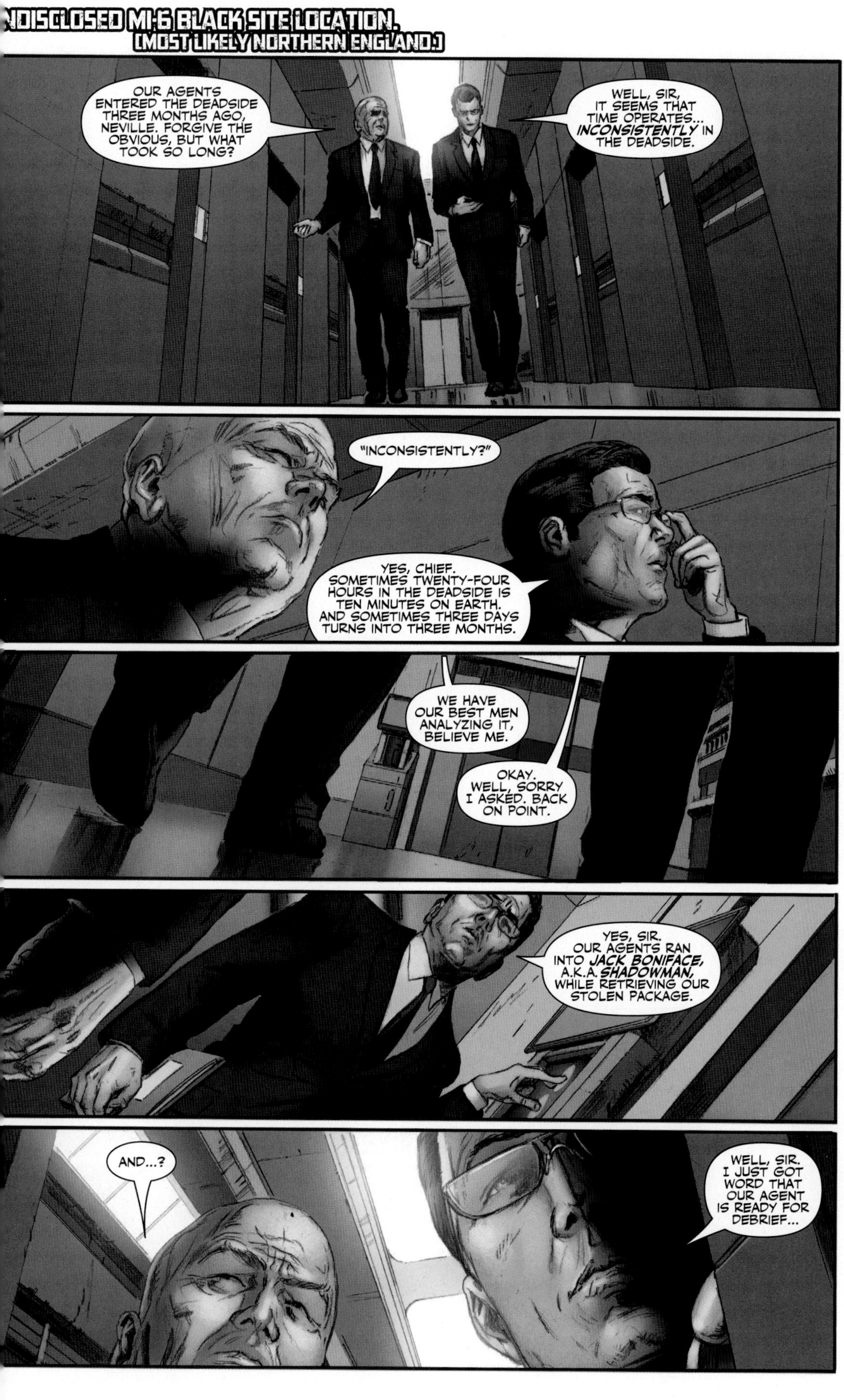

NDISCLOSED MI-6 BLACK SITE LOCATION.
(MOST LIKELY NORTHERN ENGLAND.)
OUR AGENTS ENTERED THE DEADSIDE THREE MONTHS AGO, NEVILLE. FORGIVE THE OBVIOUS, BUT WHAT TOOK SO LONG?
WELL, SIR, IT SEEMS THAT TIME OPERATES... *INCONSISTENTLY* IN THE DEADSIDE.
"INCONSISTENTLY?"
YES, CHIEF. SOMETIMES TWENTY-FOUR HOURS IN THE DEADSIDE IS TEN MINUTES ON EARTH. AND SOMETIMES THREE DAYS TURNS INTO THREE MONTHS.
WE HAVE OUR BEST MEN ANALYZING IT, BELIEVE ME.
OKAY. WELL, SORRY I ASKED. BACK ON POINT.
YES, SIR. OUR AGENTS RAN INTO *JACK BONIFACE,* A.K.A. *SHADOWMAN,* WHILE RETRIEVING OUR STOLEN PACKAGE.
AND...?
WELL, SIR. I JUST GOT WORD THAT OUR AGENT IS READY FOR DEBRIEF...

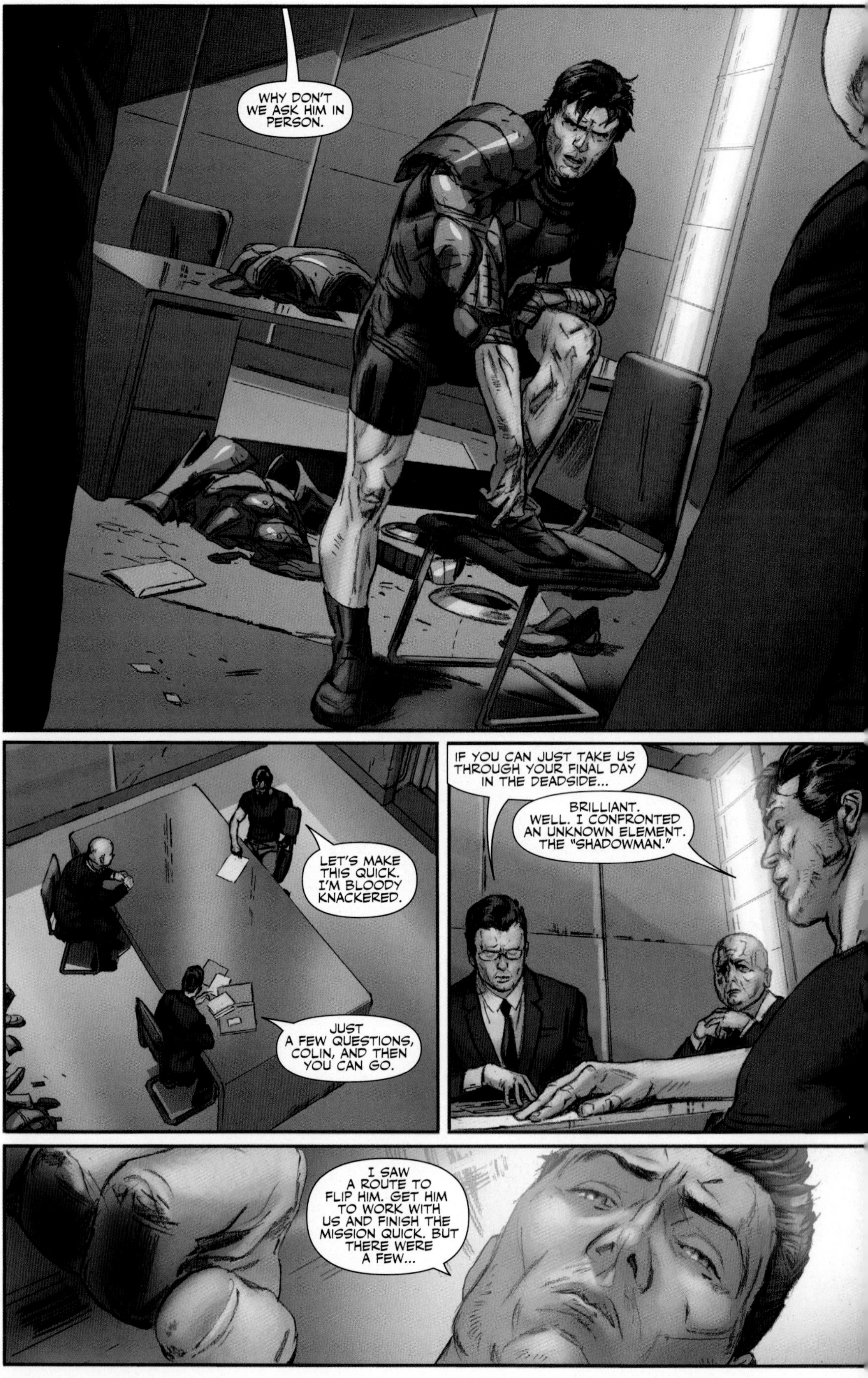
WHY DON'T WE ASK HIM IN PERSON.
LET'S MAKE THIS QUICK. I'M BLOODY KNACKERED.
JUST A FEW QUESTIONS, COLIN, AND THEN YOU CAN GO.
IF YOU CAN JUST TAKE US THROUGH YOUR FINAL DAY IN THE DEADSIDE...
BRILLIANT. WELL. I CONFRONTED AN UNKNOWN ELEMENT. THE "SHADOWMAN."
I SAW A ROUTE TO FLIP HIM. GET HIM TO WORK WITH US AND FINISH THE MISSION QUICK. BUT THERE WERE A FEW...

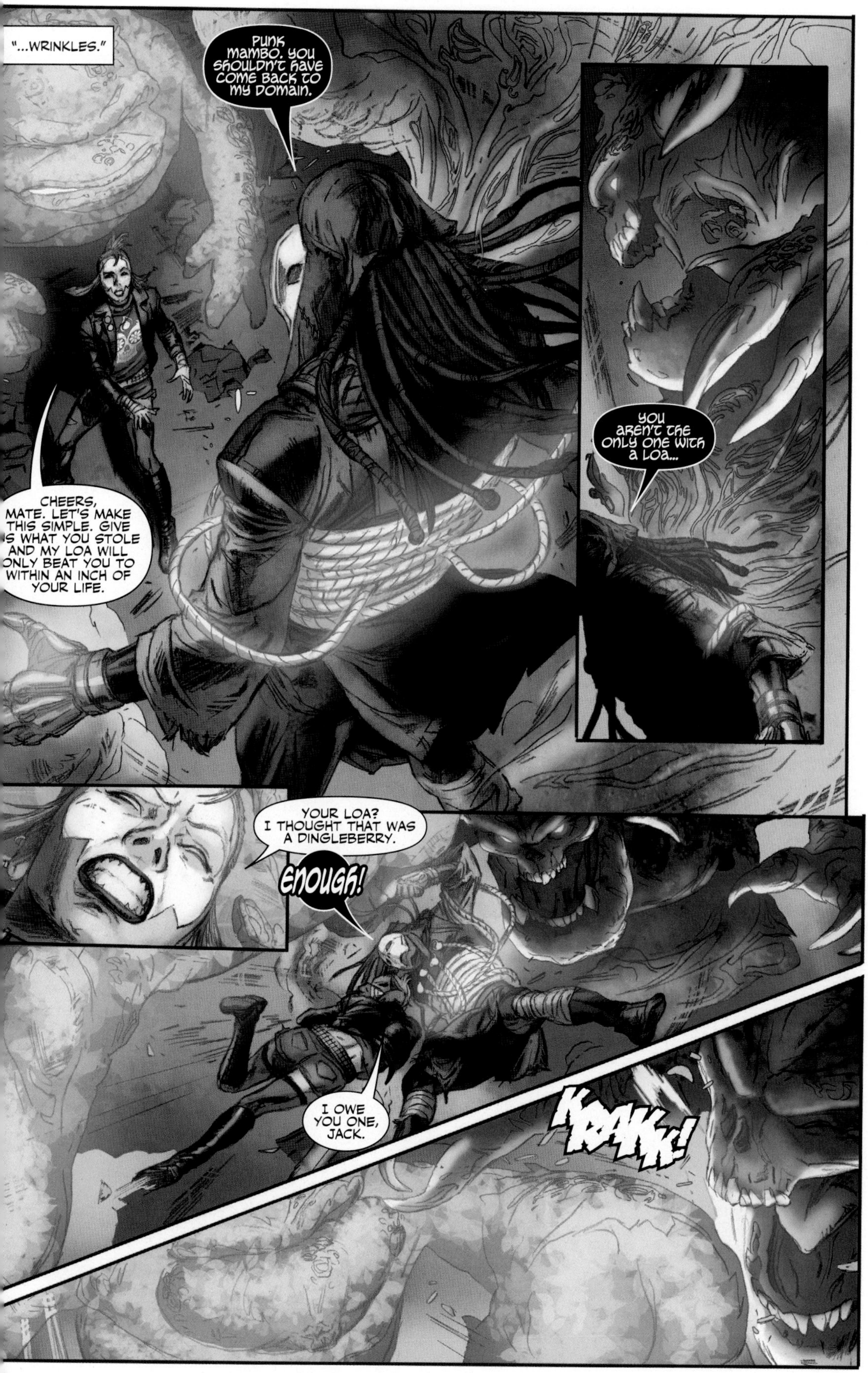
"...WRINKLES."
PUNK MAMBO. YOU SHOULDN'T HAVE COME BACK TO MY DOMAIN.
CHEERS, MATE. LET'S MAKE THIS SIMPLE. GIVE US WHAT YOU STOLE AND MY LOA WILL ONLY BEAT YOU TO WITHIN AN INCH OF YOUR LIFE.
YOU AREN'T THE ONLY ONE WITH A LOA...
YOUR LOA? I THOUGHT THAT WAS A DINGLEBERRY.
ENOUGH!
I OWE YOU ONE, JACK.
KRAKK!

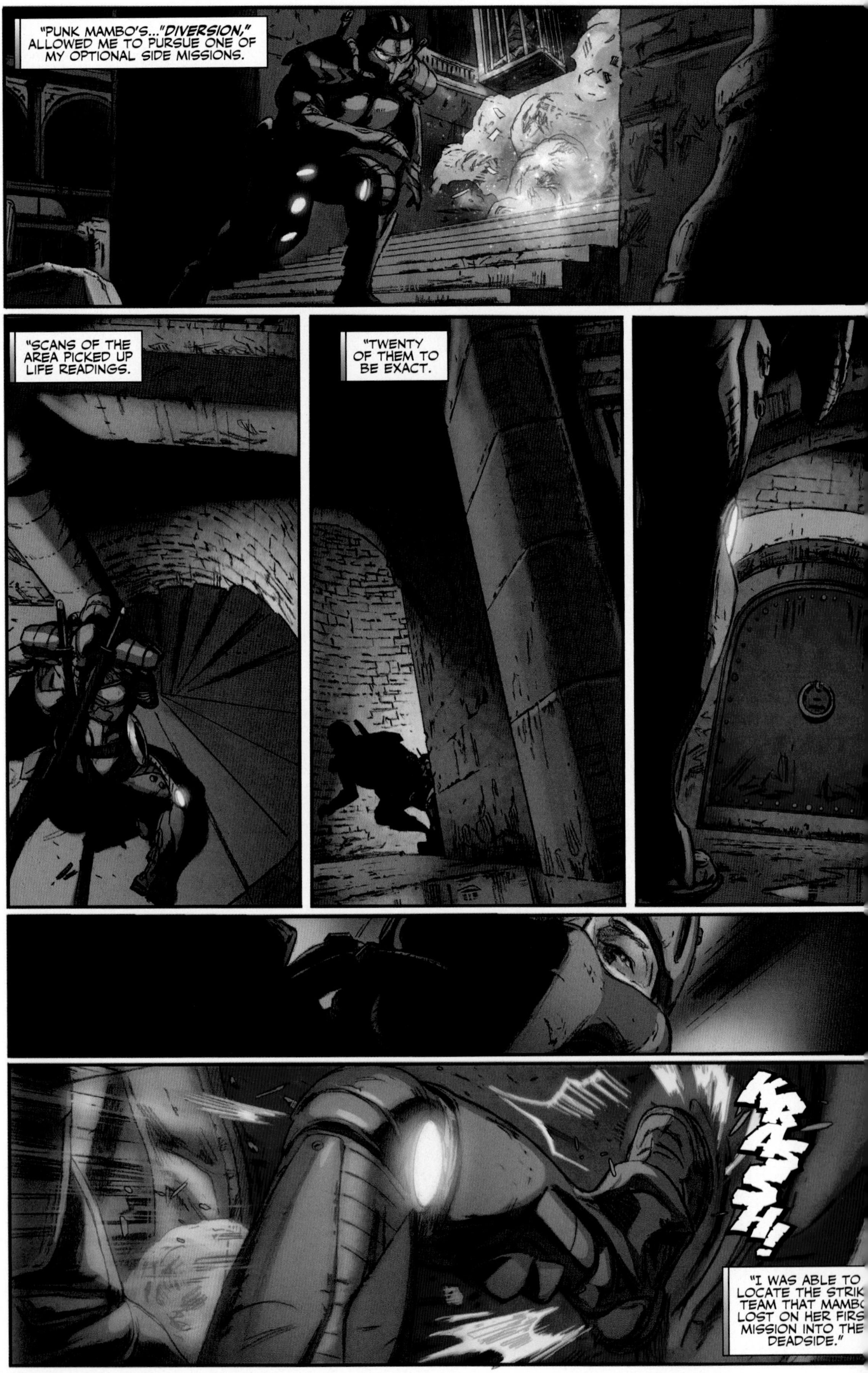
"PUNK MAMBO'S..."DIVERSION," ALLOWED ME TO PURSUE ONE OF MY OPTIONAL SIDE MISSIONS.
"SCANS OF THE AREA PICKED UP LIFE READINGS.
"TWENTY OF THEM TO BE EXACT.
KRASSH!
"I WAS ABLE TO LOCATE THE STRIK TEAM THAT MAMB LOST ON HER FIRS MISSION INTO THE DEADSIDE."

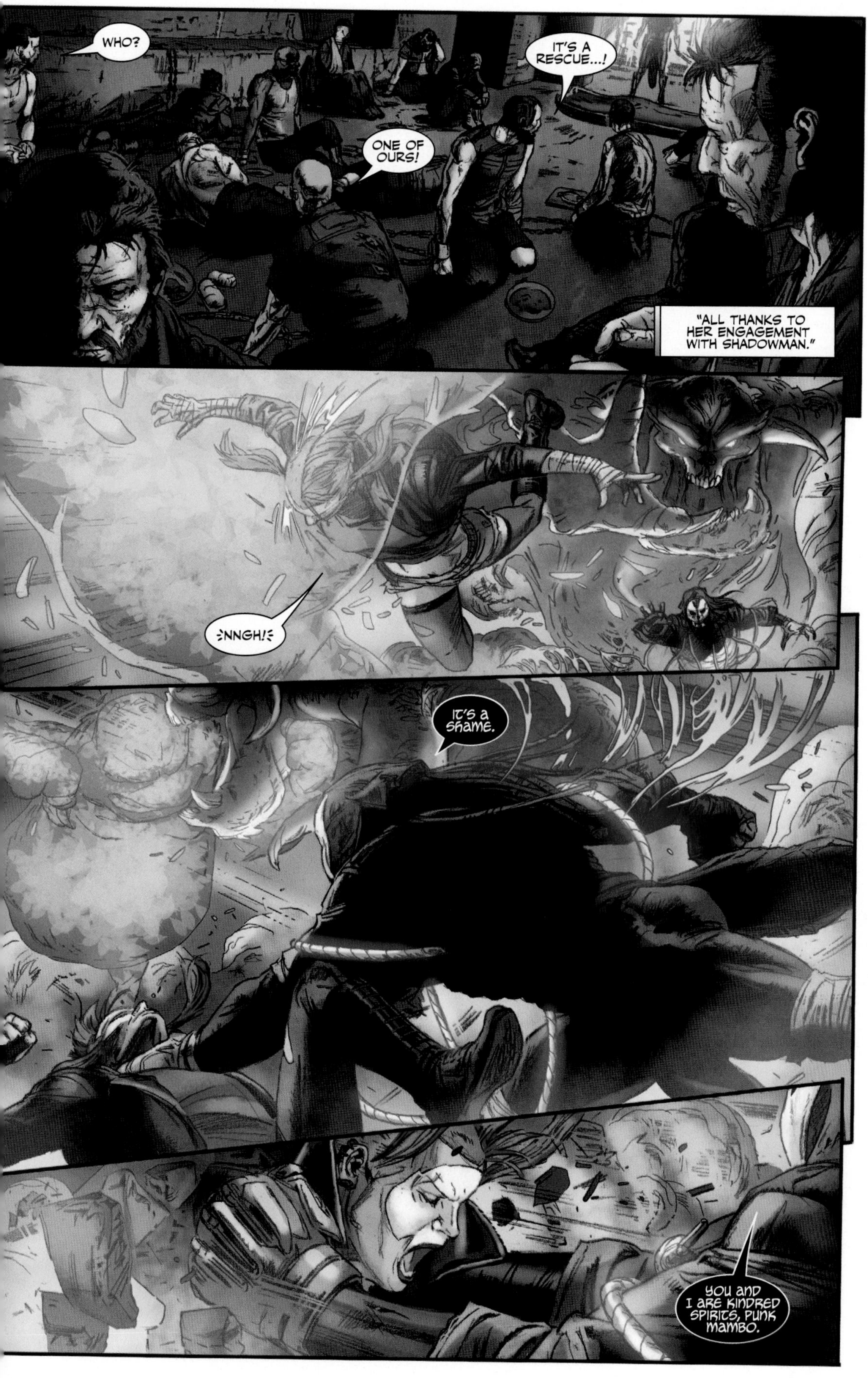
WHO?
IT'S A RESCUE...!
ONE OF OURS!
"ALL THANKS TO HER ENGAGEMENT WITH SHADOWMAN."
NNGH!
IT'S A SHAME.
YOU AND I ARE KINDRED SPIRITS, PUNK MAMBO.

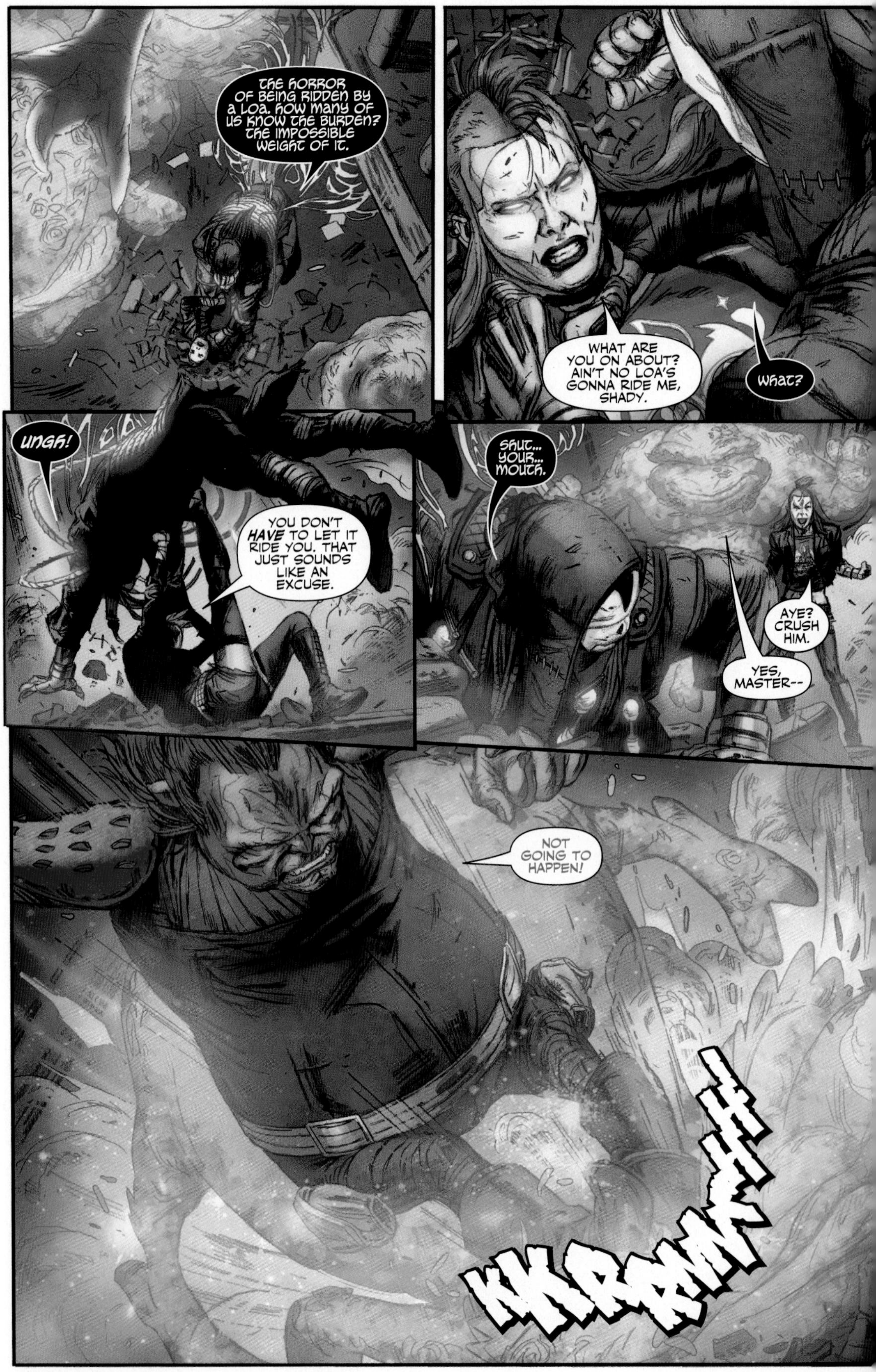
THE HORROR OF BEING RIDDEN BY A LOA. HOW MANY OF US KNOW THE BURDEN? THE IMPOSSIBLE WEIGHT OF IT.
WHAT ARE YOU ON ABOUT? AIN'T NO LOA'S GONNA RIDE ME, SHADY.
WHAT?
UNGH!
YOU DON'T HAVE TO LET IT RIDE YOU. THAT JUST SOUNDS LIKE AN EXCUSE.
SHUT... YOUR... MOUTH.
AYE? CRUSH HIM.
YES, MASTER--
NOT GOING TO HAPPEN!
KKRAMM

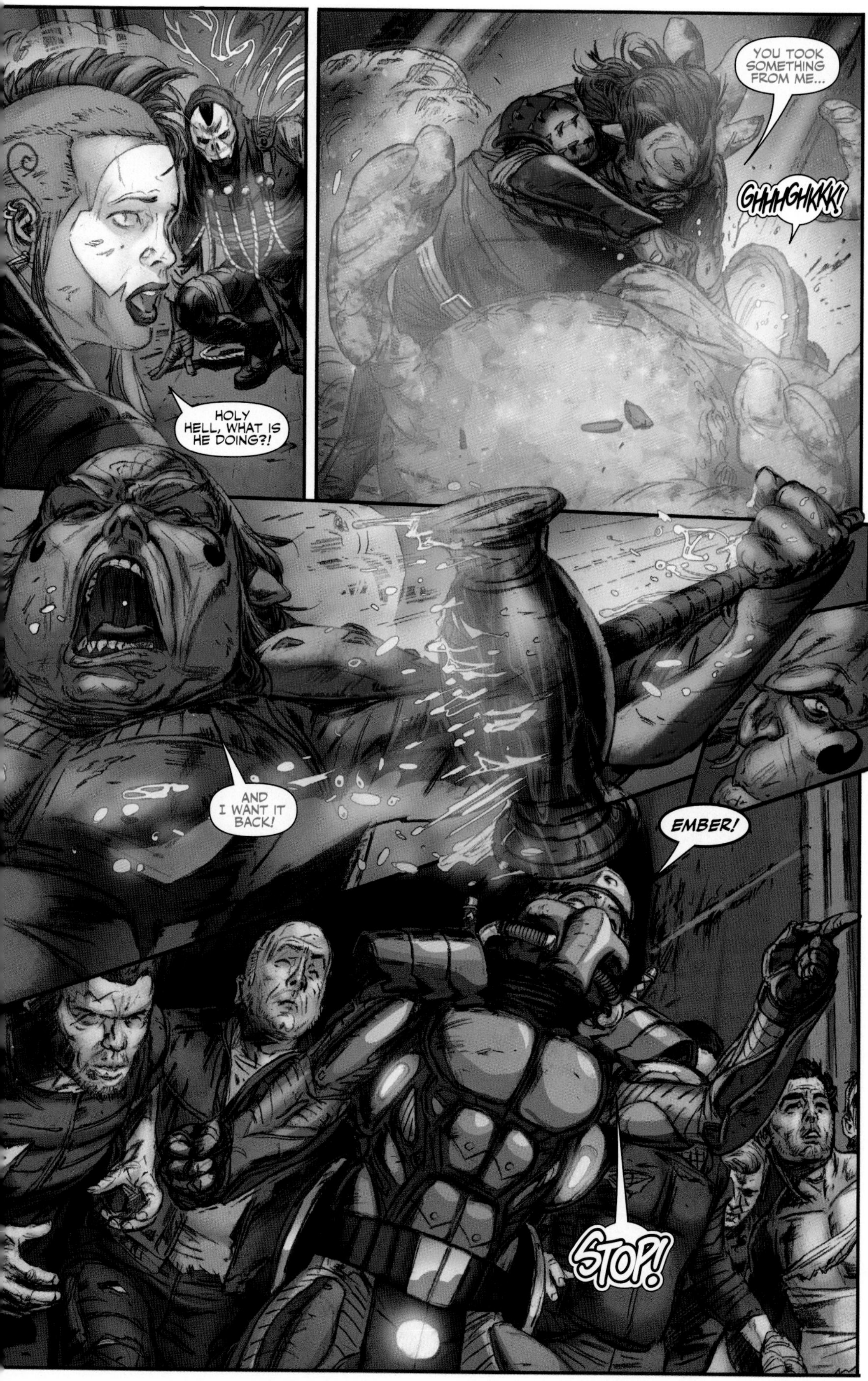
HOLY HELL, WHAT IS HE DOING?!
YOU TOOK SOMETHING FROM ME...
GHHHGHKKK!
AND I WANT IT BACK!
EMBER!
STOP!

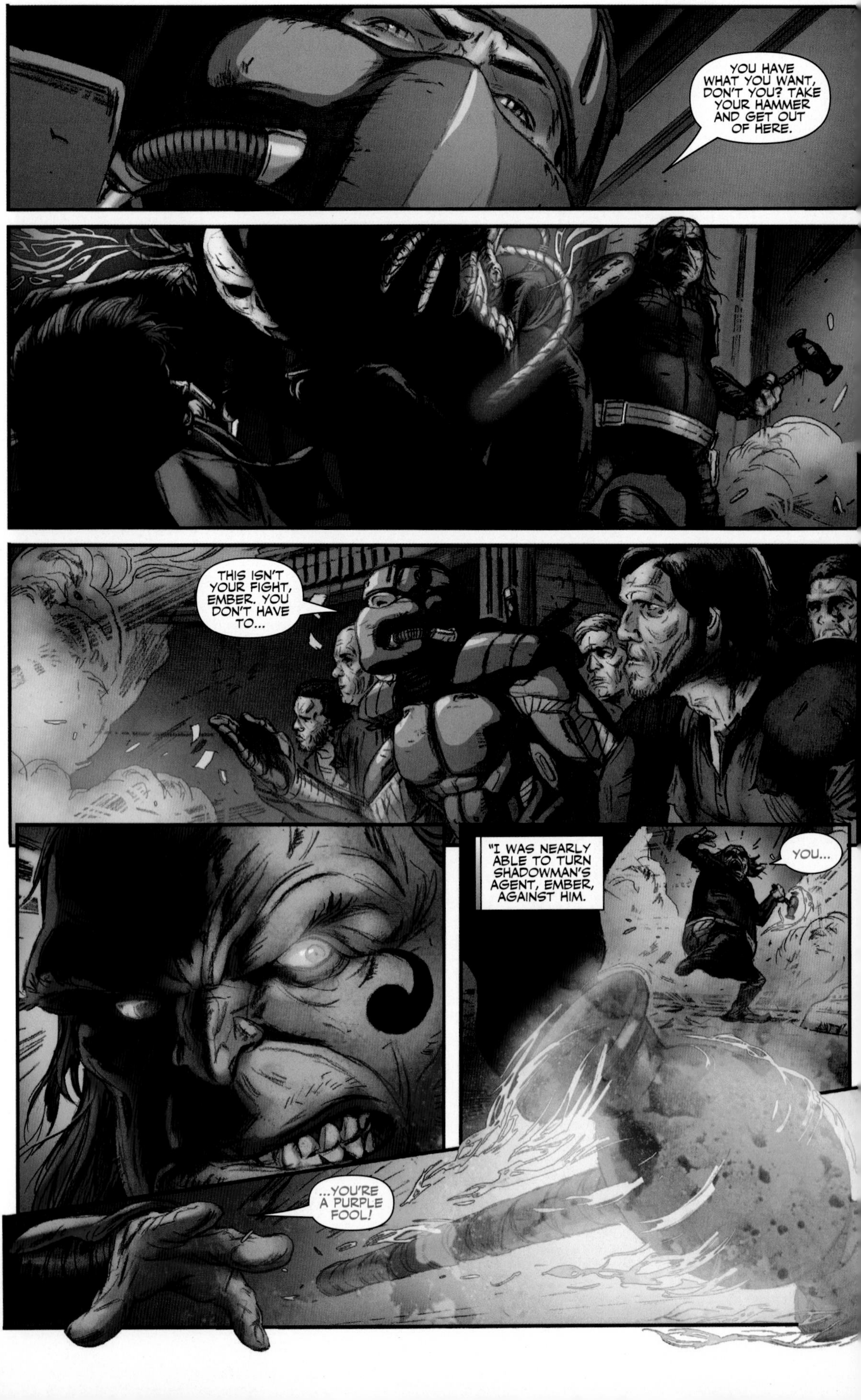
YOU HAVE WHAT YOU WANT, DON'T YOU? TAKE YOUR HAMMER AND GET OUT OF HERE.
THIS ISN'T YOUR FIGHT, EMBER. YOU DON'T HAVE TO...
"I WAS NEARLY ABLE TO TURN SHADOWMAN'S AGENT, EMBER, AGAINST HIM.
YOU...
...YOU'RE A PURPLE FOOL!

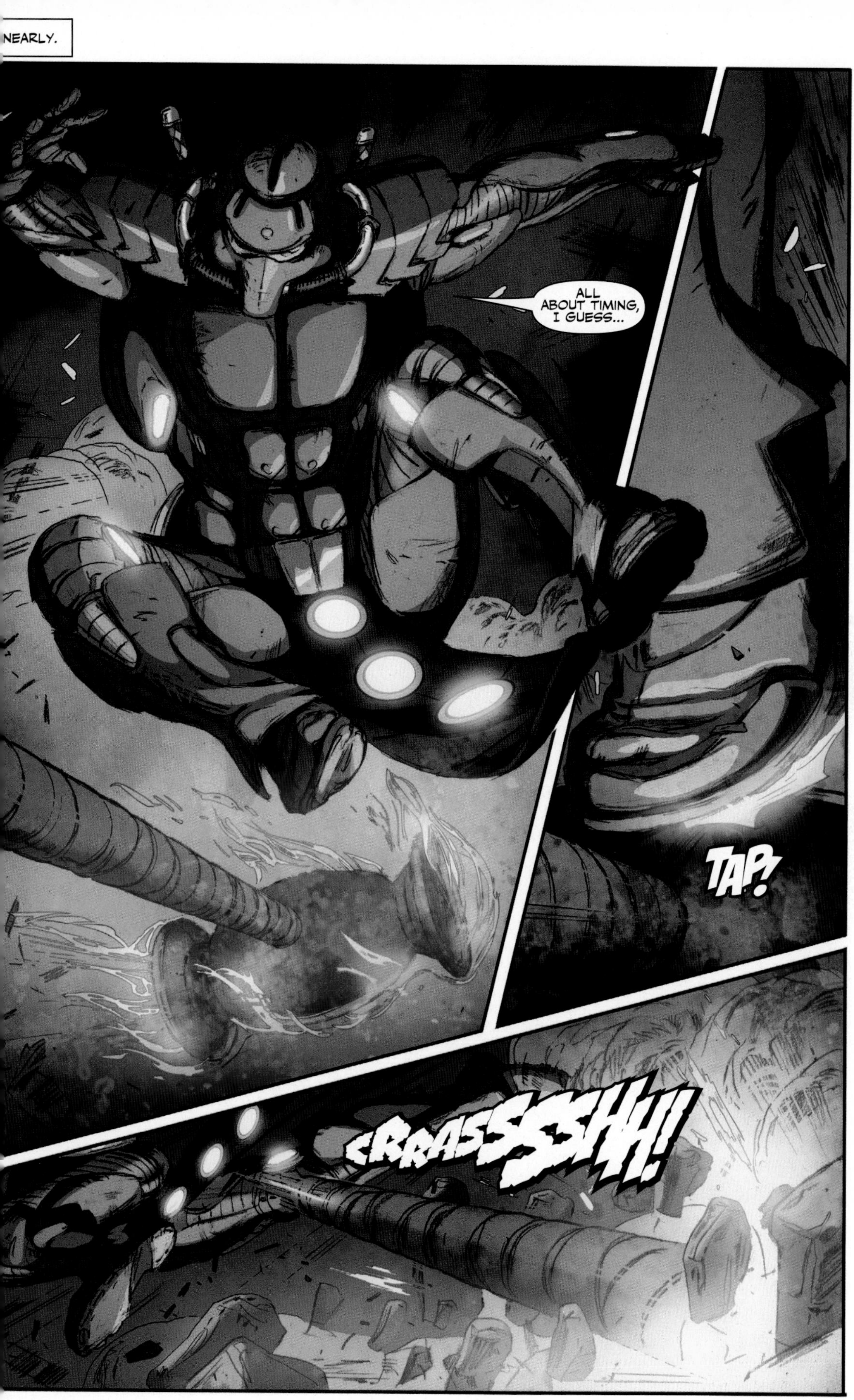
NEARLY.
ALL ABOUT TIMING, I GUESS...
TAP!
CRRASSSSHH!

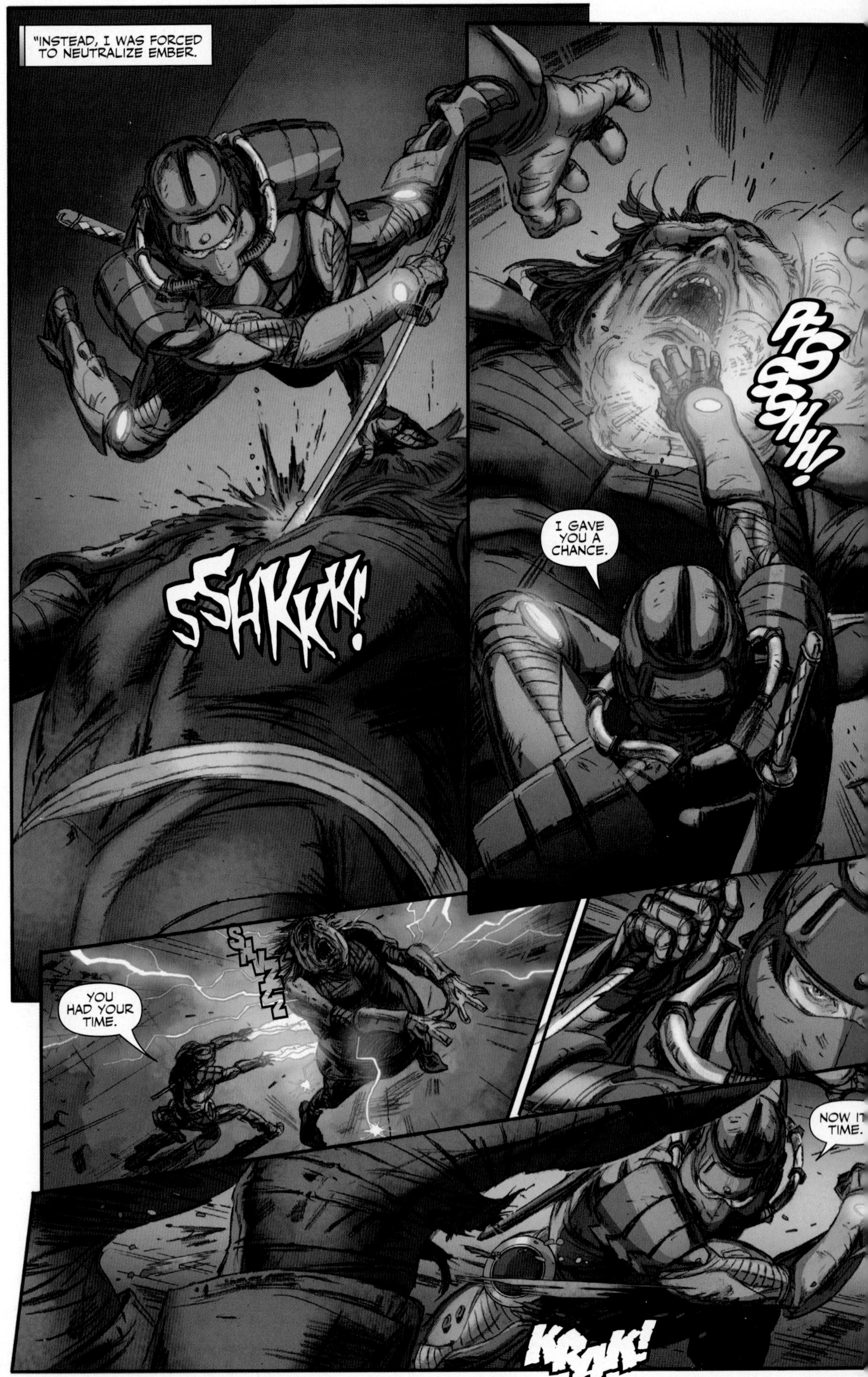
"INSTEAD, I WAS FORCED TO NEUTRALIZE EMBER.
SSHKKK!
PSSSHH!
I GAVE YOU A CHANCE.
SHZZZ
YOU HAD YOUR TIME.
NOW IT TIME.
KRAK!

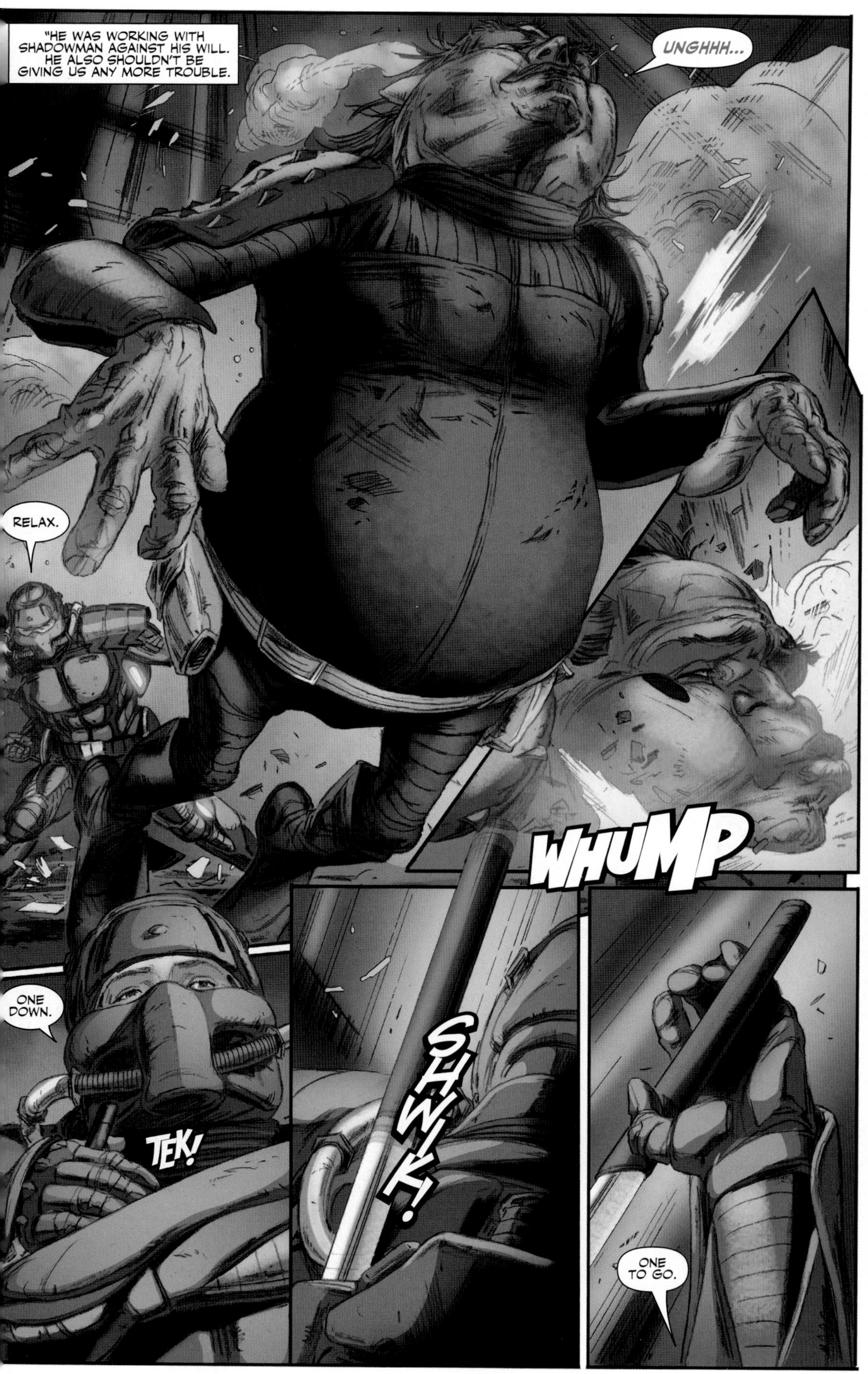
"HE WAS WORKING WITH SHADOWMAN AGAINST HIS WILL. HE ALSO SHOULDN'T BE GIVING US ANY MORE TROUBLE.
UNGHHH...
RELAX.
WHUMP
ONE DOWN.
TEK!
SHWIK!
ONE TO GO.

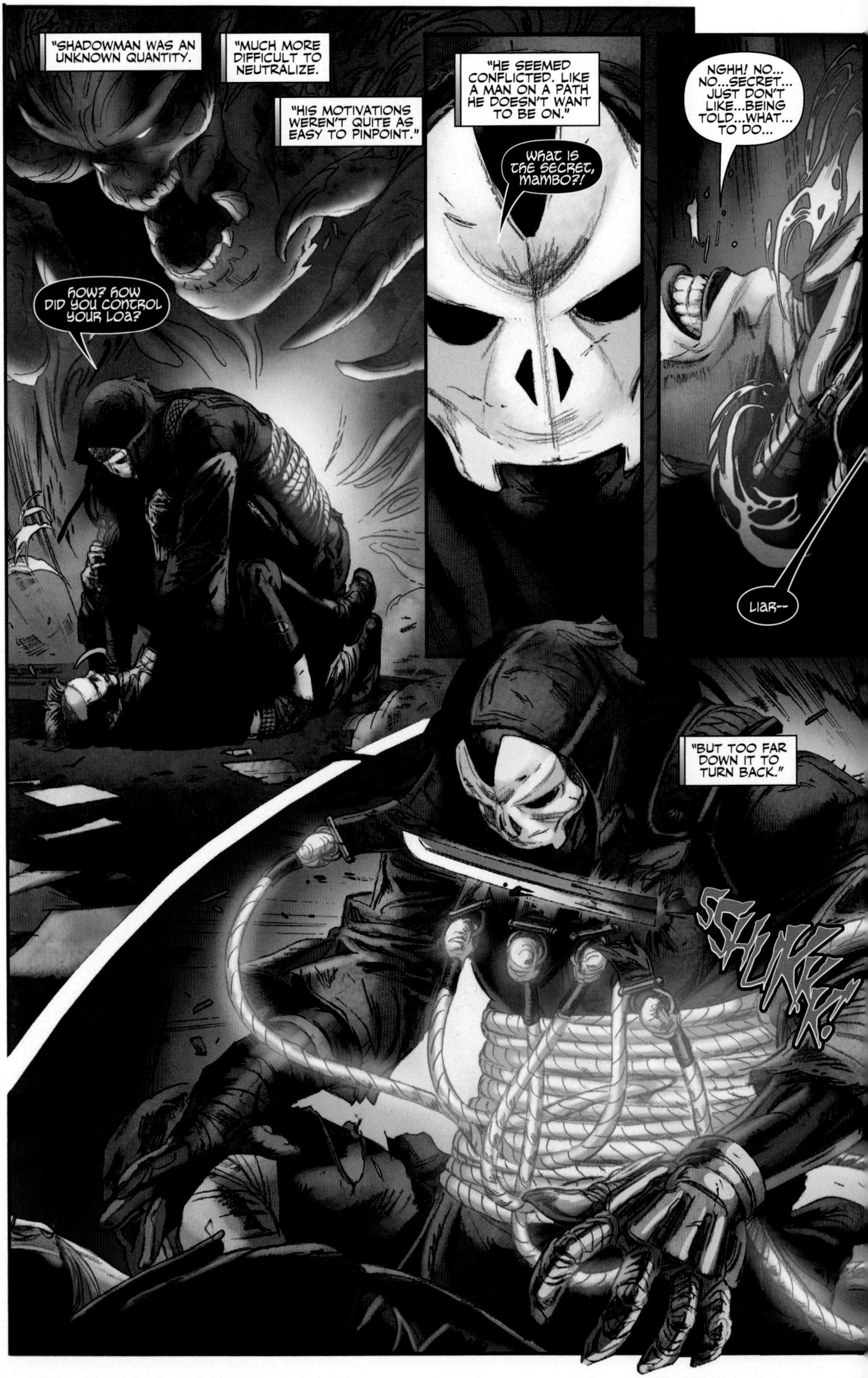
"SHADOWMAN WAS AN UNKNOWN QUANTITY.
"MUCH MORE DIFFICULT TO NEUTRALIZE.
"HIS MOTIVATIONS WEREN'T QUITE AS EASY TO PINPOINT."
HOW? HOW DID YOU CONTROL YOUR LOA?
"HE SEEMED CONFLICTED. LIKE A MAN ON A PATH HE DOESN'T WANT TO BE ON."
WHAT IS THE SECRET, MAMBO?!
NGHH! NO... NO...SECRET... JUST DON'T LIKE...BEING TOLD...WHAT... TO DO...
LIAR--
"BUT TOO FAR DOWN IT TO TURN BACK."
SSHUKK!

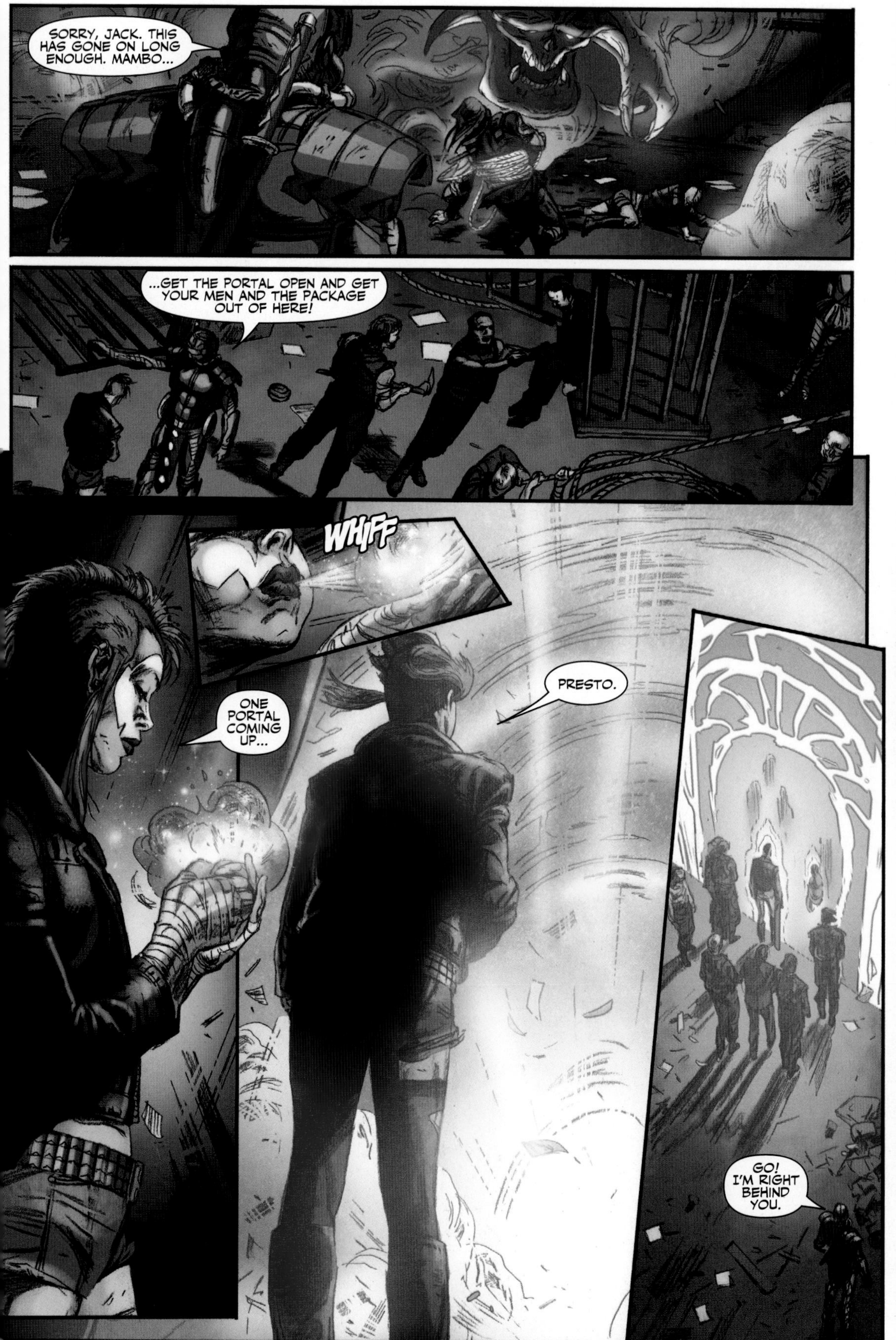
SORRY, JACK. THIS HAS GONE ON LONG ENOUGH. MAMBO...
...GET THE PORTAL OPEN AND GET YOUR MEN AND THE PACKAGE OUT OF HERE!
WHIFF
ONE PORTAL COMING UP...
PRESTO.
GO! I'M RIGHT BEHIND YOU.

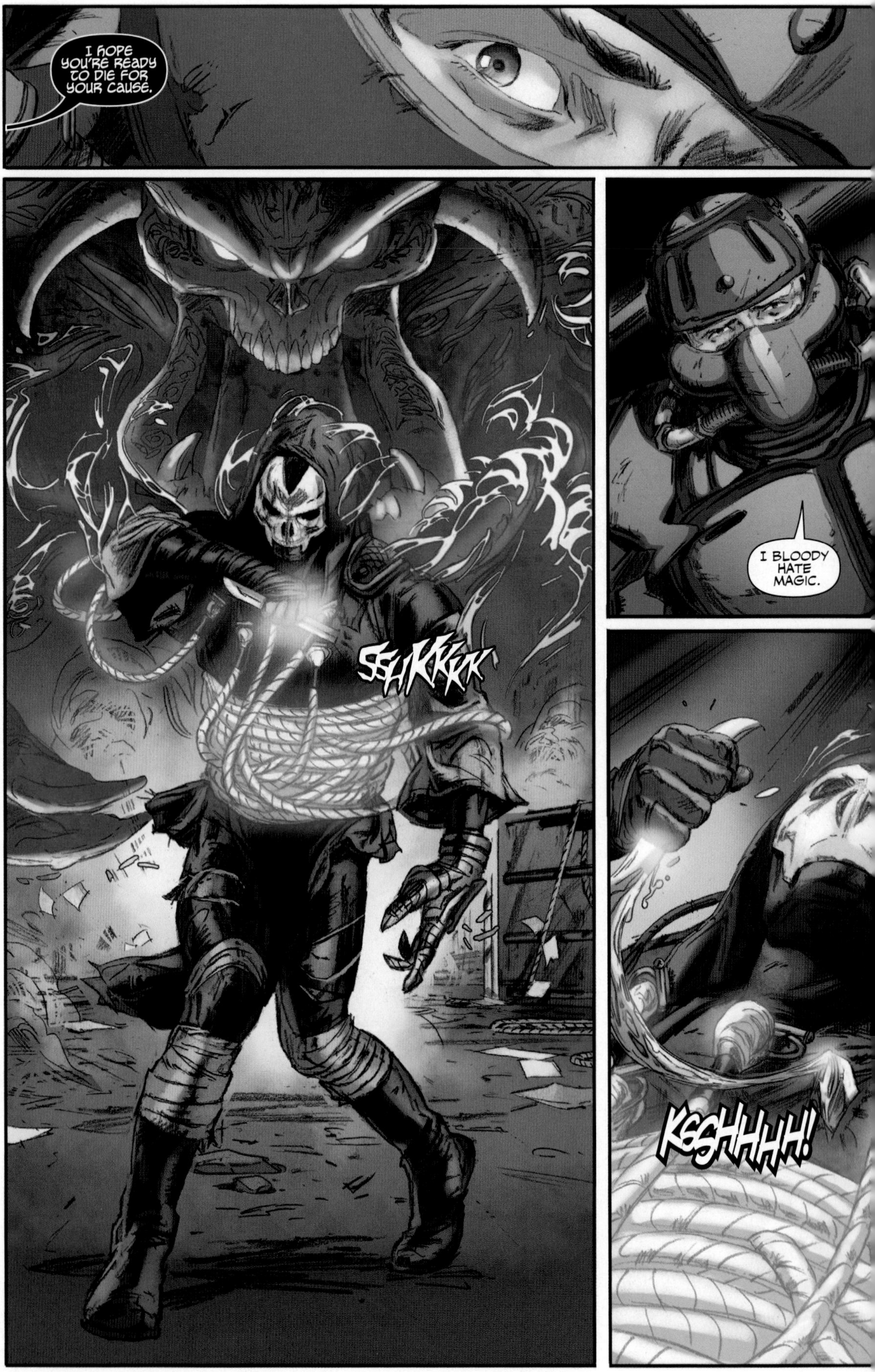
I HOPE YOU'RE READY TO DIE FOR YOUR CAUSE.
SSHKKKK
I BLOODY HATE MAGIC.
KSSHHHH!

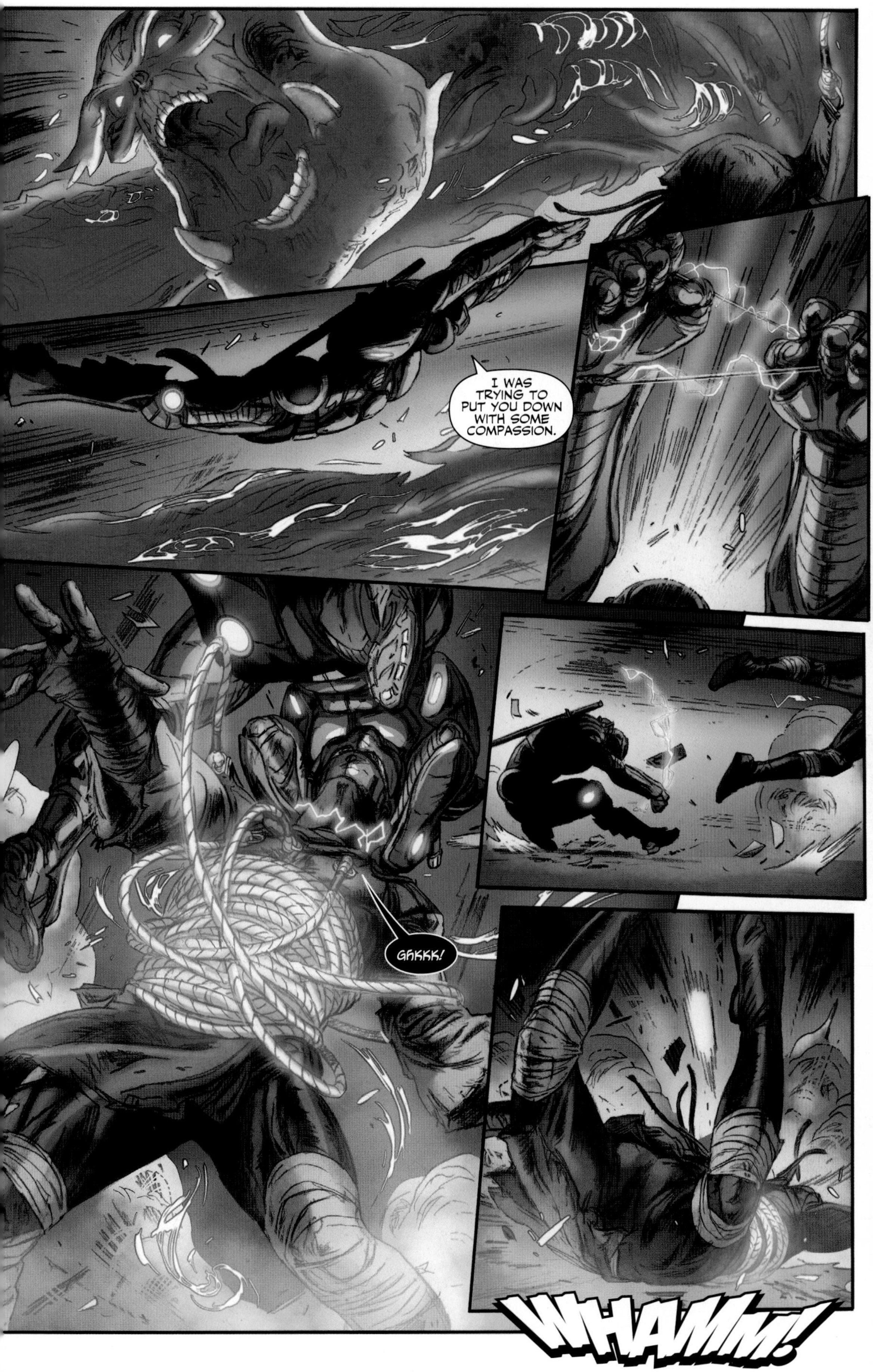
I WAS TRYING TO PUT YOU DOWN WITH SOME COMPASSION.
GRKKK!
WHAMM!

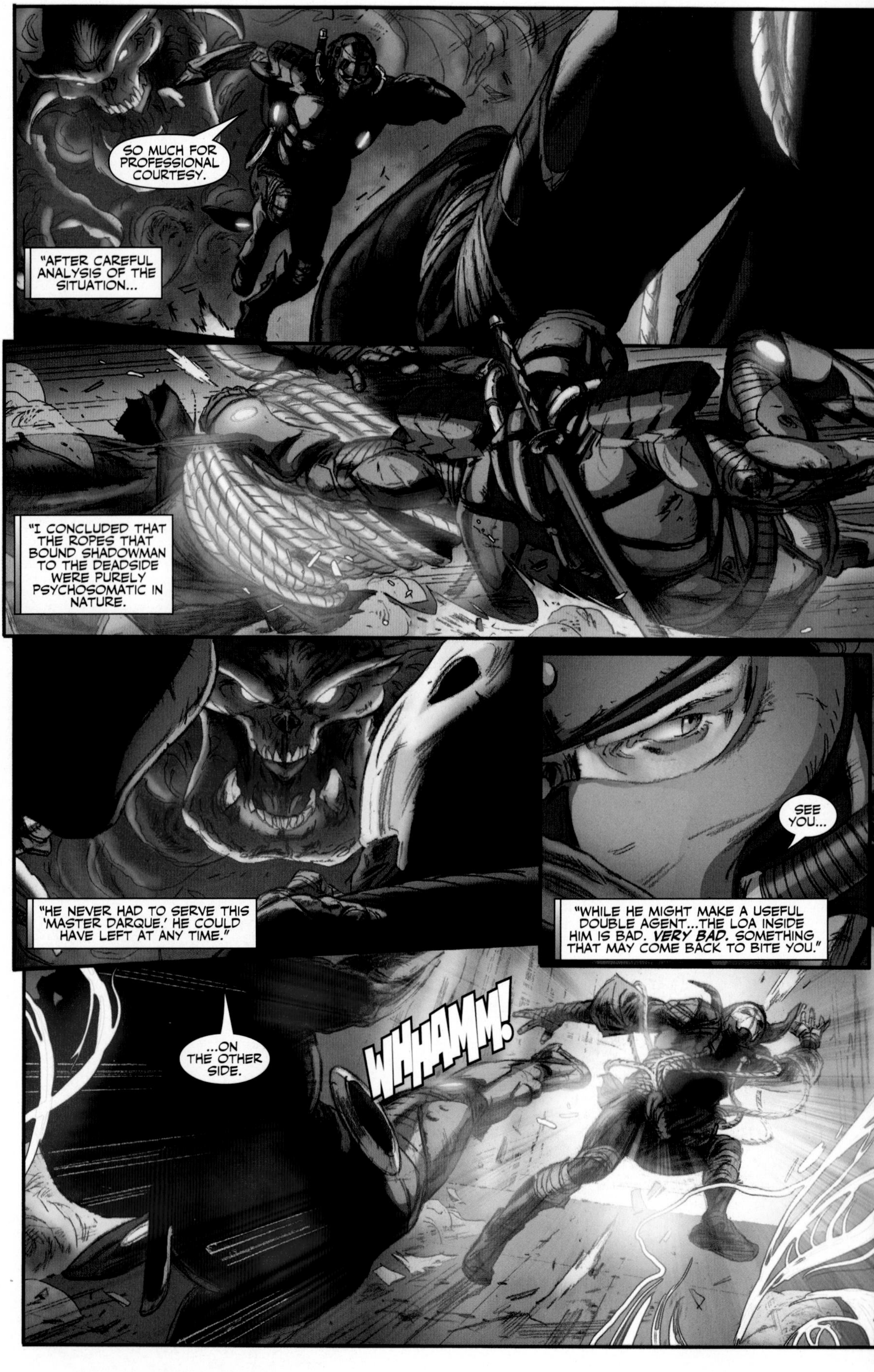

SO MUCH FOR PROFESSIONAL COURTESY.
"AFTER CAREFUL ANALYSIS OF THE SITUATION...
"I CONCLUDED THAT THE ROPES THAT BOUND SHADOWMAN TO THE DEADSIDE WERE PURELY PSYCHOSOMATIC IN NATURE.
"HE NEVER HAD TO SERVE THIS 'MASTER DARQUE.' HE COULD HAVE LEFT AT ANY TIME."
SEE YOU...
"WHILE HE MIGHT MAKE A USEFUL DOUBLE AGENT...THE LOA INSIDE HIM IS BAD. VERY BAD. SOMETHING THAT MAY COME BACK TO BITE YOU."
...ON THE OTHER SIDE.
WHHAMM!

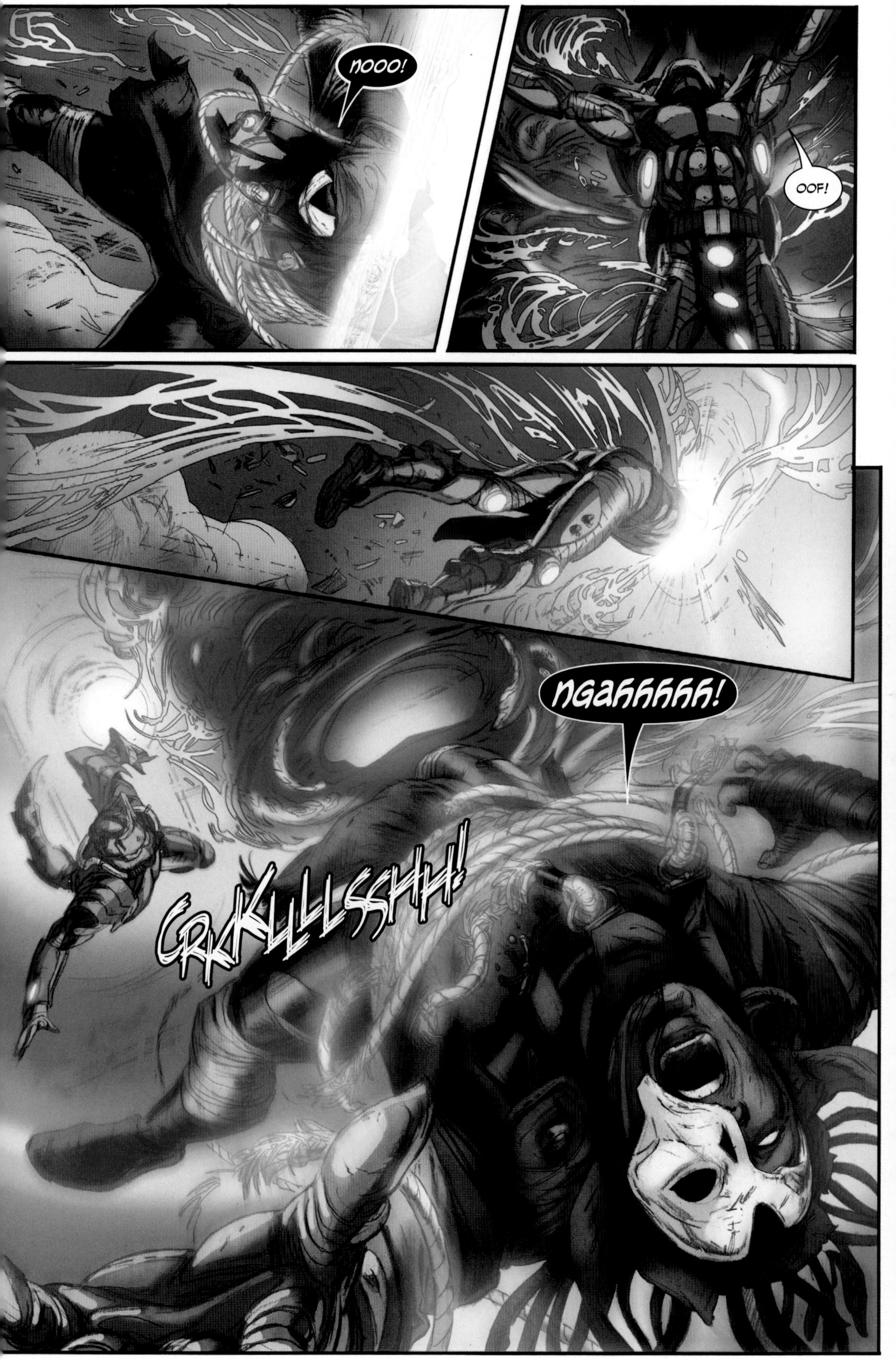
NOOO!
OOF!
NGAHHHHH!
CRKKLLLLSSHH!

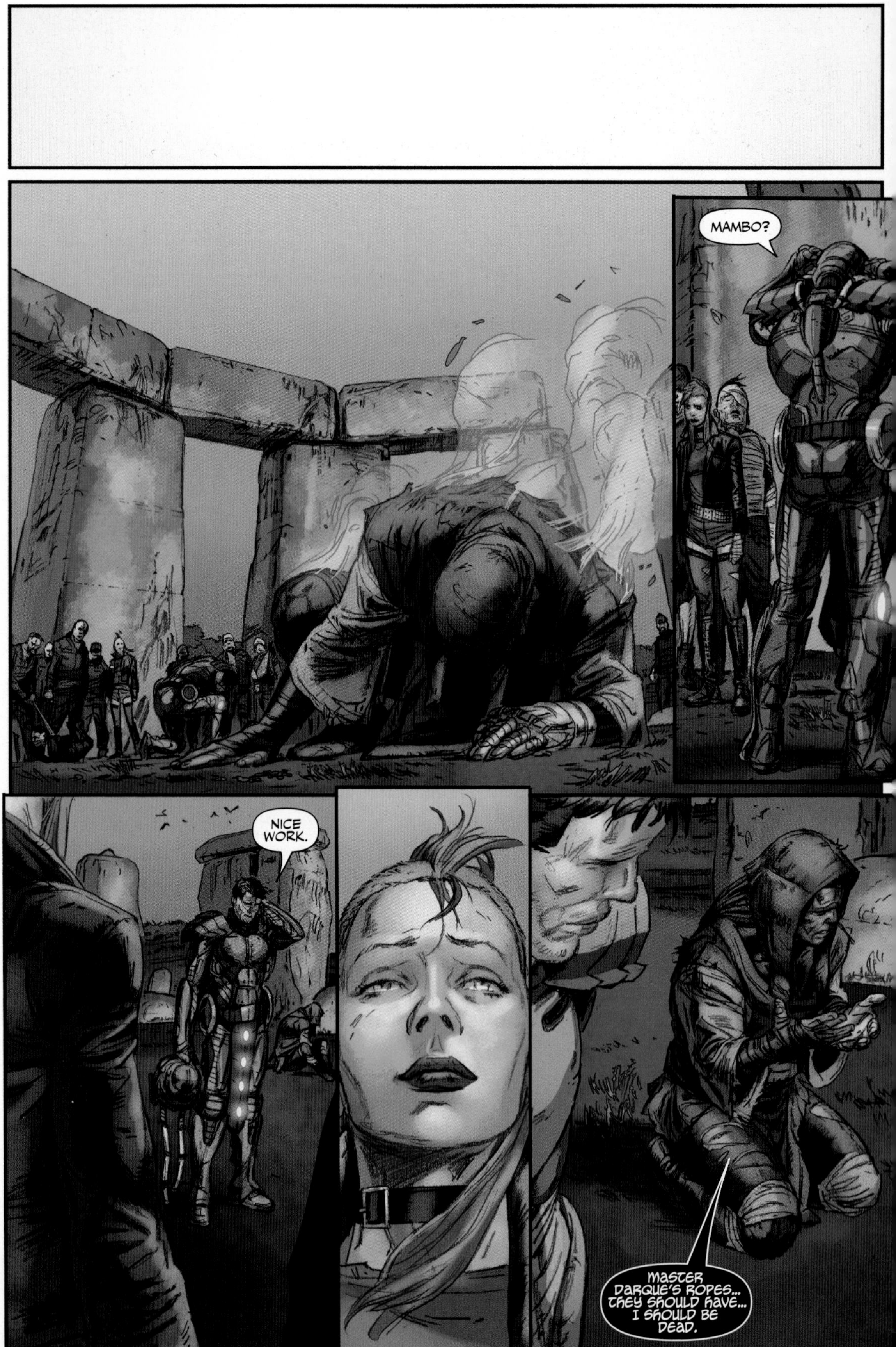
MAMBO?
NICE WORK.
MASTER DARQUE'S ROPES... THEY SHOULD HAVE... I SHOULD BE DEAD.

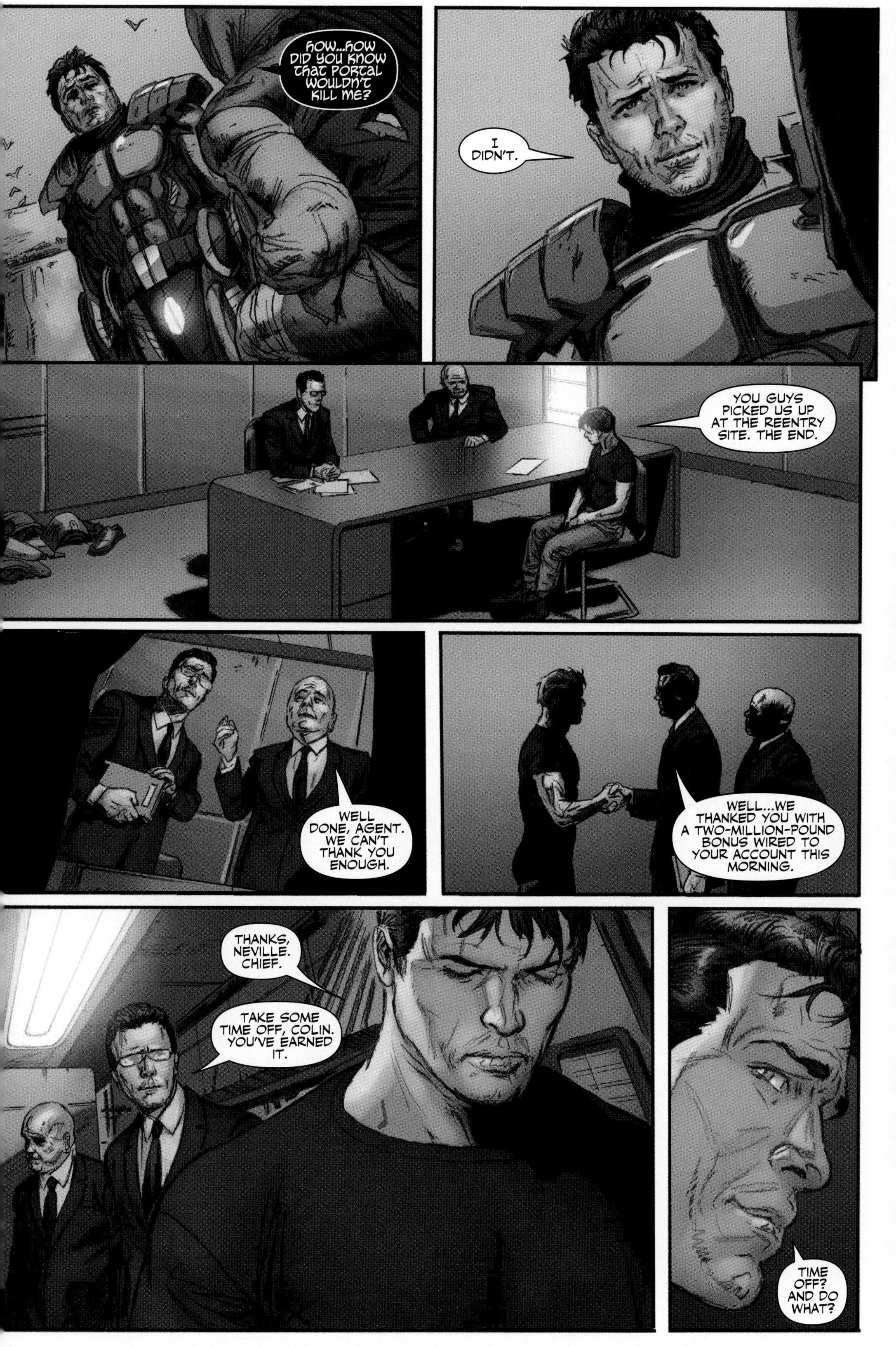
HOW...HOW DID YOU KNOW THAT PORTAL WOULDN'T KILL ME?
I DIDN'T.
YOU GUYS PICKED US UP AT THE REENTRY SITE. THE END.
WELL DONE, AGENT. WE CAN'T THANK YOU ENOUGH.
WELL...WE THANKED YOU WITH A TWO-MILLION-POUND BONUS WIRED TO YOUR ACCOUNT THIS MORNING.
THANKS, NEVILLE. CHIEF.
TAKE SOME TIME OFF, COLIN. YOU'VE EARNED IT.
TIME OFF? AND DO WHAT?

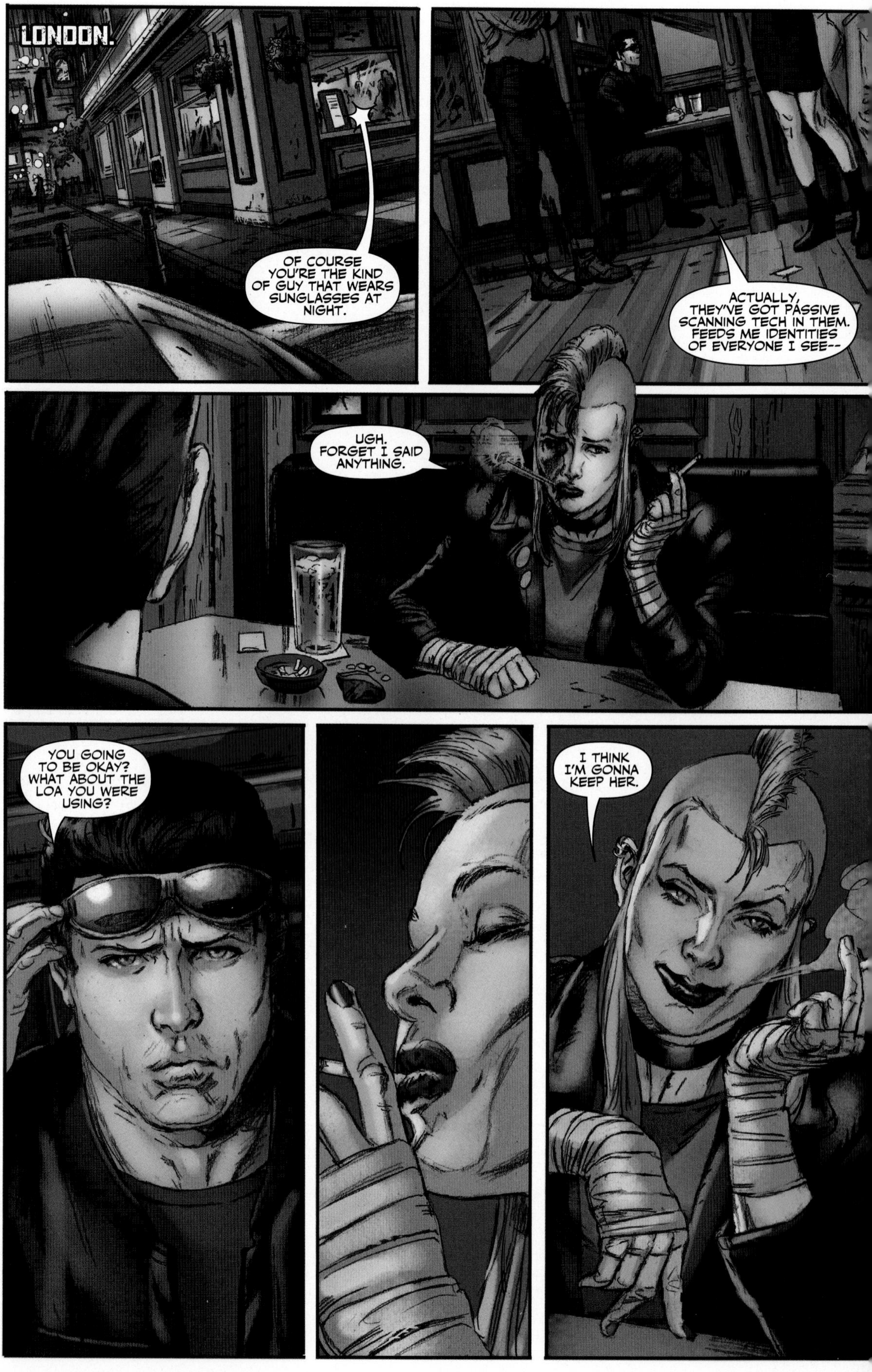
LONDON.
OF COURSE YOU'RE THE KIND OF GUY THAT WEARS SUNGLASSES AT NIGHT.
ACTUALLY, THEY'VE GOT PASSIVE SCANNING TECH IN THEM. FEEDS ME IDENTITIES OF EVERYONE I SEE--
UGH. FORGET I SAID ANYTHING.
YOU GOING TO BE OKAY? WHAT ABOUT THE LOA YOU WERE USING?
I THINK I'M GONNA KEEP HER.

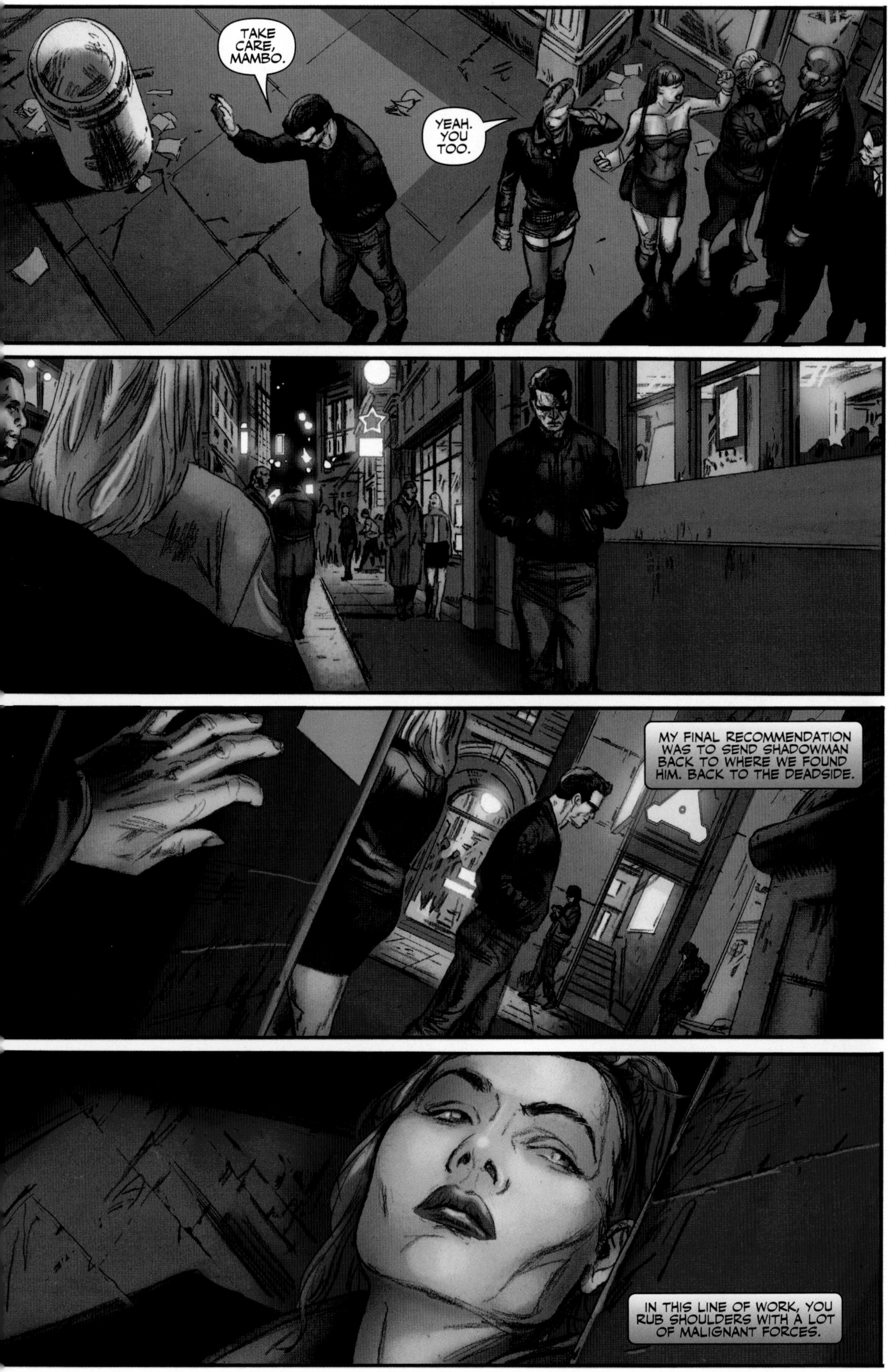
TAKE CARE, MAMBO.
YEAH. YOU TOO.
MY FINAL RECOMMENDATION WAS TO SEND SHADOWMAN BACK TO WHERE WE FOUND HIM. BACK TO THE DEADSIDE.
IN THIS LINE OF WORK, YOU RUB SHOULDERS WITH A LOT OF MALIGNANT FORCES.

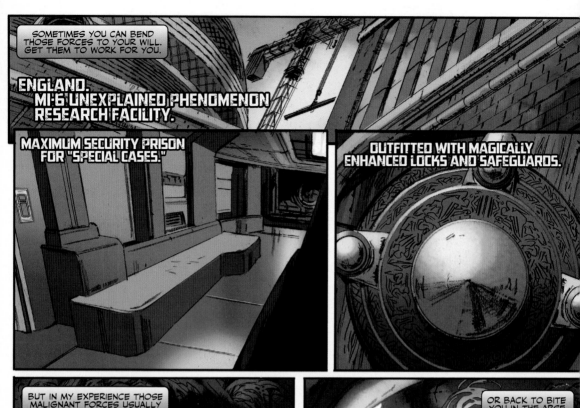

SOMETIMES YOU CAN BEND THOSE FORCES TO YOUR WILL. GET THEM TO WORK FOR YOU.

ENGLAND.
MI-6 UNEXPLAINED PHENOMENON RESEARCH FACILITY.

MAXIMUM SECURITY PRISON FOR "SPECIAL CASES."

OUTFITTED WITH MAGICALLY ENHANCED LOCKS AND SAFEGUARDS.

BUT IN MY EXPERIENCE THOSE MALIGNANT FORCES USUALLY COME BACK TO HAUNT YOU...

OR BACK TO BITE YOU IN THE ARSE.

NEXT: The SIEGE of King's Castle

BONIFAC

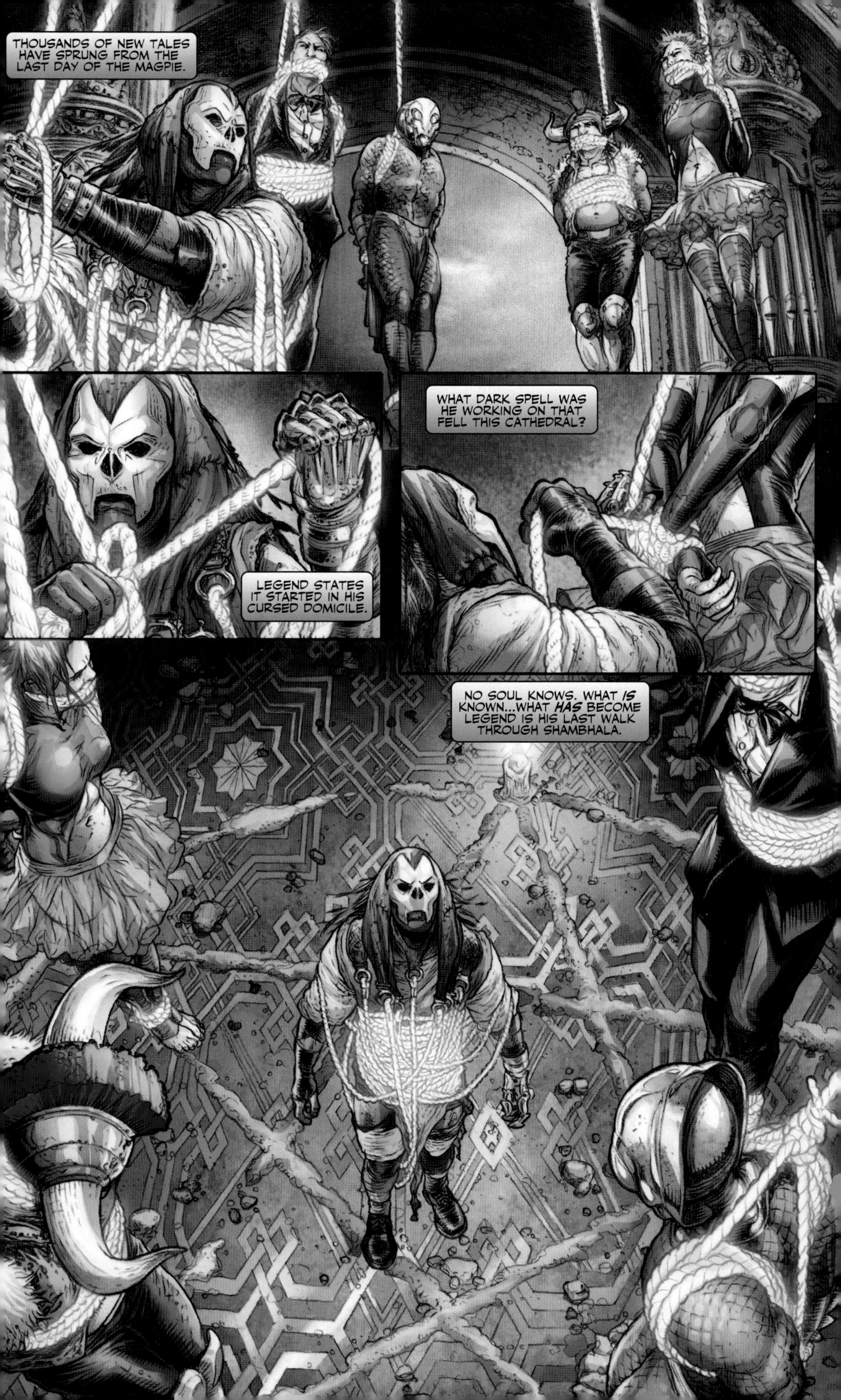
THOUSANDS OF NEW TALES HAVE SPRUNG FROM THE LAST DAY OF THE MAGPIE.
LEGEND STATES IT STARTED IN HIS CURSED DOMICILE.
WHAT DARK SPELL WAS HE WORKING ON THAT FELL THIS CATHEDRAL?
NO SOUL KNOWS. WHAT *IS* KNOWN...WHAT *HAS* BECOME LEGEND IS HIS LAST WALK THROUGH SHAMBHALA.

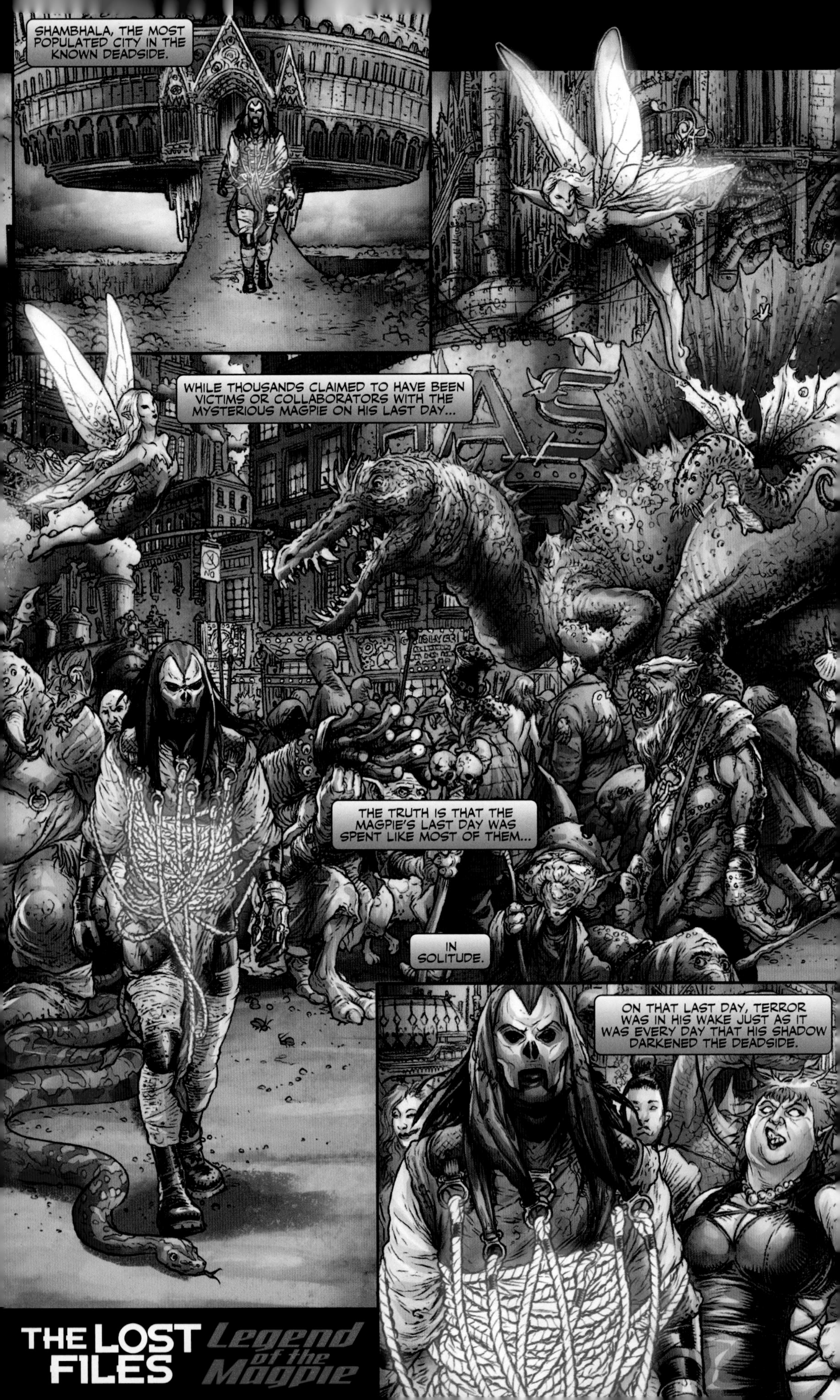

SHAMBHALA, THE MOST POPULATED CITY IN THE KNOWN DEADSIDE.
WHILE THOUSANDS CLAIMED TO HAVE BEEN VICTIMS OR COLLABORATORS WITH THE MYSTERIOUS MAGPIE ON HIS LAST DAY...
THE TRUTH IS THAT THE MAGPIE'S LAST DAY WAS SPENT LIKE MOST OF THEM...
IN SOLITUDE.
ON THAT LAST DAY, TERROR WAS IN HIS WAKE JUST AS IT WAS EVERY DAY THAT HIS SHADOW DARKENED THE DEADSIDE.
THE LOST FILES
Legend of the Magpie

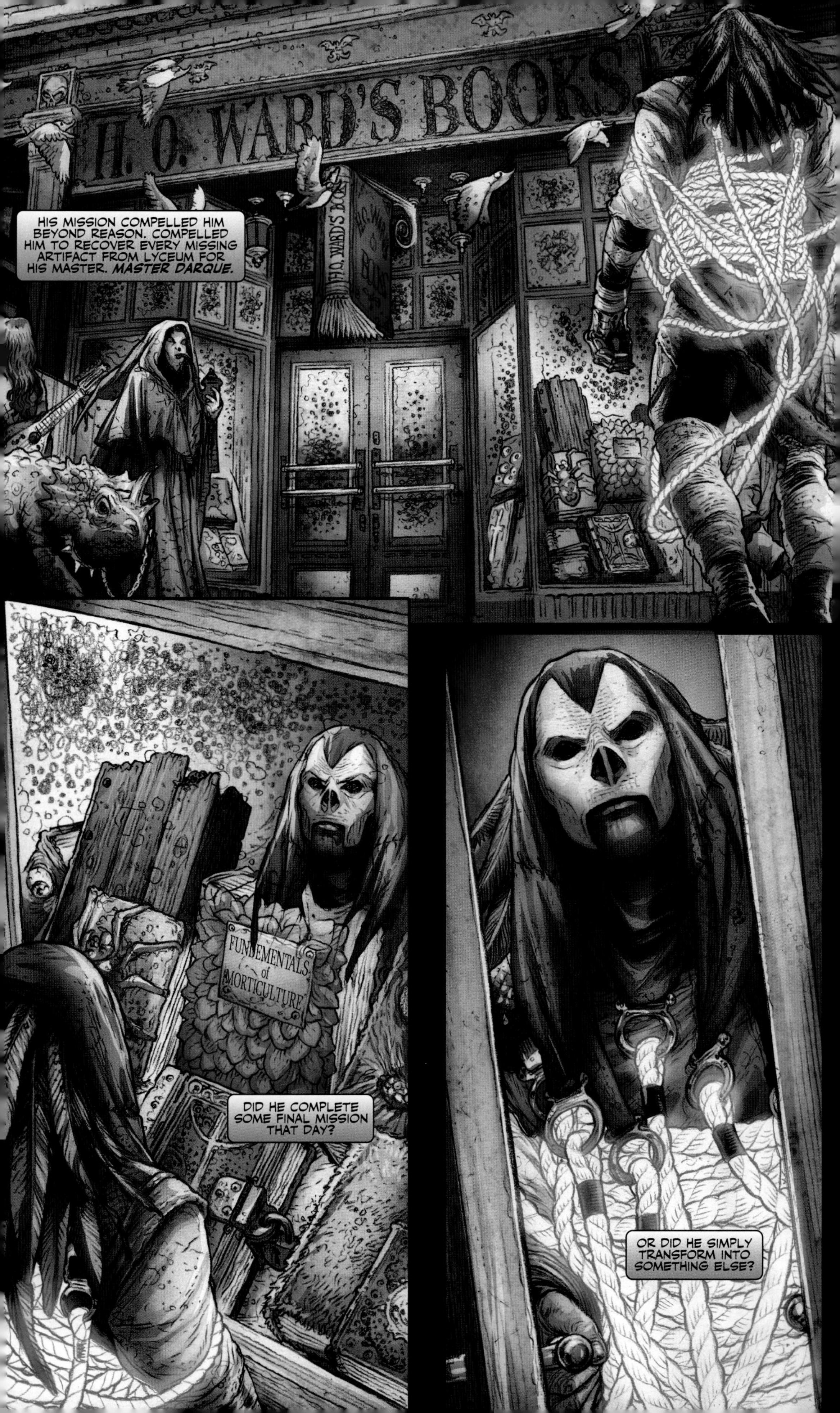
H. O. WARD'S BOOKS
HIS MISSION COMPELLED HIM BEYOND REASON. COMPELLED HIM TO RECOVER EVERY MISSING ARTIFACT FROM LYCEUM FOR HIS MASTER. *MASTER DARQUE.*
FUNDEMENTALS of MORTICULTURE
DID HE COMPLETE SOME FINAL MISSION THAT DAY?
OR DID HE SIMPLY TRANSFORM INTO SOMETHING ELSE?

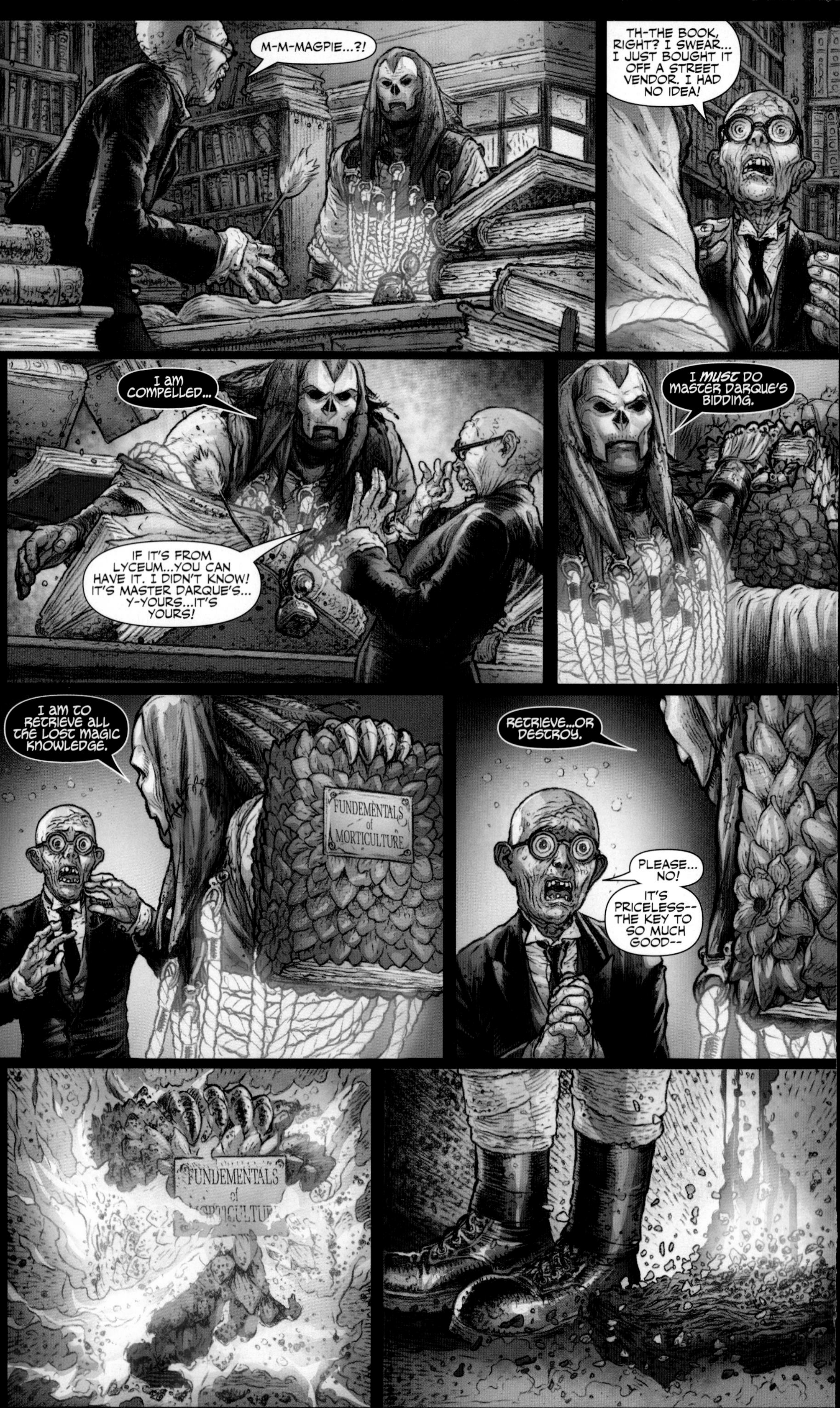
M-M-MAGPIE...?!
TH-THE BOOK, RIGHT? I SWEAR... I JUST BOUGHT IT OFF A STREET VENDOR. I HAD NO IDEA!
I am COMPELLED...
IF IT'S FROM LYCEUM...YOU CAN HAVE IT. I DIDN'T KNOW! IT'S MASTER DARQUE'S... Y-YOURS...IT'S YOURS!
I MUST DO MASTER DARQUE'S BIDDING.
I am TO RETRIEVE ALL THE LOST MAGIC KNOWLEDGE.
FUNDEMENTALS of MORTICULTURE
RETRIEVE...OR DESTROY.
PLEASE... NO!
IT'S PRICELESS-- THE KEY TO SO MUCH GOOD--
FUNDEMENTALS of

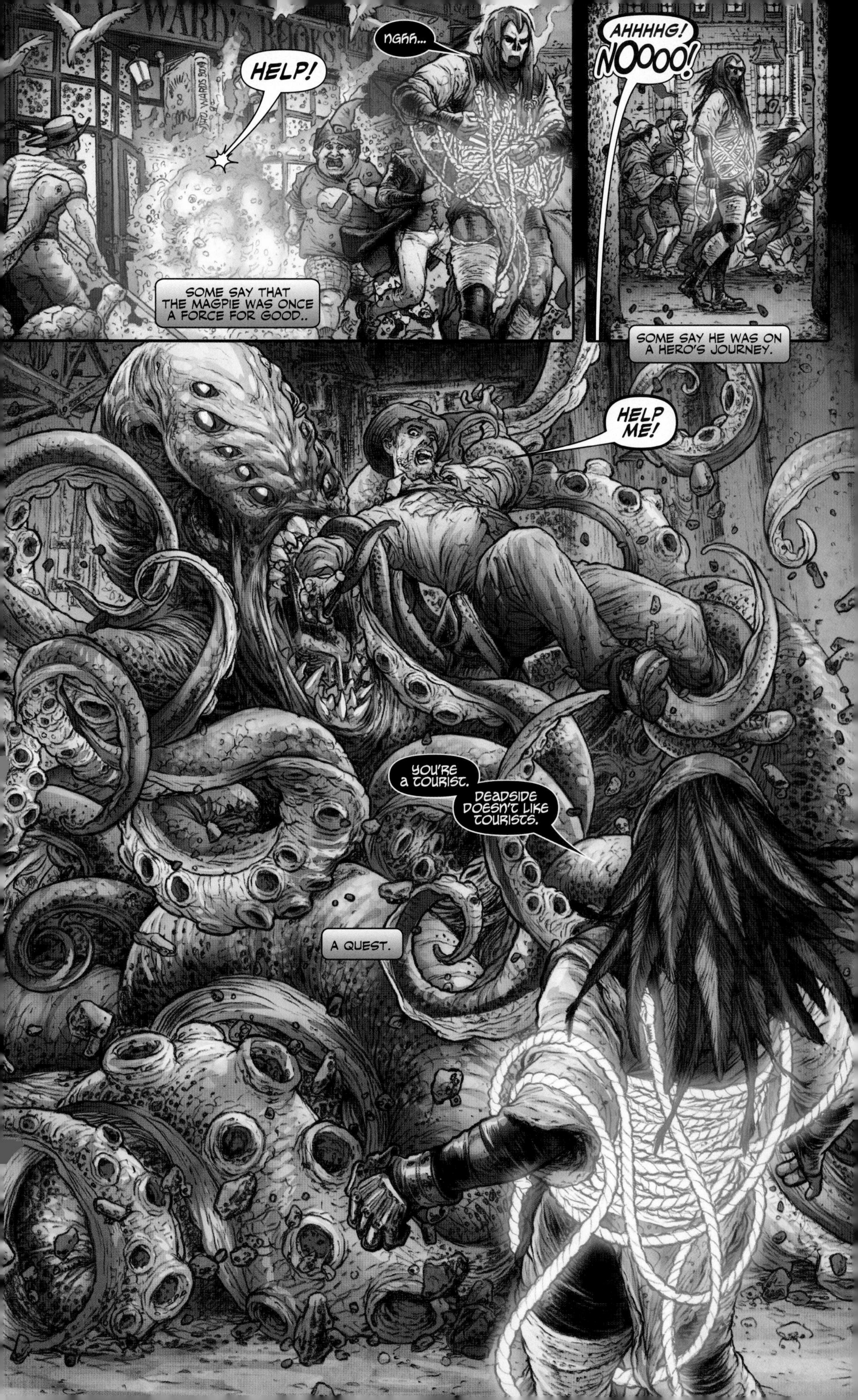
nghh...
HELP!
SOME SAY THAT THE MAGPIE WAS ONCE A FORCE FOR GOOD..
AHHHHG! NOOOO!
SOME SAY HE WAS ON A HERO'S JOURNEY.
HELP ME!
YOU'RE A TOURIST.
DEADSIDE DOESN'T LIKE TOURISTS.
A QUEST.

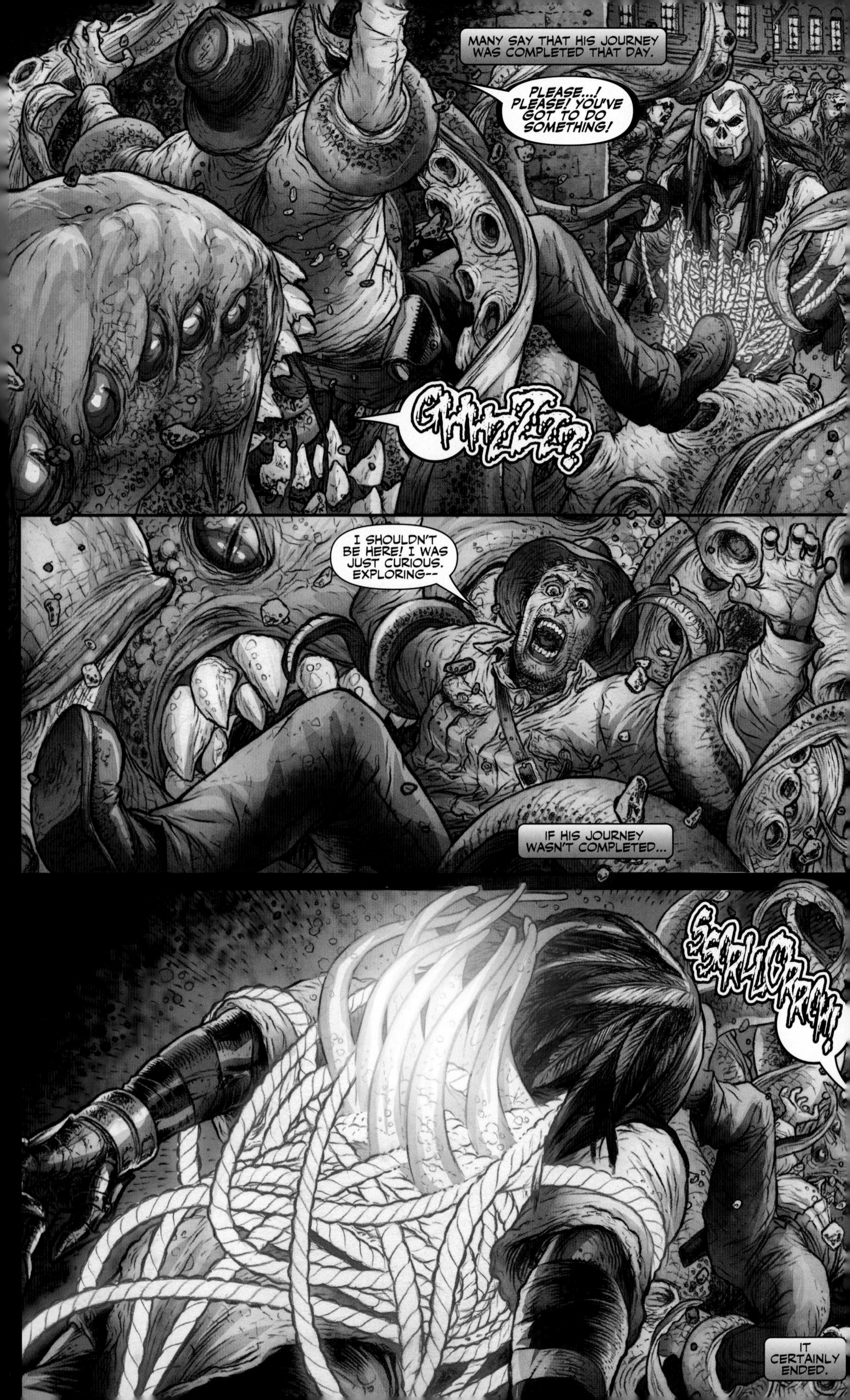
MANY SAY THAT HIS JOURNEY WAS COMPLETED THAT DAY.
PLEASE...! PLEASE! YOU'VE GOT TO DO SOMETHING!
I SHOULDN'T BE HERE! I WAS JUST CURIOUS. EXPLORING--
IF HIS JOURNEY WASN'T COMPLETED...
IT CERTAINLY ENDED.

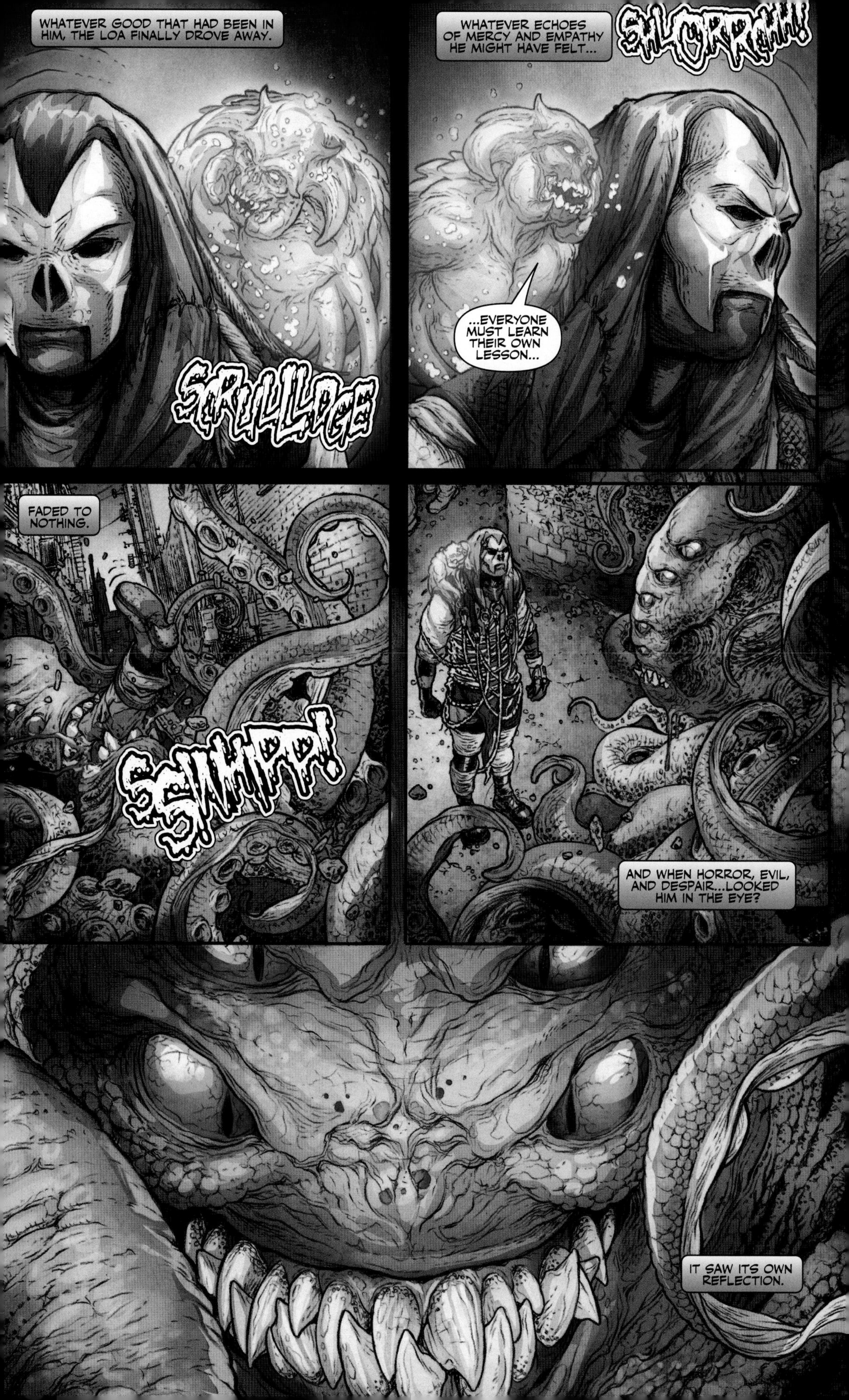
WHATEVER GOOD THAT HAD BEEN IN HIM, THE LOA FINALLY DROVE AWAY.
SCRULLLDGE
WHATEVER ECHOES OF MERCY AND EMPATHY HE MIGHT HAVE FELT...
SHLORRCHH!
...EVERYONE MUST LEARN THEIR OWN LESSON...
FADED TO NOTHING.
SSWHPP!
AND WHEN HORROR, EVIL, AND DESPAIR...LOOKED HIM IN THE EYE?
IT SAW ITS OWN REFLECTION.

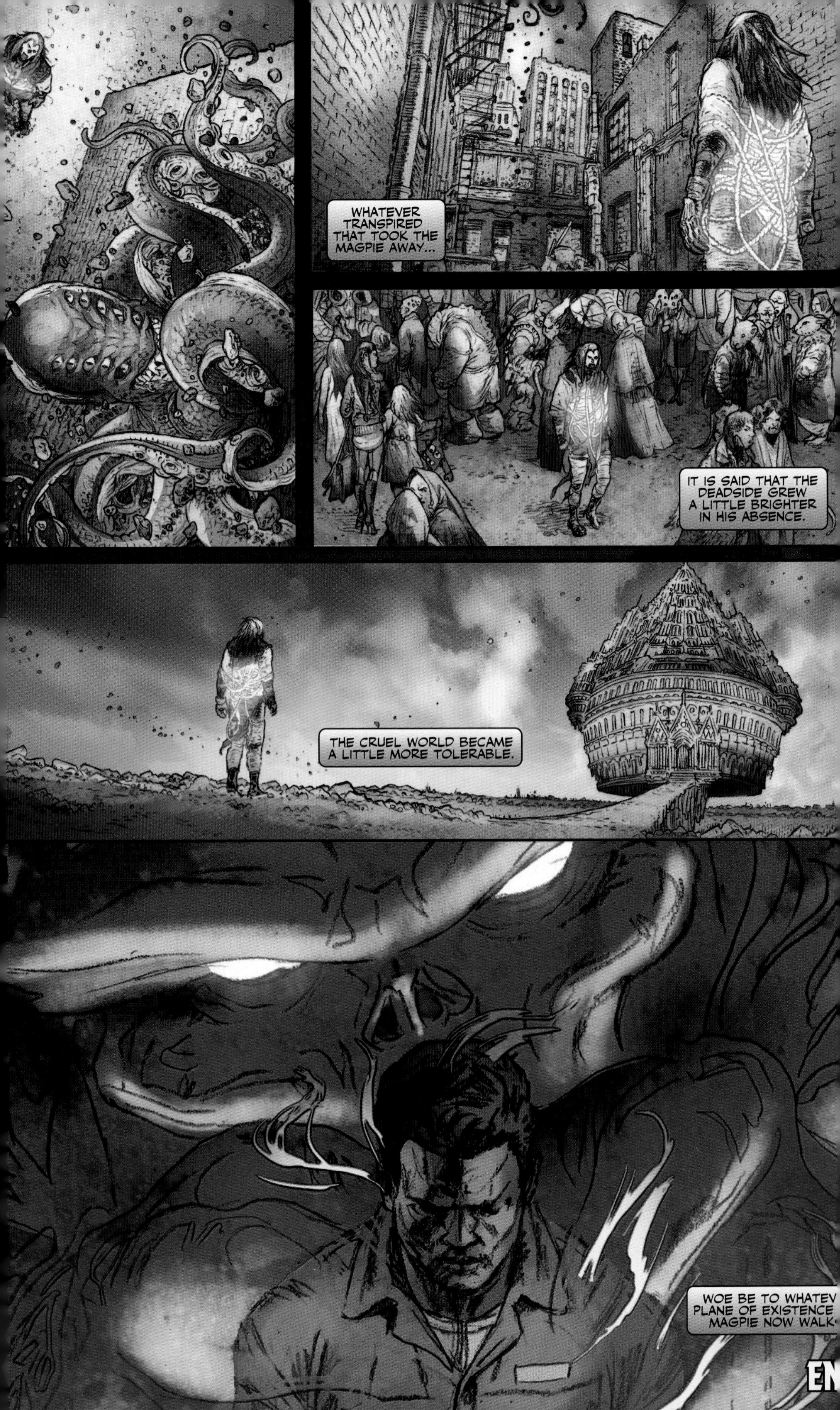
WHATEVER TRANSPIRED THAT TOOK THE MAGPIE AWAY...
IT IS SAID THAT THE DEADSIDE GREW A LITTLE BRIGHTER IN HIS ABSENCE.
THE CRUEL WORLD BECAME A LITTLE MORE TOLERABLE.
WOE BE TO WHATEV PLANE OF EXISTENCE MAGPIE NOW WALK.
EN

GALLERY

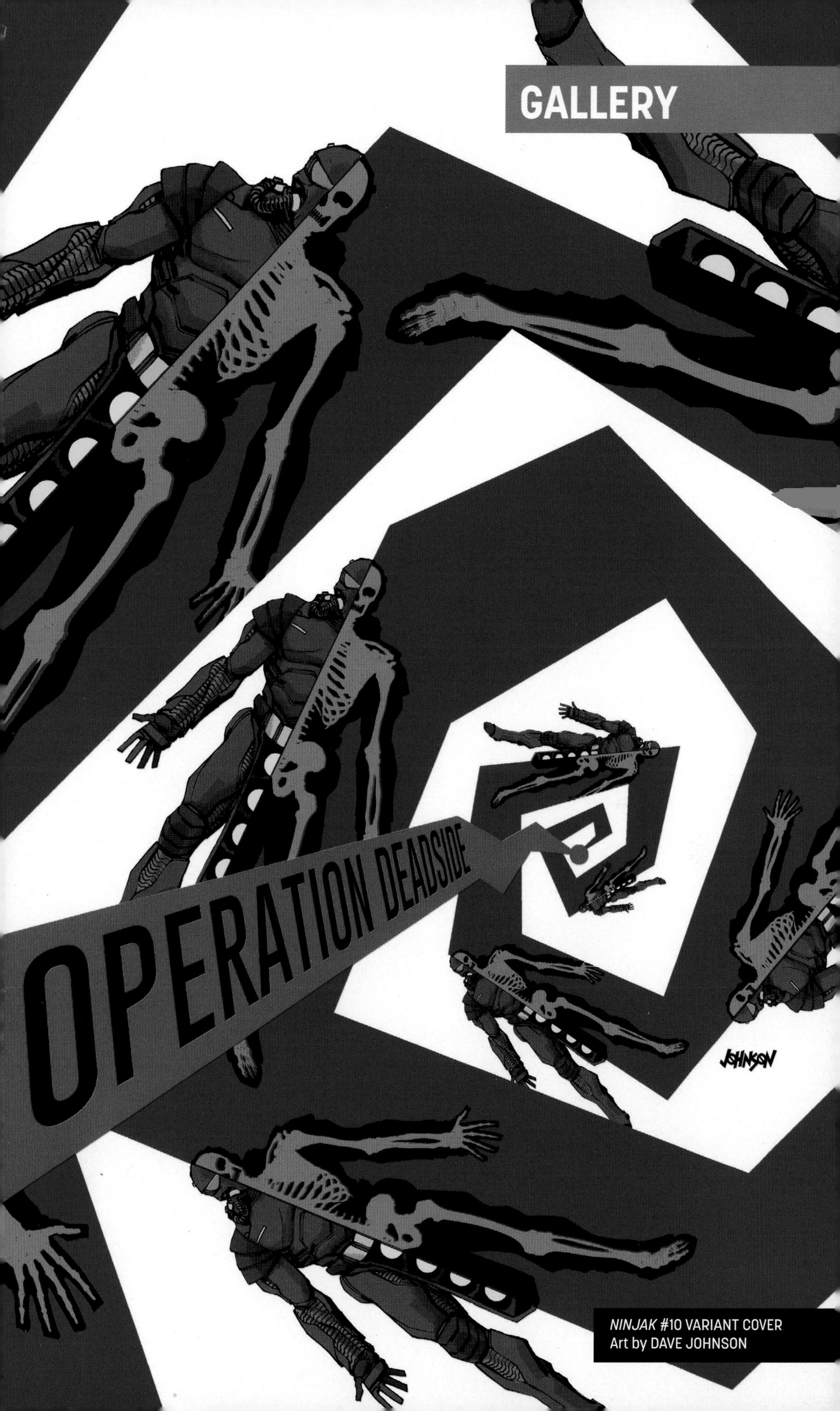
OPERATION DEADSIDE
JOHNSON

NINJAK #10 VARIANT COVER
Art by DAVE JOHNSON

NINJAK #11
CHARACTER DESIGN VARIANT COVER
Art by TREVOR HAIRSINE

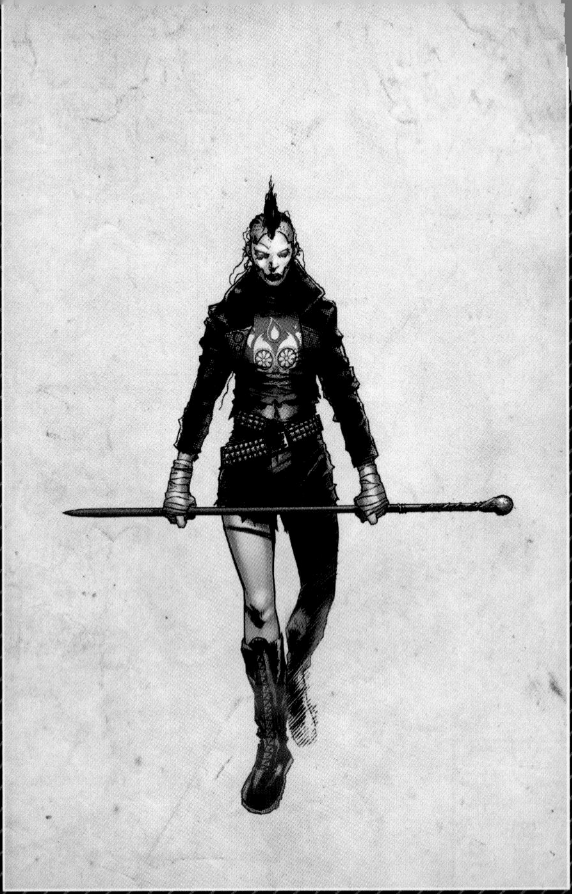

NINJAK #12 COVER B
Art by TOM RANEY with BRIAN REBER

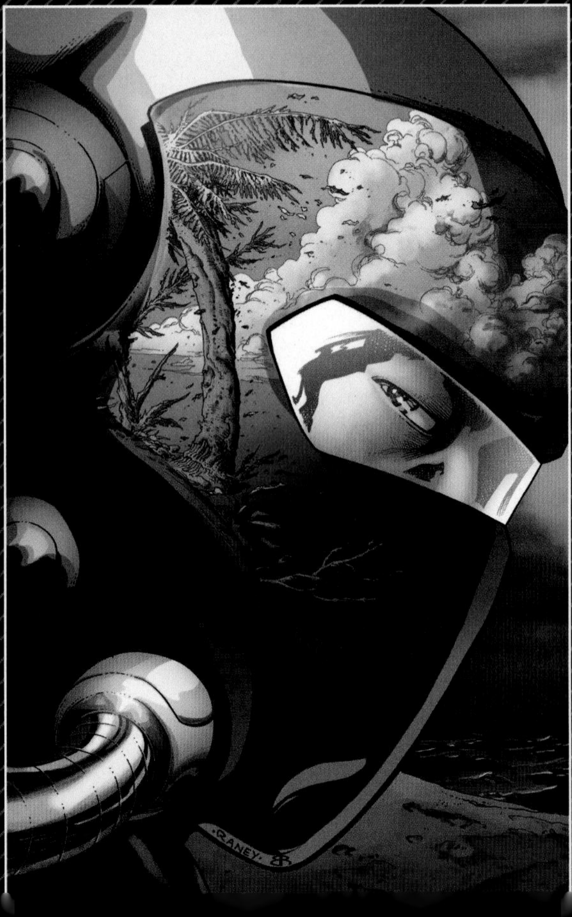
RANEY

NINJAK #11 COVER C
Art by CLAYTON HENRY

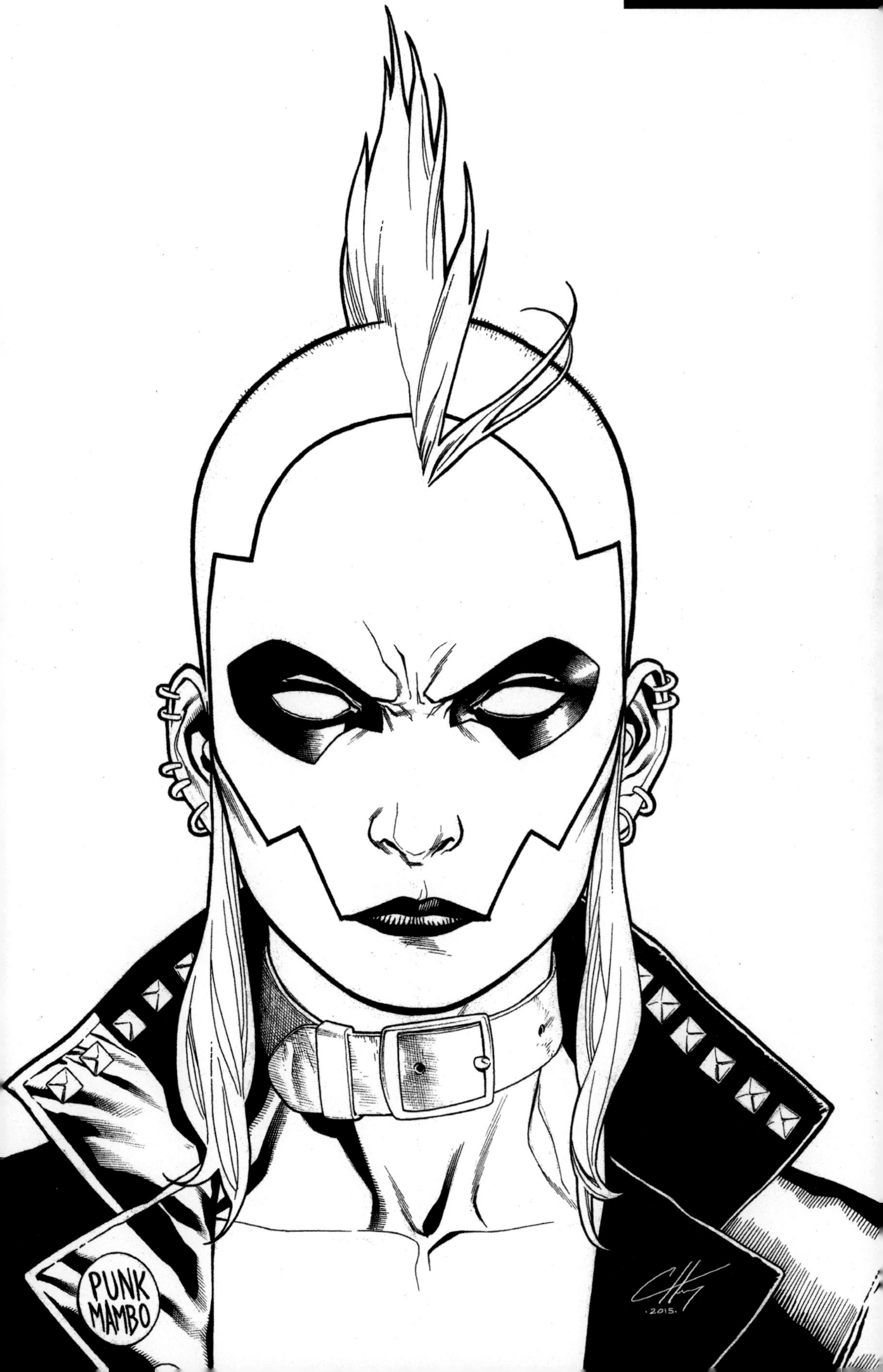
PUNK
MAMBO
·2015·

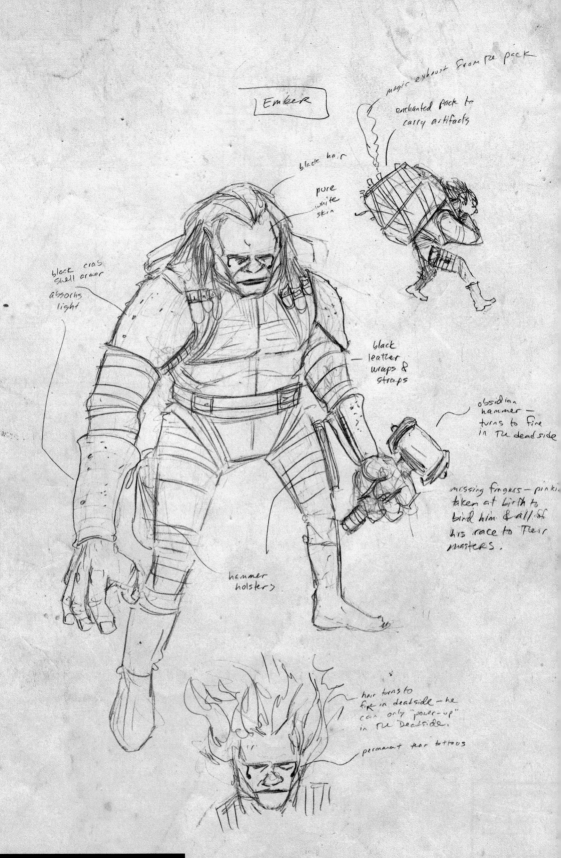

Ember

magic exhaust from the pack

enchanted pack to carry artifacts

black hair

pure white skin

black crab shell armor absorbs light

black leather wraps & straps

obsidian hammer — turns to fire in the deadside

missing fingers — pinkie taken at birth to bind him & all of his race to their masters.

hammer holsters

hair turns to fire in deadside — he can only "power-up" in the Deadside.

permanent scar tattoos

NINJAK #13
CHARACTER DESIGN VARIANT COVER
Art by MATT KINDT

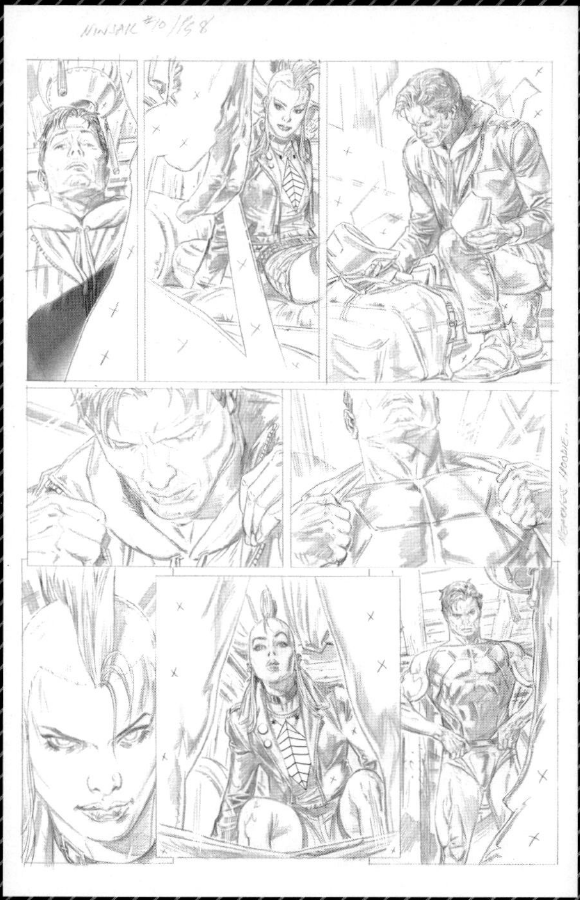
NINJAK #10 / PG 8

NINJAK #10, p. 8
Art by DOUG BRAITHWAITE

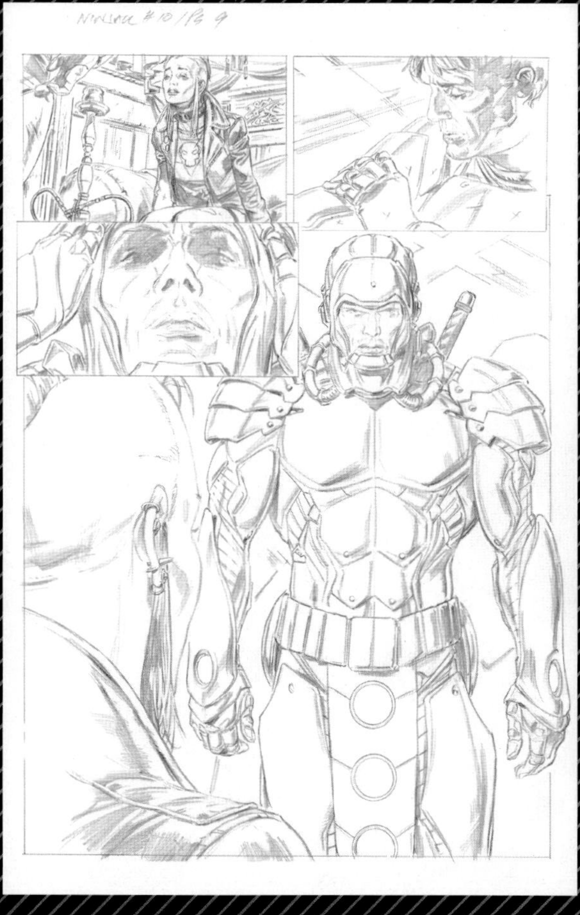
NINJAK #10 / PG 9

NINJAK #10, p. 9
Art by DOUG BRAITHWAITE

NINJAK #13, p. 7
Art by DOUG BRAITHWAITE

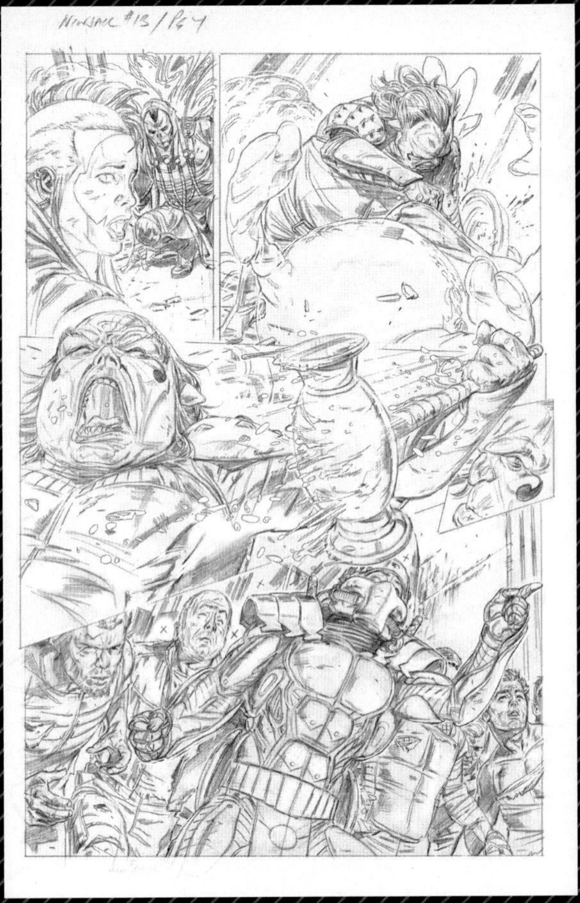

NINJAK #13, pages 12 and 14 (facing)
Art by DOUG BRAITHWAITE

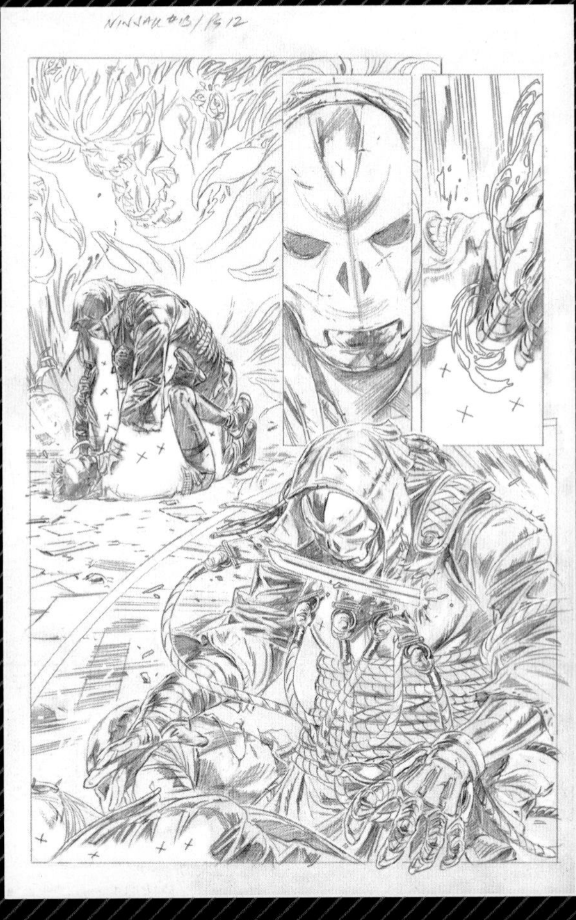
NINJAK #13 / Pg 12

NINJAK #13 / Pg 14

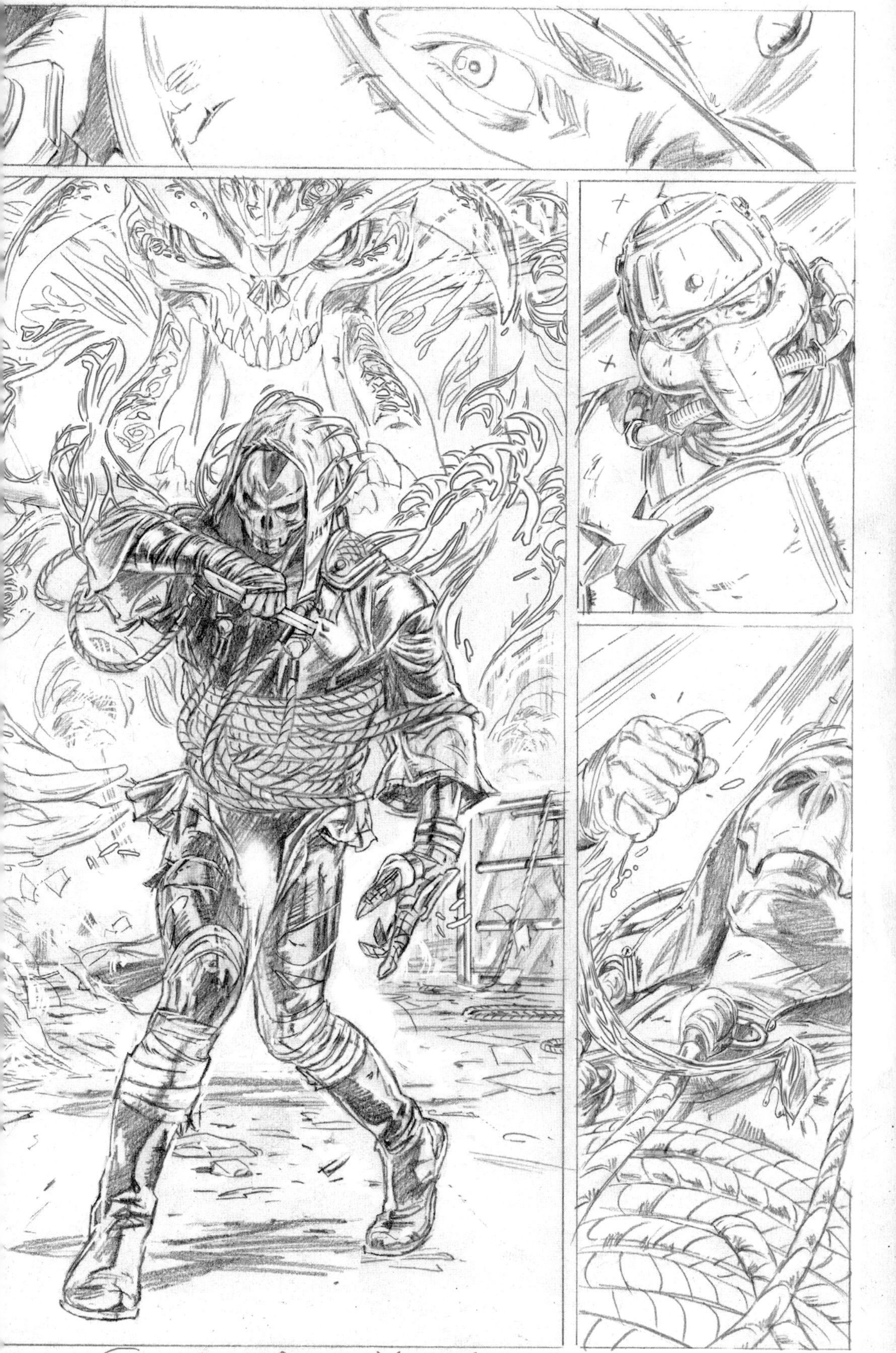

(SFX) = GLOW AROUND THE HAND/SWORD BLADE.
HAZY/INTENSE.

EXPLORE THE VALIANT UNIVERSE

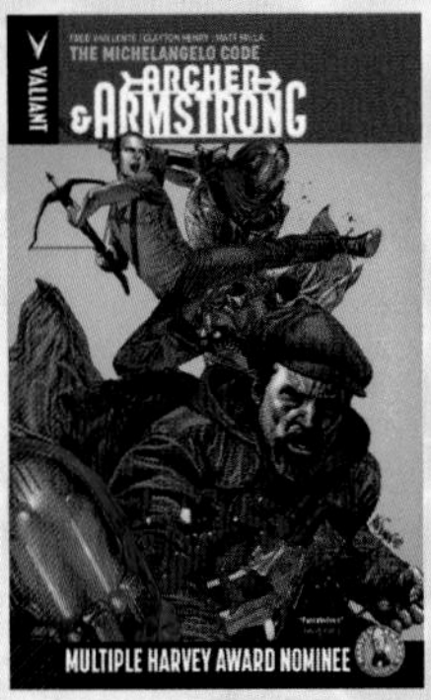
VALIANT
THE MICHELANGELO CODE
ARCHER & ARMSTRONG
MULTIPLE HARVEY AWARD NOMINEE

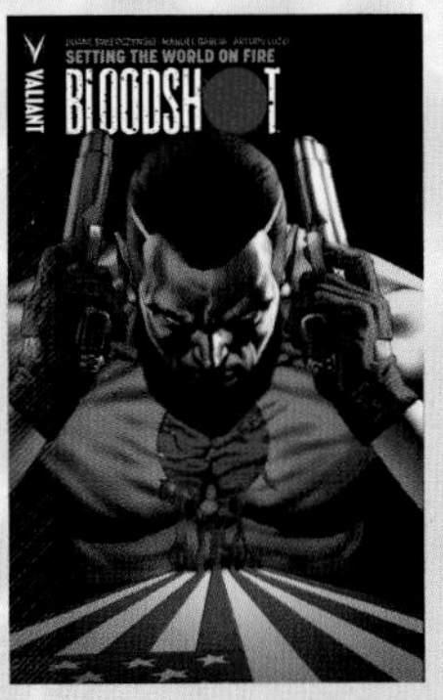
VALIANT
SETTING THE WORLD ON FIRE

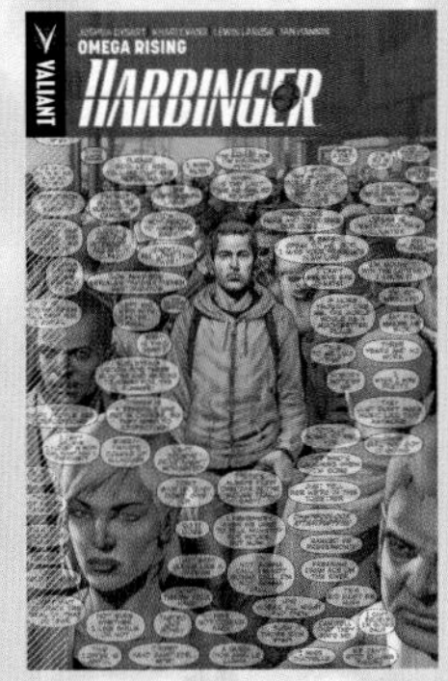
VALIANT
OMEGA RISING
HARBINGER

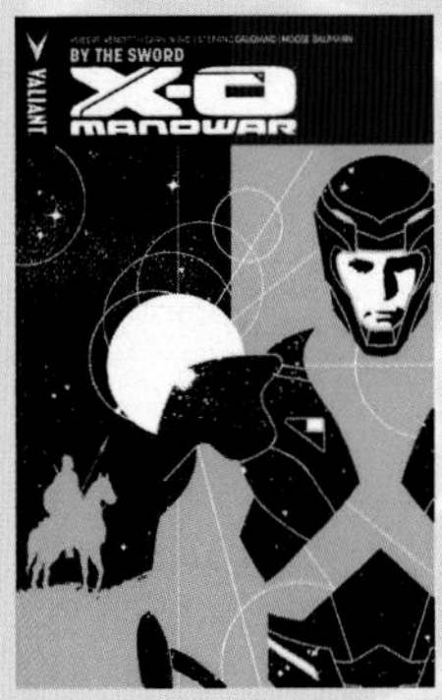
VALIANT
BY THE SWORD
X-O MANOWAR

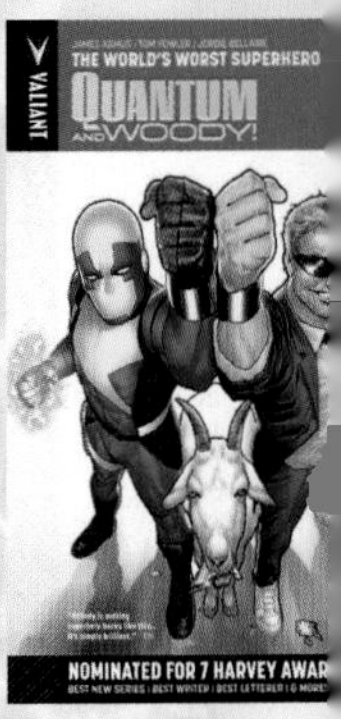
VALIANT
THE WORLD'S WORST SUPERHERO
QUANTUM AND WOODY!

ARCHER & ARMSTRONG

Volume 1: The Michelangelo Code
ISBN: 9780979640988

Volume 2: Wrath of the Eternal Warrior
ISBN: 9781939346049

Volume 3: Far Faraway
ISBN: 9781939346148

Volume 4: Sect Civil War
ISBN: 9781939346254

Volume 5: Mission: Improbable
ISBN: 9781939346353

Volume 6: American Wasteland
ISBN: 9781939346421

Volume 7: The One Percent and Other Tales
ISBN: 9781939346537

ARMOR HUNTERS

Armor Hunters
ISBN: 9781939346452

Armor Hunters: Bloodshot
ISBN: 9781939346469

Armor Hunters: Harbinger
ISBN: 9781939346506

Unity Vol. 3: Armor Hunters
ISBN: 9781939346445

X-O Manowar Vol. 7: Armor Hunters
ISBN: 9781939346476

BLOODSHOT

Volume 1: Setting the World on Fire
ISBN: 9780979640964

Volume 2: The Rise and the Fall
ISBN: 9781939346032

Volume 3: Harbinger Wars
ISBN: 9781939346124

Volume 4: H.A.R.D. Corps
ISBN: 9781939346193

Volume 5: Get Some!
ISBN: 9781939346315

Volume 6: The Glitch and Other Tales
ISBN: 9781939346711

BLOODSHOT REBORN

Volume 1: Colorado
ISBN: 9781939346674

Volume 2: The Hunt
ISBN: 9781939346827

Volume 3: The Analog Man
ISBN: 9781682151334

BOOK OF DEATH

Book of Death
ISBN: 9781939346971

Book of Death: The Fall of the Valiant Universe
ISBN: 9781939346988

DEAD DROP

ISBN: 9781939346858

THE DEATH-DEFYING DOCTOR MIRAGE

Volume 1
ISBN: 9781939346490

Volume 2: Second Lives
ISBN: 9781682151297

THE DELINQUENTS

ISBN: 9781939346513

DIVINITY

ISBN: 9781939346766

ETERNAL WARRIOR

Volume 1: Sword of the Wild
ISBN: 9781939346209

Volume 2: Eternal Emperor
ISBN: 9781939346292

Volume 3: Days of Steel
ISBN: 9781939346742

WRATH OF THE ETERNAL WARRIOR

Volume 1: Risen
ISBN: 9781682151235

HARBINGER

Volume 1: Omega Rising
ISBN: 9780979640957

Volume 2: Renegades
ISBN: 9781939346025

Volume 3: Harbinger Wars
ISBN: 9781939346117

Volume 4: Perfect Day
ISBN: 9781939346155

Volume 5: Death of a Renegade
ISBN: 9781939346339

Volume 6: Omegas
ISBN: 9781939346384

HARBINGER WARS

Harbinger Wars
ISBN: 9781939346094

Bloodshot Vol. 3: Harbinger Wars
ISBN: 9781939346124

Harbinger Vol. 3: Harbinger Wars
ISBN: 9781939346117

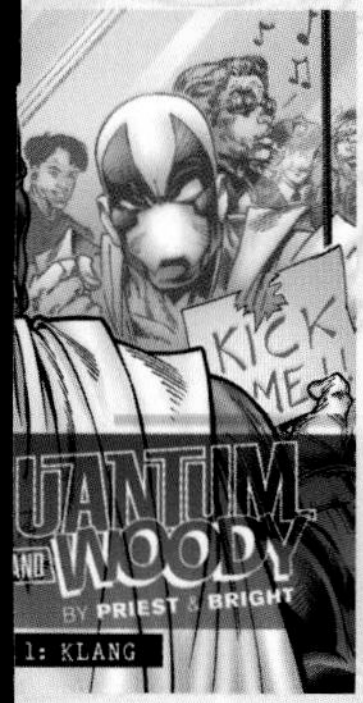
KICK ME
UANTUM AND WOODY
BY PRIEST & BRIGHT
1: KLANG
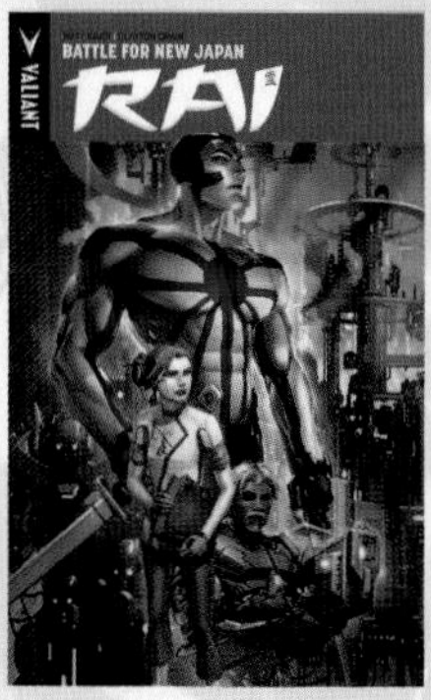
VALIANT
BATTLE FOR NEW JAPAN
RAI
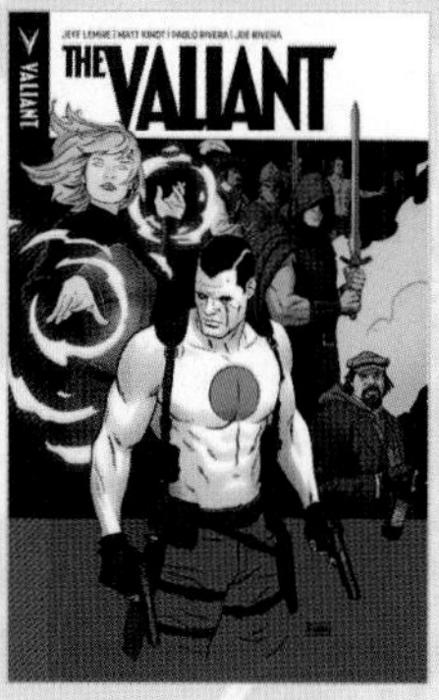
VALIANT
THE VALIANT
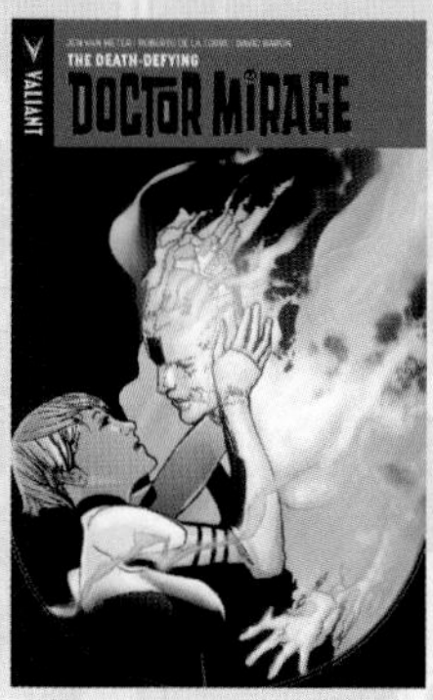
VALIANT
THE DEATH-DEFYING
DOCTOR MIRAGE
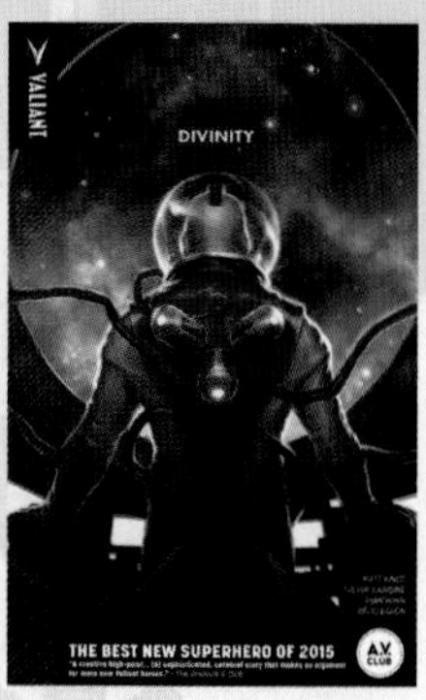
VALIANT
DIVINITY
THE BEST NEW SUPERHERO OF 2015

PERIUM

ne 1: Collecting Monsters
9781939346759

ne 2: Broken Angels
9781939346896

ne 3: The Vine Imperative
9781682151112

NJAK

ne 1: Weaponeer
9781939346667

ne 2: The Shadow Wars
9781939346940

ne 3: Operation: Deadside
9781682151259

ANTUM D WOODY

ne 1: The World's Worst Superhero Team
9781939346186

ne 2: In Security
9781939346230

ne 3: Crooked Pasts, Present Tense
9781939346391

ne 4: Quantum and Woody Must Die!
9781939346629

ANTUM AND WOODY PRIEST & BRIGHT

ne 1: Klang
9781939346780

ne 2: Switch
9781939346803

ne 3: And So...
9781939346865

ne 4: Q2 - The Return
9781682151099

RAI

Volume 1: Welcome to New Japan
ISBN: 9781939346414

Volume 2: Battle for New Japan
ISBN: 9781939346612

Volume 3: The Orphan
ISBN: 9781939346841

SHADOWMAN

Volume 1: Birth Rites
ISBN: 9781939346001

Volume 2: Darque Reckoning
ISBN: 9781939346056

Volume 3: Deadside Blues
ISBN: 9781939346162

Volume 4: Fear, Blood, And Shadows
ISBN: 9781939346278

Volume 5: End Times
ISBN: 9781939346377

IVAR, TIMEWALKER

Volume 1: Making History
ISBN: 9781939346636

Volume 2: Breaking History
ISBN: 9781939346834

Volume 3: Ending History
ISBN: 9781939346995

UNITY

Volume 1: To Kill a King
ISBN: 9781939346261

Volume 2: Trapped by Webnet
ISBN: 9781939346346

Volume 3: Armor Hunters
ISBN: 9781939346445

Volume 4: The United
ISBN: 9781939346544

Volume 5: Homefront
ISBN: 9781939346797

Volume 6: The War-Monger
ISBN: 9781939346902

Volume 7: Revenge of the Armor Hunters
ISBN: 9781682151136

THE VALIANT

ISBN: 9781939346605

VALIANT ZEROES AND ORIGINS

ISBN: 9781939346582

X-O MANOWAR

Volume 1: By the Sword
ISBN: 9780979640940

Volume 2: Enter Ninjak
ISBN: 9780979640995

Volume 3: Planet Death
ISBN: 9781939346087

Volume 4: Homecoming
ISBN: 9781939346179

Volume 5: At War With Unity
ISBN: 9781939346247

Volume 6: Prelude to Armor Hunters
ISBN: 9781939346407

Volume 7: Armor Hunters
ISBN: 9781939346476

Volume 8: Enter: Armorines
ISBN: 9781939346551

Volume 9: Dead Hand
ISBN: 9781939346650

Volume 10: Exodus
ISBN: 9781939346933

Volume 11: The Kill List
ISBN: 9781682151273

VALIANT
HARBINGER
DELUXE EDITION 2

VALIANT
ROBERT VENDITTI MATT KINDT JOSHUA DYSART JOE HARRIS ROBERT GILL DOUG BRAITHWAITE DIEGO BERNARD TREVOR HAIRSINE STEPHEN SEGOVIA
ARMOR HUNTERS
DELUXE EDITION

VALIANT
JIM SHOOTER | DAVID LAPHAM
CHILDREN OF THE EIGHTH DAY
HARBINGER
VALIANT MASTERS

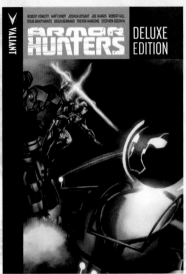

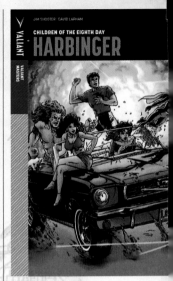

Omnibuses

Archer & Armstrong: The Complete Classic Omnibus
ISBN: 9781939346872
Collecting ARCHER & ARMSTRONG (1992) #0-26, ETERNAL WARRIOR (1992) #25 along with ARCHER & ARMSTRONG: THE FORMATION OF THE SECT.

Quantum and Woody: The Complete Classic Omnibus
ISBN: 9781939346360
Collecting QUANTUM AND WOODY (1997) #0, 1-21 and #32, THE GOAT: H.A.E.D.U.S. #1, and X-O MANOWAR (1996) #16

X-O Manowar Classic Omnibus Vol. 1
ISBN: 9781939346308
Collecting X-O MANOWAR (1992) #0-30, ARMORINES #0, X-O DATABASE #1, as well as material from SECRETS OF THE VALIANT UNIVERSE #1

Deluxe Editions

Archer & Armstrong Deluxe Edition Book 1
ISBN: 9781939346223
Collecting ARCHER & ARMSTRONG #0-13

Archer & Armstrong Deluxe Edition Book 2
ISBN: 9781939346957
Collecting ARCHER & ARMSTRONG #14-25, ARCHER & ARMSTRONG: ARCHER #0 and BLOODSHOT AND H.A.R.D. CORPS #20-21.

Armor Hunters Deluxe Edition
ISBN: 9781939346728
Collecting Armor Hunters #1-4, Armor Hunters: Aftermath #1, Armor Hunters: Bloodshot #1-3, Armor Hunters: Harbinger #1-3, Unity #8-11, and X-O MANOWAR #23-29

Bloodshot Deluxe Edition Book 1
ISBN: 9781939346216
Collecting BLOODSHOT #1-13

Bloodshot Deluxe Edition Book 2
ISBN: 9781939346810
Collecting BLOODSHOT AND H.A.R.D. CORPS #14-23, BLOODSHOT #24-25, BLOODSHOT #0, BLOODSHOT AND H.A.R.D. CORPS: H.A.R.D. CORPS #0, along with ARCHER & ARMSTRONG #18-19

Book of Death Deluxe Edition
ISBN: 9781682151150
Collecting BOOK OF DEATH #1-4, BOOK OF DEATH: THE FALL OF BLOODSHOT #1, BOOK OF DEATH: THE FALL OF NINJAK #1, BOOK OF DEATH: THE FALL OF HARBINGER #1, and BOOK OF DEATH: THE FALL OF X-O MANOWAR #1.

Divinity Deluxe Edition
ISBN: 97819393460993
Collecting DIVNITY #1-4

Harbinger Deluxe Edition Book 1
ISBN: 9781939346131
Collecting HARBINGER #0-14

Harbinger Deluxe Edition Book 2
ISBN: 9781939346773
Collecting HARBINGER #15-25, HARBINGER: OMEGAS #1-3, and HARBINGER: BLEEDING MONK #0

Harbinger Wars Deluxe Edition
ISBN: 9781939346322
Collecting HARBINGER WARS #1-4, HARBINGER #11-14, and BLOODSHOT #10-13

Ivar, Timewalker Deluxe Edition Book 1
ISBN: 9781682151198
Collecting IVAR, TIMEWALKER #1-12

Quantum and Woody Deluxe Edition Book 1
ISBN: 9781939346681
Collecting QUANTUM AND WOODY #1-12 and QUANTUM AND WOODY: THE GOAT #0

Q2: The Return of Quantum and Woody Deluxe Edition
ISBN: 9781939346568
Collecting Q2: THE RETURN OF QUANTUM AND WOODY #1-5

Rai Deluxe Edition Book 1
ISBN: 9781682151174
Collecting RAI #1-12, along with material from RAI #1 PLUS EDITION and RAI #5 PLUS EDITION

Shadowman Deluxe Edition Book 1
ISBN: 9781939346438
Collecting SHADOWMAN #0-10

Shadowman Deluxe Edition Book 2
ISBN: 9781682151075
Collecting SHADOWMAN #11-16, SHADOWMAN #13X, SHADOWMAN: END TIMES #1-3 and PUNK MAMBO #0

Unity Deluxe Edition Book 1
ISBN: 9781939346575
Collecting UNITY #0-14

The Valiant Deluxe Edition
ISBN: 97819393460986
Collecting THE VALIANT #1-4

X-O Manowar Deluxe Edition Book 1
ISBN: 9781939346100
Collecting X-O MANOWAR #1-14

X-O Manowar Deluxe Edition Book 2
ISBN: 9781939346520
Collecting X-O MANOWAR #15-22, and UNITY #

X-O Manowar Deluxe Edition Book 3
ISBN: 9781682151310
Collecting X-O MANOWAR #23-29 and ARMO HUNTERS #1-4.

Valiant Masters

Bloodshot Vol. 1 - Blood of the Machine
ISBN: 9780979640933

H.A.R.D. Corps Vol. 1 - Search and Destroy
ISBN: 9781939346285

Harbinger Vol. 1 - Children of the Eighth Day
ISBN: 9781939346483

Ninjak Vol. 1 - Black Water
ISBN: 9780979640971

Rai Vol. 1 - From Honor to Strength
ISBN: 9781939346070

Shadowman Vol. 1 - Spirits Within
ISBN: 9781939346018

NINJAK | READING ORDER

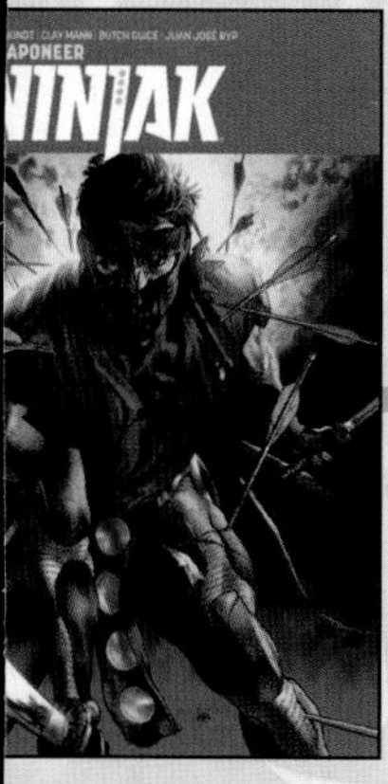
WEAPONEER
NINJAK

Ninjak Vol. 1:
Weaponeer

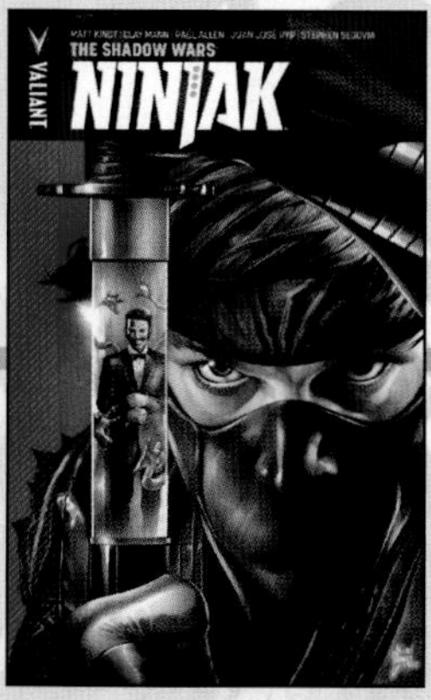
THE SHADOW WARS
VALIANT
NINJAK

Ninjak Vol. 2:
The Shadow Wars

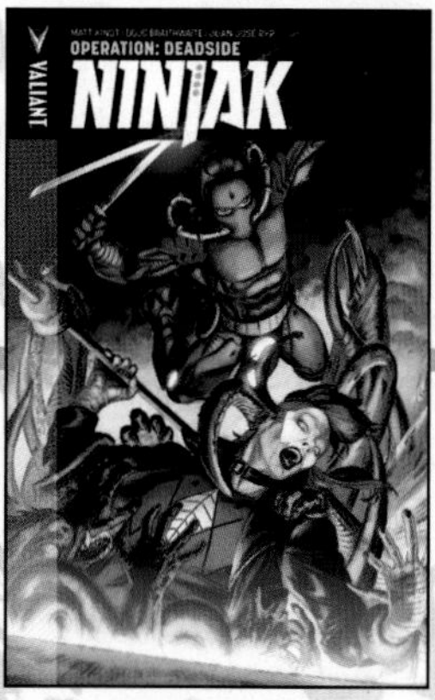
OPERATION: DEADSIDE
VALIANT
NINJAK

Ninjak Vol. 3:
Operation: Deadside

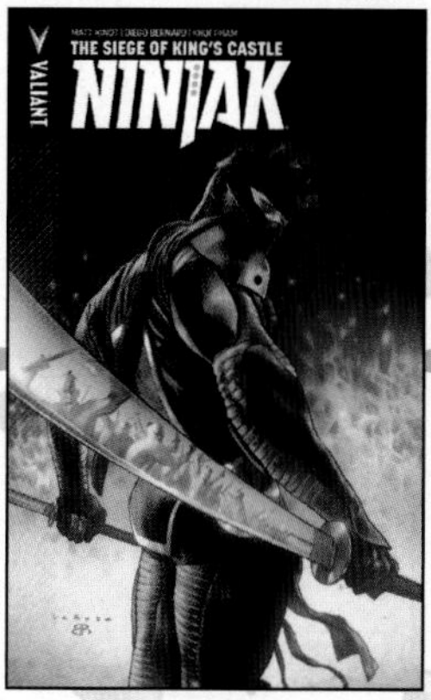
THE SIEGE OF KING'S CASTLE
VALIANT
NINJAK

Ninjak Vol. 4:
The Siege of King's Castle

Read the smash-hit debut and earliest adventures of the Valiant Universe's deadliest master spy!

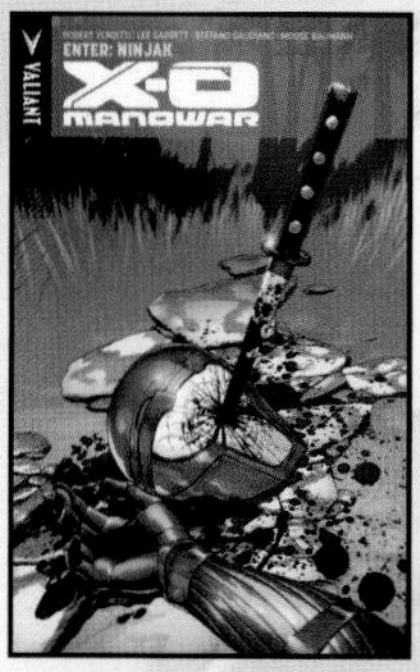
ENTER: NINJAK
VALIANT
X-O MANOWAR

X-O Manowar Vol. 2:
Enter Ninjak

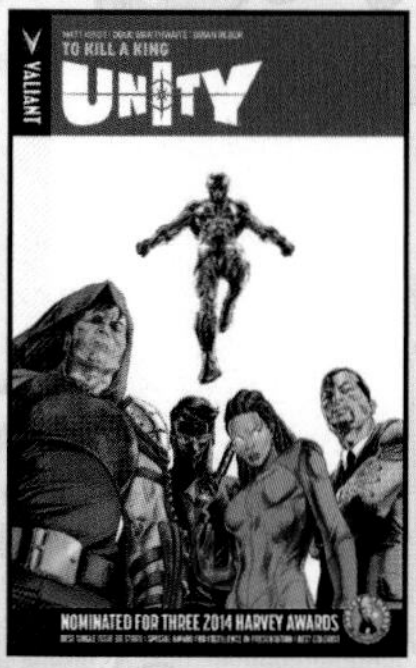
TO KILL A KING
VALIANT
UNITY
NOMINATED FOR THREE 2014 HARVEY AWARDS

Unity Vol. 1:
To Kill a King

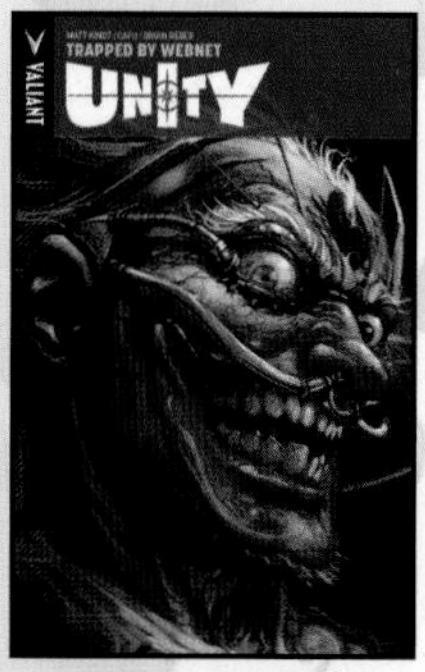
TRAPPED BY WEBNET
VALIANT
UNITY

Unity Vol. 2:
Trapped by Webnet

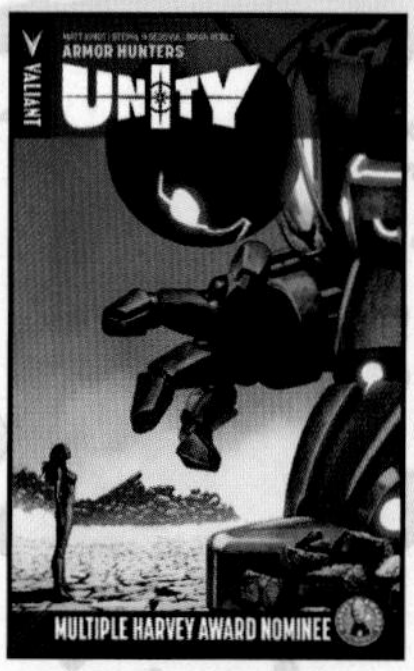
ARMOR HUNTERS
VALIANT
UNITY
MULTIPLE HARVEY AWARD NOMINEE

Unity Vol. 3:
Armor Hunters

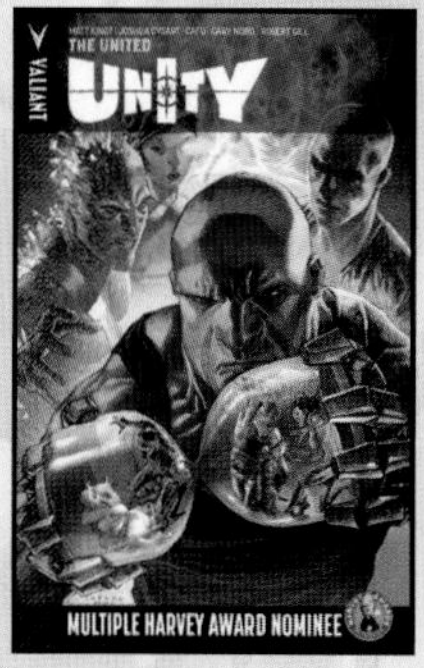
THE UNITED
VALIANT
UNITY
MULTIPLE HARVEY AWARD NOMINEE

Unity Vol. 4:
The United

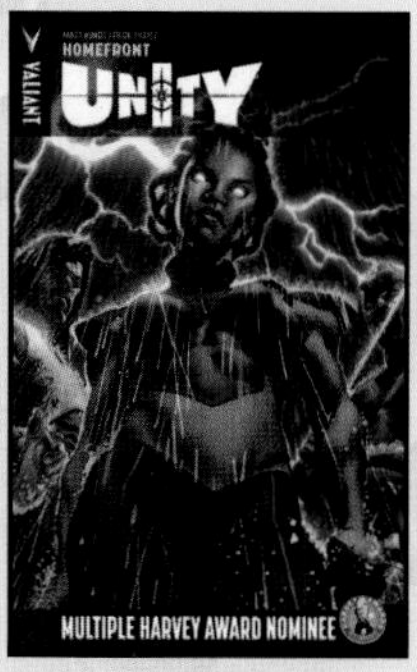
HOMEFRONT
VALIANT
UNITY
MULTIPLE HARVEY AWARD NOMINEE

Unity Vol. 5:
Homefront

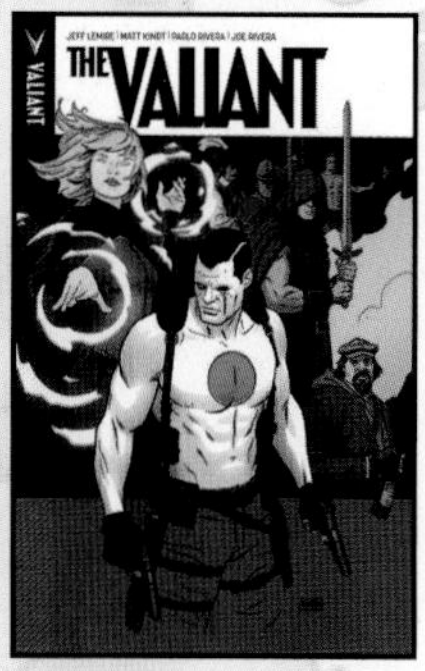
VALIANT
THE VALIANT

The Valiant

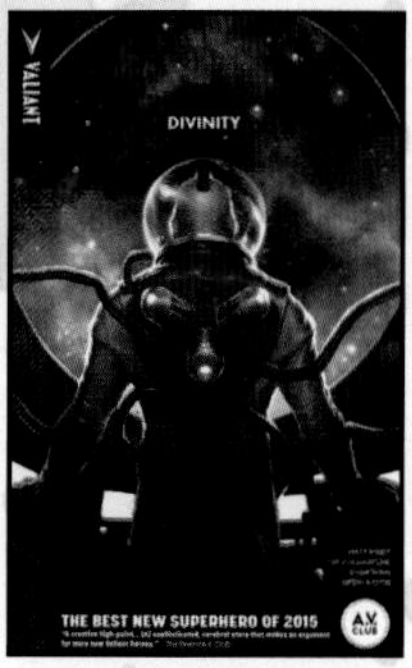
VALIANT
DIVINITY
THE BEST NEW SUPERHERO OF 2015

Divinity

VALIANT®

NINJAK®

VOLUME FOUR: THE SIEGE OF KING'S CASTLE

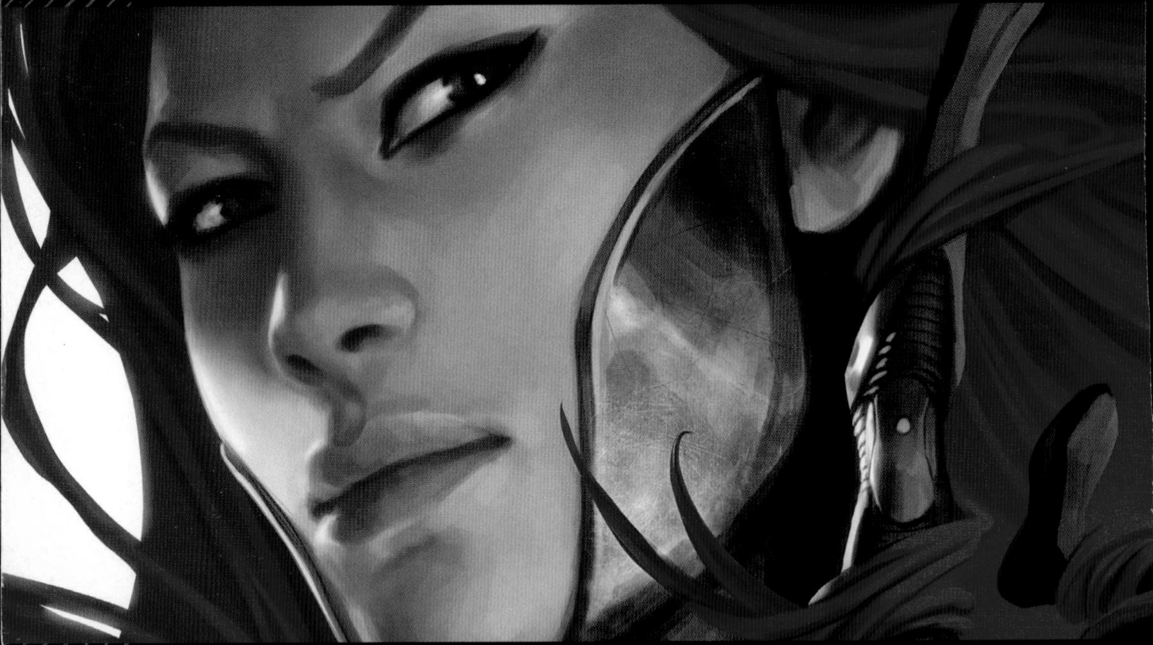

THE LAST STAND OF COLIN KING!

Colin King, the elite MI-6 intelligence operative codenamed Ninjak, has confronted his past. He's survived the gauntlet of the Shadow Seven. He's walked into the Deadside and returned a changed man. Now his greatest trial yet will come to pass as the ruthless assassin called Roku returns to lay siege to Ninjak's present and future by destroying his life from the inside out – and only the death of Colin King will stop her.

New York Times best-selling writer Matt Kindt (DIVINITY) and rising star Diego Bernard (X-O MANOWAR) charge into a new blockbuster story that will leave no one unscathed!

Collecting Ninjak #14-17.

TRADE PAPERBACK
ISBN: 978-1-68215-161-7

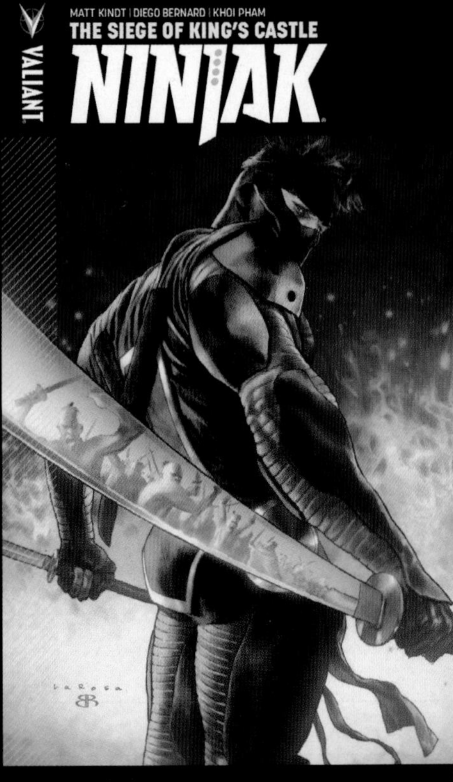
MATT KINDT | DIEGO BERNARD | KHOI PHAM
THE SIEGE OF KING'S CASTLE
NINJAK
VALIANT